Praise for Ana Manwaring's
JadeAnne Stone Mexico Adventures

Coyote
Recipient of the Literary Titan Silver Award for Fiction 2022

Literary Titan Review

The author has sent her characters on a heart-pounding mission in the fourth installment in her series. The ensemble cast and suspenseful story remind me of the consistently entertaining *Fast and Furious* series... [*Coyote*] successfully brings together action and adventure in this explosive thriller set against the unique backdrop of Mexico.

US Review Kat Kennedy

This novel, with its backdrop of human trafficking, is a riveting read that puts one into the center of Mexican culture with its descriptive narrative of landmarks and cuisine.

Nothing Comes After Z
Recipient of the Literary Titan Silver Award for Fiction 2022

Literary Titan Review

Nothing Comes After Z is a riveting crime thriller with a strong female protagonist. I appreciated the grounded nature of the crime and how it relates to some headlines we see in the news today. Before she can safely leave Mexico and return to her life, she has to uncover some hard truths and catch the perpetrators. I enjoyed how well the emotion is weaved into this action novel because it ensure we're invested in the protagonist and we're biting our nails when the action intensifies. Author Ana Manwaring knows how to create a storyline that easily sets up the hard-hitting action.

M.M. Chouinard, USA Today bestseller of the Jo Fournier Mystery series

"A well-written, engaging story with a bad-ass protagonist I loved spending time with. Bring on more JadeAnne!"

The Hydra Effect

Lisa Towles, Bestselling and multi-award-winning author of Hot House, Ninety-Five, The Unseen and Choke

"*The Hydra Effect* sizzles with action, tension, and peril. Great writing combined with regional flare and international intrigue make this sequel a delightful ride!"

Jan M Flynn, award winning author

"JadeAnne heads to Mexico City for a break from her partner and now ex-boyfriend. But her sharp intelligence, curiosity and inability to stay in her own lane land her in a snarl of trouble. In short order she's evading cartel thugs, uncovering a human trafficking network and confronting high-level Mexican politicos with questionable connections, all in a lushly realized setting one can just about smell. And taste—JadeAnne might be in the middle of a gunfight, but she's never immune to the temptation of a good plate of tacos al pastor. She and her loyal dog Pepper are a team you can't but cheer for."

Set Up

Heather Haven, multi-award-winning author of the Alvarez Family Murder Mysteries

"This is a blowout of a story. It starts on the backroads of Mexico in the middle of the night—just a woman, a dog, and Mexican Banditos—and escalates from there. If you are looking for a fast-paced, action-filled thriller about the adventures of a young PI and her lethal but well-trained dog, this will be your cup of tea. Or should I say Margarita? Jack Reacher step aside. You have met your match in JadeAnne Stone.

Judy Penz Sheluk, Amazon international bestselling author

"In her debut mystery novel, Author Ana Manwaring offers up more twists and turns than a Mexican rattlesnake. Fast paced, with well-crafted characters and a strong female lead, there's plenty to like about this world of power, politics, and Mexican money laundering. I especially enjoyed the strong sense of place, which Manwaring uses to great effect. Well worth adding to you TBR pile."

Praise for Ana Manwaring's Memoir of Living in Mexico

Saints and Skeletons

Recipient of the Literary Titan Gold Book Award 2023

Literary Titan Review

Saints and Skeletons is a captivating and introspective work that encourages readers to embrace life's complexities. Ana Manwaring's unflinching honesty and willingness to bare her soul are both brave and inspiring. This memoir stands as a testament to the transformative power of storytelling and the remarkable human capacity for growth and resilience.

Nannette Rundle Carroll, Author of The Communication Problem Solver

"Your writing is so immediate! I feel like you brought me along on the trip."

Lisa Towles, Bestselling and multi-award-winning author of Salt Island, Hot House, The Ridders, and Ninety-Five

"There are so many things I loved about this engrossing memoir. If I knew nothing of the author beforehand, I wouldn't be surprised to learn that she's a lifelong poet and an award-winning crime novelist. Too often, you find a book with beautiful language that plods forward slowly and deliberately, or a crime novel with lots of pace and adventure but lacking in soul. This book has it all - beautiful execution along with interesting peril that the author faced on this adventure of a lifetime. Love story, travelogue, and survival story, this book is an exciting chronicle of a gutsy woman's search and personal transformation across unfamiliar lands. But the best part is the fictional JadeAnne Stone series that evolved from this experience. Highly recommended for readers seeking meaningful adventure."

First Edition November 2023
by Indies United Publishing House, LLC

Cover design by Vila Design

This is a work of fiction. Names, characters, places, and incidents are either the product of the author's imagination or are use fictionally, and any resemblance to actual persons, living or dead, business establishments, events or locales is entirely coincidental.

ISBN: 978-1-64456-659-6 [Paperback]
ISBN: 978-1-64456-660-2 [Mobi]
ISBN: 978-1-64456-661-9 [ePub]
ISBN: 978-1-64456-662-6 [Audiobook]

Library of Congress Control Number: 2023946974

INDIES UNITED PUBLISHING HOUSE, LLC
P.O. BOX 3071
QUINCY, IL 62305-3071
indiesunited.net

The JadeAnne Stone Mexico Adventures

To

Harold R. Miller

Thanks for sharing your Nam vet buddies and all your
experiences in Saigon as it fell.
Y muchas gracias por nuestros viajes a México.

Acknowledgements

My deep gratitude for the special folks whose support, consideration, care and hard work have guided this series. Especially to Lisa Towles for... everything! And to my 9:00 p.m. writing partner, William Bruce Johnson, IT consultant, brainstormer extraordinaire, and brilliant company for late night writing.

Again thanks to ace critique giver, Mark Pavlichek. You've lifted JadeAnne from idea to series. Now you've brought Quint to life! I can't imagine writing without you. Also much gratitude to Mac Daly, my first declared fan and topnotch Beta Reader. All your feedback has been invaluable.

I've dedicated the book to Harold R. Miller, but want to thank him again for sharing what he could of his top secret assignment in Vietnam and introducing me to two of his 'Nam vet drinking buddies, Jim Bell and Tony Lazzarini. A few beers, and you three had given Quint his service, rank and big trouble! Thank you.

As always, a special shout out to my editor, Cindy Davis, The Fiction Doctor. You're curing me of all my bad writing habits. I can't imagine doing this without you. Or you, Lisa Orban, my publisher at Indies United Publishing House. You keep me laughing!

Finally, I couldn't do this without my husband David Prothero and our family for their love and encouragement. That includes Alfie and Beto Feral who purr while I write and "walk me home" from my studio when the session is done. You're the best!

BACKLASH

Venom and Vengeance from 'Nam

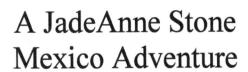

A JadeAnne Stone
Mexico Adventure

ANA MANWARING

INDIES UNITED PUBLISHING HOUSE, LLC

Chapter 1

The Past is Always With You

Saturday, September 29, 2007

Jackman Quint hovered outside the TSA checkpoint at the Denver airport, despondency a blue funk like Tule fog swirling around him. JadeAnne was leaving—going home. He felt his heart cracking open. After he'd finally found his daughter, lost to him before her birth, JadeAnne was flying back to her home in California. He hadn't expected to feel like this.

Obscured behind the snaking line of travelers inching through the TSA checkpoint, he watched JadeAnne slip back into her shoes, scoop up her small carry-on, and take her boyfriend's hand. They headed into the wide hall toward the train to Concourse C. Quint tracked them until they were swallowed by the crowds. His eyes stung. He already missed her—even the dog. Would she come back? He shuddered, gulping to stifle his sorrow, then swiped away the visible signs of emotion from his face. *Get a grip, soldier.*

Irritated at acting like a broken-hearted teenager, he

exhaled striding toward the drop-off area in front of Jeppesen Terminal East. Horacio would be navigating back around the airport loop to pick him up. He couldn't keep his partner waiting any longer, or risk a ticket and police interest. It would be gamble enough driving back to El Paso in the shot-up SUV, and Nader, one of the traffickers, was still in the wind.

Anyway, public displays of emotion weren't his thing. The first time he'd lost her—the last time he'd cried—it was either buck up or bitch up. He wouldn't be anybody's bitch. At least JadeAnne and Dylan were safe. He blew his nose on his Starbucks napkin. No, he wasn't going to start blubbering now. He dropped the empty coffee cup with the soiled napkin into a receptacle then pushed through the revolving door onto the wide sidewalk crammed with luggage and travelers scurrying to check-in to their flights.

But the question, *would she return to their home and business in Mexico City?* pecked at his thoughts. Would she? A series of honks startled him back to the airport. A man, scooting out of a black SUV, its side riddled with bullet holes, gesturing.

"Quint. *¡Queent! ¡Aqui yo!*"

Quint waved his arm, and broke into a jog, shoving his sadness into a dark crevasse of his heart to inspect later. They had a long drive ahead. The sooner they dumped the SUV with his contact on the border, the sooner they could get back to Colonia Roma. Work would take his mind off JadeAnne.

Horacio held the shotgun door open. A sudden sharp crack rang through the departure area, sending Quint diving into the SUV, ducking below the window. Horacio slammed the door behind Quint and stumped around to the driver's side, sliding his ogre bulk behind the wheel.

"Thanks, H. What was that? Backfire?"

"*Tal vez.*"

"Well, they're off. Let's get out of here. Dump this SUV. You okay to drive?" he asked, straightening up, nodding toward the makeshift dressing under his partner's shirt, covering the bullet wound from the attack two nights before.

"Only hurts when I laugh, *jefe.*" He grinned, shifting into drive as the ping of metal on metal rang out. Then another.

"What the hell—"

"Get down, *jefe,*" Horacio shouted. He floored the gas pedal, cutting off arriving travelers to honks and shrieking brakes.

The vehicle shot into the left through-lane then the curve as the rear window spider webbed, but held. H laid on the horn as they blasted away from Denver International to loop onto Peña Blvd.

Quint craned around in his seat. "Can't see a damned thing out the rear. Anything chasing us?" He peered through the side mirror. The white peaked roofline of DIA, like a giant circus complex, receded into the endless blue sky spread over the prairie.

"Nothing going as fast as we are," Horacio said. "The sniper wasn't in a vehicle. Not a moving vehicle."

"Parking garage?"

"*Sí.*" His answer slipped into the sibilance of air breeching the cracked glass.

"Get off the road at the next opportunity."

"On it, *jefe.*"

The SUV's body might look like hell, but the engine hummed. Quint wouldn't have considered anything less of his El Paso contact. They'd worked together several times. Quint knew from experience Gonzo was a pro: ran a tight ship, regardless of his outward appearance as a gangbanger. He would be pissed. Quint resigned himself to buying Gonzo a new vehicle. But only if he agreed to help catch the bastards who shot up the car: Nader and the criminals operating the human trafficking ring. They'd form a joint taskforce—as it were.

Quint stiffened. "*Oye* H. If Nader followed us here, do you think he followed us to the Medina's?" After everything…what if Nader had snatched the teen they'd rescued? Sold her back to the cartel.

"We weren't followed, Quint. Nader knew the plan from

3

the start. He was watching the airport." He tapped the gas and spun around a slow-moving truck carrying bottled water. "He's acting alone. I shot the fourth man. The other two are dead—"

"He'll have a new crew." Quint dropped his head into his hands. Muttered, "I was a fool."

"*No te castigues por eso*, don't beat yourself up. What's his angle, do you suppose?"

"I haven't a clue. I thought we were something like friends. He was my CO back in 'Nam." Quint paused, looked out the window at the interstate businesses rushing past. "Take that second exit in a half mile—Tower Road—" He pointed north. "Sign says there's a Walmart Superstore." He paused, peered through the side mirror again. A Denver City patrol car was coming up fast. "You see that? Exit now!"

Horacio grunted and swerved off the highway as the patrol's lights came on.

Quint nodded. "Okay then."

"We need gas," Horacio said, inching the vehicle toward the right-hand lane through the thickening morning traffic on the exit.

"We'll probably find a station nearby. Let's get to that Walmart."

Horacio turned right and made the first left to parallel the highway. Tower Road intersected in several blocks. Besides the usual gastrointestinal distress cluster of Burger King, MacDonald's, and Taco Bell, they saw two of Denver's finest squatting on Walmart's coat tails.

"Turn left!" Quint growled.

H turned and stepped on the gas. One of the patrols turned on his lights and made a U-turn on Tower chasing after the SUV. H blasted through another left, circled the block to double back into a neighborhood. The scent of tortillas and chilis wafted through the window. Horacio sniffed. "Maybe we should eat before hitting the Interstate." He pulled into the parking lot behind a restaurant, a ramshackle-looking affair tucked into the edge of an equally downtrodden housing district, and backed the SUV between two jacked-up pickup trucks. They slouched down as the patrol cruised past.

Quint chucked. "Good work, H. Yeah. it's a long drive. Let's eat." He nodded his head toward the back door as a pair of mestizo-looking men in cowboy hats and boots sauntered out. One carried a cup to go. Quint heard a snippet of Spanish as they passed by.

Horacio squeezed through the narrow door opening only after shedding his jacket. A tight fit, but no one looking for it would see the SUV.

"H, if you eat two orders of *huevos rancheros*, you aren't going to fit back into the vehicle."

Horacio bellowed his infectious laugh. "True dat."

Quint snorted. "True dat? You been taking English lessons from Chucho? Speaking of Chuch, I should call. See if everything is okay at the office."

"Mrs. P will keep him in line, *jefe*."

"True dat," Quint retorted, grinning as Horacio pulled open the back door to the enticing steam. Quint almost felt at home. *Damn. I'm getting too comfortable in Mexico.* There was no telling where Senator Aguirre's op would take him. So why was he obsessing over Jade's return?

Three orders of *huevos rancheros* later, with a thermos full of black coffee and two paper cups, the men eased out into the weedy parking lot. Quint felt better. Maybe his emotional weakness had been brought on by hunger. One of the trucks was gone, but the other remained, protecting the bullet-ridden side of the SUV. Probably belonged to the two guys in the corner flirting with the middle-aged proprietress. Regulars. If he was staying in Colonia Roma to finish his work for Senator Aguirre, Quint needed to find a local breakfast dive with good food and a cheerful staff.

Reading his mind, Horacio said, "You know there's a place two blocks from the office even better than this one for breakfast. A lot cheaper, *tambien*."

"Well, this is the U.S. Everything costs more."

They pulled up to pump 6 at the EXXON Mobil on Tower Rd. "Grabbing supplies, H," Quint said. "I'll pay inside. Keep your eyes open for the cops. Last thing we need is to be delayed explaining the bullet holes in the side of this SUV. "

When he'd finished filling the tank, Horacio putted over to the Tower Liquor. Quint clambered in. He held up a bag of hot chili Cheetos and a Coors. "Snacks. Ever try the Rockies' best? Made from pure Rocky Mountain spring water."

"Ay, that piss water? *No gracias.*"

"Good thing I got these." Quint grinned and pulled two bottles of water from his shopping bag, settling them into the cup holders. "By the way, I called Medina. Warned him to be careful."

Horacio slowed for a red light. "I thought you might. What did he say?"

A low rider pulled up in the left lane and stopped next to them. Four gangbangers stared at the side of the SUV. The kid riding shotgun cocked an air AR-15 making like he was blasting them. Quint heard the laughter over the booming bass. Horacio finger-blasted back. The light turned green; the kids roared ahead, fingers cocked.Another patrol car appeared from nowhere and raced up behind the gangbangers.

"We're drawing attention. *¿Qué piensas?* The *entrada* to I-25 is coming up."

"I dunno. Which is worse? Explaining what happened to the police when we're pulled over in town, or risking a run-in with Nader? The thing is, Nader knows where we're going and where we'll end up. He'd be insane to attack us here. Too much traffic. Too many witnesses. He'll wait until we get to El Paso or hit us on the interstate. There's a lot of empty country before the border. But I-25 is the fastest route."

Horacio nodded and pulled over then veered onto the southbound entrance ramp.

Quint pushed down his seatback, closed his eyes. "Wake me up when you want to switch drivers."

"Where are we?" Quint yawned, rubbed his eyes, and sat up. "It looks like a desert out there."

"We're almost in Santa Fe. Just past the halfway mark. You've been sleeping for five hours."

"Didn't get much sleep last night. Want to trade now?"

"No, I'm fine. I'll take us into Santa Fe. We can get out. Stretch. I'll swap then. I could eat."

Quint fished around behind his seat to grab the bag of snacks. "Cheetos and beer?"

"I was thinking about some of that famous *carne adovada* with Hatch chilis."

"How do you know about New Mexico food?"

"My wife and her sisters took a trip to Santa Fe. She's still raving about a restaurant called Cafe Pasqual's in the old town. Here's the map." He handed Quint a new road map with city maps of Santa Fe and Albuquerque. Quint flipped to Santa Fe.

"Where'd you get this?"

"Stopped at a visitor center when we crossed into New Mexico, *jefe.*"

"Damn. I must have been tired. Sounds good, *amigo.* Let's find those Hatch chiles."

The SUV garnered a ration of stares and glares. Quint wanted to pin his credentials to his shirt or shout, *We're the good guys here,* but kept his head in the map, trying to ignore the tourists. Horacio looked nonplussed. Maybe he didn't realize they were being taken for narcos. But inside the quaint adobe restaurant, the food was worthy of remembering; the other diners at the long communal table were congenial. A Russian woman, her American daughter, two gay men from California, one a muckety-muck in high tech, a couple from Toronto celebrating their thirty-fifth anniversary, and a young German running a humanitarian aid organization for immigrants displaced by wars and poverty, who was traveling with his vivacious Italian girlfriend. Quint relaxed, enjoying the lively talk, the exchange of ideas, observations, and, of course, the food. Horacio proved to be a warm, entertaining, social addition to the group. For a moment, Quint's sadness lifted.

After a bison burger and two servings of toasted piñon ice cream with fleur de sel caramel sauce, Quint was ready for another nap. "*Amigo*, I've got to walk off some of this food."

"All for it, *jefe*. I need to pick up some trinkets for *mi marida y hija*."

"Let's go. We walked by plenty of shops on the plaza."

Thirty minutes later, Quint had a stunning silver necklace of green turquoise and Mexican jade for Jade's birthday. Horacio bought a silver ring inlaid with turquoise and coral for his girl, and a handmade silver and turquoise bracelet set with several tiny sapphires, her birthstone, for his wife. Everything had been made locally.

When Quint and Horacio returned, two local officers were inspecting the SUV, their patrol car double-parked, hemming in the vehicle.

"Can I help you, officers?" Quint asked, his tone mild.

The younger officer's hand hovered over his gun. The older man asked, "This your vehicle?"

Quint replied, "No, sir. Borrowed." He patted his pockets.

The younger cop rested his hand on the butt of his revolver. "License," he said.

The older cop nodded. Quint pulled out his wallet, handing over his driver's license, carry permit, and a second ID. Quint noted the man's nametag: Quintero.

"You're attached to the State Department? You carrying?" the cop asked, handing the IDs over to his partner.

"Not on me. Glove box. I'm on loan to the Mexican government, actually."

The cop eyed Quint skeptically. "This is *New* Mexico. What happened to the vehicle?"

"Registration's in the glove box. H, give the man the keys." Quint replied, ignoring the question. The younger patrol's hand tightened around the gun. Quint swung his chin toward Horacio. "My assigned minder. Horacio, *dale al oficial las*

8

llaves."

Horacio fished the keys out of his pocket, tossing them to the younger cop who let go of the sidearm to catch them. *Good thinking, H.* A tourist family with three school-aged kids flowed around them, the kids gawking open-mouthed.

"Your man don't speak English?"

"Nah, but my *español* is improving."

"Ask him for his papers," Quintara demanded, waving Quint toward the side of the SUV. "Hand them to Herdez."

"*Horacio, muestrale al hombre tus papeles.*" Again, he gestured with his chin.

"*Claro, jefe,*" Horacio replied as he handed over his passport to the junior patrol.

Herdez nodded to his partner and unlocked the door, reaching into the glove box. He retreated to the patrol car with the registration and Quint's gun, checking the license plate on the way.

"What happened to the vehicle?" Quintara demanded a second time.

"We're guessing they were gangbangers. Shot it up while we ate breakfast in a dive in Denver. Maybe thought we were someone else."

"Make a police report?"

"No. I can't talk about the mission. You'll have to call to verify. Partner's got the number." Quint tossed his chin this time toward the kid in the patrol car.

The older cop motioned to Horacio to stand next to Quint. "Is he carrying?"

"No sir," Quint snapped back. "Not authorized in the U.S." He prayed they wouldn't search the SUV. The cache of weapons would boggle the bored tourist cops' minds. And probably land them in jail.

"So what're ya doing in Santa Fe?" the man asked, obviously making small talk until the plate was run.

Quint chuckled. What did anyone do in Santa Fe? "Lunch at Cafe Pasqual's. Shopping for the girls." He held up his gift bag from Malouf's. Quintero raised his eyebrows, gave a quick

9

nod.

Herdez returned and leaned toward his partner. In a low but audible voice he said, "All clear, Quintero. Vehicle checks out. It's a Fed permit to carry. Matches the ID. Only problem I can see is the SUV could be connected to the shootout in Hernandez—black, shot up. Whadda we do?"

Car tires squealed around the corner; its motor revved as it peeled away from the plaza. A second car in hot pursuit.

"Let's go!" Quintero sprinted to the patrol car. Herdez thrust the papers and gun into Quint's hand and ran.

Quint settled behind the wheel and shifted into gear. "Someone is watching over us, H. Let's blow this town. Five more hours, if the gods continue to clear our path."

"Police are the same everywhere. It's why I quit. What did they want—money?"

"Not so common in the U.S. You didn't hear the young guy. He made the SUV for the one in Hernandez. Someone saw what went down. Or Nader made a report."

"He would have known the *placa,* license plate."

Quint shrugged. He turned left toward I-25. Traffic was light pre-rush hour. "I dunno, H. Nader was never the most observant character. If he'd reported the plates, we'd be in the back of that squad car, cuffed." *But now they have the license plate.*

The men sank into silence as Quint maneuvered them onto I-25 and set the cruise control to 75 mph, the posted limit. He punched on the radio, dialed in a jazz station to some peppy driving music. Lots of clarinet. The station identifier cut in. "103.7 The Oasis. We'll take care of your thirsty ears. Your best stop along Route 66."

Horacio dropped his seatback and stretched out as far as he could. "Wake me up when we get there, *jefe.*"

Fifty minutes later, the SUV snarled into Albuquerque afternoon traffic. Quint kept an eye on the signs for the throughway to Las Cruces, the termination of I-25 at the Texas border. He'd pull off. Contact Gonzo to expect him. Maybe have a coffee. They could eat in El Paso at the airport before flying. If all went well, they'd be home in Mexico City before morning.

Outside the windshield, the urban landscape morphed into a dun-colored drone of emptiness bordered by dark crags and monotone peaks. Along the highway, he could see evidence of irrigation, but this late into the year, most of the cultivation would be done. What did they grow in New Mexico, anyway, besides chilies and corn? Goats probably. After all, he was essentially in Mexico. Listen to the ads: Valencia sopapillas. Even the city names: Santa Fe, Las Lunas, Belen, Las Cruces. No question who immigrated here first. Were there missions like in California?

Further south, the scenery began to resemble a moonscape. Dry. Bare. Rocky—driving him into the blue funk again, but now the mists morphed to dusty haze. He could always fly to California. Beg her to come home. *But Sausalito is her home.* Quint had a hankering to pull over, dial JadeAnne's number, ask about the dog. Dylan. Their trip. But he had another two hours and forty-seven minutes of this mind-numbing scenery to go before Las Cruces. He hoped to arrive before dark. Easier to see attackers during daylight. *Would Nader be so stupid?*

Convinced Nader hunted him, he pondered why. *Why would Nader hate me?* What nagged at Quint was, he'd done time for Nader's operation. He'd never given him up. Quint never revealed the kingpin—and Nader walked scot-free while, for five years, he languished in Lompoc. Lost his commission. Dishonorable discharge. Everything expunged if he signed on with NSA. Everything he hated—dirty dealing—spying on citizens—assassinations—you name it. Only, you didn't name it. Top secret. Few with clearance. Not even Nixon was privy to what those fuckers were up to in Vietnam, Laos, and Cambodia. Or, maybe the politicians just didn't want to know. Still didn't, for that matter. Not that Quint was NSA anymore. He'd completed his indentured servitude. Got out. *But did I really get out?*

The radio program changed, with a new DJ coming on shift. An evening program. Mellow. Easy. So unlike Quint's life. He'd paid his dues. Why was Nader after him now? "Hold on! Because I know the truth. I know everything!" he bellowed.

Horacio stirred, snuffled, and shifted his weight toward the door, but didn't wake up. "Sorry, man," Quint whispered and punched the door lock. Didn't want to lose his partner, but he did want to lose Nader. They'd never really been friends. Nader played him back then just as he was doing in Mexico City before showing his true colors and attacking them outside Hernandez three days ago.

How long had the man been looking for him? *Congratulations, asshole. Took thirty-three years to find me—* now that Quint had something to lose. Nader knew Jade was flying back to California. No coincidence he was shooting at him, or had he been waiting to kill JadeAnne? Maybe he planned to hop a flight to San Francisco. Quint banged the steering wheel. The vehicle shimmied and swerved into the right-hand lane, cutting off a farm truck piled with hay bales. He stepped on the gas and moved back into the fast lane. Horacio snored.

A dark blue SUV shot up behind them, tailgating. Quint adjusted his mirrors to see into the vehicle. No luck. Too dark as the sky streaked pink, orange, and purple between the peaks as the western mountains shadowed to black. He sped up, the SUV dropped back but kept pace with him. Quint needed a telephone. But there wasn't any cell service in this God forsaken desert. Anyway, who would he call? He was still a half hour from the Texas border. He reached over his sleeping partner and retrieved his gun from the glove box. If the vehicle came any closer, he'd wake H.

Horacio woke up chipper at the Shell station just off I-10 East outside Las Cruces.

"Good morning, *amigo.* We're being followed. Get your

weapon."

"*¿Qué hora es, Queent? ¿Dónde estamos?*"

Horacio put his seatback up and swiveled to see the blue SUV pulling into the station behind them. It drove around the pumps and stopped in front of the convenience store. Three kids piled out. Quint blew out a clenched breath and circled to a pump.

"The border. Las Cruces. I figured it out, H. Nader. I have to call Jade. Need a pit stop? It's another fifty minutes to El Paso."

"*¿*Pit estop?"

"*Baño.*" He opened his door and dropped to the ground.

Horacio called across the seats, "I'll be back. Want anything? How much on the gas?"

"Forty. Thanks. I'll park over there." He pointed to the front of the convenience store, then extracted his cell phone from his jacket pocket. Three bars. He dialed.

"It's Quint. Heads up, I'm in Las Cruces. One hour. You ain't gonna be happy, Gonz." He disconnected. The pump was ready and he filled the tank. At least Gonzo would get the SUV back with a full tank.

Quint hung up the nozzle and capped the tank. Horacio hadn't returned, so he moved the vehicle to a parking space then wandered into the store. H appeared with the bathroom key. *Might as well hit the john.* "Grab something if you're hungry. We'll eat dinner at the airport in a couple hours."

In the bathroom, Quint dialed JadeAnne. No answer. They had to have arrived. Maybe out grocery shopping. Or...he let the thought hang unfinished. He couldn't go there. She and Dylan would be doing something. Visiting her friends or her parents. Her parents. He should have raised her. He should have rescued *Thuy*, Jade's gentle mother. He didn't even know she was pregnant. Because of Nader and his "mission" he was pulled out of Saigon, sent to Laos to move heroin into Vietnam. White-hot hate boiled through him, scalding his veins. Charley promised to protect Thuy, had tried to find her as the NVA swept toward Saigon, but it was too late. She was dead.

Quint slammed his fist into the metal bathroom door, splitting open his knuckles. The pain soothed him. It was real. He was a free agent. He could do something about the tragedy of his life. Not like 1975—addicted, incarcerated, and disconsolate. Quint had been helpless. He signed over the papers for Charley Stone to adopt his baby. He hadn't even read the documents to find out the child's gender. But now he'd found her. His flesh and blood. He'd be damned if anyone was going to take her away from him.

Pounding on the door. "*Queent*? You okay in there?"

Quint washed his bloodied hand, looked for towels, then wiped his palms across his jeans, and opened the door. "The big question, H. Why'd Nader turn up right when I found JadeAnne?"

Chapter 2

Out in the West Texas Town of El Paso

Back on the street, Quint found the Interstate entrance and set the cruise control. He needed Horacio's help. He said, "I don't know why, but Nader has me in his sights. I'm afraid he's going after Jade."

"*Tal vez, jefe.* I'm worried about it too."

Quint glanced sideways at his companion. Horacio leaned forward, his eyebrows raised expectantly. It was time to share his story. "It all goes back to Vietnam."

"I figured that, *jefe. ¿Qué pasó?*"

"I graduated from college in '71 with degrees in engineering and computer science. I was young, sixteen, when I started university. I believed in my country. The government." Quint grimaced. "I believed in democracy and freedom—that the government had the citizens' backs. It was my duty to preserve these ideals. I joined the ROTC. When I graduated, I enlisted in the Army knowing I'd be deployed to Vietnam; I was going to be a hero," he said, voice dropping.

"Rough home life?"

"Anything was better than going home. My father was a mean bastard."

"*Lo siento, mano*. I know how hard that is. You hate 'em and love 'em."

"No love lost between us. It was always Dad and my older brothers against me. I never went back. He died recently."

"*Lo siento.*"

Quint shrugged but remained silent. The radio softly played static.

Horacio prodded. *"Entonces,* what happened?"

"Because of ROTC and my degree, I entered as a Second Lieutenant close to the end of the war. Ya know, the Vietnamese call it the American War—ain't that irony?"

"I don't know too much about it, Quint. More than seeing *Platoon* and *Apocalypse Now.*"

A moonscape of barren land dotted with dark outcroppings of shrubs or rocks sloped up to jagged coal black teeth against the milky way. Headlamps tracked stretches of interstate, a river of light cutting straight south in the late evening traffic. Quint felt his energy draining, his mood ebbing.

"It was hell, man. I landed on a hellish plain of dust, mud, heat, stench, and noise. Helicopters night and day. Guns. Sweat. I was assigned to manage a reconnaissance unit—make sure the men were trained, plan missions, man the comms. Hell. I was barely twenty-one, no experience. The non-com sergeant was a *pendejo* on his third tour. Fucker loved war. Loved the hyper tension, killing the gooks, or Charley as he called 'em. I wasn't fighting for democracy, I was fighting my father and brothers all over again. Fighting for command of my unit. Stingray he called himself," Quint mused. The tires hissed over the asphalt.

"Our job was to scout out Vietcong strongholds, tunnels, ammo dumps, camps, trails. I monitored and reported, managed the personnel, gave orders. Or that's what I was supposed to do. Stingray made it impossible. No respect from the men. Humiliation, sweat, bug bites was all.

"We marched, if you can call hacking back jungle with

16

machetes all day, marching. We'd follow trails, but they were often booby-trapped. We'd sleep in shifts. The enemy slithered through the jungle like snakes. They could be on us before we knew they were around, crawling out of their holes like ants swarming out of ant hills, biting. Everything biting. And it pissed down rain. Men were wet, chafed, skin rotting. I tell ya, H, be glad you didn't go." He lapsed into silence again as he overtook a slow semi.

"Had a couple of months of missions. Always the same. Found tunnels and supply dumps. Sometimes a small Vietcong patrol. Fool Stingray, ordering the men to engage and kill anything that moved. Sometimes women and kids. Never took a prisoner. We might've gotten intel—that was the job. No—kill and count—that was his mandate. When we found anything of significance, I radioed the coordinates. Base sent out the 'copter gunships to destroy the infrastructure and supplies. They annihilated everything. And if the choppers couldn't do it, the B-52s and Agent Orange could. The noise was terrible. I can't take loud noise anymore." He stopped talking to fiddle with the radio, landing on Garth Brooks, *More than a Memory.* *Yeah, Thuy is more than a memory.*

"*Pues*, what happened? You got out."

"Yeah, I got out." He punched off the radio when a string of commercials came on. "They booted me out. Did a stretch in the Federal penitentiary."

"What? No!"

"Yeah. Third month in-country. Late March '72. We'd been whacking our way through the jungle when we came into a clearing with a small cluster of bamboo and thatch structures. Homes. We entered through a small plot of vegetables where some women and a few old men toiled. Kids playing, laughing. It looked peaceful. I thought the people seemed happy to see us. But as we advanced, I started to see fear. Of course we didn't have an interpreter and no one had more than a few words of Vietnamese. Our orders said we were to inspect any village we came across for the enemy or evidence of the enemy. These folks were poor, skinny. Few men or teens. But

17

I'd seen men from the edge of the jungle. It was like they'd evaporated. I ordered Stingray to organize a house search but, before I could set up my comms, the village was on fire and my men were shooting down the people. Mothers. Grandmothers. Babies—I've never seen such savagery. Yelling, 'Where are the NVA? Where are the men?'"

Quint gripped the wheel, clenched his jaw as the memories flooded back. "I tackled Stingray. Got him down. But it was too late. The damage was done. He'd kicked the hornet's nest and the angry swarm came up from its hidey-holes. I radioed for back-up. Armed men and boys as young as ten. Our men fought valiantly, but there were too many. Five down. Only five to hold off the horde. Stingray in the middle of the fray charging the enemy even as I commanded the platoon to retreat into the jungle. Maniac.

"Bastards cut him down. But we don't leave our wounded or our dead. I believed that. Who was the maniac, Horacio?" he asked, leveling a pained expression on his partner.

Horacio shrugged.

"I lobbed two grenades, charged, spraying the enemy with bullets. A round caught me in my thigh, but I made it to Stingray. He was alive. I dragged him back through the vegetables into the trees under cover of my remaining five men, then three of us ran back for as many of the rest as we could find. Four dead. One more wounded but alive. We felt the chopper blades whomping the air before hearing them and hauled ass out of danger as far from that village as we could get."

Quint's hands shook the steering wheel. The SUV wavered. Horacio reached over and steadied the wheel. "*Todo esta bien. Take a breath.*"

Quint sucked in a lungful of dry desert air and breathed deeply for several breaths. They had reached the northern outskirts of El Paso. Descending the valley, El Paso's lights reminded Quint of a flowing river, although he knew the river was the black line at the bottom of the light flow. The border. A dark no man's land of terror sucking the light of the city into its depths, and he was headed straight toward it.

"H, we're almost to our turn-off. I've been thinking about the airport attack today. I don't think Nader has gone after Jade —yet. He knows we have to come here to return Gonzo's SUV."

"*Por supuesto, jefe.* You never told me how you and he are connected. What does Nader hold against you?"

"I've never talked about Vietnam to a civilian before. In the slammer I saw a shrink."

"A shrink?"

"Sorry, a *sicologico,* psychologist. He was a Stanford student studying shell shock and some experimental therapy. Talked a lot. There's a new name for it these days. Ever heard of PTSD?"

"No."

"Well, I'll try to explain it later. Here's the exit. We need a plan," Quint said.

"Pull over. This is a tough neighborhood. You keep watch; I'll drive," Horacio countered.

"You sure?"

"*No te preocupes*, I can find the chop shop, *jefe.*"

Quint veered into the parking lot in front of a rundown liquor store. The windows were filled with beer and bottle advertisements but metal window grates obscured most of the information, if it could be called information, Quint thought as he walked around to the passenger door.

"Hey mister. Spare some change?" A staggering kid, maybe twelve, in the uniform of whatever local street gang ran the territory—sagging pants, muscle tee, red bandana—held his palm open.

"Sorry kid." He got in the SUV, slamming the door as Horacio turned the key. "Get going." He nodded at the three men, possibly armed, piling out of the store. Same clothes. Same colors. Looking for trouble.

Horacio threw the vehicle into reverse and backed around, laying a patch of tire as he sped off. "*Pinche, pandilleros,*" he muttered.

"Yeah. Street gangs. Kid was a set-up. As soon as I pulled out my wallet the men would have robbed me. Gangs're everywhere."

"*Claro.*"

"Listen, Nader didn't get me this morning. He's going to be waiting."

Horacio grunted in the affirmative.

"We need to surveille the area. Circle, ease in. We see any suspicious men lurking around, we back off. Not worth getting killed. We can leave the van at the airport if we have to, but I'd rather make it to Gonzo's and take my punishment now."

Horacio snorted. "I'll turn at the next block. Drive slow, look mean. This district is no Del Valle."

Quint pulled a black ballcap out of the door pocket and pulled it low over his face.

The turn made, they continued straight for a half mile. The road sloped and narrowed through a ramshackle neighborhood of primarily adobe or stucco homes. Some lights were on, but much of the area was dark. Few street lamps illuminated the road as it deteriorated into a pitted lane. Under the few lights, a kid or a couple men loitered, the red glow of their cigarettes or joints brighter than the lamps. More red bandanas.

"Turn left."

The street widened. A few more street lamps lit a sort commercial center. Mostly bars, rent-by-the-hour motels with scantily clad Latinas strutting around or lounging in small groups against the sides of the buildings. Some of the women made catcalls or beckoned them over. "Lookin' for a fiesta, boys?" called a curvy, black-haired woman wearing skin-tight spandex below the ugliest face Quint had ever seen. Horacio saluted but drove on.

"I hate seeing this, Quint. Some of these are barely teens. Look at her—" he glanced at a woman who could easily been in her fifties, scrawny, wrinkled, grey hair thinning.

"She's probably a meth head and twenty five, H."

Horacio sighed. "I hate it *jefe*. I've never met a woman who woke up one day and said, 'I'm going to be a street whore.' It's the punks we're fighting. We've got to shut down the trafficking."

"I wish we could. But we're not going to even make a dent in it. If we succeed in closing down the BLO supply chain and the Zeta demand connections in the capital, they'll only move somewhere else. How many of these women are cartel-controlled do you think? Half? Two thirds? More? Indentured slavery for bringing them across. Rosi is the one with the statistics. This is one of her neighborhoods. She pulls the women out, smuggles them back to Mexico, puts them in programs to help them detox, heal, and learn how to have a decent life. It has to be heartbreaking work. Make a left." He stared out the window, pensive, but alert.

Quint watched a couple Beemers and a Cadillac idling at the curb. Goods being exchanged, deals made. Not anyone looking for him. As they cruised, he saw one whore hand over her cash, or he presumed it was cash, to the driver of a fancy lowrider pickup vibrating to the bass of a rap tune. Another woman got into a Toyota with a man in a ten-gallon hat. Horacio sighed again.

"Turn right."

They plunged back into patchy darkness. Blinds closed, doors bolted against the evils of the night. The smell of sewage floated into the cab. "Smells like home," Horacio joked.

"Except without the tortillas cooking. Another right." No one loitered on this street.

They angled through the neighborhood as they cautiously approached the garage. "We're almost there." Quint reached around the seat, grabbed one of the two AR-15s he'd dug out of Gonzo's secret storage under the back seats while at the gas station. He patted his shoulder holster for his 9mm Luger. "I haven't seen any scouts," he said.

"Any of those whores could have been *halcones*."

"Sure, H. Anything is possible, but would Nader have connections to...what is it here? Barrio Azteca?"

"*No sé.*"

"Left. Gonzo's is two streets away, around to the

21

southeast." They patrolled without headlamps. The lack of streetlights kept the bullet holes from standing out. "Maybe we should park, call Gonzo now. Down that alley, H," Quint commanded. "Leave the engine running and watch the rear."

Quint scoped out the area in front of them as he dialed. "G. I'm behind the garage. We might have a problem." He briefly related the situation, listened, then hung up. "Said he'd send some men into the neighborhood to check things out. Call back. We wait."

He handed Horacio the other AR-15 and the men slouched into their seats. The night was dark but the brilliant stars illuminated enough to make out houses and parked cars. A light flared in one of the cars. A cell phone? A match? Someone was in that car. His heart started pounding. "H, left 45 degrees."

"Saw it, *jefe*. Doesn't look like they know we're here."

"No." A shadow passed behind the car. They heard the muffled sound of a silenced gun. The shadow moved out of view. In the distance shouts. Gun shots. A scream. A vehicle's engine revving. Squeal of tires. Silence.

The phone buzzed. "Yeah." Quint listened again. "Okay, coming in." He hung up. To Horacio, he said, "The neighborhood has been cleared, but Gonzo thinks it was Nader getting away. Let's go. Be ready to peel out of here if Nader makes us. Take a right, then left. You'll see the garage. Flash the lights; he'll open the door."

Chapter 3

Gonzo's

Quint's AR nosed out the vehicle's window as they inched around the block, the atmosphere heavy with tension, even the air on high alert. Quint slipped on his NVGs, night vision goggles, then passed a pair to Horacio. The street lit up, a martianscape out of a futuristic world—or Iraq. Nothing moved. No lights. Quint felt his heart step up a beat, then another. His blood pounded. Lights danced before his eyes. Energy shot through him, even as he stiffened, poised. Ready. He remembered the moment before attack. The fear, the palsy, the panic, then the motivation to live. A green shadow moved in his peripheral vision. Quint's paralyzation vanished as the rifle swung up and spit fire. The shadow dropped. Hell broke loose.

Quint threw off the NVGs. Guns blazed from a derelict warehouse. Horacio stepped on the gas as bullets sprayed the passenger side of the SUV. Ahead, a pileup of SUVs blocked the street. Quint watched the mirror. More vehicles closed in behind them. The barrage from the warehouse continued.

"The garage, H!" Quint yelled. He pointed. The door was rolling up. Gonzo and his men stepped out, armed and firing.

Gonzo waved. Horacio swerved into the dark garage, screeched to a stop. The metal door squealed down, lights flipped on. Quint was out of his door, pounding toward a set of stairs behind Gonzo and his men. "Roof!" Horacio grabbed his AR-15 from the floor and sprinted after the others. A hail of bullets pelted across the metal door.

On the roof, the team spread out, snipers taking pot shots at anything moving. The rest spraying the warehouse with rounds of ammunition. Two young men set up Stingers. Within moments, the eastern blockade exploded in a fireball of burning metal. Quint heard the ruckus of the westerly line of defense fleeing. The Stinger launch onto the warehouse set it on fire. Screams of injured and burning men filled the night. Quint and Horacio picked them off as they ran. It was 'Nam all over again. He slumped to the roof. Out of ammo. Out of energy.

Gonzo signaled his crew. The battle was over. "Quint, my guys will go down, search the remains with you. I'll inspect the SUV. It looks like you ran into some trouble; I'll write up an estimate while you take care of your shit."

What could he do? Quint nodded. "Yeah, Gonz. Sorry about the damage. I appreciate the vehicle though. Well armored. Decent drive. Come on, H. Let's get our kits out and see if Nader wants to tell us what this is all about."

"Hughie, Toño," Gonzo shouted, beckoning to the men. "Grab the Stingers. Yo! Lobo. Mac. Go with them." He nodded toward Horacio and winked. "Keep him alive. I need 'im to pay for the repairs." He guffawed. The men snapped to attention.

"Follow us," a desert-camo clad youth ordered.

"I need ammo, G."

"No worries. Mac, hit the armory on the way out. AR-15? Got you covered, man."

"Thanks."

Their footsteps clattered down a set of metal stairs on the back side of the building. The lead ducked through a metal fire door. Quint realized the building had a metal sheath protecting it. Who the hell were these guys? Well, it didn't matter as long as he and H arrived safely back in Mexico.

"Hey… sorry, I don't know your name."

The putative leader grinned, extended his hand. "I'm Lobo. Looks like you had some problems." He laughed, displaying a mouth full of canine-looking teeth.

"Quint." He held out his fist for a bump. "Yeah. But I have a bad feeling the problem wasn't out there." He turned to Horacio. "Whaddya think?"

"*De acuerdo, jefe.* Nader wasn't on the street."

"*No habla inglés, carnal?*" Lobo asked. The sounds of sirens wafted in on the night breeze from a distance. No one seemed concerned. Quint let it go.

"My partner is shy, aren't you, H?"

Horacio let loose with one of his famous Shrek belly laughs and shrugged.

"Let's go get you some ammo."

Lobo led the unit past the garage through a set of doors to another part of the building. The man called Mac inserted a card into the electronic lock and shouldered the door open. "Hughie, put that thing down. Find the AR-15 ammo."

Quint had thought "armory" was a glib description until he saw the room. Horacio's chin dropped. He gaped. Gonzo had armaments and ammunition enough for a war. He hadn't seen a depot like this since 1974, Saigon. Hughie, with the kid in camo, returned the Stingers to their location, then Hughie rustled around until he came up with two boxes, handing them to Horacio.

"Thanks, man," Quint said. "Hughie, is it?" The young man dipped his head. Not a talker. "So you guys preparing for an invasion or something?"

The camo kid laughed. "Just G's hobby— collectin' guns n' stuff."

No one seemed in a hurry to go anywhere. Gonzo's men took their guns to the far wall where shelves housed cleaning supplies and proceeded to clean their weapons. Quint and

Horacio sat down, joining them, to reload several cartridges.

"I was here when you swapped vehicles. You get your girls where they were going?" Lobo asked?

"Yeah. The teen's back with her family. Put my daughter and her boyfriend on a plane this morning."

"The injured guy you left with us when you picked up the SUV, he split. Stole a car. G wasn't so happy about that."

Quint spun toward Horacio who frowned. "You hear that, H? You mean Chuck Nader? Did you men find him or the car?"

The sounds of cracks, clinks and the familiar smell of gun oil filled the space. "Car has a tracker. Went to Denver but it's back now. Figure your guy has something to do with the attack."

"Yeah. But who were the rest of them?"

"Cartel affiliates. Nasty people. Take your pick. Bloods, Crips, Barrio Azteca, Zetas, North Side Locos."

"Who's got red bandanas?"

"Crips are blue. Where'd you see bandanas?"

Quint released the magazine, grabbed a handful of bullets from the box and started loading them. "At the liquor store. Kid panhandled me then three gangbangers appeared."

"Yeah, those would be North Side Locos. Petty crime, a little dealing for the Barrio. The attack? Those assholes were organized and armed. Probably Barrio," camo kid said.

Quint slid the loaded magazine back into the magwell with a snap then pulled the charging handle, chambering a round. He held up the rifle, sighting down the barrel, his finger poised above the trigger as he thumbed on the safety. He lowered the gun and doublechecked the safety lock. Satisfied, he leaned the rifle against the bench at his knee. Horacio continued to buff the stock of his weapon with a fresh rag passed by the man called Mac. The atmosphere had shifted from the easy camaraderie of the locker room. Quint felt tension stiffening his spine, his limbs, and saw it in the postures of the men. He tasted the sweetness of iron, the acid of cordite, and fear on his lips. The rot of death. This wasn't over. The unit knew it. He took the proffered rag and wiped down his rifle. No one spoke, each man attended his weapons, cleaning, loading, securing. The camo kid affixed a bayonet to his. He had a second weapon strapped to his ankle. At some silent command, the men retrieved bullet proof vests, helmets from hooks, and put them on, adjusting night goggles, queuing up the commlinks. Lobo tossed vests and helmets to Quint and Horacio.

War. Quint had signed up once, but not this time. What was Nader's problem? Wasn't Vietnam over and done? He stood up, slipping into his vest, goggles, taking charge of the unit. "Everyone armed?"

The team nodded, camo kid grinning broadly. *Christ, that kid can't be more than sixteen.* "Then let's do some reconnaissance. I want to know who these people are, what the fuck they want from me. You men ready?"

Lobo looked around the group, silently communicating with his people. As one, Gonzo's men raised their weapons in solidarity for a beat then headed for the door.

"Lobo, you men have a plan, here?" Quint asked as the ammo depot door clanged shut. "It's your territory."

"Sure do, boss. This isn't our first rodeo with these guys. Gonzo is pissed. They've broken our truce. They know what's going to happen, and we know what to do. You and Horacio there, be our rear guard. Watch and cover. Got enough ammo?"

Quint nodded. "H?"

"*Sí, jefe. Listo,*" he replied as Gonzo's men moved into the parking area and lined into a single file formation to skirt around the building to the street. Quint and Horacio fell in at the end.

Mac took forward lead, edging into the street with Hughie behind. Quint stepped out from the shadow of the building, alert for any movement from the warehouse. Smoke rose from the rear quadrant, but he saw no sign of flames. Nothing moved. Mac inched ahead, Hughie three yards behind to his left. Quint fell back into the right flank. Exposed. *Could be walking into a trap.*

The other team dropped into formation, Horacio covering the advance, and proceeded toward the smoking SUVs. A quick glance told Quint to call for an ambulance, but neither Mac nor Lobo seemed to care about the bodies. Quint got the idea Gonzo's outfit was happy to see its enemies contorted and bleeding to death on its doorstep.

They'd reached the edge of the warehouse without shots fired. The enemy was gone, only the bodies remained. Quint stepped over a soldier, a child really, crumpled in a pool of his blood. The kid didn't even shave yet. This was how Nader operated in 'Nam. Preyed on the weak, the ignorant. The young. Getting them to do his dirty work like transporting the drugs. Quint wondered what Nader had done to get all these kids to join him in his vendetta. It had to be Nader. Jade had been right when she mistrusted him. She'd said to leave him at the storm drain. Why hadn't he?

Mac stood back and Hughie stepped into the warehouse, disappearing into the black. Quint advanced to second position, covered by Mac. They split up to search. The dusty, shadow-filled space housed an assortment of mostly road building equipment: excavators, loaders, rollers rusting, caked with dried adobe. A couple of cranes, a row of graders, a pile of asphalt mixers. Along the wall, forklifts. In the back, piles of crushed road rock. The air thickened with smoke. The Barrio, or whoever had attacked, could have used the equipment for protection—heavy equipment lined the boarded-over front windows. But they'd shot from the roof. He twisted around looking for stairs, keyed the comms. "Roof." He headed up.

The heat rose and the air filled with smoke. The fire was on the upper floor, illuminating the hall. Quint fished a handkerchief from his cargo pocket, tied it around nose and mouth. He climbed the rest of the stairs. Mac followed. On the landing he saw the fire licking at the old dry wood, crackling, spitting, advancing on the stairs. He trotted toward the roof access visible through the smoke at the end of the corporate offices. Jade's voice told him to turn back, get out of there, it was too dangerous, but he had to know if Nader had gotten away. He had to document the dead before the flames erased their existence.

On the roof, he found three bodies scattered, victims of the Stinger, near the corner now blazing. Another kid hung over the side of the building, his too long belt caught in an exhaust vent. He dragged the body over the parapet toward the stairs. Mac tugged another body, Hughie a third. Gonzo's men ferried the corpses down to the now nearly engulfed second floor, taking a second set of stairs to the warehouse floor. Quint wrestled the fourth body down. The second floor was giving way, burning beams crashing onto the abandoned equipment. If anyone was hiding in the building, either they were injured or out of ammo. There wasn't time to search. The men created a bucket line to ferry the dead to the street.

Outside, Mac contacted Lobo. "Four dead. We've deposited them on the street. The building is on fire. Call the fire department?"

Quint couldn't hear the reply, but no sirens wailed into the district. They approached the blasted SUVs. Horacio hefted a body from one of the vehicles to lay it on the sidewalk next to five others. One of the bodies groaned. Alive. The camo kid stuck his bayonet into the injured man and grinned at Quint, then returned to collecting weapons, some exploded beyond recognition, let alone usefulness. Quint's gut roiled with his anger as the senselessness of this mushroomed. Still, no Nader.

Gonzo pulled out of his garage in a tow truck and began the process of hauling off the destroyed vehicles. Quint jumped in with him. They towed three of the vehicles to a wrecking yard on the outskirts of the district. The sign read, Gonzo Wrecking.

By the end of the night eleven kids were dead and unidentified, a warehouse had burned to the ground, and the last two blockade vehicles had disappeared. Filthy, stinking of smoke, Quint and Horacio, were no closer to answers than at the airport when the sniper shot at Quint.

"You men can billet here tonight. Dorm's over there." Gonzo pointed his thumb toward a door. "Shower's down the hall."

"Thanks, man. We have a flight in the morning. Can you

get us to the airport by seven?"

"Sure, Quint. I'll bill you for the work when my van is repaired."

"Gonz, why didn't the police or fire show up?"

"Hell man, they don't come into my neighborhood. But I'll make a report tomorrow. Looks like we have a new gang moving in. None of the bodies belonged to Barrio. I don't know all the gangbangers, but those kids had guns and no training. I'm hoping you brought the trouble and you'll take it away, bro'."

"Yeah. What happened to the bodies? Some families are gonna be real unhappy."

"Ambulances. The hospital isn't afraid to come into the barrio."

"Why do you stay in this neighborhood, Gonz?"

"Cheap land. Lawless. Nobody keeping an eye on me. It's great cover. Let's go eat. Chef has stew."

They ascended the stairs, landing in a back hall and followed the scent of cooked meat and vegetables to a cafeteria style room with food and metal tables. A dozen men, including Lobo and Hughie hunched over trays, spooning hunks of what Quint thought was pork and hominy in a green sauce into their mouths. A portly man wearing a chef's hat with tattoos of cuts of meat up and down his arms, ladled stew into bowls the size of wash basins to the men queuing to eat.

"You always eat so late?"

"Third seating. Bigger than usual for you guys who missed dinner. Chef, give my friends a nice full bowl of that slop. Smells great. Boys, grab some bread and drinks. He gestured to another table next to a small glass-fronted refrigerator filled with beer, energy drinks, and water. Three coffee urns stood on the table.

The cook slopped a couple of pounds of stew into Horacio's bowl. He held out a dish of sliced jalapenos. "Chilis?"

"*Claro, gracias compa.*" The chef dumped half the bowl over Horacio's meal.

"You *amigo?*"

"Thanks. About half that amount. No chilis." Quint was handed a normal-sized bowl of stew, as was Gonzo. They grabbed a basket of bread, beers and sat down at a table with a couple of the men sopping the dregs of stew from their bowls.

The room buzzed with quiet conversation punctuated with the scraping of metal chairs over the vinyl floor and occasional bursts of laughter. During lulls in the conversation, Quint heard the comforting sounds of cutlery on plates and smacking lips. A few belches. It felt relaxed yet an underlying current of tension ran through the room, reminding Quint of Lompoc once he'd been bumped to minimum security.

Gonzo greeted the diners, but made no attempt to introduce his guests to the sandy blond with SEMPER FI tattooed down his arm. Instead, he said, "Laith, you know who those kids are? Any buzz on the internet?"

"No. Everything is quiet. No one has come forward to claim the hit. I haven't made any identity matches. I'm judging they aren't from around here. Like a boys' school of wannabes —no tats, no scars. A lotta dead though. Whoever ordered these boys to attack has a heart of ice. Or was totally ignorant of who they would be up against."

"Very curious, indeed," Gonzo muttered, glaring at Quint. "Man, could your guy be that cold?"

The more he found out, the more Quint was convinced this was all some sick vendetta on the part of his superior officer, his handler, after he'd been transferred to intelligence. "Colder, Gonz."

"So you know this baby killer?" the marine asked.

"'Nam. What about you?"

"Gulf, bro'"

"I'm guessing we all know something about killing babies, but my CO didn't get his hands bloody. Left it up to the men under him. Believe me, thinking back on it, the man's hands were in the muck to his armpits. Asshole used his intelligence resources to get something on you, or threatened to, and forced you into his dirty game." Quint stopped, stared at his forkful of chayote dripping in a spicy tomatillo sauce. He put it in his mouth and chewed as though he'd realized something, or come to some determination for action.

The men at the table watched him. He put down his fork. "I did some shitty things during that war. The whole thing was a lie. Vietnam was hell. I let Nader blackmail me into drugs and moving Vietcong opium through his network to the States. Got caught. Did time. But there was more. Secrets. I never put the timing of my bust together with Nader's activities. I can't say how or what, but my gut is telling me they're connected."

"You mean this Nader clown is after you for some intel you have on him from what 1970?" asked Laith.

"'72 through four. I was arrested, discharged, and convicted in fall of '74. And yes. but I don't know what or why. If I was likely to reveal my Vietnam secrets, I would've done it long ago."

"I'll look into him. Full name? Service? Rank?" Laith offered.

"Charles 'Chuck' Nader. Spook. NSA."

"Ah, man, even I can't dig into NSA files. I'll try, but don't get your expectations up."

"I'll have my IT guy work on it too. My daughter's office has a good hacker on payroll. Maybe between all of you, we can stop whatever is going on," Quint said. "Gonz, you okay with this?"

"That the asshole shot up my van?" Quint nodded. "Hell yeah, I'm okay with taking him down. We go back, Quint. I got no beef with you. As they say, 'the enemy of my friend is my enemy too'. I sure don't need a bunch of kids killed on my doorstep, bringing me headaches."

Quint scraped away from the table. "Thanks Gonz. Laith I'll text you information as soon as I get back. H, you finished? I'm headed to the bath house. Wash the stench off." He stood up, grinning. "Any place I can burn my clothes?"

"I'll give you plastic bags to put them in. Your duffels are on your beds. See you here at six. We leave at six-thirty for the airport."

Horacio stood, too and shook their host's hand. "Thanks for everything, Gonzo."

Quint grinned. "Visit us sometime. Laith, I'll text you my contact info. H and I are based out of Mexico City."

The fifth man had remained silent through the conversation, his chin resting in his hand, elbow propping him up. He raised his head and spoke in a slow drawl, "Y'all can search, but ya ain't findin' no information on a 'Nam spook. He gonna be wrapped up in government secrets so tight he mummified."

"Yeah, yeah, Weevil, we don't need your negative world view," Laith said.

Quint thought this Weevil might be about his age. "You a vet?"

"Yep. 'Nam, just like you. Right at the end."

"What branch?"

"Now wouldn't y'all like to know. But if I tell ya, I'd hafta kill ya."

Gonzo shot his man a look Quint couldn't interpret."

"I'm serious gentlemen. Ya don't mess with NSA," he said and returned to his dour pose.

Chapter 4

Safe Return

Sunday, September 30, 2007

Quint slept through the Aero Mexico flight into Mexico City. Horacio stared out the window at the geography of his country, something he'd seldom experienced. He elbowed his boss to wake him up when the plane started its final descent into the Valley of Mexico. He'd never seen Popo's and Ixtla's snow-covered peaks so close before.

Chuhco met them at the curb in front of baggage claim. Horacio jumped in front. They rode in silence as he concentrated on maneuvering Horacio's limo through the mid-afternoon traffic clogging exhaust-filled Viaducto headed toward Colonia Roma.

As they approached their exit, Quint spoke from the backseat. "Chuch, thanks for picking us up. How have things been at the office? Any trouble?"

"No, Mr. *Queent*, it's been quiet. I came by every day, but I slept at my apartment. I miss Lily and JadeAnne. How'd it go for you?" He made eye contact through the rearview mirror.

Quint mentally rebuked himself for not calling the staff. Of course they worried. "A success. Lily is safe with her family."

"*Felicidades, jefe. Y JadeAnne?*"

"We put Jade, Dylan, and Pepper on a flight to California yesterday. I don't know how long they'll be gone." He paused. Chucho shot him a questioning look. "Jade has to sell, or rent her houseboat, terminate her partnership at Waterstreet Investigations and close out her life in Sausalito. It's a big job," he said, unwilling to tell the young man how bereaved he felt.

"Good. They made it through the storm drains. How did Javie do? He was pretty excited about the mission."

Quint couldn't answer. What would he say? *Javie is dead, kid. Gunned down by a man you knew.* Which man was it? Anibal or Nader? Instead he replied, "You're handling the limo very well. I didn't know you drove."

"*Aye, jefe,* Horacio started giving me lessons long ago. I've got my license. I'm saving up to buy a car. I'm tired of wasting my time on *pesera*s to get to school."

"Speaking of school, how are you doing? Caught back up?"

"No, *jefe*, it's only been a few days. But I got permission from all my professors to be late. At least my Computer Science professors. I'll need your signature, though. You'll sign, won't you?"

"Of course. I'll support my head of IT in any way I can," Quint said, and winked. "But you better get back to classes. By the way, Chuch, I have a task for you. Ever heard of the NSA?"

"No. ¿*Qué es?*"

"A U.S. security agency created to spy on the world and know everything going on. A lot of their work is top secret or black ops. I need to know about a man who worked for NSA in 1974. He was in Vietnam. You'll have to hack their files," he said, adding in English, "You can't get caught."

Chucho grinned. "Right up my *callejon, jefe.* I'll get started right away. What's his name?" he asked as he pulled the limo into the alley behind the residence.

"Toss the keys to H. Let's go up, see if there's anything to eat. Did Mrs. P stock the pantry?"

"*Sí, jefe*," he said, nodding.

"Good. I have a long story to tell you. H, you want to come up?" Quint asked before stepping out onto the cobbled drive.

Horacio leaned forward. "No. Better I show my face at home." His voice was low, strained. He knew what Quint was going to do to young Chucho. Javie was his buddy.

Quint nodded, slid out, meeting Chucho at the stairs. At the top, Mrs. P flung open the door.

"Mrs. P! I'm so glad to see you. I was just thinking about your *albóndigas*. What's for lunch?"

The housekeeper's face turned a rosy shade of pink to match her apron, but her smile showed her pleasure. "Would you like a sopa and quesadillas or cold tuna-stuffed-poblanos, Mr. Queent?"

"Mrs. P, I'm happy with whatever you serve. Anything you make will be delicious. I haven't had a decent meal in a week."

She beamed and led the men into her kitchen.

After *almuerza* and Quint's story of Javie's death, Chucho went to class. Mrs. P shopped. It was obvious their pleasure at Quint's and Horacio's safe return had been destroyed by the loss of the young marine. Quint lay down, still exhausted, to ponder the situation. The residence felt empty, his mood dark. Why was Vietnam rearing its ugly head now? Hadn't he paid the penalty already? He needed someone to talk to. *Rosi?*

A warm glow ignited in his gut, calming him. How could she be so positive doing the work she did? Combatting the buying and selling of people as though they were cattle—worse than cattle. Rosi fought every day to rescue victims of human trafficking, primarily sex slavery—an industry as old as men and women, uglier than the ugliest thing he could imagine. She knew it was a losing battle over greed, lust, and the insane delusion one human had rights to own and profit from the misery and degradation of another.

His daughter was just like her. Integrity. A strong sense of right and wrong. Humanity. A crusader. Jade wasn't going to stop now. She'd won a skirmish—vowed to win the war. Jade would come home. *How did a guy like me ever get connected to women like them?*

Jade's mother was another strong woman with the conviction and moral fiber to fight for a better world. Look what Thuy had done for him. She'd healed him. He was a foreigner invading her country, wreaking brutal, deadly havoc in the name of freedom. What freedom did his kind bring the Vietnamese people? Death!

Thuy had nursed him for six weeks in the hospital after he was shot. He was lucky he hadn't lost his leg, already infected by the time he was airlifted to the 17th Field Hospital near Saigon. *Damn rotting jungle, rotten country.* The place was overcrowded, but they had long- term treatment—and pretty Vietnamese, volunteer nursing assistants.

A nursing student at the university, Thuy came from a village near Da Nang. She'd grown up in a war-torn country, but she believed she could alleviate the suffering she saw around her. She made him laugh. With Thuy encouraging his exercising, he regained almost one-hundred percent usage of the leg. But the real healing had been her help to accept the horror of what he'd done. *I may not have pulled the trigger, but I gave the order.* Thuy loved him anyway, and he hated himself a little less.

He shuddered as he undressed for bed. Quint had lost her through his connection to Chuck Nader. Now, here was Nader, and again he had someone to lose.

Chapter 5

Quint's Tour of Duty

Monday, October 1, 2007

He woke up chilly in the dark bedroom. The empty residence echoed street noise—a kind of static matching his muddled thoughts. He'd had another Vietnam nightmare. Always the same: shadows creeping toward him, silhouetted against a wall of fire, the roaring of the flames drowning out the sound of rescue, the sound of his men dying, the heat waking him drenched in sweat. In the distance, a siren wailed. Quint sucked in a deep breath and blew it out, partially clearing the remnants of the dream from his mind, but the fear continued to clutch at him. His heart raced. Always an enemy lurking just out of his sight. Always dogging his footsteps. He inhaled again, holding it for several beats, feeling his blood pressure drop.

He should get up, take a shower, call Jade, see how things were going. Get her IT man onto the hack. He turned on his bedside lamp. The clock read 7:30. Maybe too early in California. Would Jade be showing Dylan around San

Francisco or the coast? Dylan would make her come home. Quint would talk to the doctor when he called Jade. Meanwhile, he'd check his mail. Catch up on the work he'd missed. He hadn't been online since he flew to Juarez. His op with Senator Aguirre needed attention. After the shower.

And he'd call Rosi. Maybe he should invite her for dinner. No, too late. Dinner tomorrow. That's it. Not good to look too eager. He'd call. Ask her to go out tomorrow. Tonight he'd heat up Mrs. P's *albóndigas.*

In the shower it occurred to him he hadn't inquired about the security. Did they still have security? Nader twisted in the wind somewhere. Was Nader the dark shadow he couldn't see and couldn't shake? Was he in Mexico? Quint needed to talk to the ambassador. Tell him about Javie. And Nader. If Ambassador Garza hadn't pulled the marines from guard duty, he sure would now. *What a fucking shitshow.* Well, that was for tomorrow. Today he needed to come to terms with an empty house. Always a loner, he should be happy, he told himself. Maybe Chucho would move back in. Mrs. P would be coming to cook and clean, but with so few people around, how often would that be? Horacio made it clear his wife wanted him home at night. *I don't blame him.*

His office hadn't changed. The same sticky notes littering the desk. The blank agenda. The open file folder. The dark computer screen. He booted up. Caught some news.

> **12 Tourists injured in Male, Maldives blast**
> **Chinese trading company Htoo closes doors,**
> **paying employees two month's salary**
> **Robert Levy, mayor of Atlantic City, New**
> **Jersey embellished a Vietnam War record**

"Christ. Vietnam. Can't I forget it?"

"Forget what, *jefe*?" A familiar voice drifted through the open door.

"Chuch, that you?"

"*Sí, soy,*" Chucho said, from the doorway.

"Have a seat. I was thinking about you. Isn't it a little early for you to be here?"

Chucho lowered himself onto the settee. He cast his eyes into his folded hands. "I, ah...I was using the computer to do homework. *Lo siento, jefe.* Maybe it's not okay."

Quint laughed. "Why wouldn't it be okay? I was thinking, now that I'm back, you might want to move into your room in the residence. You can park in the garage."

"*Jefe?* I don't have a car."

"Neither do I, kid. But I was thinking we need one for when Horacio is busy. What should we buy?"

"BMW?" Chucho responded, half smiling, eyebrows raised.

"Maybe used. We'll have it armored. You can use it for school when we're not busy."

"*¿De veras?*" The joy radiating from Chucho's face convinced Quint. They both needed a car; a small car would be way easier to park in crowded Mexico.

"Want to google some ads?"

"Joo becha boss." He leapt to his feet.

"Whoa, hold your horses, man. What about moving back here? I could use some company. Ultimately it's safer if the place looks occupied." Chucho sat again, nodded. "Is that a yes?"

"*Tal vez.* I like my apartment. With a car it would be easier to get here," he said then paused, his expression neutral.

"Why do I feel a negotiation coming on?"

Chucho grinned. "If I lived here I could use the computers as much as I want for anything?

"Don't you already? Yeah, sure. I don't care what you do as long as you do your work. And your homework, Chuch."

"You're not going to make me pay rent are you?"

"Why would I do that? I'm not going to make you work extra, either. But I am going to ask you to continue to act as security. Chucho, before you decide, I gotta tell you about the trip." Quint checked his watch. "First I want to talk to Jade."

Again Chucho stood up. " No, sit down. Don't you want to say hi?"

"*Claro.*" He tossed himself onto the settee for the third time.

Quint dialed, switching to speaker phone. It rang six times before JadeAnne's voice said, "Hello?"

"Hello, daughter. How are you? How was your flight?"

"Dad! It was uneventful. I slept... Dyl! It's Dad. Come say hi." Pepper woofed in the background. "Pepper says hi, too. We miss you."

"I've got you on speaker phone. Say hi, Chuch."

"Hi, Jade. Hi Dylan. I miss you guys and Pepper. When are you coming home?"

Pepper woofed again. Jade and Dylan chorused their hellos. Chucho mouthed, "Shall I leave?" Quint shook his head.

"Listen kids, I want to warn you to be careful—"

"What do you mean, Dad?" Quint heard the apprehension in Jade's voice.

"At the airport, after you went to your gate, a sniper took a shot at me then a full attack was mounted on us as we arrived at Gonzo's garage. Odds are it's Nader. H and I are fine, but frankly, Jade, I'm worried. He's got some vendetta against me. He might try to get to me through you—"

Dylan interrupted. "*Jesus Cristo, Queent—no nos digas.* Aren't we over this. Anibal is dead."

Chucho bolted upright, his lips forming an "O" to match his wide eyes. Quint held up his palm.

"This is speculation Dylan, but we can't ignore his alliance with Anibal. My gut is telling me this has something to do with my tour in Vietnam—what else could it be? I haven't seen or heard of the man since 1974."

JadeAnne responded, "You treated him as a good buddy."

"That I did, Jade."

"So what happened, *jefe*?" Chucho asked.

"Raced us down I-25 to El Paso. Attacked as we were pulling in."

"No, I mean in Vietnam. You were there? In the American War?"

"I'll tell you after we hang up. Now, let's ask Jade to start Qadir on the hacking job. Chucho, I want you on it. too."

"*Aye, claro.* Maybe we could consult?"

"That's the idea," Quint said.

"What do you want Qadir to do? Nothing illegal. I hope."

"Jade, would I do that?"

She made a derisive sound with her exhale.

"Okay, I want him to hack the NSA employee records from 1972 through 1974 and find out anything he can on Nader. Especially what he was doing in Vietnam and what he was supposed to be doing with me. He's got to be very, very careful. If he will, I want him to team up with Chucho and a guy called Laith in El Paso. I'll send you everything I know tomorrow."

"You and Nader were mixed up together in the heroin trafficking," Jade speculated.

"Among other things."

"Why, Dad?"

"Blackmail."

"Nader *blackmailed* you into—what?"

"Loading body bags with NVA opium, mainly."

"Were you stealing it?"

"Hell, no. Nader was sent to 'Nam to collect intel on Khun Sa's network. They ran seventy-percent of the world's supply. He used me because my unit worked reconnaissance in the region the drugs were carried through. Not only was I transporting drugs for sale, I was handling payments to the enemy. The opium was put on mules and moved into the Mekong Delta. Put on fishing junks. It was fucked up, Jade. He threatened to get me busted if I screwed up. He'd cut-off my supply, send me to prison. Dishonorable discharge. Lose my commission. Those days I still thought I was doing something good for the world. Fighting for freedom."

"You were addicted?" Dylan asked.

"Drug use was prevalent. The military looked the other

way unless you shoved it in their face. I was a social user. Nader made sure I wasn't."

"What do you mean Dad?"

"He introduced me to heroin and opium. Made sure I was always along for parties and R & R. Encouraged me. Christ, girl, I was twenty-two years old. A decorated hero. I couldn't possibly get addicted."

"Sick."

"Me? Mebbe—"

"No, that bastard, Nader."

"Well, I wanted you to hear it from me before you read it in the NSA documents."

"Dad?"

"Yeah?"

"If Nader blackmailed you with prison, was he the one who turned you in?"

"Nah, Charlie found out what I was doin'. Didn't like it. Said if I didn't stop, turn Nader in, he'd turn us both in."

"You're telling me my father busted you?"

"It's how he became your father."

"The webs we weave. Well, *you're* my father now, Quint, we'll get to the bottom of this. I'm so *not* surprised Charles Stone, the two-faced shit, would do that to his 'best friend'. He claimed to be against drugs, but Mom was addicted to pills. He tooted coke with all the hip Mill Valley yuppies through the '80s and into the '90s. Count me in, Dad. There's an atonement due."

"Does this mean you'll be home soon?"

Dylan replied, "It's lovely here. The Sarasvati is charming, but I'm working to convince her to come back to Mexico with me."

"What does Pepper want?" The dog barked at the sound of his name. "Good boy, Pepper. Jade, your dog wants to return to us."

"All right, I'm thinking about it. We've got to go. Nice to hear your voice, Chuch. Say hi to H for me. And Mrs. P. Are you having *albóndigas* tonight?" She laughed. "I'll talk to you soon. Call Rosi."

Quint punched off the phone, slumped back into his chair. "Now you know, Chucho." He studied his reflection in the window. The spiky succulents in the patio looked like some mad hair or halo around the reflection of his head. Or maybe he was some resurrected breed of dinosaur. He felt like one.

"I read about the American War in Vietnam in a history class. You were there?"

"I was there. 1972 until I was discharged. Sent to prison at the end of '74. It was right at the end of my tour. I was about your age when I enlisted. Twenty-one. A stupid kid with high ideals. I was going to save the world from communism... " Quint's voice tapered off to silence.

Chucho quietly stood up and said, "I'll move back in, *jefe*."

Quint skipped the meatballs and turned in after checking all the doors and windows. No way could he fend off an attack single handedly. The bulletproof windows were a plus, but if Nader sent a rocket into the residence, or the office, Quint would die. He needed to see about hiring security. He needed to call the ambassador.

In the morning—*if* he was still alive.

Chapter 6

Horacio Agrees

Tuesday, October 2, 2007

Horacio showed up at the kitchen door with a bag of *pan dulces* at eight, chipper as ever. Quint was feeling better. The coffee helped. "Morning, H. You look like you're well rested. Coffee?" Quint said, taking the bag.

"*Sí, Por favor.*"

Quint plated the sweet rolls, retrieved the cream from the fridge, poured them each a cup, then transported everything to the table. He missed Jade. "Talked to the kids last night. Dylan's pressing her to come home. She'll get her IT man onto the hack. Chucho is probably down there working on it already. He said he'd move back in. I need a roommate. Place is too lifeless with just one."

"I hear you. I'm used to a constant circus at home. I doubt I'd be able to live without it now."

"Chucho wants a car. A BMW. I think I should find one. It will be mine until he can buy it from me. He'll drive it and me when you're tied up. I was thinking, we're going to be, at minimum, a year on this op. Maybe I should encourage the kid to rent out his apartment. He lives here free. With income off the apartment, he'd get his car and be able to save for his future. I couldn't help my own kid, but I'd feel good helping this one. What do you think, H? Talk me out of it if it's a bad idea."

Horacio let loose with an ogre belly laugh. "*Jefe,* you look like a tough guy, but inside, you're a fluffy *conejo.*"

"A what?"

"Rabbit. Soft."

"Yeah. I don't know what's gotten into me. So you think I should make him work for his future?" He smiled. It was easy talking with Horacio.

"Not at all. Help Chucho. He's still suffering from the loss of the senator. In a way, Aguirre acted as a father to him. Now you do. It's all good. He's loyal, reliable, honest, and loves to work."

"Speaking of work, we need a plan. We've got enough intel. Whaddaya think, H?

"Mr. Quint, you got a big roadblock to the successful outcome of the senator's op."

"First off, H, call me Quint! We're in this together. Second, which roadblock would that be?"

His voice flattened. He spit out the word as though he'd bitten into a persimmon. Astringent. "Nader."

"Christ. You think he's part of it? It wouldn't surprise me if he had something to do with the cartels."

"I think he's out to get you. Blocking us, possibly killing you, at least sending you to prison again. That would make his day."

"Sending me to prison again? Why do you say that?"

"What do you have on this guy, Quint?

"You know—he was involved in trafficking opium and heroin from the Golden Triangle during the Vietnam War. Statute of limitations has probably run out. No one would care now. H, if I didn't spill when I went to prison in '74, why would

I now? Hell, I'd forgotten all about him."

"Maybe Jade can talk to her other father to get the truth. Maybe he didn't send you to prison."

"You mean, maybe Nader did. I flashed on that when I was talking to her yesterday."

"I didn't need to hear the conversation. I don't know what happened, but what you confided to me sounded like only part of the puzzle. That's what we need to do now. Piece it together. I'll bet you next month's salary, Nader is at the heart of it. We figure it out—take him out of the equation. We'll successfully complete the op and Senator Aguirre will rest in peace."

Quint studied his steepled hands for several minutes. Horacio sipped his now-lukewarm coffee between bites of his second *concha*. He set the half-eaten pastry onto a napkin when Quint raised his head.

"I've asked myself why Nader showed up now—I don't believe in coincidence—but I can't wrap my head around his possible involvement. Certainly not the sex trafficking." He gave his partner a piercing look. "No, he'd have turned up earlier. It's got to be—"

"*Jefe,* you've described Nader as a man without morals. Why not sex trafficking?"

"We know who brought Lily and her sister into Mexico. We know who they were selling to. Strictly cartel business. Nader isn't the type to be brought into someone else's operation. He'd want to be top dog. No Zeta's going to let him in. Maybe as a buyer. But if he was after my girls, he had plenty of opportunities without hooking up with Aguirre. If he was posing as a buyer, he'd never get merchandise without paying upfront. That was something he didn't do in Laos. He got the Sa organization opium fronted."

"How was that?"

"Sa was imprisoned in '69 for political crimes. He bargained his way out in '74, but his trade suffered. Nader had access to the U.S. While the drug lord languished in prison, I carried opium out and money in through my reconnaissance missions. I was already undercover breaking codes to send intel to the NSA, but now I know that was Nader's cover for his dealing.

After Nixon's bombing offensive Christmas'72, when most of our troops were being shipped home, I was reassigned to a base outside Saigon. Being the new guy, I landed the death detail. Nader probably pulled strings. It was a perfect setup. His mules transported the opium to me at the base. I loaded the bags and put them on the transports back to the States. It was ugly work, H. By then I was doing more than smoking weed to relax. I was paranoid. Thought my superiors were onto me. I told Nader I wanted out and tried to get reassigned. My tour only had months to go. Nader wasn't going for it. He was getting rich—I was getting scared. I told Charley Stone what was going on. He was my buddy."

"And you got *arrestado*—busted."

Quint slammed his mug onto the scarred table top. "I got busted. That bastard Stone got my kid, took her away from me. I didn't even know she'd been born until he came to Lompoc after his discharge. Had me sign over rights. I agreed to be dead to my daughter." He croaked out the admission.

"*Jefe*, Quint, I can't guess how painful this must have been. I couldn't imagine living without my *escuintlas,* but did you ever think your buddy was trying to help you? Maybe he didn't turn you in? How much did you know about Nader's operation?"

"Plenty, H. I knew he was selling intel to the NVA. He was getting it from me."

"There's your answer. Call Stone. Thank him for saving your kid."

"Christ, I don't know. Why now? Does anyone care about Nader's crimes now?"

"Did you tell Stone about his selling intelligence?"

Quint's head dropped into his hands. "I did. But Nader could have killed me. Why would he send me to prison? He's a sociopath. Doesn't care about anyone but himself. Life meant nothing to him. I don't want to talk about what I've witnessed him do."

Horacio wrinkled his forehead. "How'd he get you involved, anyway?"

"Blackmail."

"*Pues,* how are we going to stop him?"

Chapter 7

This Could be Treason

Horacio closed himself into the workroom settling at the telephone, a fresh notepad and pen ready. Susana, Senator Aguirre's assistant, would take over the running of the Roma office. But she was still closing down Senator Aguirre's homes and offices, tying up the loose ends since his murder in Tepoztlán at the hands of Z2, one of the top men in Los Zetas —the man responsible for the Mexico City human trafficking ring. Until Susana returned, Quint left it to his righthand man, Horacio.

Quint presumed Chucho still worked on the hack in the communications center. He closed his office door to make the appointment with the U.S. ambassador. Tony Garza needed to know what kind of man he'd let into the embassy. If Nader had been selling intel in Vietnam along with his drug dealing, he'd come to the right place. Plenty of drugs and guys ready to buy both in Mexico. Could he still be NSA? Was he independent— a bad actor selling U.S. intel to the cartels to get drugs to sell outside Mexico?

Mrs. Tomsky, Garza's private secretary, sandwiched Quint into a fifteen-minute slot after the ambassador's lunch. He checked his watch, dialed Horacio on the intercom.

"Yeah, *jefe*?"

"Can you drive me to Cuauhtémoc in an hour? The embassy needs to know about Nader."

"*Claro*. I called my brother. Sami agrees to represent us. I'll let him know to be here in forty-five minutes. Should I pull a retainer out of the safe?"

"Might as well. If this goes south, I'll need a U.S. attorney, but Sami can handle Mexican law. You have more calls?"

"*Sí*. I'm looking for Nader. The airlines aren't being helpful. Sami can get that maybe."

"Would Nader drive?" Quint asked.

"Twenty hours? Not too likely."

I'll check with Chucho, and call Gonzo," Quint said.

"Call Susana too. I'm useless in an office," H joked.

Quint hung up. He strolled to the comms center, knocked, and pushed the door ajar. Chucho typed ferociously, staring at his screen. "Come in, *jefe*," he said without looking up. "I've started with searching Tor for anything I can find on Nader."

"Tor? Isn't that some secret thing on the World Wide Web? How did you find that?"

"It's easy. Anyone with an internet connection can use Tor. It's just a browser like Lynx or Netscape."

"Found his file then?"

"No, I'm not in NSA. So far there's not much. I'm using the information you gave us last night."

"What time you come in?"

"Stayed." He swiveled around gesturing to a pile of rumpled blankets on a tatty couch Quint didn't remember.

"You worked all night?"

"No, *jefe*, but I have school this afternoon. I needed to get a jump on this."

"Well, okay, but go home after school. Get some rest and pack up. I'll have H pick you up in the morning. While you're at school, put up some signs to rent your place out. No reason

51

you can't get an income off it."

"Jefe, can I afford the rent here?"

"I hope so. You've just gotten a raise including full room and board. How about an extra hundred a week to help out with school costs? Or maybe you'll want to buy back that BMW." Quint grinned as Chucho's eyes lit up his entire face.

"*¡Mil gracias, jefe!* How can I thank you for this gift?"

"By being the best IT department in Mexico, Chuch. That's enough!"

Chucho paled. "I hope—"

Quint laughed. "No pressure, kid. You are the best! Let's call Jade. See if we can connect with Qadir. Find out what his luck is."

He pulled out his cell phone and dialed. Jade answered on the second ring. "It's a beautiful morning. We're drinking coffee on the deck. What's up Dad?"

Quint asked about Qadir. Jade said she had started him on the hack. She'd get back to him, or if he was at the embassy, she'd have him call Chucho. Qadir wanted to practice his Spanish anyway.

"Okay, Chuch, let's call Laith. Same time zone." He dialed Chucho's office phone; when Laith answered, put it on speaker mode, and introduced the computer geniuses. "You men know what we want. I'll leave you to it. Laith, please liaise with Chucho. He can report to me when I get back later. Be careful. After this conversation, it's probably better to use encryption on the computer. I don't need to tell you that. You're the experts." He waved as he let himself out of the room.

Quint relayed Gonzo's news to Horacio on the ride to the embassy. "Nader was shot on the warehouse roof. Nothing serious. One of his hired gangbangers drove him to a sketchy doctor in the district. He's staying in one of the whorehouses. Gonz's people are keeping an eye on him. When Nader hits the street, Gonz'll call. He's got surveillance on the airport. Says it's the best he can do."

Horacio braked in front of the embassy gate. The duty guard stepped forward. Quint clambered out and showed the marine his ID. Horacio moved off to find a parking space or double park by the restaurant. It was lunchtime. He might have to circle for a quarter hour, Quint considered as he was led through the labyrinthian maze of passages. With each step, his dread expanded. Garza was not going to take the murder of his marine well. He sure wouldn't—hadn't. Javie had been one of the good ones. Life cut off before it began. He was sweating when the guard ushered him into Mrs. Tomsky's office to await his audience with Tony Garza.

"Good afternoon, Mr. Quint. How are your lovely daughter and the poor little girl? Did you ever resolve her problems?"

"Nice to see you again Mrs. Tomsky. Yes. Jade and a coyote crossed her over the border through the storm drains. We delivered her to her family."

Shocked, her eyes widened, then she giggled. "Oh, Mr. Quint, you are a comedian."

"Not at all, Mrs. Tomsky."

Garza's secretary's face morphed from amusement to horror as her hand flew to her lips. The desk buzzer sounded. "The ambassador will see you now," she said.

Quint nodded and let himself into the office.

Garza met him mid-way to the desk, hand extended in greeting, the Angel of Independence perched on his shoulder, gleaming under Mexico's sun. "Mr. Quint. What a pleasure. Sit down, sit down. Mrs. Tomsky said you had important information for me."

"Thanks, Garza. I know you're tight on time, but before we begin, I think it best to wait for my attorney, Sami Rafiq. You remember Sami?"

"Of course, we're well acquainted, but what could you be discussing that requires an attorney?" He laughed.

Quint heard the nervous apprehension in it. He wouldn't be laughing for long. "What do you know about Chuck Nader, Ambassador?"

Garza squinted, wrinkling his nose. "Nader? A career

marine. Why do you ask?"

"What's his assignment to the embassy?"

"I don't know that I can discuss it. You'll have to talk with our intelligence division."

"Garza, why would a marine be attached to an embassy's intelligence division?"

"I'm not sure I like the tenor of this conversation, Mr. Quint. What are you getting at?"

The intercom buzzed, Garza went around his desk and pushed the button. "Yes, Mrs. Tomsky?"

"Mr. Rafiq is here."

"Thank you. Send him in."

Quint turned as the door opened. "Rafiq, thanks so much for joining us. Have a seat." He jutted his chin toward one of the chairs as he seated himself in the other.

Sami leaned across the desk, shook hands with Garza. "Nice to see you again, Ambassador. It's a fine day; the angel is radiating freedom." Sami bellowed his delight over his joke.

"So it is, Sami. The statue is catching the sun just right. She's the best part of my day."

"I thought angels were hermaphrodites," Quint mused, "but I'm guessing you'll be needing her before I'm done. Some of what I'm going to tell you incriminates me, or may. It's why I've retained Sami. You may want to record my statement, Ambassador."

"Not if you're confessing, Quint."

"Fair enough. First, may I extend my condolences on the death of your marine, Javier Mendez. Javie was the marine you sent with Nader to protect us. He was murdered in El Paso. I have reason to believe Chuck Nader or another bad actor, Anibal Aguirre, pulled the trigger."

"What the hell, Quint?"

"Javie illegally crossed the border from Juarez to El Paso through the storm drains as protection for my daughter and the trafficked girl you failed to return—"

"Now don't go putting this on me, man. My office did everythin—"

"I'm not going to bicker with you. The U.S. Embassy failed to help a U.S. citizen. We delivered her to her family. That is not the point of this conversation. Your marine was gunned down in cold blood while valiantly protecting two U. S. citizens on U.S. soil. I expect he is in the El Paso police mortuary as a John Doe. He deserves a proper burial, and his pension."

"Why would you say Nader was involved?"

"Chuck Nader was not a marine. He claimed to be NSA, which was the organization he was attached to in the '70s in Vietnam where I knew him. This is the story I want to relate to you."

"I served a tour in Vietnam. What about it?"

Quint quickly related his assignment, his medal, and his stint in the hospital. Garza drummed his fingers, impatient. "When I went back to active duty, Nader turned up. Everywhere I went, there he was. Passing the joints, buying the beers, talking up his recon work. Wouldn't I like to really do something for my country? Put the nail in the coffin of communism? I signed on, but stayed with the Rangers leading advanced recon missions. Not only was I reporting back to my commanders, I was undercover reporting everything to Nader. He was my handler. We got friendly. He brought me in deeper. About the time Nixon started pulling troops out, I got reassigned to Nader's company. By then Nader started demanding I do things: make some deliveries, pay some people. Soon I was one of his stable of mules." Quint continued summarizing, "In '74, when Sa got out of prison, drug trafficking spiked. Nader was at the heart of it. I started to back out, object. He blackmailed me to keep me in line. He got me transferred to the *death detail* packing body bags."

Garza nodded. "I remember. I spent time in '74 at that base. A hell hole. Wasn't it in August a scandal erupted over drugs and trafficking? I only heard about it. I was consulting on the border."

"Yeah. I was arrested, shipped to Fort Benning. The Army wanted me to tell what I knew, because, of course, I couldn't have been working alone. I kept silent. Was stripped of my commission and kicked out of the army. I was tried as a civilian. Served four of seven years in the Federal Penitentiary at Lompoc, California."

"Sad story, Quint, but what has this to do with Nader?"

"Nader had another sideline in 'Nam."

"What do you mean?"

"He was selling information to the NVA."

"What!? Do you have proof?"

"I can get it. I think he's doing the same thing here. If he's on some sort of drug taskforce, he's selling our intel to the cartels."

"This is a big accusation, Quint."

"Indeed. He's made it clear he's out to kill me."

"Do you know where he is now? He hasn't reported in."

"In a low-rent whorehouse on the border in El Paso with a gunshot wound."

"You shoot him?"

"No. But he was shooting at me."

"Mr. Quint, I'm not sure how much of this I should believe, or what you expect me to do. I'll notify his department to look into him and determine who he's reporting to. As far as your involvement in drug trafficking in Vietnam, you've paid your debt. What worries me is you have implicated civilians in an illegal border crossing. That is a crime."

Sami straightened up. Quint had forgotten he was in the room. Sami cleared his throat. "If I may, I don't believe a citizen crossing a border *into* his or her native country is a crime. Perhaps there's a misdemeanor for not passing through immigration; the fact that the youngster took her escape from Mexico into her own hands is not a crime on any one's part. Quint, you have nothing to worry about. Except this man who obviously wants to kill you."

"Mr. Quint is responsible for the death of my marine," Garza said.

"No, sir, the marine was on leave. He was responsible for his own actions. Further, I know Mr. Quint was against the plan from the start. It was arranged by others."

"Tony, please, this is bigger than who is responsible for a citizen crossing the border without her papers. This could be treason. At the minimum, it's selling potentially sensitive government information," Quint said. "Please take it seriously."

The intercom buzzer sounded again. "Yes, Mrs. Tomsky?"

"Your next appointment is here."

Garza rang off. "Gentlemen, thank you for coming to me with this potential breech of security." His speech sounded stiff. "I will have it looked into. Now, I must say goodbye." He reached across his broad desk and shook their hands.

El Angel de la Independencia winked under the bright midday sun.

Chapter 8

Be Prepared

Horacio idled the limo under the jacarandas. The embassy's backside teemed with cars and people out for *comida*. Quint saluted the gate guard and clambered into the front seat. Sami dove into the back.

"Little brother." Horacio greeted Sami. "How'd it go in there? Sami, is my boss going to be arrested?"

"Arrested!" His peals of laughter lightened the atmosphere. "No, Garza isn't buying the story. You have to admit, Quint, this speculation of yours is pretty farfetched."

"All true. Well, except for the reason Nader has attached himself to the embassy. But think about it. The guy sold secrets to the North Vietnamese Army. What else is going on in Mexico but the war on drugs?

"The rise of organized crime," Horacio mused.

"The cartels." Quint shook his head. "They're the one and the same—into more than drugs. We know it. Everyone knows it."

"You make a strong argument, Quint," Sami conceded.

"Have you heard anything about Nader yet?"

Quint opened his phone. "*Nada*."

Horacio said, "Home, Sami? You want lunch?"

He replied, "*Por supuesto*. Let's go to Sitti's Shawarma. The Lebanese restaurant."

"Sounds great! Quint, you like Middle Eastern food?" Horacio asked.

"Like lamb, pita bread and mint? You bet."

Horacio nosed the limo into the right lane of the Insurgentes roundabout, heading east then south, skirting Colonia Roma on the way to Navarte Poniente and Sami's office. Sami grilled Quint on his involvement in selling secrets to the North Vietnamese.

"I had no part in that. I had a legitimate assignment to gather information and report it to my superiors. It was one of my principal assignments in advance reconnaissance. NVA troop movements, Vietcong strong holds, sympathetic villages. When Nader got hold of me, I carried around a fifty-pound Nestor encryption system. I remember being pretty excited to work one of those. Codes and computers were my thing then. Operating it was complicated, but I excelled. I was proud. But the weight made it unmanageable—it's why I survived that..." He trailed off to silence. The familiar anvil weight settling onto his shoulders. "What can I say. Vietnam was hell."

"This Nestor contraption, it was coded radio communications? Who else besides your superiors received your messages?" Sami asked.

"No one. it was supposed to be unbreakable. But Nader got the code."

"How did you find out he was passing secrets to the enemy?"

"Saw him setting the machine once. He didn't have the expertise to create something I couldn't crack. I confronted him. He lied."

"Did this happen again?"

"Again and again. I read the messages. I threatened to turn him in. He offered me a cut of the profits. It's when I was transferred to his service. I was under orders. I knew everything."

"Why didn't you turn him in?"

"He had too much on me. Circumstantial, yet damning. He held it over my head. In a way, I was party to the crimes. I was also taking a lot of drugs. He held that over me, too. He supplied the drugs, by the way. And he threatened Thuy."

"Who's Thuy?"

"Jade's mother."

Sami regarded Quint, who was half-turned on his seat toward the back of the limo where Sami sprawled. "Now I understand. As far as I know, International law offers no statute of limitations on passing classified information to an enemy, Quint. I think this would fall under U.S. law."

"Then why is he trying to kill me? Why doesn't he just have me arrested?"

"He would have to implicate himself to do that. If he can assassinate you, he eliminates the threat."

"Basically, I'm fucked. All I can think of is, why now?

No one answered.

After lunch, Sami agreed to look into similar cases. Horacio dropped Quint off and drove Chucho to pick up his clothes. Quint took care of paperwork. As the late afternoon shadows reached across his desk, he called Gonzo. No answer. Quint left a message to call. He tried JadeAnne then trudged up to his room to lie down, his mood heavier with each step.

The phone ringing pulled him from a nightmare. Another war dream. All the dredged up memories raising the old nightmares. Nader was coming. Quint could feel it in his bones. He tried Gonzo again. This time Gonz answered.

"He's on Aero Mexico flight 2710, arriving at 10:30—" Quint checked the time. An hour and a half. "—and he's got three men with him. They don't look like they're going for the nightlife or beaches."

"You recognize any of them?"

"No. Ex-military types. Professional."

"Who saw them? You?"

"Yeah."

"He's seen you."

"Not like this he ain't."

"Okay. Thanks man."

"Be prepared. Good luck."

"I'll need more than luck."

Gonz clicked off, leaving Quint with dead air space. It was too late to hire a platoon of security men. He'd have to drag Horacio from his family. Omar too. Might as well contact Sami, although if any of them ended up in jail, they'd need him alive and available. Quint dialed Horacio.

The sounds of banging pots and pans drifted into his room. Chucho must be getting some food. He unlocked the gun safe he kept in his bedroom to assemble his weapons. He'd get ready for battle then eat. He wouldn't be calling Rosi tonight.

"Jefe, Mrs. P left us chicken, rice, and tomatillo salsa," Chucho said as Quint entered the kitchen.

The sauce bubbled gently on the stove. Quint could smell the chicken heating in the oven. Chuch had even set the table.

"She make salad?"

"*Claro*. I'll get it."

Once they'd sat down to eat, Quint broached the impending attack. Chucho's eyes twinkled and his grin spread across his face.

"This isn't a game, Chucho. These are trained killers coming for me, and anyone with me. Help yourself to more chicken and pass the rest over." Chucho passed the food. "Thanks. We need to secure the residence. We're fucked if they have rockets."

"They're coming tonight?"

"Tonight or early morning. If not tonight, tomorrow. Or the next. We need to turn this place into a fortress."

"What about calling the police or asking for more marines."

"No. You missed Garza's reaction to Javie's death. He's not

sending men. We're on our own. It's us and the Rafiq brothers."

"While you were gone I had the building alarmed. Every window and door. No one is getting in without tripping a loud alarm."

"Is it set now?"

"No, I waited for you. Everyone has to learn how to arm and disarm it first."

Chapter 9

Caught in the Act

Omar and Sami came in through the front door while Horacio stowed the limo in the garage. Quint and Chucho pulled the blinds, double checked all the doors and windows, then called everyone to the alarm system panel for a lesson. He rattled off the code. Each practiced activating and de-activating it. Chucho set it then they convened at the kitchen table to hammer out a strategy. It was most likely Nader would try to breech the building while Quint slept. A bombing would bring first responders. Too loud. Too messy. It wasn't Nader's style.

"He is a sneaky bastard," Quint told his team. "And he's not going to expect five of us armed. He knows the layout, so we can't be where he expects us."

"We should be on the roof. We'll see him coming."

"You offering to stand guard, Chuch?"

"Joo betcha, *jefe.*"

"Possible they'll try to come in over the neighbor's roof. Probably set a small explosive to open the kitchen door. He knows he can't get through the blast door, eliminating entry through the office. Or they'll try to come in through a bedroom window street side. Most likely option. You alarmed them too, Chuch?"

"*Sí.* All the windows have bullet proof glass. Any disturbance will set off the alarm siren and turn on the flashing outside lights."

"The tenants will love that," Horacio muttered.

"If there's a fire, we have only one way out. Follow me."

Quint led his men into the pantry. Obscured from immediate view by stacked supplies, was a covered attic access. He dragged over a stepstool, mounted to the top step, and pushed aside the cover, pulling down a hanging ladder over the front of the built-in shelving.

"There's a grated opening with a hanging ladder, which will let you climb to the street. Got it?"

Back in the kitchen, Horacio asked, "*Jefe*, where do you want us?"

"Chuch, on the garage roof. Stay down. Nader knows this is a good lookout. H, I want you in here. You're our first defense if he tries to breech the back door. Sami and Omar will take the office; I'll monitor the rest of the residence, backing up Horacio. Shoot to kill anyone on our property. Now, grab a bedroom; get a couple hours of shut eye. I'll make coffee and wake you up when it's time. I guess the good news is there won't be a full moon or an eclipse."

Quint handed an assault rifle to Chucho, who checked it then double-checked the safety was on. Horacio and Omar carried a small arsenal each of assault rifles, and handguns. H proudly displayed a grenade. "H, I'd prefer that not blow in my house." Everyone laughed. "Okay, naptime men," Quint ordered.

Three hours later, the moon rose, weakly casting its glow on the rooftops. The aroma of fresh-brewed coffee wafted through the apartment. Quint woke up his team. *The waiting game begins.* Nader was not a patient man, Quint recalled.

Unless he'd changed his spots, he would mount his attack tonight—soon. A church in the distance tolled. A bell for each of Nader's team. His men drank their coffee in silence before settling down to their watches.

Just before one, two shadows came over the neighbor's roof. Chucho keyed a code into his communications device. Quint clicked twice, sending the code to Sami and Omar downstairs. They responded with two clicks. "H, it's started," he said aloud.

"10-4, *jefe*."

He slipped his NVGs from his pocket and put them on. The familiar slime green tinted his world. And there he was. Nader —a face he'd never forget. A vaguely familiar looking man strode over the tenant's roof toward the office with Nader. But the goggles distorted things, turning men into monsters, the green casting unreality onto everything Quint viewed. Maybe he didn't know the man. Maybe he was just another face from his nightmares.

The men crept, hunched, cautious. He wanted to laugh. As Dylan would say, *capa y espada*—cloak and dagger. Their progress was slow. Chucho watched too, as did Horacio. Where were the other two men? Omar would have sent the code if anyone tried to break in. Anyway the alarm would wake the dead. Maybe he should shoot them now, get it over with. Didn't he have every right? His ex-CO had tried to kill him and kidnap his daughter. His finger drifted toward the trigger, thumb itching to flick off the safety. No, he had to wait. Shoot when you see the whites of the enemy's eyes. They had to cross onto his roof. Anyway, the bulletproof glass worked both ways. He'd have to go outside.

Quint edged to the kitchen. "H, Nader and another man are under the living room window. If I'm right, they'll be coming in through Lily's balcony window." He keyed Chucho.

"*Jefe?*"

"Can you see them?"

"No. They are up against the residence. If they come this direction, I'll shoot."

"Anyone across the way?"

"*Nadie.*"

Quint clicked once then closed the signal. "H, put on your goggles. C'mon, let's greet our guests."

"On it, boss."

They silently moved outside Lily's bedroom door. When the alarm activated, they'd go in, guns blazing. Enough firepower would break the window. Nader would cease to be a problem.

The commlink clicked three times. Omar. "What' happening down there?" Horacio asked.

"Get out. Now! I'm in the garden. They're planting explosives. They're going to bomb the residence."

"Can you shoot them?"

"As soon as you and Horacio are out."

"We're coming down now."

They veered from the bedroom door to the stairs and clattered to the first floor. Sami met them at the steel door. He tossed the grenade, catching it. Hand to hand. Again and again.

"Don't drop that thing, *Licensiado*," Quint said. Sami grinned but stopped. "Let me call Chucho." He queued twice.

"*Jefe.*"

"Get down now. They're setting charges. Come around into the garden. If you have a shot. Take it. They can't blow the building up until they are safely away."

"Coming now."

Quint and the Rafiq brothers ran to the storage room door. If the intruders saw them, they'd die. "Horacio, you go around along the garden wall. Get in position. Sami, come with me."

They returned to the entry. Quint punched off the alarm. "Sami, cover me. I'm going up there." He cracked the door open. A barrage of gunfire sprayed from across the street, bullets embedding into the heavy door and clattering off the front window. Lights blinked on in apartments across the street.

Trapped. At least the window glass worked. Quint knew where the other men were.

"Sami, go out through my office. Get into the garden. I'm

going back upstairs to come at them from the residence roof. Tell Horacio and Omar. Don't you guys shoot me." He grinned then bolted for the stairs.

In moments, Quint slumped into the doorframe of the kitchen. Winded. He paused, caught his breath, opened the door. The stairs were going to be the problem. Halfway down, he could swing onto an overhang and slip around onto the office roof. If Nader was at the stairs end, he was dead. Quint offered up a little prayer to whomever might be listening. He started down.

Movement caught his eye, the gun swung into position, his commlink clicked twice. Chucho on the ground. He crouched, using the railing as cover, dropping stair by stair until he could step across to the roof. Nader was close. He could taste him—a bitter poison. He flattened his back against the residence wall and edged to the corner. The night grew darker as clouds passed in front of the moon. *It might rain.* At the corner, Quint paused, positioning his weapon, stabilizing his feet, grounding his center of gravity. The ledge he stood on was narrow. A misstep and he'd either get shot and fall, or just fall. He took in a slow, deep breath, calming his heart then stepped around the corner and shot.

More shots, shouts, a scream. A man fell to the garden. The other slumped into the building. Quint ran forward. Shouts of "Cease fire! from below. Nader looked up. Hatred sparking from his eyes. Quint had him. He raised his handgun to Nader's chest. "Why, Chuck?"

Nader suddenly pushed himself off the wall, zigzagging across the office roof and disappearing into the tenant's stairwell, Quint's shots buzzing past.

Quint ran to the street-side roof edge. A shooter swung up his rifle and blasted. Quint dropped to the roof protected by the low balustrade. He heard return fire and the joyful sound of Sami's Shrek laugh. Then running footsteps. A car starting, the door slamming, its tires squealing around the corner, the scream of sirens closing in. He stood up. Peered over. Sami trained his gun on a man bleeding in the street on one side of the building. Chucho guarded another in the garden. Both injured. Both alive. Maybe he'd get some answers.

"Get these guys inside before the police arrive," he shouted over the comms, then scrambled back along the wall, snipping the wires connecting the explosives and cutting off the tiny receivers. They'd need an expert as soon as possible, but he doubted the devices could be set off.

The team lugged the men into the office, secured them with duct tape, then locked them into the storage room. They kept the lights off. Blood trails were a dead giveaway. They had to keep the police out.

"We need a doctor for these men. One of you have a contact?" Quint asked.

"I'm on it," Sami replied, pulling out his cell phone. He headed toward the workroom.

"Hold on Sami. The one guy isn't going to make it. I'll call for an ambulance. Get that tape off them."

The sirens' screams faded. The neighboring apartments went dark again. Chucho came in with an armload of weapons, depositing them on the worktable.

"Chuch, lock those up." Quint said. "Any of you know a bomb expert?"

"Call the police."

"And get arrested?"

Sami, hustled back to the huddle. "We're not getting an ambulance for twenty minutes. They'll both be dead by then. Back the limo up to the storage door, H, while I call my contact at the bomb squad."

In four minutes, the wounded men had been wrapped into blankets and loaded into the back of the limo. Omar had served as a medic in the military. He'd triaged their wounds, staunching the blood from the worst with tourniquets while the team created a plan of action. He bandaged as much as he could in the limo as they sped toward Hospital Maria José over on Cozumel in the colonia.

"You're a genius, Omar. Thank you," Quint said. "But why would it take the ambulance twenty minutes if it takes us five?"

No one had an answer as they arrived at the emergency room door. "We'll see you back at the house. Take care of the explosives," Sami ordered. Omar and Sami carried each man through the automatic doors. The Rafiqs had a story ready. They'd be okay.

Horacio and Quint returned to the office. In that short time it took to drive across the colonia, Chucho had stowed the weapons and washed the blood from the office floors. If a forensics team were called in, Quint doubted the cleaning would hold up. He could smell the tang of iron. "Looks clean, thanks Chuch, but don't we have any air freshener? I can smell blood."

Chucho shrugged. "I'll look, *jefe*." he said, dashing to the cleaning supply closet, returning to the entryway empty handed. "I can open the windows. It should air out by morning. Are we calling in the police before then?"

"We're first taking care of the charges Nader set. Sami called a contact from the car. He should get here in about fifteen minutes," Quint said. "He's with the police, Chuch. We don't want any complications."

"*De veras.* I'll see what I can do."

Horacio turned on the lights and monitored the door. He and Chucho had a story, too. Chucho was taking care of the place while the *jefe* was away. He heard noises, saw two men setting the charges. Other men came, he wasn't sure how many because he hid in the pantry during the gun battle on the roof. Chucho had called Horacio, the manager, who called an ambulance and his brother, an attorney. They carried the wounded to the hospital. No, none of them knew who these men were or why they had targeted their office and the boss's residence.

The brothers arrived by taxi moments before Sami's contact from the municipal police rang the doorbell. Sami greeted him, introducing Señor Vega as they climbed the kitchen stairs and crawled onto the connecting roof.

"Is this how these men got on the roof?" Vega asked as he inspected the charges. "There's enough plastic here to drop the entire building," he muttered.

"No señor, I only saw them because they came over from the neighbor's roof. See—" Chucho pointed to the access stairwell.

"Who lives there?"

"No one. It's a business. He's a tenant of my employer, Mr. Quint," Horacio said,

"What kind of business?"

Omar answered. "Insurance. His name's Quiñones. I've run into him before."

"Your business?"

"No, I have an accountancy firm over in La Condesa." He held out his card. "Omar Rafiq, *a sus órdenes*."

Vega studied the card for a moment. "Rafiq. Unusual name. You related to Sami?"

"We're brothers. This is Horacio, manager here."

Vega and Horacio shook hands.

"*Pues*, I'm going to remove the charges. I need to get into my protective gear. You lot wait across the street. By the way, who cut the wires?"

"I did señor. Picked up a bit of bomb knowledge in the service."

"Tricky business. Well done."

It didn't take long for Vega to collect the explosives, making quick notes into his notebook. He took the explosives, transmitter, and paraphernalia away in evidence bags.

Sami walked him to the street door after Vega declined a drink. "*Pues*, it's three in the morning. A little early for drinking," he said and laughed. "The boy will have to come in to make a statement."

"I'll bring him in tomorrow." He held out his hand. The men shook. Vega returned to his car; the team followed the sound of the engine until it faded into the city noises.

"Chucho, you'll have to go in tomorrow. I'll take you. We'll see another contact I have for our district."

"I have classes tomorrow until three."

"No worries. We'll go after dinner. I have clients tomorrow and a court appearance. I need to go home and get to sleep. You'll be okay here, Chuch, or do you want a ride to your apartment?"

"Sami, I think I'll take Chucho to my house tonight. How about it, son?" Horacio said.

"Thanks, H. Let me get something to wear, and my books." He darted up the stairs, returning a few minutes later. "I turned out the lights. Everything is locked. Let me double-check down here."

"I've done it. *Vamos.*"

"*Oye*, what about Mr. Quint?"

"He's gone to a hotel. Until this attack is reported, he's out of town. Don't forget."

They locked the door behind them then strolled to the limo purring at the curb. The street was silent, only the hum of a city of almost twenty million people charged the atmosphere.

Chapter 10

Gunmen Attack Limousine in Colonia Condesa

Wednesday, October 3, 2007

Quint woke up disoriented, the phone ringing, his stomach growling. "Yeah," he said.

"Quint, it's Horacio. When should I come for you? It's eleven-thirty. I took Chucho to my house last night; Amina got him off to classes. Sami is taking him in to make a statement after supper."

"I've got to call Garza. What were the explosives? Any determination?"

"No, Vega will try to figure out a signature but the cut wire will make it harder for him to ID a maker. My guess, C-4."

"We know who it was. Probably came from China."

"Nader is a bomb maker?"

"Why not? He's a spook. Nader knows plenty of tricks. Did you ask about fingerprints?"

"We probably fucked that up dismantling the charges. He

took all our prints last night."

"So when do I get back to town? Where have I been?"

"Good question. Witnesses in Tepoztlán? Pueblo? I got it. Vera Cruz. I can get Leon to corroborate. I'll set it up for you."

"How soon 'til you get here?"

"I'm outside."

"Five minutes. Did you bring coffee?"

"Claro que sí, jefe."

The aroma of good coffee filled the limo, enveloping Quint as he settled in. He buckled the seatbelt. Horacio handed him a tall cup with La Selva printed on the side.

"You bought the good stuff. Thanks."

"I stopped in after dropping Chucho at the metro. Read the paper."

"Anything interesting going on?"

"Nothing to do with us."

"H, why wouldn't the neighbors call the police to report the disturbance?"

"Someone probably did. Don't worry, Sami will know everything when we see him."

"If he can find out, can't Nader? Has Nader put my neighbors at risk?"

"Nader has no way to get information out of the local police. Sami has friends, he'll have lunch wherever the cops go."

"You don't know?

"I can guess. Omar is going over to make nice with your tenant, Quiñones. He's either taking bribes, or needs better security. Sami will find out and try to keep him in the building."

"Bless him. That's the tenant who has threatened to break his lease. I can't lose the income. We need some paying work, H."

"The Rafiqs are on it, *jefe*. Let's get some lunch."

"I need to see Garza."

73

"Let's eat in Cuautemoc then. Call. Invite him to join us. Call Rosi, too."

Quint felt little prickles of hot perspiration beading along his hairline. "Turn the air on, would you?"

Horacio laughed. "A certain little *señorita* making you nervous, Quint?"

"Am I that transparent? Why don't I call her. She can cajole the ambassador into joining us. Pull over at the park. Under the trees."

Horacio found a parking space along the shady side of Parque Mexico near La Selva. He put up the privacy window before going for more coffee. Quint made himself comfortable in back and dialed.

Rosie answered on the third ring. "Jackman, you're home. I've been waiting to hear. How did it go?"

"Our girl is back with her family, but we had trouble. It's a long story. I've shared some of it with Garza, but we've had new developments. I need his help."

"And you want me to get him on board."

"If you don't mind. I'd like to see you anyway. H and I thought we'd invite you both to lunch at that place behind the embassy. I could catch you up. You could put some pressure on him." Quint laughed. "That is, if you will. But aside from some business, are you free for dinner tomorrow?"

"Yes to both. Give me a hint. What happened?"

"Remember my buddy from Vietnam? He hooked up with Aguirre. One of them murdered young Javie at the drains. My buddy was shot and I left him with a contact. He and Aguirre ambushed us up north. Aguirre is dead. The other wired my house with explosives last night."

"*Dios mio*, Quint. Is everyone all right? The house?"

"Yes. But I need this guy stopped. I don't know what the hell he has against me. I think he's selling information to the cartels."

"Hmmm. Tony won't like that. How would he get anything worth selling?"

Knocking on the privacy window startled Quint. Horacio

held up a fresh cup; Quint lowered the window.

"What was that?" Rosi asked.

"H just handed me a coffee."

"*Entonces*, drink your coffee while I call Tony and make a reservation. I'll call back with the time. It's good to hear your voice, Jackman."

He could hear the smile in Rosi's voice and grinned.

"Conversation go well?" Horacio asked when Quint rejoined him up front.

"Very well." There was that prickly sweat again, but Quint felt too happy to care.

"I'll drop you back at the hotel then get you some clothes. What do you want? You can't go back to the office until tomorrow or maybe Friday."

Quint looked at his shabby, gum-soled shoes good for climbing onto roofs, and the wrinkled, chambray work shirt he'd tossed on the night before, now blood-stained. "Slacks, a pressed shirt. I think there's a pastel one. The tan loafers and linen blazer. And my razor."

A young teen, no more than a hundred pounds with her plaid school uniform rolled over her bony knees, was pulled past the limo by six panting dogs, ranging from a Yorkie up to a giant bearded Bouvier, straining on leads. Shouldn't the kid be in school?

"Skip the razor. Go for the Miami Vice look. Women like that scruffy masculinity." Horacio tried to keep a straight face.

"That's so nineties. I'll shave. Women like to stroke a smooth cheek, too." He wiggled his eyebrows.

"*Pues*, good luck with that. American TV is slow to arrive in Mexico," Horacio added, shifting the car into gear.

Idly observing the park passing by his window, Quint was overcome with melancholy. Parque Mexico teemed with walkers, dogs, a clown. Near the bandstand, a man with a bouquet of balloons. He smelled popcorn and the sweet scent of churros. Red flowers stood out against the dark green trees. He wished he could be a regular citizen. One who saw the beauty in life. A man who could stroll in the park, smell the roses. But he came from the rotted underbelly of civilization. Why would a woman like Rosi Orozco be interested in him? He looked for the worst in every situation. And the greater loss —JadeAnne. Beautiful Jade. So much like Thuy. His heart sank. A weight in his chest. What reason did she have to come back to him? He hadn't saved her mother. He hadn't been her father. No, Quint was a loner; it was better that way. People like Quint made it possible for regular folks to enjoy the park on an almost clear, sunny day.

They caught a red light at the end of the park. When it changed, Horacio started forward, braking suddenly. A black car ran the light, almost ramming into the limo. It screeched to a stop. "¡*Hijole! Cabrón!*" Horacio yelled over the cacophony of horns blaring.

Quint jolted from his reverie. Nader was behind the wheel. "Run him down, H!" he yelled.

The doors flew open. Nader and three men with assault rifles poured out, aiming at the limo. Horacio stepped on the gas, swerving headlong into the oncoming traffic. The limo clipped the black car's rear taillight. He accelerated along the next block, swinging the wheel side to side, dodging cars, horn blasting. Bullets rained against the rear.

The limo took the next left on two wheels, leaving a snarl of traffic and the shooters in Condesa. He headed toward Constituyentes circling back toward Quint's hotel through Zona Rosa. They were not followed. The men released the breaths they held.

"*Jefe*, how did they find us?"

"Did you go by the office today?"

"No, straight to the hotel. I wasn't followed that I know of."

"Were you watching?" Quint squinted at his partner.

"I always watch."

"They've got *halcones* then. Probably made the plate while we had coffee. How safe is the hotel?"

"Safe enough. Nader hasn't had time to put together a team. I recognized one of those *pendejos*. Gun for hire. Not organized. Not affiliated. Those guys were no militia." Horacio's tone sounded derisive.

"So you're saying the hotel is safe?"

"I'm saying I know a back way into the garage."

"Of course you do," Quint said.

In a few minutes Quint stood in the underground parking garage for his hotel. Horacio was already on his way to pick up clothes for the luncheon. He hurried up the ramp to the hallway and punched the elevator. Shortly he was in the shower lathering his hair with the grassy-scented shampoo. He wished he had his razor.

He dried off, putting on the complementary robe to await his clothes. His phone rang. Rosi.

"Good news?" he said.

"We have a reservation for four at two-thirty."

"Four? Who else is coming?"

"Doesn't Horacio want lunch?"

"Sure, I'll ask him. I'm waiting for him to deliver my luncheon clothes. But wouldn't Sami be a better choice?"

"Sure. Ask him too. We can squeeze in a fifth."

"I'll call now. I need to talk to him anyway. We just were shot at near Parque Mexico."

"What? In the middle of the day? Did you see who?"

"Yeah—a shootout at high noon. Four guys—one of them Nader. H recognized one of his men. A low level gun for hire. I want to get Nader into a torture room and beat the truth out of him," he said, his voice a growl."

"Don't talk like that, Jackman. You are not like them."

His voice softened. "I don't want to be like them."

"Then don't sink to their thuggish mentality."

"Rephrasing, I want to sit in a garden with tea and discuss, as gentlemen, Mr. Nader's motivation for coming after me thirty some years after our association ended."

Rosi's bell-like laugh tinkled through the receiver. "This is what I like about you, Jackman. You are such a card."

"An ace, I hope."

"I'll see you there at two-thirty—Ace," she said. The line

went dead.

A light tap on the door wiped the grin off Quint's face. He approached it and quickly looked through the peephole. Horacio stood outside holding up a bag and a hanger with his jacket. Quint ushered him in, snatched the clothes then stepped into the bathroom to dress. "Have a drink if you want, H. Oh, and Rosi wanted to know if you'd like to have lunch with us?"

"Thanks *jefe*. Parking will be a bitch. I'll grab something at a street vendor and circle."

"Better idea. Pick Chucho up. Don't let him go to the office. He'll be hungry. Meet me back here at six," he called through the door.

"Good plan, I'll call right now."

"Call Sami, too. We want him at lunch. Two-thirty at La Casa de los Abuelos."

Quint put on his shirt and fished in the bag. "A tie, Horacio? Where are the socks?"

Chapter 11

I Need Proof

Sami and Rosi chatted under the portico at La Casa de los Abuelos, a cream-colored, two-story building across Reforma on Hamburgo. Horacio, barely stopping, let Quint off at the curb, shooting back into traffic to pick up Chucho at the metro stop. Rosi's smile welcomed Quint as he sauntered over to them. She stepped back, giving him the once-over. "You clean up well, Jackman.

He grinned, and gave her a peck on each cheek. Although he wore the tie loose like the hip kids, it was the right touch, he thought. "*Hola,* Sami." The men shook hands. "Glad you could make it. I hope you brought your appetite. And your law degree. We're waiting for Garza?"

"Yes. Our table will be ready momentarily. Tony is on his way."

"This isn't the restaurant I remembered. A long time ago I ate at a place that resembled a Swiss chalet. We sat outside. I could have sworn it was right behind the embassy."

"I don't remember that one, Quint. So you've been to

Mexico City before."

"Early '90s. I had an assignment here. That operation led me to Senator Aguirre, actually."

"I was in law school back then. Starving student and all. Didn't eat in Cuautemoc."

Garza strode up. "Hello, hello. I hope I haven't kept you waiting," he said, shaking hands around the small circle. "Rosi, you look lovely today."

"Thanks, Tony. Let's go in, they should be ready for us. I asked for a private table."

Quint held the door, following the group to the reception desk. A waiter grabbed menus and said, "Right this way, Señorita Orozco."

"They know you here?" Quint asked after they were seated at a table tucked at the back of the second floor dining room.

"I used to come here often." She smiled at Garza. "Tony you still come?"

"Sure. Great food and it's not 'over-filled' with embassy people. I see them at work." He laughed then held up his finger. A waiter scurried over. "A scotch and soda, please." He gestured to the others.

"*Tequila añejo* with tonic for me, with a squeeze of lime and a dash of orange bitters," ordered Rosi.

"Modelo Negra, *por favor*," Sami said.

Quint said, "I'll try what the lady is having. What do you call it?"

"A Shazam."

Lunch ordered, drinks in hand, Quint and Sami related the evening's events. Quint added the story of the shooting in the intersection in La Condesa.

"You're sure it was Chuck Nader."

"Absolutely, Ambassador. He was my CO. Back then I knew him well. He's a little more wiry and has grey hair, but he's the same man. I don't have a beef with him, or I didn't, but he has a big problem with me. I shared with you my take on his purpose."

"Mr. Quint, if I didn't take you seriously enough yesterday,

I do now. I don't understand what his assignment here has to do with you, however."

Rosi reached across the corner of the table to lay her hand on Garza's arm. "That's the point, Tony." She smiled. "His assignment is either irrelevant, his purpose is to pursue his vendetta against Jackman, or once he discovered someone from his past with knowledge of his traitorous actions was here, he decided to take him out. You must talk to his division. Discover what he's doing here. That will help us know how to handle him. Jackman can't live like this, Tony. Two men have already been hospitalized. We don't know how many people were injured or killed this afternoon in Condesa."

Garza visibly melted under Rosi's persuasion. They'd dated, he was sure of it. Quint reckoned Rosi was the one to break it off. Might she realize her mistake? Go back to him? She was obviously fond of the ambassador.

"Quint! Quint, do you want dessert? The flan here is terrific," Sami said.

"Flan, please," he replied to the waiter. "Sorry, I was thinking about what Rosi said. Yeah. One of those two scenarios is the key. But it all goes back to 'Nam. God, I don't want to have to think about that hell again."

"I've already spoken to the division chief. Apparently the mission is top secret. We're assisting CIA in an investigation. From what I extrapolated from the conversation, it has something to do with the rise of the Sinaloans. Our government is unhappy with the implications of weaponizing criminal gangs. Already the death toll has topped two thousand people this year due to cartel activity. It's Calderon's war on drugs. But there has been no slowdown of drugs crossing the border."

"He's CIA? I'm surprised. What did he say about Nader?" Quint asked.

"That's just it. Nader *was* placed by the NSA; you were correct. Our people have no jurisdiction over him. The chief doesn't know exactly what the op is, or so he says."

Sami asked, "Is it common practice to run ops without your knowledge, Ambassador?"

"Frankly, Rafiq, I'm unhappy at the usurping of my authority. I've spoken to Nader. A diplomat he is not. I see why you don't trust him. There's something squirrelly about him—spooks in general."

"NSA follows its own rules. Nader breaks those." Quint said. "They tried to recruit me after I was released. I turned them down."

"So what are we going to do, Tony? If Jackman is correct, Mr. Nader is aiding and abetting our enemy, Joaquín "Chapo" Guzmán by selling him information of the Mexican government's movements against him."

Quint held up his hand. "Hold on, Rosi. How would Nader have intel of the Mexican government's operations if he's stationed in the U.S. Embassy? Tony, does your division work with the Mexicans?"

"Of course. It's intelligence."

"In light of last night's, and today's, attack in public, which is probably on CCTV somewhere, don't you have authority to throw him out of your embassy?" Sami wanted to know.

"I wish I could, *licensiado*. I wish I could throw you all out. You folks are a thorn in my otherwise blemish-free ambassadorship. I need proof of Nader's activities. With it, I'll have him arrested—NSA or not."

"We'll get your proof," Quint said.

"Sami, can you check on the CCTV? Do they actually have it here?"

"Yes. But I don't know how extensive it is. I can check. What I can't do is offer you any solutions on how to deal with NSA. I've heard talk about its operations. Mythology. Urban legends."

Rosi said, "I can attest to their unconventional methods. I've stepped on some toes in my work."

They huddled at the corner near the restaurant waiting for Horacio to arrive to drop Rosi at her car and take Sami back to his office. The rush hour had begun. Traffic streamed by in both directions.

"Do you think Garza will actually do anything if we can get proof?

"Absolutely. He's an honorable man, Quint."

"Like he did for Lily, hey?"

"That's not fair, Jackman. We asked him to break the law."

A horn beeped. The limo. Quint held the door for Rosi and Sami, hopping in behind them.

"How was lunch?" Horacio asked, as he laid on the horn, bullying his way from the curb into the traffic.

"Productive. Hi Chuch, Horacio buy you lunch?"

"*Sí, jefe.* Thanks. Hi *señorita, licensiado.*" He grinned, waving from the front seat.

Rosi smiled, "*Hola, Chucho.*" Sami waved back.

"Chuch, You mind sleeping at your place tonight?"

"It's cool, *jefe,* I have a lot of studying to do."

"Good. Catch up. I'll be at the hotel if you need me."

Due to the one-way streets, Horacio made a large circle to get back to Rosi's car. Quint helped her out. "So I'll see you tomorrow night, Rosi? Anywhere you've been wanting to try?"

She clasped his hand and squeezed it. Hers was warm as was her smile. "I'm looking forward to it. Since you asked, I'm dying to try Pujol on Tennyson in Polanco. It's been rated by your Wall Street Journal as the best restaurant in Mexico City."

"I'll wear my suit. Pick you up around seven-thirty?"

"Give Horacio the night off, Jackman. I'll pick *you* up at your office at seven-thirty."

"It's not safe for you to go there, Rosi."

"Or for you, my friend. I'll see you tomorrow night." She reached out, slipped her hand behind his neck, pulling him down to her height and kissed him,"

Quint flushed, grinning . "See you tomorrow night."

"Okay, men. How are we going to stop Nader?" Quint asked, as soon as the car door slammed shut behind him.

"As your councilor, I advise you not to kill him."

"I have no intention of killing him, Sami, I want to know what his vendetta against me is. Once I find out, then I'll kill him." Quint's lips twitched as he suppressed a laugh.

"I did not hear that, Quint."

Horacio and Chucho hooted from the front.

"Bring him on, *jefe*. He's evil. *Oye,* let's plan a trap," Chucho joked.

"Maybe call him at work at the embassy—invite him over for *churros*?"

"Tequila, *jefe*. To talk it over. We'll spike his drink with truth serum, tie him to the chair, and ask why he hates you. If he doesn't answer, we'll waterboard him."

"That's illegal, Chucho," Sami said, with mock seriousness.

"No, really, I saw it in a video on Blog de Narco."

"Like those people do everything by the book," Horacio quipped.

"And after the waterboarding, Mrs. P would kill *us*. Water all over her kitchen. I can see it now. It ain't pretty, kid."

"No, not in the kitchen," he said, "In the garden. If he doesn't tell us what we want to know, we'll put him in a barrel of acid."

The conversation stopped for a silent beat.

"Ah, jeeze, Chucho. Where did you get that idea?" Quint asked.

"It's what they did in the video," he said, defensively.

"Why would you watch crap like that? You'll give yourself nightmares."

"It's not real, Quint. It's a video."

Sami's voice was grave. "*Hijo*, that blog documents real cartel activity. I want you to research it. It's anonymous. I challenge you to use your hacking skills to uncover who produces the vile stuff. Do it for your term project. The authorities have not been able to identify the bloggers or suppress the site. It's an abomination. The cartels are an abomination. I never want to hear of you watching that kind of thing again. The senator will turn over in his grave if he finds out. You know one of the cartel leaders killed him in cold blood. What has our society come to?"

"You sound like an old fart, Sami. Is this what law school does to people? I remember when you took a keen interest in gory deaths," Horacio taunted his brother.

"When I was eleven or twelve, *hermano*. You too." He snorted. "Remember that time we went with Dad to some store, and we found the *dueño* in the back, turned blue, bleeding foam from his mouth? You and Omar touched him. You didn't stop looking at the guy. Talked about it for months. We never told *papi*."

"What happened to the guy?" Chucho asked.

"It was in the papers. He ate rat poison."

"Ew, gross," Chucho said in accent-less English.

"You miss Lily, don't you."

"She was teaching me English."

Quint roared, laughing until his eyes watered.

Chapter 12

Bugged

Thursday, October 4, 2007

Quint slept well, relaxed in knowing his team was safe. He woke up refreshed, anticipating, not the return to his building, but the dinner with Rosi, although with mild trepidation. He hadn't gone on a proper date with a woman in years, perhaps since Thuy in 1972. He'd been content with casual relationships—mostly "friends with benefits". Maybe he'd stop at the barber on the way back to Roma. The reflection staring back at him in the steamed bathroom mirror said he could use a trim. H would know of a good place.

Women scared Quint. They were so capable and assured. Rosi was no different. She could handle most anything, he guessed. Like his daughter, he thought as he pulled on his shoes. He dialed room service for a carafe of coffee, a plate of *huevos rancheros,* and the morning paper. Then called Jade. She'd be home. It was only seven a.m. in California.

"Hullo?" a sleepy voice answered.

"Daughter, my breakfast is about to arrive. I thought I'd take it with you. Make some coffee while we talk."

"Uh, sure, Dad." Quint heard the bedclothes rustle and Jade's voice say "it's Quint" then the sound of a door closing.

In a moment, Jade said, "You sound chipper today. All going well?"

"I have a dinner date with Rosi tonight." Quint's excitement spilled over into his voice.

"That's wonderful, Dad! So all is going well then?"

"That's going well. I think she likes me."

"I know she likes you. What's not going well?"

"You better sit down."

"That bad?"

"Worse. Yesterday Nader and some thugs blocked traffic at an intersection in Condesa. Started shooting. If the limo wasn't bullet proofed, H and I would be dead."

"Oh. My. God. So he's not seriously injured and has followed you back to Mexico? Did you go to the police?"

"You forget where we are. They were probably off-duty cops with him. Rosi, Sami, and I met with Garza again yesterday. Over lunch. But it gets worse—"

"What. Something else happen?"

"Yeah. The night before last he attacked the residence." Quint went on to detail the events. "I'm in a hotel now. Chucho is in his apartment. Mrs. P isn't due until tomorrow."

"When do you go back?"

"Soon. I'm not in a rush. I thought I'd get my hair cut on the way."

Jade replied, her voice teasing, "So you'll look good for Rosi?"

"Something to do to put off the inevitable. And yes." He laughed. "I feel like a teen going on my first date."

"When was the last time you dated someone?'

"Possibly not since your mother."

"You're kidding!"

Room service knocked on the door. Quint ushered in his breakfast, pouring his first cup of coffee. He could vouch that this place served an excellent brew.

"Dad, do you want me to let you eat?"

"No, tell me everything you're doing. How is Dylan enjoying himself? How soon until you come home?"

"We're having a lot of fun, but I have to get going on the moving plan. What did Garza say?"

"He didn't offer me any marines for protection. He says he can't do anything without proof. H is checking to see if there's CCTV at the intersection. With proof Nader is causing deadly mayhem, Garza can arrest him. Send him back to the U.S. to trial."

"Why not in Mexico? He deserves an extended stay in a Mexican jail. I hear they don't feed the inmates." She laughed, then coughed. "Oops, coffee down the wrong pipe."

"I didn't ask, but anything that gets him out of commission works for me. Garza determined he *is* working for NSA."

"Say hi to Dylan, Dad. Keep me updated." The air went dead for a beat.

"*Hola Quint. ¿Qué tal?* It's great here. We've been to the beach, Muir Woods, and today we're going to the Napa Valley to taste Cabernet Sauvignon. On a train."

That's great, Dylan, but don't like it there too much," he said through his grin. "I want my girl back in Mexico soon."

Dylan laughed. "I do, too. I do, too. Tomorrow we have a meeting with her partner to discuss her contract."

"You think he's going to let her go? Or maybe I should say, buy her out. Jade will do what she wants."

"*Hijole*, you got that right. My breakfast has arrived, let me say *adios* for now. Have a good day, Quint." Dylan hung up.

Jade was planning on coming home. That news, along with his date with Rosi, buoyed his mood. When Horacio arrived, Quint was ready to get to work.

Horacio's barber turned out to be quite a character, and he was a CI. "You didn't tell me you have confidential informants. How did that come about?" Quint asked once he settled back into the limo.

Horacio replied, "The senator needed to know the talk in the street. I set up a network. *Negro* is one of my best. He hears everything. He's one of the top barbers in the city."

"*Negro*? He's as pale as a ghost."

"Albino."

"Odd nickname then. I'm impressed with the depth of his report. He must have his own network."

"He does. But this still isn't the proof we need. Nader's hired gun is in custody."

"Good news. His statement will be proof. How'd you find out?"

"Sami. But he's not talking."

"He will be when we put some pressure on him. Can Sami get us in to see him? I feel like kicking ass today. You?"

Horacio nodded and pounded his fist into his cupped hand.

"I was thinking more of rebar, but fists and feet might do nicely. All we need are the names of the other two men."

"Maybe the license plate will turn something up. I'm betting it's a rental though. Nader drove."

"*Negro* didn't say if it was a government plate, did he?"

"No, but I'll call my contact from the office. We're almost there. Shall we stop for some takeout lunch?"

Quint nodded. Without anyone coming after the girls, they could start enjoying the neighborhood restaurants. But it was a toss-up with Nader on the streets and dangerous. The last bunch wanted to snatch Jade and the trafficked girl. Now the bad guy wanted to kill *him*. He sighed. How had he chosen this life? The tree-lined streets of Roma slipped past his window as he thought of the long road to get here. He hadn't saved the world from anything. No one lived free. He chuckled, more a low grumble than mirth.

"What's so funny, *jefe*?" Horacio asked as he double parked outside a tiny restaurant advertising tortas. "Grab me a couple of *jamón y queso y bifstec*. Add a tamarindo." He pulled some pesos out of the console, shoving them at Quint, who nodded, holding up his hand in a no-need gesture.

"Business expense. I'll be right back."

Bag in hand, Quint jumped back into the car eight minutes later. "Let's go. Some clown inside took too much interest in me. I didn't want to start something in the neighborhood, but I snapped a couple of photos. I forget these iPhones do everything now. I should have taken a picture of Nader yesterday."

"It's hard to snap photos in the heat of the attack. Let me see who it is." Quint queued up the shot. He held the phone across the seat. "He's one of the men from yesterday—driver's side rear. I got a clear look at him for a moment. Nader is staking out the neighborhood. What do you want to do?"

"Put the limo in the garage. I'll make some calls; get us security. This is draining our reserves. It needs to end now! Put Chucho on the license plate as soon as he arrives. I think he's done at school and on his way," he said, checking the time.

Horacio pulled away from the curb aiming toward the office. Quint watched the parked cars and pedestrians for surveillance and lookouts. He didn't identify anything out of the usual, but a tracking device could be on the car, or maybe the siting in the sandwich shop had been a random coincidence. He still eschewed that word—coincidence. Not likely. Joe Blow was in *his* colonia to report to Nader. Nader would be on his way. "When we get in, we'll arm ourselves. I won't accept that siting was random."

"*Yo tampoco, jefe.*"

Inside, the office suite felt like an ice cave. Jade was right about those marble floors. Cold. Their shoes clattered, echoing through the empty space. Quint didn't like it, but at least the place hadn't been disturbed. He feared boobytraps, but the alarm wasn't sounding. The little tell-tales he'd left were in place. So far, no one had entered. The residence might be another matter. Horacio went to the workroom and settled in front of his computer. Quint continued to his office. He switched on the lights. Again he didn't notice any disturbances.

He found the rubber band he'd left under the second desk drawer in place. His papers remained in order. He sat down, booted up his laptop with no idea what he needed to do. Make a plan, he guessed. He gazed out the windows. Mrs. P was a stickler for clean windows. She'd scrubbed the dirty city air and street dust off them, polishing to crystal clear. A ray of sunlight illuminated fingerprints around the lock. He stood up, stepped across the small space. Yep, he'd come over the wall. Jade's succulents crushed into two shoe-shaped depressions in the garden bed. Nader knew how to break and enter—they'd done it together once or twice. He knew how to find the tell-tales. Hell. Quint had learned most of his tricks from the man. He stormed back to the workroom.

Horacio looked up from his screen. "*Jefe*?"

Quint put a finger to lips. Picked up a pad and pen and scribbled: *Nader's been here. Don't speak. Don't use the phone until we sweep for bugs.*

Horacio nodded then shrugged, a quizzical look on his face. He took the pad and wrote: *What about the alarm? It was set.*

Nader was good with alarms, as I recall.

Should I get someone to sweep?

Thanks, H. I'll do it, Quint replied. He'd start in his office.

It took him twenty minutes to search all the nooks and crannies Nader had taught him to bug. Of course he'd put one in the telephone receiver. Another in the ceiling light fixture. A third in the electrical outlet. The surprise was the bug planted in the casing for his laptop. Nader had probably hacked it anyway.

"*Buenos tardes,* Horacio," Chucho yelled as he let himself in the front door. Quint rushed down the hall waving him off as Horacio barreled out of the workroom motioning silence.

Chucho looked confused. "*¿Hola?*"

Both men put fingers to lips. Quint guided the young man back outside. In a low voice, he said, "Chuch, Nader broke in. I've found four bugs so far. He opened his hand to display the tiny transmitters. I need you to search everywhere in your office. Open the computers. I'm going to call for someone to sweep, but let's get as many as we can. Don't talk inside until we know we're clean. No talking in the residence either. Don't use your computer until you've checked it out. He might have had it hacked or something. Chucho thumbed up and disappeared inside to his IT department. Quint disabled them.

Christ, this is just what I needed today. That bastard.

Quint received little consolation from the thought that Nader wouldn't have found any information on his work. Since they'd moved in, everything had been about getting Lily back to her family. Maybe Nader wanted that information. But no, it didn't make sense. Nader wanted Quint—or Quint's mission. If he wanted intel, killing him was a poor way to acquire it.

He unlocked the stairs door and started up. He'd make a cursory assessment of the apartment then go out on the roof to check it. That asshole might have re-planted explosives. He'd make his calls from the roof.

Like the office, nothing appeared to be touched. The back door hadn't been jimmied; he found no bugs, and all the windows were intact. Nader wasn't interested in his wardrobe or the contents of his pantry. He climbed over the railing onto the lip of the roof, following the wall around to the street. Nothing but residue of the adhesive Nader used. Did the neighbor refuse him access? Nader on the roof during the day would attract attention. At night he could come up the *callejon* unseen and climb the two walls to break in. Quint leaned over the edge, checked out the garden. No footprints, but the limb reaching over the back corner looked easy to reach. That's how he got in.

"*Jefe*, I've found five more bugs. I've run diagnostics. Our system is intact. Horacio found two bugs. My check of his laptop, and yours, say they are free of malware," Chucho called up from Quint's patio."

"This is good?"

"*Sí*. We haven't been hacked. What shall we do with the bugs?"

"Put them on the workroom desk. I'll be down soon. I'm

worried about you staying here while Nader is on the loose. Can you look into him at home on your laptop? I want every shred of info you can find. I need to figure out what the *cabrón* wants."

"Sorry, Mr. Quint. I forgot to report. I got information on Nader through the university's computer. Did you know he was in prison from 1975 to 1981? He was charged with espionage and drug trafficking. I found trial records. My English isn't good enough to read them, but I downloaded the files for you."

"Chucho, you're brilliant! This is what I needed to know. Now I understand. Or I might understand."

"Understand what, *jefe*?"

"I'm coming down. Get Horacio. Meet me in the garden." He turned to climb back onto the stairs.

"Grab chairs, gentlemen. Our brilliant information technician has cracked the case."

Horacio and Chucho pulled lawn chairs close to Quint and sat down.

"Chuch, tell Horacio about your successful search."

The young man reiterated what he'd told Quint, adding, "He wasn't fired. I found files on his assignments: all active war zones: Korean DMZ 1966 to 1969; Lebanon 1982; Grenada 1983, Libya '86, Persian Gulf, Panama '89-'90, The Gulf War, Iraq, Somalia, Bosnia. It doesn't end, Mr. Quint. The *hombre* has spied on every conflict your country has been involved with. Haiti, Kosovo. Afghanistan. I've never heard of some of these places. What does he do?"

"That's the sixty-four thousand dollar question, men. What does Nader do? Why does he think I'm in his way?"

"I think the question should be, if Nader is collecting data on enemies, why is he in Mexico?" Horacio asked.

"Easy. Both our presidents have declared a war on drugs. I know from 'Nam he acts as a consultant by setting up networks and collecting intelligence to give our allies an advantage. Or that's the theory. I was part of the network."

"Does he speak Spanish?"

"He doesn't speak any languages besides English that I know of."

"Doesn't make sense. How's he going to get intel if he can't talk to the people?"

"Go back to Chucho's report. Why is Nader in the field at his age. He's got to be sixty something. Why hasn't he moved up in the agency? I'm betting prison held him back. I know my conviction hurt my chances of promotion." Quint's smile a wry smear across his lips. "He must be bitter about it, Chucho. I know I am. I need those trial records to confirm my theory."

Chucho rose, but Quint threw out his arm to stay him. "Hold up, Chuch." He surveyed the faces of his team and grinned. "Boys, Chuck Nader thinks I sent him to prison."

Horacio cocked his head, brow wrinkling. "Why, *jefe*? You were already in prison."

Chucho snickered. "It's why Mr. Quint wants the trial records. Maybe somewhere somebody mentions who accused him."

"Yep, you got it. I'm betting Nader, not Charlie Stone, put me in prison." He leveled a hard look at the men. "I can call Stone for confirmation, leaving us the task of determining why Nader thought I was a threat in 1974."

"Knowing isn't going to stop him trying to kill you, or give us the evidence for Garza to act," Horacio said.

"Knowing gives us leverage. Strategy. We find out his weakness and we can poke it with a stick. He'll make a mistake then we can put him away for good. He's already out of control. This is a vendetta against me—we've all said it—it's personal.

"Chuch, get me the transcripts. While you're at it, find the transcripts of my trial. Let's see what went on. I've wiped that part of my life out of memory. When I found out Thuy had died, I went crazy angry. Depressed. Charley Stone visited me, assured me he'd take care of JadeAnne, raise her as his own. I signed his papers, agreed I'd never contact my child. I was so deep in the pit, all I wanted to do was die. It seemed like the right decision." He looked down, contemplating his clenching hands and shuddered. "What a mistake. What a fool."

Alarmed, Chucho said, "Don't worry *jefe*, I'll find you the records."

Quint swiped at his eyes and looked up. "I know you will, Chucho. I'm going to call Stone. You two carry on, but no talking inside. I'll get a sweep taken care of—you have a contact, H?"

The trio sat in silence for several minutes, virtual wheels turning. They'd come up with answers and strategy. Chuck Nader wasn't going to win.

Chapter 13

It Wasn't Charley

Quint paced the small garden. He prided himself as a man willing to take calculated risks. One who faced danger without a qualm. Honed by the military, Vietnam, prison, and his own sense of justice, he was a man who would not hesitate to act to right a wrong. His gut churned. His muscles clenched. He felt almost light-headed. The way he'd felt going into a battle. Fear, he realized. Quint feared speaking to his army buddy, feared the reception Stone might give, feared what he might find out. He paced faster, shaking his hands, rolling his shoulders.

He dialed Jade, halting his pacing around the fountain when she picked up saying she was in the middle of something.

He interrupted. "I need to talk to Stone. Will he talk to me?"

"How would I know, Quint? What's that sound I hear?"

"Long story. I'm outside by the fountain. Will you call him for me? Check him out?"

"Dad, I'm at the office negotiating my buyout."

"So, no?"

JadeAnne blew out an exasperated breath. "Look Dad, you need to do this one yourself. I'll be in touch later. Qadir has turned up some information for you."

"That's good news. Chucho, too."

"Oh? How is Chuch? Tell him hello. Gotta run, Dex is giving me the evil eye."

His tension soared. He had to loosen up, prepare a calm front to meet an old adversary. Quint had harbored an ember of anger toward him since 'Nam. The man had turned him in—or had he? Quint needed to find out; he couldn't let the ember flame into a confrontation. *Calm down, man.* He remembered Jade's yoga breathing and sucked in a slow breath. Held it. Exhaled a metered stream of air. His shoulders immediately dropped along with his blood pressure. He did it again then dialed Charley Stone's direct line.

"Good timing, Quint. My client just left. What can I do you for?" Stone's voice carried a forced joviality.

"Charley," Quint greeted his old pal. "Jade called you?"

"Yes. I've expected to hear from you for, what—about thirty years?"

"It's been a long time, Charley," Quint replied, softly.

"I could sue you."

"She's an adult. She can make her own decisions now. I followed the agreement while she grew up. You don't know the hell I suffered, knowing I had a child and having that child dead to me. You made sure of that, didn't you? But you were right, Charley. I wouldn't have been able to parent her."

"Ah, the day of reckoning has come."

"I was on the air field, a Huey landing with wounded aboard. A couple of body bags. I was assigned to the death detail. My job to pull the bags, get 'em lined up for transport home.

You came up. Caught me loading the opium, threatened to have me arrested. Next thing I knew, I landed in court. Court marshalled. Kicked out of the service and tried as a civilian. Short trial, Vietnam vets were hated. The war was hated. They convicted on hearsay. Got a couple of guys I'd served with to testify they'd seen me load the bags. I spent four years in a federal pen, as you well know. You visited me once. Why, Charley? To get my girl?"

"I always thought you blamed me. No, Quint. I did not turn you in." He paused. Quint's heart raced. "I couldn't let that baby, my best friend's child, be left to probably die at the hands of the VC. I took Jade to relieve your mind. You knew we'd care for her."

"This the truth, Charley? You didn't turn me in?" Quint smiled.

"I did not. But I wondered. When I was discharged and began my practice, I looked into your case. You don't know?"

"I have a good idea—beyond a reasonable doubt—in fact. A spook called Chuck Nader."

"Yes."

"Why did you never contact me? Tell me?"

"I didn't think it was fair to the child. She struggled enough thinking her parents were dead. Bringing you in would have just complicated things."

"Well, I'm in now. Have you talked to her?

"Not really. She called me a couple of months ago when she met you."

"Ah, Charley, you need to have dinner with her. Tell her the story. Tell her you didn't turn me in. She's met Nader."

"Hold on. What was that NSA spook to you? I learned he turned you in, but that's it."

"It's a long story. The upshot is, Nader has a vendetta against me. He's tried to kill me. I don't have time for the long version now. I've got to stop him. My team is trying to figure it out. You've answered a big question. I believe Nader blames me for his prison term. A term for a term, so to speak. But it wasn't me. Do you know who turned him in?"

"I'll check into it for you."

"Thanks, Charley. Call Jade. She and her boyfriend, Dylan, are in Sausalito. She's planning on coming back to Mexico. They're hinting at making their relationship permanent. Welcome him in, Charley. He's good people. A U.S. trained surgeon from a good family."

"I'll invite them to dinner, tell her history. I'll call when I have information on Chuck Nader. Good luck, Quint." Stone hung up.

Charley Stone had not turned him in! Nader. It kept coming back to Nader. It puzzled Quint why the man would screw up a good smuggling trade, bringing him beaucoup bucks. Obviously Nader feared Quint would turn on him. With the blackmail Nader held over him? Idiot? Or paranoid. Quint was in it too deep to turn on his handler. He would have been implicated. The minimum term he'd have received was ten years. Or it might have been a charge of treason. What would have happened then? When did they stop hanging traitors? Quint was thinking when he pushed through the blast door into the office.

Horacio looked up from his computer. He tipped his head toward the window. A "come here" gesture. He had something. Quint hurried into the workroom, shrugging in the universal *what?* Horacio pickled up his pad. Jotted: *Sweep at three-thirty.*

Quint thumbs upped. It was almost three. He took the pad and wrote: *Not Stone—he looked into my arrest. Nader turned me in. Stone reviewing Nader's arrest and trial.*

H replied: *The pieces of the puzzle are beginning to fit.*

Quint grinned, wrote: *What next?* He jerked his head toward the stairs and pointed up. Horacio made the beer-time sign, raising his eyebrows. Quint mouthed *Yes.*

The sweep turned up three more bugs. None from the residence. Quint invited the tech, Cuetzpallea, Pali for short, to a beer.

"Interesting name, Pali. *Náhuatle?*" Horacio asked.

"Yeah, my parents, Lupe and Rafael were hippies—I grew up on the *conchero* circuit. They joined the movement back to our indigenous roots in the '90s. My name means lizard. You can imaging the flak I got for that in school." He laughed. "But it is apropos of my work now. A gecko on the wall." He held out the three bugs.

Chucho held up his bottle. "To a successful sweep. Let's end this with a bang. Are those things active?"

"Not these, why?" Pali asked.

"Hold on, I'll be right back." Chucho ran downstairs, retuning in a few minutes with the box of bugs and an old fashioned claxon. "Found it in the storage room." He gently lined the bugs onto the table, whispered, "Cover your ears," aimed the bell toward the bugs, and squeezed the rubber bulb. A piercing honk blared from the horn. He repeated the noise twice more, then gathered up the devices, dumped them in the sink, running the faucet over them, hopefully shorting out their function. The men hooted in laughter.

"I hope Nader was listening," Horacio said. "That noise might blow out your eardrum."

"If it didn't damage his hearing, it certainly let him know we're on to him," Quint said.

Pali's smooth forehead wrinkled. "You know who placed the bugs?"

"Oh, yeah, *compa*, he's a bad, bad man, but we're going to get him," Chucho bragged.

"Why don't you bug him? Find out what his plan is? I could help." Pali cocked his head. Chucho grinned. They turned to Quint.

"*Pues*, why not, *Quint*?" Horacio raised his eyebrows, grinning.

The earnest enthusiasm of the young men, boys, really inspired him. He'd been like that, full of good humor. Ready to jump in to right the world's wrongs. It wasn't a bad idea. "Pali, how do we get bugs here?"

"I can make them and plant them. How many do you need?"

"How do we hear them?"

"Easy. They transmit to a receiver in range with a digital relay. You can pick them up on a computer."

"*Jefe*, can I show Pali my operation?"

"Sure. Why don't you two go hash out a plan while H and I talk. Take another beer."

Horacio smiled as the young men thudded down the stairs. "That was nice of you, *jefe*. I don't think Chucho has many friends. Law enforcement, a good choice for our Chuch."

"What I was thinking. Were we ever that young? They remind me of puppies," Quint said. "Smart ones. I rely on Chucho. He's got skills."

Horacio suggested, "We should offer Pali payment if he works with us."

"I was thinking the same. But if we're going to bug Nader, we need to find out where he's operating. Garza's not letting us bug the embassy."

H snorted. "I doubt Nader spends any time in the embassy —more than to get the secretaries to type up his required reports."

"You got that right," Quint said.

"Let's find him then."

Quint called down to the IT department.

"*Jefe*."

"Do a little digging. See if you can find out where Nader is staying."

"We're already on it. Pali is searching the CCTV footage for the beige car's *placa*. We can follow it through the city cams once we have a starting point, through the police's system."

"How's that?"

"Pali is a hacker, too."

A match made in heaven.

Chapter 14

A Date with Rosi

Quint waited in the office lobby when Rosi pulled up to the front door promptly at seven-thirty. She beeped. He'd hired a security detail during the afternoon. Another expense his group could hardly afford but Garza had been adamant he wasn't loaning any more marines to him. Quint didn't blame Garza. He texted the unit lead leader, Chepe: *Street safe?*

Sí, señor Quint.

Entonces, me voy, Quint texted and cracked open the door. Rosi had the passenger door open; he rushed in. Quint looked up to the roof as they pulled away and saluted.

"New security?"

He leaned over; gave her a peck on the cheek. "Thanks to you. Chepe rounded up some men. We've got two shifts of three for round-the-clock monitoring over six days. It shouldn't take six days—"

"But better safe than sorry, right?"

"Exactly," he said as he gave Rosi an approving once-over. "You look lovely."

Her face lit up in pleasure. "Thanks. Like I said, you clean up well, Jackman. I didn't know you had a suit."

He laughed. "Of course I do. It's required in court," he deadpanned.

She tried to hold back her laughter and failed. They rounded the corner at the end of Calle Tobasco giggling like kids. Quint relaxed, a warm glow in his chest. He liked Rosi. She was the first woman Quint felt wholly comfortable with since Thuy. She reached over to grasp his hand.

"Quint, I like you. I'm glad we've connected but I look forward to continuing our work. I think we can do a lot of good together in this greedy, immoral world."

His heart sank, as his pulse rose. What was she saying? He'd better stick to work. "Speaking of work, how are you coming along in the new offices?"

"I made headway while you were gone. I won't move until I'm completely set up, of course. I need personnel, computers, furniture—a name! I've moved my old office goods and set up my space. Can you think of a good name?"

"I'll consider it. But you're still operating from home?"

"Dining room table."

"Yeah," he chuckled. "More of our work goes on at the kitchen table. Have the funds been disbursed yet?'

"No. It will take months. Trusts are tricky. Rafiq's brothers are working on setting up a new trust for the non-profit. When Polo's trust closes, the new trust will fund. Meanwhile, I operate as I always have. On a shoestring."

"I know your parents support you. That helps. They're lovely people," Quint said, reflecting on the help they willingly gave to get Lily across the border when Quijada's people were after them.

"They are. They do so much for our work, but they take such a great risk. I have begged them to come here with me. Papi is too old to run that farm. With the narcos at each other's throats, I worry constantly. If Quijada gets wind you lot escaped to my parent's farm, he'll do something heinous. He's been after me for a long time."

"How so?"

"Dinner. A gallery opening. Theater. Barcelona—you name it. I refuse everything. He's scum."

"Is he trying to quash your trafficked persons rescue?"

"Of course. He's losing money. He might fancy himself Mexico's transportation baron, but he's really Juarez's whorehouse master." She checked her mirrors, flicked on the blinker to get into the left lane, and cut up Reforma. A car honked in her blind spot. "He owns most of the whorehouses in the city. Probably is itching to put me into one of them for all the girls I've rescued. I'm a little too well known. My family have been civic leaders in the area for centuries."

"Centuries? You're exaggerating!"

She blinked again, making a smooth lane change in time to turn left. Reforma was congested, but moving rapidly. "Not at all. Mexico is an old country. *Pues*, not like Europe, but the Europeans came five hundred years ago and established the hacienda system. Not that it benefitted the indigenous peoples, but *sí,* over three hundred years."

"On the same land?"

"More or less. It was a huge parcel originally. But through the years pieces were sold off. The hacienda burned down in the early 1900s. My grandparents built the house my parents live in."

"Whose side of the family?"

"My father's. Land passed father to son for the most part. Mom's family came from another big landowning family. Here's our turn." She flipped the blinker for a right off the glorieta at *el Monumento a Simon Bolivar* to angle onto Calle Julio Vern. They crossed a small park then Avenida Presidente Masaryk onto Alejandro Dumas.

Quint started to catch on. "I'd never noticed the streets in Polanco are named for writers."

She replied by saying, "Look for parking. We'll probably have to walk. Yes—writers, poets, philosophers. It was a lovely colonia. Now it's the chichi shopping district. The Rodeo Drive of Mexico City. With great restaurants."

"I know about the restaurants. The senator and I ate at many."

Rosi trolled the neighborhood. "And you didn't notice the street names?"

"Not really. I knew where I was going and Horacio was driving."

"So do I, if I can find us a parking space. We're due now." She turned right then right again down Tennyson past Pujol. A space opened up.

"There!" Quint pointed. He was glad it was getting dark. The sun had gone down about thirty minutes before. Twilight was short at Mexico's latitude. They had only a stroll to the restaurant, but he couldn't be sure they hadn't been followed. Hard to concentrate around this lovely woman. He envisioned a mass shooting at the restaurant—rival cartel style. Nader would walk away—disappear. The BLO and Zetas blamed.

"Rosi—"

She was already stepping through the door an older couple held for them. She smiled that welcoming smile. "*Gracias.*"

Quint followed her to the receptionist. "A reservation for Rosi, party of two," he said.

The receptionist, an attractive forty-something in a sophisticated grey silk sheath under a modern updo, smiled. Welcoming them, she ask if this was their first visit as she gathered menus. "Please, this way." She led them through the restaurant. Rosi looked like a queen crossing the room. She held her head high, her graceful gait measured in her high heeled sandals, a flowing skirt swirling around her shapely calves. Quint wanted to follow her forever. The receptionist stopped at a quiet corner away from the kitchen. Rosi smiled as Quint seated her then took his chair—positioned to see the room including the entry.

"This is a beautiful restaurant, Rosi. Thank you. How did you get this spot?"

"The parking?"

"No, the table."

"Oh, I assumed you'd be uncomfortable sitting in the

middle of the room. We'll both keep watch."

Except it wouldn't be Nader. "Nader will engineer an attack to look like something else. He knows the girls were running from the BLO and the Zetas. Look around. See any familiar faces?"

Rosi surveyed the room over the rim of her menu. Tipping it down, she smiled at Quint, murmuring she'd like the tuna tostada with avocado and kimchi, while pointing to something on her menu. "Hector Beltrán and his simpering beauty queen are dining at three-fifteen. Keep your back turned. Keep your smile on. What would you like to order?"

"We should leave."

"Are you armed?"

"Of course."

"You can see the entry, I can see the kitchen. We'll keep watch."

"And if men come in shooting?"

"You will shoot them. So will Hector. So will I."

"You have a gun?"

"Never leave home without it."

"That's an American Express card."

"I've got that too. Why? You short?" She giggled at her joke.

"Okay. Kidding aside, I hope the food is as good as the prices. I don't quite understand the menu."

Rosi flagged down a waiter, ordered two margaritas without worms, or *chapulines*, and asked him to explain the menu as she translated.

"They're all small plates. Order several. I'll order several. We'll share. The rock fish, seabass and softshell crab all sound good. I love cauliflower. I think *mole* comes with everything."

"I'm easy. I'll let you order."

She flagged the waiter a second time. He appeared after delivering the bill to Beltrán's table. They were leaving. If gunmen showed up, only innocents would be injured or killed.

"Relax, Jackman. You'll recognize anyone who doesn't belong. No one here has tattoos."

She had a point.

The waiter collected the bill and came over ready to take their order. Quint was certain Rosi had ordered one of everything. The Beltráns made their way across the dining room. Four men, diners from tables near the entry, rose as the kingpin reached the middle of the room. Two of the men exited. The other two fell-in ahead of their boss. "Security. Hector isn't taking any chances," Quint observed.

The couple stepped into the foyer. The shooting started. Three guns. Someone screamed.

"Rosi, get under the table!" Quint shouted. He flashed on the elegant receptionist.

Quint stood up, aimed, waiting for the automatic gunfire to stop. Uzi, he reckoned. The attacker was the rear flank of Beltrán's crew. A turn-coat. Mayhem overflowed the elegant dining room. Diners dove to the floor or ran toward the kitchen or patio. Women screamed. Fleeing patrons ran into each other, knocking some down, and trampling them in a mad escape. The stench of sweat and fear tainted the atmosphere souring the enticing smells of the food.

Another burst of gunfire then the firing stopped leaving a trail of gun smoke to drift through the doorway into the dining room. The receptionist was either the assassin or dead. Quint could hear only whimpering from the couple under the next table. He held his aim on the dining room door. A figure appeared. Rosi was correct, besides the weapon—a big give away—the shooter didn't fit the upscale look of the patrons of Pujol. The room resembled a Bosch painting Quint had seen in Madrid as the panic escalated. Rosi tugged on his pants, yelling. He couldn't make out the words in the din of misery and horror.

Concentrating, he slowed time. All the mayhem was a backdrop for what mattered. He was going to take this asshole alive then torture he truth out of him, if he had to. No one threatened *his* dinner date. *Come on, sucker. Another step into the room—I've got you.*

The man entered the room, Uzi ready, head swinging,

searching. The screaming intensified but any patrons still standing dropped to the floor. The man watched the mayhem, grinning. His gaze fell on Quint. The grin turned into a growl. Quint felt his manic energy, his intent—the shooter was coming for him.

"Lower your weapon, soldier."

The Uzi swung toward him, spitting bullets. Quint shot it out of the man's hand.

Another single shot rang out from under the table. Quint glanced down. Rosi held a pistol. The assassin dropped in the doorway howling as he grabbed his knee. Guns trained on the shooter, Rosi and Quint advanced. The man reached for the dropped Uzi with his good hand. Quint shot the gun. The man roared, crab-scuttled into the foyer, but Quint held his Luger on him. "Rosi, find something to tie him up with." She backed out, running to the kitchen dodging diners getting off the floor.

The empty kitchen was a shambles from the exodus of staff and diners. Rosi found a huge roll of plastic wrap and scissors. She carried them to Quint, pushing through the crowd forming in the dining room doorway, gawking and snapping photos as he wrapped the man's legs while Rosi held the gun. He roughly twisted the man's arms behind him, then wrapped his wrists.

Rosi handed the gun back to Quint. She pushed open the front door. "No sign of the Beltráns," she said, returning to the foyer and shaking her head.

She peered behind the podium to find the receptionist quaking on the floor, but unharmed. She led the woman into the dining room to an empty table and told her to stay put then Quint heard her shout, "Everyone sit back down. Wait for the ambulances."

It took ten minutes for the ambulances to arrive. Paramedics, police and the fire department converged on the restaurant. The shooter and his allies were arrested and whisked away. Quint was detained for carrying a gun.

Chapter 15

Not The Dessert I Anticipated

Garza met them at a bar in Condesa.

"I appreciate you sorting this out, Ambassador," Quint said.

"Thanks for coming, Tony. We're grateful you're taking over," Rosi chimed in.

"What a cluster-fuck. Exactly what I said Nader would do, wasn't it, Rosi?"

"Mr. Quint, we have no proof Nader had anything to do with this. It may have been what it appeared to be. A hit on Beltrán."

"Then why wasn't Beltrán a bloody corpse in the entryway? The shooter knew Quint. I could see it in his face," Rosi protested. "How do you suppose Nader got Beltrán there?"

"Rosi! There is no evidence—"

"Sure there is, Tony. You have him plastic wrapped—ready to freeze."

"Give him a few a hours in the deep freeze. He'll tell you the whole plan, Garza."

"I'm going to pretend you didn't say that, Mr. Quint. But I'll get the appropriate people to have a talk with him before we bounce him back to the police. I wouldn't count on much. These people are fiercely loyal. Ready to do time for their gangs."

"Nader hasn't had time to develop a security team, any more than I have. The actor you have is a hired assassin."

"Why do you say that?"

Rosi answered, "Tony, Nader showed up in time to go to El Paso. He was chasing Quint's crew through New Mexico, Denver, and back to El Paso. Jackman gets home—Nader is planting explosives on his residence."

"And this means he hasn't put together a crew?"

"When would he have time? Doesn't he have a job with embassy intelligence?"

"Ambassador, look at it like this: a rival cartel would send a team to take out Beltran. This guy was alone, corroborated by the receptionist and witnesses. On top of that, Nader has had different men with him at each incident. The two in New Mexico were killed. Two were killed on my roof. We know which gang he affiliated with in El Paso, but none of those people are the people we've seen here. Nader is a loner, hiring what he needs as he needs it. Just like in 'Nam. Don't forget, I was coerced into his drug trafficking scam. I've seen up close personal how he works. He bugged my place after the attack. Probably heard me make the reservation."

"Or he had your phone tapped," Garza said

"Or mine," Rosi said, face thoughtful.

"No, I used my cell phone."

"You think NSA can't tap a cell phone?"

"You've got a point."

The barmaid stopped at the table and cleared the empty glasses. "Bring you folks another drink?"

Rosi raised a finger, widened her eyes. Quint nodded.

The server looked at Garza expectantly.

"No, I should be getting back. I'll get right on this. Goodnight, Mr. Quint. Rosi." Garza pushed up from the table.

"Two of the same, then?" the waitress asked.

Rosi nodded.

"Make mine a bourbon and soda," Quint said, standing to shake Garza's hand. "Thanks, Mr. Ambassador. We appreciate all you can do."

"Get me evidence, Quint," he said, saluted, then headed for the door.

"That was disappointing," Rosi said.

"Aw, he's got to watch his diplomat back. We'll get the proof he needs."

The server returned with their drinks. Rosi dimpled, eyes twinkling. "Here's to our successful mission." They clinked glasses.

For another half hour they sipped and strategized. Making plans was calming, taking the sharp edge off their nerves. Quint felt his blood pressure easing back to normal, but the noise in the bar ramped up as a rowdier clientele trickled in. "Looks like it's time to go, Rosi."

"How about that dinner? I'm famished. Funny how a shoot-out makes you hungry. I know a good place nearby. It's open late. We can walk."

Quint signaled the waitress for the check before draining his glass. He needed food to soak up his three drinks. The woman brought the check and her card reader. Quint pulled out his card, but Rosi said, "No, let me get the drinks, Jackman. You get dinner. Let's not talk about work." He acquiesced.

She led him out to the sidewalk, took his arm, and together they ambled a couple of blocks before turning left another block, although Quint kept a sharp eye on their surroundings. It felt safe walking arm-in-arm with Rosi, but until Nader was neutralized, he'd remain vigilant.

The restaurant was a two-story affair backing onto a walled, wooded garden on Avenida Michoacán, covered in ivy with window boxes spilling plants. Rosi claimed there was no access to the garden, blocked by an apartment building. Rosi

111

asked for a table in the back window in what would be a sunny, yellow-painted room in the morning. Quint did his best to relax.

They shared a *queso fundido* to start, dipping chunks of bread into gooey melted Oaxaca cheese and feeding bites to each other. Rosi ordered a sopa for their first course, a *fideo seco*, something Quint had never tried. It turned out to be a pasta dish with soured cream and avocados with a rustic cheese. Very tasty. Conversation turned to their families. Quint found himself telling her too much about his upbringing. The tops of his ears burned.

She laughed and covered his hand with hers. "Jackman, don't be embarrassed. I'm a good listener. I won't judge you. We can't pick our families. Mine was venerated for longevity, but we weren't rich. I was lucky to have loving parents who approached life together as partners. My *papi* was no *macho*. He encouraged my mother to pursue her interests. He was the one to insist I go to university. *Papi* managed the farm, but *Mami* oversaw it. She knew every job and did them when hands were needed. *They* taught us to care for the animals, to plant, harvest, and maintain and operate all the equipment. *Mami* taught us how to store the harvest, can, pickle, and cook. My brothers too."

"How many brothers do you have?"

"Three. They are three years apart. Güicho is the oldest and has his own farm. Meme is an engineer working for a firm out of Monterrey. Neto we don't talk about."

"The bad seed? What did he do?"

"Neto studied accountancy at Texas A & M. He met a girl at university and married her. Her family was very rich, oil, cattle, real estate, trafficking. Neto's brilliant, creative mind, shady contacts from Juarez—a great friend of Dylan's uncle, Quijada—introduced the father-in-law to a whole new level of profits. Neto runs his money laundering business. But in Neto's favor, he abhors human trafficking. He helped me set up the cross border network to get victims back to their families. Out of his own dirty pocket he funds much of my work. I'm not proud. I'll take it. My parents won't take a peso from him. Not even a Christmas gift. But I believe he protects them. He's got wealth and power."

Quint set his fork across the scraped-clean painted *barro* plate his *pollo crujiente con mole de guayaba*, a crispy fried chicken in a guava sauce, and licked his lips. "That was delicious—worth every *centavo*. I'm betting this joint is way better than Pujol. Although I feel responsible for bringing a disastrous evening down on them. How was your *chipotle* dish?"

"Absolutely wonderful, thank you. But, Jackman, it's not your fault. Stop thinking like that. It's Chuck Nader's fault. What do you want for dessert?"

Quint accepted the proffered dessert menu and scanned the offerings. He was no longer hungry but the mouthwatering food was too good to pass up. "The cheesecake in a fig reduction sounds good. You?"

"That's what I would have ordered. Shall we split a piece?"

Quint nodded and reached for her hand and squeezed it. The waiter returned with two espresso coffees, the cheesecake and two forks.

"Anything else, *señor*?"

"*No, gracias, solamente el recibo*," Quint replied, regret tinging his voice. He wasn't ready to leave this woman's company or the warm ambiance of Fonda Garufa, but it was clear the restaurant had closed some time before. Their waiter wanted to go home. Quint left a healthy tip.

"Jackman, I'm concerned about you staying at the residence tonight. Why don't you come home with me. I have a spare room," Rosi said, turning a soft smile on him as they started back to the car.

He bent down, gathered her into his arms wanting to say yes, but hesitated. Was this too fast? Or was she just being kind? She kissed him before he could answer. Soft, then more passionate. They kissed long and deep standing on the corner of the street. When they came up for air, Rosi said, "There's more where that came from."

They crossed, arm in arm, walking slowly until Quint pulled her in again, whispering into her ear. Rosi giggled and grinned.

On the short ride back to Roma Norte, Quint checked his texts. The head of the new security team, Chepe, had left a message an hour earlier. *Jefe, your man dropped by after eight. We detained one of his team, but the others got away. Your man was wounded.*

Quint texted: *Sorry for the delay. Attack at the restaurant. I'm on my way. Chucho went with Horacio?*

Chepe responded right away. *We're fine. The men are gone. I'll see you shortly?*

Quint: *I'll be there.*

"Nader paid my offices a visit around eight-thirty. Chepe thinks he's wounded. He detained one of the accomplices. I should—"

"Oh, Jackman. I'll run you by, but you will not stay there."

"No?"

"It's final."

Chapter 16

Leo

Friday, October 5, 2007

After midnight, Rosi pulled up in front of the office. Quint sprang around the car and escorted her to the front door, which he opened. Inside he texted Chepe, who showed up a few moments later.

"Hey man, thanks for being vigilant. Let's go talk to Nader's accomplice. This is Rosi, by the way."

Rosi and Chepe shook hands before he led them to the garage where a dark complexioned youth glowered from his sitting position tethered to the central roof strut, a shock of wavy hair hanging over one eye.

"Mr. Quint, meet *la comadreja*."

The boy spit at Quint's feet. "The what?" Quint asked.

"Weasel. His gang name," Chepe clarified.

The boy's pinched, long-nosed face resembled the animal. Quint doubted he'd get much out of him. "What's your real name?"

115

"*Chinga tu madre.*"

"I doubt my mother has much to do with it," Quint replied acidly. "Take him into my office."

"We know who hired you. Is he worth going to jail for?"

"*Pinche pendejo*, you know nothing."

"A *vaboso gabacho* who ran, leaving you to take the blame is worth protecting?" Chepe asked the boy. "We're willing to help you if you help us."

"You're all *pinches gabachos.* Why should I trust you?"

Rosi stepped forward. She quietly said, "*Hijo*, I'm as Mexican as you. I head an organization which helps Mexicans in trouble. Chepe works for me. We are here looking for the *gabacho's* daughter who has been kidnapped. Maybe you know something about that. Can you help us?" She smiled sweetly, impressing Quint with her smooth ability to lie.

Her soothing voice calmed the gangbanger, but he said, "Why would I know anything about that?"

"The man who hired you, Nader, is responsible. She's only eleven. Don't you have sisters?" La Comadreja nodded, avoiding eye contact. "*Hermano*, what would you do if he took one of yours?"

"I'd kill him."

"And you think a *gabacho* loves his daughter less? Help him find this Nader and his girl."

The dark head sank lower. Rosie was a master at shame, Quint thought. He better stay on her good side. She hunkered down next to the boy. They sat in an almost companionable silence for a few moments. The tension in the garage thickened as La Comadrejo grappled with some decision. His lips tightened as his eyes squeezed shut. Quint noticed a tear cut a channel down his dirty cheek.

"You know what he feels. You've lost someone. To trafficking?"

He nodded, the tears now streaming. Hot. Inconsolable. Rosi put her arm around his shaking frame, murmuring into the boy's ear. He slowly stopped crying. Rosi released him.

"They took my sister. She's a drug addict and a whore, a slave to the cartel. I'm trying to get her out, but I need money."

"My organization can negotiate her sale if you will help us."

His anger exploded. He thrashed against the post, the restraints holding fast. "How can I trust you? You rich people all the same. Promises until you get what you want. Then what? Nothing for a kid like me."

"How old are you, *hijo*?"

"I'm fourteen. I'm a man," he retorted.

Quint squatted, pulled a roll of bills from his pocket. "How much money do you need?"

The boy's eyes bugged. He tried to snatch the roll, but Quint hovered just out of range. "How much do they want for her?"

"Fifty thousand pesos, but I have to work for them, too." He slumped back into a dejected pose. "I will never make that."

Quint peeled five one-hundred-dollar bills of the roll, fanning them in his hand. "Where is she? Who has her?"

"They're going to sell her to Los Zetas."

"How do you know?"

"I hear him talking on his phone."

"You work for them?"

"No. He lives with my mother."

"How did Nader find you?"

"My *jefe*."

"Who's that?" Quint asked, exasperated. He turned to Rosi. In English he said, "It's like pulling teeth. Maybe you'd have a better time of it."

"*Hijo*, tell me who your *jefe* is."

"*No es importa más*. He's dead. Now I work for the man you call Nader. I think Nader killed him. He wants to take the trafficking."

Quint spun back to face the weasel, grabbing his shirt, shouting, "Anibal Aguirre?"

The boy blanched, fear turning him rigid. Rosi pushed

117

between them." Quint, stop it this moment." He let go; the boy thumped back to the floor. "Untie him and bring him into the house. He needs food."

"Rosi, he's a gangbanger who came here to harm me."

"He's a fourteen-year-old kid who's scared and confused. Regardless how he got here, he's been abandoned."

"Chepe, check him for weapons. Keep his hands tied. Take him up to the kitchen. Go with him Rosi." Quint stomped out, found the other two security guards and gave them instructions.

When Quint arrived in the kitchen, Rosi had opened the refrigerator. She pulled out covered dishes and peeked into each. "This looks like enchiladas. You hungry, Leo?"

"*Si Señora.*"

She dished up a large portion, put it in the microwave, then pulled out salsa and a Fanta. "Chepe, would you like some?" she asked.

"*Sí, por favor.*" She fixed him a plate.

"How about your men, Chepe?" she asked as she unbound Leo's wrists.

"*Por supuesto, jefa.*"

"I'll take plates to them if you promise not to rough up, Leo," Rosie said.

Quint got himself a beer and sat down. The boy shoveled in the food like he hadn't eaten for days. He probably hadn't.

"How much did Aguirre pay you?"

"Depended on what I did."

"Did you know he worked for the U.S. government?"

Leo's jaw dropped then snapped shut. "He was a *pinche traficante*. Nader killed him."

"No, Leo. Someone else did."

"*No te creo.*"

"Believe what you want. I have a proposition for you. I will pay you fifty U.S. dollars a day for ten days, plus expenses of 50 pesos daily to travel and eat, if you will gather information for me. You have a phone?"

"No, why?"

"At the end of each day you will call me with what you've found out. If your information pans out, and if I am able to get proof of Nader's illegal activities I will pay you a bonus of $500 U. S. dollars when he's arrested. You might consider buying yourself a burner phone."

Leo's eyes bugged, but he remained sarcastic, cautious. "You *el tamarindo*? What kind of information?"

"Where he goes. Who he meets. Where he plans to go the next day. Get me my information and you'll be able to buy your sister. But no, I'm not a cop."

Rosi handed a steaming plate to Chepe.

Quint pulled fifty pesos from his pocket and handed it to Leo. "An advance on tomorrow." Leo nodded. "Do you have somewhere to stay?" Leo nodded again. "Does Nader know where you stay?" This time Leo shook his head.

Rosi heated the last plate, fixing a tray for the guards. She discovered a vanilla cake in the cupboard, adding slices to each plate. Chepe took the tray out to his men. Leo's eyes lit up when Rosi put a huge piece of cake topped with a scoop of ice cream in front of him.

Once the kitchen was cleaned up, Quint quizzed Leo on his association with Nader until he had a rough picture. He said, "Rosi, give me a minute to collect some things and let's go."

Leo, working on a second bowl of ice cream, looked up in alarm. "You can't leave me here."

"Hadn't planned on it, Leo. Rosi, we can drop him off?" They both looked expectantly at her.

"I guess we'll have to. Where do you live?"

"It's far. I can go to my friend's over in Tepito just off Reforma."

"Quint, it's a terrible neighborhood at night," Rosi said, her English accented.

"I'll bring a gun."

Leo swung his head back and forth between them as they spoke in English.

"I think he's lying. Homeless kids sleep under the tarps at

119

the flea market."

"What do you want to do then?"

"Why are you speaking *ingles*?"

"Leo, I don't think you have a place to sleep. We'll take you to a friend with a room for you."

"I do too have a place." he said, fear rolling over his boyish face.

Rosi gently said, "The *tianguis* is no place for a kid."

Leo blushed.

Forty minutes later, Leo was bathed and tucked into a warm bed at Horacio's house with the promise Horacio would bring him back to Roma Norte in the morning to start his new job. He was to meet Nader outside the embassy to see if there were any errands. Rosi drove them back to her house. It was already one-thirty in the morning. "Do you think Leo will stay?"

"I don't know. The question is, if he does stay, will he try to steal anything? Will he do the job?" Quint said.

"It's a lot to ask of a youngster."

"It's late, let's worry tomorrow," he said, kissing her.

She pulled away. "Quint, I'm calling for a re-do on tonight. Let me get you some towels and show you to your room."

His face fell, but he kissed her lightly on the cheek. "You're right. It's late. Thanks for all the help." He followed her down the hall.

Chapter 17

A Double Agent

Rosi dropped Quint off during the morning shift change. Chepe gave him the report: no nocturnal activity. Quint thanked the men. They would return at eight that night. Chepe's cousin headed the day shift. Quint explained who was authorized to go in and out. Mrs. P for one. He looked forward to seeing her. She wouldn't have much housework to do, but maybe he could call Jade and let Mrs. P talk to her. That would make the housekeeper happy.

Horacio honked the limo's horn when he turned into the *callejon*. Quint looked out the window. Good. Leo was with him, looking much less like a weasel and more like a fourteen-year-old boy wearing some of Horacio's boy's clothes. They came up the back stairs as Mrs. P rang the office doorbell.

"All go well last night, H?" Quint asked? He looked Leo over. "You're looking smart, Leo. Good night's sleep?"

"*El señor es muy amable.*" He held up a sack with his dirty clothes. "*¿Dónde?*"

Mrs. P chuffed in from the steep climb. She paused to catch

her breath and inspected Leo. "*¿Quien eres, muchacho?*" she demanded.

"*Bienvenidos,* Mrs. P. I'm so glad to see you." Quint pulled out a chair for her. "Coffee?"

"*Qué amable,* Mr. Quint." She handed him her coat then sat down. Horacio poured her coffee, delivering it and a plate of *panes* to the table while Quint stowed her belongings in the back hall.

"Are either of you boys going to introduce me?" she asked.

"This is Leo. He's doing a job for us right now. Leo, this is our *ama de casa.* You can thank her for those delicious enchiladas last night. Leo stepped forward and shook her hand gently. "*Muy ricas enchiladas Doña. ¡Y la salsa!*"

Mrs. P beamed, glad he liked them. "What a nice boy, Horacio. He's not yours is he?"

"*Lástima,* no. He's much politer than mine."

"*Doña, dónde quedo mi ropa sucia?*"

Over by the washer." She pointed to the porch. "I'll wash them with Mr. Quint's clothes. You have a suitcase full?"

"Already in front of the machine. I thought I'd call Jade today. Would you like to talk to her?'

"Oh yes. *Gracias.* What do you want for dinner? How many people?"

"I'm not sure, but we have three security men who will need lunch."

"I'll make a list before I shop. Do you want breakfast?"

"No, Rosi and I ate together earlier. H, you and Leo eat?"

"*Señor Quint, la señora* made my favorite, *chilaquiles con pollo.*"

"So, everyone is well fed. It's almost nine. Don't you have a date with Nader, young man?"

"Yes sir, br-bring it on," he stammered in English.

"Nader! I don't trust him. How can you send this boy to him?" Mrs. P was obviously appalled at the idea.

"Leo is working undercover for me. I'll tell you after they leave. Drop him on the far side of the *tianguis* in Tepic, H. Be sure you aren't followed. Leo, *es un operación encubierta*—an undercover op. *Cuídate hijo*."

Leo quivered like an excited puppy.

"Mrs. P, we are not safe here. If you want to go home, I won't blame you. Since we got back, we've been attacked here twice and twice outside the property." He proceeded to tell her of the trouble. She listened calmly, taking in Quint's story without interruption.

"I'm not sure how you can use a young boy like that against that man."

"Leo has a story, too. He's already working for Nader. Now he's a double agent."

The doorbell buzzed three short blasts. In moments, Chucho bounded into the kitchen.

"Hi Mrs. P, *jefe. ¿Que pasa?*" He poured a coffee, helping himself to a *pan dulce*. "I like this continental style better than waiting to the afternoon for my *panes*."

"After you eat, I want you to meet the new security guards. But take your time, I'm filling Mrs. P in on all the excitement."

Chapter 18

But Can You Trust Him?

Shadows angled across the room between rays of late afternoon sun. Quint thumbed the desktop rhythmically—tap-tap-tap, pause, tap-tap-tap— his forehead furrowed in concentrated thought. He straightened. "I don't have any other ideas." He shrugged, looking directly at Horacio. "What do you propose?"

"But Quint, can you trust him?" Horacio asked. He rubbed his palm over his chin and blew out a short breath. "Leo was out of the limo, disappearing into the market before I could stop the car. I suspect he was on the run with your fifty pesos."

"It's fifty pesos, H. I piss that much away every day. Did the kid say anything? He's got street tats. Who is he affiliated with?"

"They're amateur, drawn on. I'm pegging him as a wannabe truant from school. Although I wonder if he's living on the street. You saw the state of his clothing."

"He denied it, but why would he want to be dropped in Tepito in the middle of the night? It's a rough neighborhood."

"Five to one he's sleeping in the market, feeding out of the market garbage with the *corrientes* and rats."

"If the bundle he left for Mrs. P to wash are an indication, I'd agree. Smelled like garbage. But it's to our advantage. We can work this."

"Only if he comes back. If we can trust he's not playing us. The delinquent could have run straight to Nader."

"He could have, but you didn't hear his story about his sister. The kid cried."

"Oldest trick in the book, Quint. *Hijole,* when I was on the beat, I heard every story. Some of those liars should have gone on stage. Leo is a con man."

"Let's wait 'til tonight. If he doesn't call, do we have resources to raid the market in a few days? Flush him out? Grab him? If there was any way to get him into a juvenile detention—is there juvenile detention here?"

"Sure, but not for sleeping in the Tepito market."

"Then, if Leo doesn't pan out, what's our next solution to getting intel on Nader? Every move I have—he taught me. Well, almost. I know how he operates. He knows I know."

"The solution is to figure out what he has against you—what he's going to gain by taking you out." Horacio flipped on the table lamp next to him, which shed a warm yellow circle onto the side table and couch. Around the pool of light, the room shifted and slithered with the creeping shadows. "Why don't we ask our tech genius to search for recent records on Nader. Has there been any luck with the trial transcripts?"

"He's already working on it. Maybe we should look more closely into my trial. Charley Stone denies turning me in. If not Charley, then it was—"

Horacio's head snapped up. They chorused, "Nader."

"But why? I was making him rich, packing those bags with his Triad opium. Heroin, too. I was getting drugs from him—not likely to make trouble for him. I had Thuy to worry about. Nader blackmailed me with threats to my girl if I stepped out of line."

"Do you have any proof?"

"None." Quint punched the intercom. Chucho answered.

"How's the search for info on Nader coming?"

"Working on it," Chucho's voice sounded tinny over the intercom. "I've got a little info."

"Why not run up for beers. Come back. Let's talk about what you've found."

"On my way *jefe.*"

The men sank back into silence. Quint jumped when he heard a knock on the door. Mrs. P tentatively pushed through and scanned the now nearly dark room beyond the circle of light thrown off by the lamp. She flipped on the overhead light. Quint blinked. Horacio shielded his eyes.

"Mr. Quint, I'm off now. I wanted to give you young Leo's clothes. They've been washed, but I couldn't get the smell of rotting vegetables out. What on earth has the boy been doing?"

"Horacio thinks he's sleeping in the Tepic market."

"Yes, that would account for the stench. I found these in his pockets." She held out a cheap pocket knife, a small heart carved from jade, several business cards, and a folded paper. "I'd burn the clothes, but he probably wants his possessions back."

"Thanks, Mrs. P. He probably does." Quint reached out to take the meager collection.

"What's the folded paper?" Horacio asked.

"*Pues,* I didn't open it," the housekeeper said.

Quint carefully opened the paper. He grinned. "Bingo!"

"Bingo?" echoed Horacio and Mrs. P.

"Never mind. It's Nader's address with his cell number. So the kid lied about knowing where Nader is.

Horacio's eyes twinkled. "We've got him then. What are the other cards?"

Chuch came in with a tray of four beers, a bowl of salsa, and a bag of tostadas. He set it down on the small table in the corner. "Mrs. P, may I offer you a beer?"

"Gracias, *hijo,*" she said, accepting the glass he poured her.

He handed out the bottles. "*Salud.*"

A hearty, "*Salud*" rang out as each tipped their beer to the others.

The team chatted and munched chips for a bit before Mrs. P glanced at her wristwatch. She said she had to go home. "Mr. Quint, I've left a pan of chile rellenos, arroz, refritos *y* tortillas for you and the security guards. There's an *agua fresca* in the refrigerator. Can you heat the tortillas? The rest can go in the microwave or the oven. The flan is on the counter."

"You did all that for us, Mrs. P?" Quint asked. "You're a marvel!" He helped her up from the low chair. "*Gracias*. Is someone coming for you?" He gave her a one-armed hug.

"No, I'll catch the six-forty-five pesera."

Quint looked at Horacio.

"Mrs. P, why don't I drop you off on my way home? *Mi marida* is expecting me for dinner so it's no problem at all."

"H, can you drop me off, too?" Chucho asked.

"Oh, dear, it looks like you'll be alone for dinner, Mr. Quint."

Horacio smiled at Mrs. P. "Chuch, why don't you stay for dinner. I have to come back to finish up some work. I'll take you home later." He guided Mrs. P to the door.

"Sweet." Chucho called after Horacio.

"You been watching American TV again, Chuch?" Quint said, lightly punching his shoulder.

"Learned it from Lily," he replied, hanging his head.

"You've talked to her." It wasn't a question.

Chucho mumbled something Quint took to be 'she called me'. "Son, it's best not to have any contact with her. You want her to be safe, don't you?" Quint asked. Chucho grunted a pained sound. "They could find her through you. You know that."

"I know. But she misses us. She's unhappy. Her sister's funeral was today."

"Has she gone back to school?"

"No. Her aunt wants her to heal first. She goes to a psychologist all the time."

"Christ." Quint grunted. "Let's go up, get some food."

Chucho heated the tortillas on the *comal* while Quint

127

microwaved the food. He got out a towel to wrap the hot tortillas then set two places with silverware and glasses and poured what looked like Mrs. P's *jamaica* water. She did something special to it. Cinnamon, maybe.

The microwave dinged. Chucho slapped the last tortilla into the towel. They sat down to eat.

"Chucho, I'm waiting on a call from Leo. I need your help with him."

"How do you mean, *jefe*."

"He needs someone young to relate to and learn from, that is, if we can pull him off the street." For the second time that day, Quint related Leo's story along with the details of the evening's adventures.

"Horacio is worried. Doesn't think he'll be back. Mrs. P found evidence corroborating his connection to Nader."

"What?"

"In his pants pocket. Nader's address and phone number."

"What kind of evidence is that? You already knew he came here with Nader. What did the kid say they were going to do?"

"He didn't say. I wanted more evidence of Leo's connection—more than Leo was caught and Nader escaped when the guards turned up. That's Nader's MO—he's an escape artist."

"M-O?"

"Modus operandi, or way of operating in Latin."

"Good word. M-O. But Nader didn't get away in '75," Chucho said.

"What have you learned?"

"He was charged with Possession of Narcotics with Intent to Sell, Crossing International Borders with Illegal Substances, and something else I can't remember. The last one was dropped. Oh, yeah, passing secrets to the enemy."

"You're translating all this?"

"Yeah, *jefe*. I might change my major to English. Get a job as a translator." He laughed.

"You're too good with the computer to be happy with that. Have you seen anything saying how he got caught?

"No, but I've barely made it through the first page. It takes a long time to translate."

"I'll be. Why don't you give me a copy. I'll see what I can do with it."

"*Sí*. I'll go get it, but first, what are we doing about Nader's address? We going for him? Can I carry the Uzi?"

Quint's eyebrows leapt up. He shook his head. "No! Of course not. Chucho, we aren't like those people."

"Sorry, *jefe*. But what *are* we doing?"

"Intelligence gathering. It's what I do, how I earn my living. Information is the best weapon—"

"Unless some *pendejo* is trying to shoot you," Chucho muttered, frowning.

"Then you may carry the Uzi. *If* you know how to use it. What we are going to do is run surveillance on Nader, tap his phones, find out what he's up to. You are doing a valuable job, Chuch, finding out what the connection is to his being in Mexico and me. I wanted to talk about that with you and Horacio earlier."

"But Mrs. P came in."

Quint grinned. "No need to scare our cook away. What would we do without her fine meals? Speaking of which, we need your intel. Go tell the security to come eat." He started heating up plates for the men.

Chepe's cousin came in with another man, ate, reported, and carried the last plate to the remaining sentry with a thermos of coffee and three mugs. Horacio had arrived but disappeared downstairs to what would eventually be Susana's office, if she ever came back. It had been a month since the senator's funeral. How long did it take to close down an apartment? It hadn't been so bad with Jade handling the administrative work. He checked the wall clock as he cleaned up the dishes. Eight. It would be six in Sausalito. He wished Jade would hurry back. Where was Leo? Quint considered his wager with Horacio. He may have been right, Leo played him. Quint grabbed another carafe of coffee to take back to his office. It would be a late night.

He knocked on Horacio's door and poked his head into Chucho's room to let them know he was ready. He set his coffee tray onto his office table with the now-stale chips. Before the men joined him, he closed the blackout curtains and turned on all the lights. They had plans to make, assignments to divvy up, information to interpret. Chucho had a point. What exactly should he do with Nader's phone number?

Horacio came in first. He sprawled on the couch. Chucho, carrying a ream of printouts, dropped into the chair Mrs. P had vacated. Quint wheeled his chair around the desk with his laptop, which he handed to Chucho. "Men, we need a plan. As it is, we're on a tight time budget to get this office organized and running. My clients expect some results, but I have to stop Nader. We've been distracted since August. It's the middle of October."

"*Jefe*," Horacio said, "it would help if we had someone to run this office. I bumped into Susana the other day. She's barely a quarter of the way through the Polanco flat. She has the farm, too, said it's the office that's taking the time, but she's almost ready to hand over the files we need."

"Has she been hassled by the senate officers?"

"Quite a bit. She placates them with inconsequential papers. She admitted the apartment was entered, but nothing taken. She thinks someone was after information. The culprit might have photographed papers, but she said most of ours are safe."

"When did this occur?" Quint asked.

"Right before we left for Denver."

"No break-ins since?"

"An attempt. She's got a team staying there 24/7 now."

"We need our files."

Horacio countered, "Susana says with all the trouble we've had, they're safer where they are."

"I'd have to agree."

"She also says she's not going to come on full-time for at least six more months."

"Then I've got to get Jade here. When was Dylan due

back? Let's all put pressure on him to convince her," he replied, voice light.

The Quint's cell rang. He picked it up. "Yeah." He listened for a few moments, then said, "hold on a minute" and covered the receiver. "Chucho, could this phone be tapped?"

"A burner? No, *jefe*. Call back to verify."

"*Lo siento,* I'll have to call you back. What's the number?" He scribbled while the speaker dictated and hung up.

Quint frowned, the lines along his chin deepening. "Something off about that."

"What do you mean?" Chucho asked.

"It was Leo, although he called himself by another name. He said he couldn't meet me for dinner, he's tied up. He called me *Papi*."

Horacio jumped up, grabbed the number. "He's in trouble. Chucho, can you do a trace?"

"Sure, come on." He bolted for his office, flinging himself in front of the computer. In moments, he had the software running. "Gimme the phone." He wiggled his fingers at Horacio who had followed him into the communications room. H passed it over. Chucho performed some magic and handed it back.

"What next?" Quint asked from the doorway.

"Dial the number. Keep him on the line for as long as you can. Horacio, you do it. If Nader is there, he's less likely to recognize your voice. Pretend to be a dad. Play it out—this takes a couple of minutes."

Horacio dialed. The phone rang too many times. He was shaking his head, about to hang up, when Leo answered. "*Hijo,* what's this about skipping your sister's birthday dinner?"

"Dad, I'm tied up at somebody's house. We have a big project due, I can't get free until it's done. I may not even get home tonight. Tell *mi hermana feliz cumpleaños.* I'll see her in the morning. Probably early."

"We're all sorry you'll miss your mother's *tres leche*s cake. Shall I save you a piece?"

"I wish you could bring us some, but I'm over on the other

side of the city. Santana lives in Satélite." Quint checked the paper from Leo's pocket. He gave a thumbs-up.

"*Pues, hijo*, I'm disappointed in you. This meant a lot to your mother and sister. I hope you plan better in the future." Chucho gave the signal. He'd captured the location. "Good luck on your project, *hijo*."

"*Gracias, Papi*. See you soon."

"We got it. He's in Satélite like he said. The address matches. Let's go."

"Who's Santana?"

Quint bellowed laughter. "Where've you been? Carlos Santana—the musician?"

"He's at Carlos Santana's house? In California?" Chucho said, puzzled.

Quint's eyes twinkled. "Come on, brainiacs, think! Santana—Carlos, a nickname?" he paused.

"Chuck!" Horacio finished. "That kid's smart. Knows more English than we thought, too."

"So Leo is being held at Chuck Nader's place. Nader is planning a move on us tonight or early in the morning. Leo is not able to get away. But Nader can see he called us," Horacio said.

Chucho replied, "*Ni modo*. It's a burner, not linked to Quint."

"Get the weapons and your bags, men. I'll find Chepe. I'm bringing him along. Meet in the entry. Two minutes." Quint sprinted outside. He speed dialed his security chief. "Chepe, we have trouble. Need you and your best man to come with us. Maybe you should drive. Out target knows the limo."

"Sure, *jefe*. Martinez, double-shift tonight. You're driving."

"Where to?"

Quint said, "Satélite," and read off the address. "We're cutting off the crew planning to attack us tonight."

"We're not going to pass them on the way are we?"

"Not according to our CI."

Chepe gritted his teeth, nodding. "Suit up. You two in position here. We'll see you when we get back."

Chapter 19

Breaking and Entering

The famous Torres de Satélite, designed by architect Luis Barragán, loomed in the middle of the *Periférico* marking the Satélite turn-off. Chucho directed Martinez to take the exit, turn west then angle south toward Naucalpan. "*Jardines de San Mateo, Calle Orquídeas.*" The white utility van wove through a dark middle class residential neighborhood for a few minutes. "There." He pointed to a house.

"Pass. Pull over out of sight," Quint ordered.

A light glowed around a curtained window behind an overgrown bush on the ground floor of the two-story house. The tall pink walls and security gates prevented Quint from seeing beyond the front of the nondescript house in a neighborhood of mostly nondescript houses.

"Are we waiting or going in?" Chepe wanted to know.

Quint said, "We'll observe the activity first. Our target knows us. Can you scout around back?"

"I'll try, *bossman*. The left side isn't going to work, but I might be able to get into those trees and onto the wall on the right. What am I looking for?"

"There's a kid, looks like a weasel. He's being held unlawfully. We want a way in. But we need to know who is there, what kind of weapons they have, and what they are planning to do with them. I know it's a tall order," Quint said. "H, set Chepe up with a commlink. You used these before?" Chepe said he had. "Good, then keep Horacio posted."

He handed Chepe a cap with a camera clipped on it. "Keep this on. Look at everything. Chucho will monitor, tell you what to do with what you see. Martinez and I are going to be standing by to advance when you give the clear sign—two clicks. Good luck." Quint said.

Chepe pulled on heavy leather gloves, saluted. He crept out of the vehicle.

"We're interested in taking the people alive. Only shoot if you have to."

Chucho got the surveillance cams running as Chepe disappeared into the neighbor's tree. The rest clustered around the computer screen, watching his progress. He made it onto the wall, picking his way gingerly along the top to pass around the corner of the house. Now Quint could see lights on in the back.

Martinez said, "You know that wall is topped with glass shards."

"Good man for the job. I'm guessing Chepe has experience with glass-topped walls."

Chucho snorted.

Chepe's progress slowed. Chepe looked around, capturing video of the side of the house and the backyard. He looked over the wall into the neighbor's yard. Clearly a *callejon* ran down the middle of the block. Both yards backed up on it with gates leading onto the properties. Nader's yard had a free standing garage, lights on. Activity inside.

"Chepe, get off the wall. Drop into the neighbor's yard through the gate. See if you can look into the garage. Click once if you copy," Quint commanded. The commlink clicked. Chepe eased himself back to the edge of the house over the lip of the wall. For a moment, all they saw were the vines.

"*Jefe,* I'm going around to find the entrance to the callejon. I'll back Chepe up." Horacio grabbed his assault rifle and climbed down from the truck.

"Maybe I should go around the other way?"Martinez asked.

Quint, still watching Chepe's slow progress getting out of the yard, turned around. "No, you and I are breaking into the house as soon as Chepe finds Nader."

Chucho reported the action on his screen. "He's in the alley, *jefe.* There's a lighted window high up. Something under it. A dumpster. He's getting on it. Look Mr. Quint—it's him."

Quint spun back to the screen, "Leo?" he said into the commlink. three clicks for no.

Chucho pointed, "Nader. Square jaw, paunch. There's another guy with him. They're loading wood crates into the SUV."

"Chepe, Horacio is coming around to back you up, Martinez and I are going in through the front. Horacio knows what to do. Remember, shoot only if they threaten you. Try not to kill anybody. Keep your cam on. I'll be wearing one, too. Chucho will monitor. He'll pick us up if we need him. Two clicks."

Quint and Martinez walked to the house, guns held close to their sides. Quint approached the door. Locked. He pulled a lockpick kit from his jacket and, with cover from Martinez, quickly opened the door.

A living room and dining room took up the front half off either side of the entry. Empty. Quint planted a listening device in the living room lamp. Martinez fitted another in the telephone on a table in the entry. A hall ran straight back from the entry with three doors off it: a cloak closet, a locked room, and the room with the light. The men got into position. Quint swung open the door, stepped in, gun ready. An office. Empty gun cabinet open. They bugged the desk phone and the lamp.

Quint motioned Martinez out. They continued to the kitchen door. It too was empty. Quint planted a device into the light switch. No doors led to a basement. He pointed the barrel of the gun up. Martinez lifted his chin. They moved silently to the stairs.

Quint had learned somewhere to tread only on the outside of the step to keep the stair from creaking. Soundlessly they crept up, ready to shoot. Two bedrooms with a bathroom at the end of the hall. Quint pointed to the right, at himself, then tipped his head at Martinez while thrusting his gun left. Martinez thumbs upped. Quint counted with his fingers: one... two...three. They kicked into the rooms.

Leo lay on the floor gagged, feet bound, hands tied behind his back. He looked scared.

"I got him!" Quint called out in a hoarse whisper. Martinez rushed into the room. "Help me untie him," Quint said as he pulled off the gag. "You okay, kid?"

"Mr. Quint, I didn't think you understood. I thought you weren't coming." His fear and relief were palpable.

"It's all right, Leo. We're here. I need you to go with Martinez to the truck. Take him to Chucho then cut around to the alley. I'll plant the rest of the bugs."

"Yes, sir," Martinez replied and helped Leo up. "Come on *hijo*, let's get you to safety." He led the boy down the stairs. Quint planted three more devices.

In the utility truck Chucho hunched over the computer screen.

"Jefe, the *callejon* is mostly access for the garbage collection. Cans, debris boxes. No cars parked, no obvious places to hide. About half the houses we can see have detached garages. The best cover is right at Nader's garage." He switched to another screen and scrolled back, stopping at Chepe's video inspection of the area around the structure, Leo hovering over his shoulder.

Quint could see the garage set lengthwise terminating at

the alley. The garden wall terminated several yards in, rather than on the alley. A dumpster sat along the garage wall with the window placed just under the roofline. On the main screen, Martinez darted into the bushes planted around the perimeter of the yard. "Chepe, Martinez is in the bushes on the other side of the door." One click sounded. "Horacio, where are you?"

Horacio spoke in a low voice. "I'm in some trees on the west side of the *callejon* about a door down. I can see the garage door—new roll-up. Lots of locks."

"Can they see you?"

"Only if they are looking."

"Bad joke."

"Chepe, can you hear them? How many?"

On the main screen, they watched Chepe's progress to the window. Then the bright fluorescent lighting. A grainy shot of Nader tossing a ball, or, no! a grenade up and down as a stocky man heaved a crate into the open side door of the SUV."

"Chuch, stop the feed. Do I see Asian markings on the side of that crate?"

Leo leaned in. "He's got a bunch of wooden boxes like that. They're Chinese."

"You know that, Leo? Or guessing?"

Chucho zoomed in on the markings. Quint recognized characters. "Zoom out again. Down in that corner—" he pointed to the left— "can you bring it up? Leo, tell me what you know." He continued inspecting the marking. It was familiar.

"He met a man, a *chino*. They talked, partly in some *chino* language, but when they talked in Spanish it was about a shipment the *chino* was arranging. He doesn't speak Spanish much."

Chucho interjected, "*Jefe*, in Mexico, *chino*, applies to any Asian, not just Chinese."

Quint pursed his lips. "When was this, Leo?"

"*Tal vez, ¿tres semanas?*"

"Did you see what's inside?" C-4, Quint thought. Where else would he get it?

The boy shook his head. "But some of the boxes were longer."

Probably assault rifles—unlicensed knock-offs of the QBZ-97 variants coming out of Cambodia and Myanmar. That's why he recognized the logo. Back to 'Nam. He shivered. Quint had blown up caches of weapons in crates with this same logo in the jungle. Nader had passed intel to the NVA. Was he still connected? But what did Quint have to do with it? He made a quick reassessment and decision.

"Chepe, Martinez, make your way back to the street. You too, H. I want Chepe observing at the east end of the *callejon*. H, you to the west. Martinez, come around the front. Get out of the yard. All of you, get moving. We'll pick you up. Watch where the SUV goes," Quint said. He moved to the driver's seat and cranked over the ignition. Leo jumped into the passenger seat. "No, stay in back, Leo. Might be trouble when Nader discovers you're gone. Can't let anyone see you."

Leo returned to the back. Quint shifted into gear. The truck lumbered away from the curb, following the gently curving street to the corner. He turned right, idling at the intersection with the alley. In moments, Horacio slid into the passenger seat, shaking his head. "Nothing yet, Quint."

Eyes on the alley, Quint filled him in.

"A Vietnamese arms distribution outfit? Thirty years?" H said, voice sounding incredulous. "The guy has a big grudge, or he's dealing arms in Mexico. We have video."

"Bingo!" they said together, grinning. This was the break they needed, the proof Garza demanded.

Horacio said, "I wondered why you pulled us out."

"They're loading the SUV. Instead of attacking them—"

"We follow them."

"Quint, isn't this truck a little too noticeable?"

Chuch called from the back. "*Jefe*, Chepe is in position, Martinez is headed around the block. I have no eyes on the garage."

A clock on the dash read one-fifteen. The neighborhood was quiet. A dog barked several blocks away. The distant din of traffic on the *Periférico* receded into a lulling background. A sense of middleclass security pervaded until the familiar scraping rumble of a metal garage door opening shattered the calm.

"He's on the move, men. Keep vigilant. Stay out of sight."

One click replied.

"Can you see which way he's turning?"

"Not yet, *jefe.* Headlights on, but hasn't appeared—no, here he comes. Turning right."

"Chepe, he's headed your way. Tell us which way to turn. Martinez, step on it. We're around the corner."

"SUV stopped. The helper is locking up..." Chepe reported, the sound of the vehicle's engine pinging in the background."

"*Pendejo* needs to maintain his vehicle," Horacio observed.

"It's moving...passing me...turning right."

Quint threw the truck in gear. Something hit the side. He stepped on the brake, grabbing for his gun as the back opened. Martinez dove in. Quint dropped the gun and stomped the gas, circled the block, and skidded to a stop when Chepe raced out of the *callejon.* Leo threw open the back, tugging him in as the truck gained speed.

"He's headed for the *autopista,*" Martinez said. "If you get a red light, change places with me, *jefe.* I know this city like the freckles on my arm."

Nader didn't enter the highway. For once the lights remained green. Quint stuck to the *lateral* crossing left, the floodlamps on the top of Arena CDMX illuminating it in the distance.

"Not going to Roma then," Horacio commented.

Quint sped through a yellow light. The next would be red. They'd lose their prey. No question Nader was selling arms to someone, but who? Quint's immediate guess was one of the cartels. BLO had the biggest influence in La Capital, but Los Zetas wanted control. What he heard lately, that Chapo character intended to take over control of the entire country. Was Nader fomenting a turf war? "What the hell do I have to do with Nader's arms trafficking?" he muttered, mostly to himself.

"*No sé*, boss," Martinez said in Spanglish. He leaned through the curtain separating the cargo area from the cab. "You'll catch the next light. The SUV is cutting onto Autopista Naucalpan-Ecatopec. We'll catch up to him. He won't be able to exit for a while."

The light turned red. The three cars ahead of the utility truck blasted through, horns blaring. Quint stopped, threw the gears into neutral and lurched out of the seat as Martinez scrambled in.

Quint slammed the side door behind him. "Where are we?" he asked.

"Tlalnepantla headed onto the *autopista* east. We could be going anywhere."

Horacio grunted. "That's an understatement. He pushed back into the cargo hold. "*Oye*, Chuch, you mapping this?"

"*Claro. ¿Como te ayudo?*"

"Where might we be headed?"

"When someone knows, I should call Garza."

No one spoke for a few minutes. Quint watched the SUV, a diminishing black hole in the distance.

"Here's where I'm sure he's not going: Magdalena de las Salinas," Martinez volunteered.

"Why's that?" Quint asked.

"The Basilica of Guadalupe? No *Mexicano* would taint that sacred place with an arms deal," Chepe yelled from the back.

"Okay, then where might such a transaction take place?"

The SUV moved into the right lane, slowed as though it was exiting.

"Something wrong," Martinez said, alarmed. "*El esta parade. No hay salida.*"

"*Pásalo Martínez. Pasa. Pasa*," Horacio ordered.

"We'll lose him, Horacio."

"Quint, he's made us," he replied as they sailed by. Horacio ducked.

Martinez said, "*Lo engañaremos*, we'll fool him, Horacio."

He took the next exit, stopped in front of a store, then

pushed into the back where he rummaged around until he pulled out a stack of magnetic signs from a built-in cabinet. "Help me, kid." He handed several to Leo. "C'mon."

Within three minutes, they'd transformed the bland white utility truck into a colorful ice cream truck, complete with a window to hand out the cones—if no one looked too closely—and jumped back in.

Martinez started up, swung a U across the boulevard onto the *autopista,* accelerating. They were no more than five minutes behind the SUV, Quint thought. The universe willing, they'd catch up. Leo laughed and jabbered in rapid Spanish to Chucho. Someone was enjoying the chase.

Chapter 20

Setting the Stage

Their luck held. About fifteen minutes later they sighted the SUV as it exited onto 57D south. They paced its speed.

"Ciudad Neza, *jefe,*" Chucho yelled. "Worst part of Mexico City. Nobody would go there at night if they didn't have bad business."

Quint turned. Searched Horacio's face for confirmation. H grimaced. "*Es verdad.*"

"Why would an ice cream truck be in the district at this time of night?"

Martinez grinned. "It wouldn't but a vehicle with gang tags would."

"You have another set of decals, man?"

Chepe laughed. "I wouldn't contract with an amateur."

They had entered a large dark park. "Wildlife refuge," Chucho said. "We'll cross into another park, which dumps us into Ciudad Neza—Ciudad Nezahualcóyotl—to be exact."

"Any of you men ever been here before?" No one answered.

57D curved east again at an interchange at the bottom of the park. The SUV was no longer in sight. "I think our luck has run out. Martinez, whadaya think?"

"*Aqui es la salida.* I'm getting off. We'll pull over. Change signs, continue south." Chucho said, "Ciudad Neza is a little farther."

"*Jefe*, if we don't find the contact this time, we will soon. You and Martinez planted the bugs, didn't you?" Horacio asked. "We'll go back, plant more in the garage and in the SUV. Catch him *con las manos en la masa*. Get the proof."

"I hope so, H.

"Mr. Quint, Martinez and I can go back tomorrow as TelMex employees. I'll go up a pole, look busy. Tell Martinez when he can get in."

"You two have quite an operation," Quint said.

Martinez pulled over again. Leo helped him swap signs. The truck now looked like a vandalized derelict. Graffiti, painted-out graffiti, dirt, dents. He reached under the rear to disconnect a length of tailpipe, chucking it back into the cargo hold. Finally, he swapped out the taillight cover for a smashed one. Everybody got out to inspect the transformation.

"Amazing!" Quint said. "Look, he's even put a crack in the windshield. It's a totally different truck."

"As long as they didn't get the *placa, jefe*," Chucho pointed out.

"Taken care of." Martinez waggled a different plate. "Magnetic."

"I'm beginning to wonder what you men do. *Este es un trabajo de estafa.* A con job."

Chepe grinned. "We get things done for our clients."

"You two always work together?" Horacio asked.

"*Cómplices.*"

Leo laughed. "It's like theatre."

Chapter 21

Kabuki Dance

Saturday, October 6, 2007

From the *autopista* turn-off, they bore left onto Avenida Bordo de Xochiaca, then right at Avenida General Lázero to Plaza Neza. Martinez turned into the dark parking lot surrounding the businesses anchored by a Mega store. He turned off the headlights, crawling around the mall, checking every loading dock and shadowy nook. The plaza ran right into another center with a Cineplex. Some cars were parked near the theater. More could be seen in the next plaza where The Home Depot anchored the bottom.

"Why are we at a shopping plaza?" Leo asked. "Everything is closed."

"If you were going to make an illegal sale of something, where would you do it? Drive to the buyers house? Risk the buyer's buddies coming out, ripping off your merchandise?"

Leo agreed. "*De veras*. I guess I'd go somewhere where I could see who was coming."

144

"And have room to move quite a few crates from one vehicle to another without *miradas indiscretas. ¿No*?" Chucho added. "What do you see, Chepe?"

Quint and Horacio now sat in back with Chucho and Leo. Nader would recognize them.

"*Todavia nada*," Chepe said. "!*Espera! Alla, Martinez*." He pointed toward the buildings.

Quint parted the tarps, following Martinez's finger. Sure enough. The SUV met a second SUV. Two men with guns on either side of Nader, and a short man. Quint fished the telephoto lens and his camera out of his duffle. "We need a diversion. Go closer to The Home Depot so I'm not shooting into the light. Stop. Get out, stagger around. Toss out some beer cans or bottles. Have any?"

"We got this down, *jefe*. The drunk act. We'll piss on the truck. Let them see us. How long do you need? He pulled next to a lamppost facing the SUV and cut the engine."

Another man had appeared with a case. Nader turned to the door, sliding it open.

"It looks like they're about to make the transfer."

Chepe pulled a beer bottle from somewhere, opened his door, kicking the bottle onto the pavement. "*¡Chingao! Mi cerveza*," he wailed, half falling out of the truck onto the ground, staggering to the back of the van to urinate on the tire.

Nader and his contact turned to the commotion but turned away quickly, dismissing the drunk from the trashed vehicle. The short man looked into Nader's SUV, held out his hand. The assistant placed what Quint thought was a crowbar into it. He pried open a crate of grenades, plucked one out, inspected it, holding it up for Quint to make a perfect video.

Chepe yelled for Martinez to get him another beer. Martinez grabbed two and staggered around the front of the truck to Chepe. They made a little scene, shouting, swearing, slurring. Quint videoed the inspection of the guns. He was right —looked like Chinese QBZ-97s, or an upgrade. It had been a while since he'd thought too much about China's and Southeast Asia's weaponry. The buyer smiled, caressing the assault rifle

145

like a lover. Nader grinned, said something. The buyer's assistant carried the case to Nader who opened it. Nader reached in, pulled out a bundle, fanned it, made a quick count, then returned the bundle to the case. They shook hands. Nader placed the case in the cab. He and his helper began handing crates out to the buyer and his assistant, who stashed them in their vehicle. Quint counted twelve crates of grenades and twenty of guns. He had proof—live action on video. He'd visit Garza in the afternoon.

Nader and his contact shook hands again. The buyer held up the grenade he'd inspected. They looked toward the truck and laughed.

Quint cracked open the passenger door, hissing through the commlink, "Time to go, boys. Get in now." He slipped into the back. Chepe and Martinez hooted, smashed their bottles, staggered back into the truck and wove off.

"What now? Change the truck art? Follow the buyer?" Chepe asked.

"Would it be worth the loss of sleep, *jefe*?"

"I shot the license plate. Let Garza's people track it down. I'm bushed."

Leo regarded Quint quizzically. "You're an *arbusto?*—like a plant?"

"Idiom for tired, Leo. Let's go home. Leo, you're coming with us tonight. We're going to have a chat in the morning."

"Am I in trouble, Mr. Quint?"

"You might be," he said, grinning.

About thirty-five minutes later, the utility truck pulled up outside the office. Everyone piled out. Martinez and Leo pulled off the magnetic signs while Chucho collected his electronics.

"Chucho, can I give you a lift?" Horacio asked.

"Thanks H, but I'll stay here tonight. I've got a big job getting set up for the recordings from the listening devices."

"Everyone is going to bed. I don't want to see you back here before lunch, H. Martinez, thanks. We'll see you for the night shift?" Quint asked.

"You got it, Mr. Quint," he said in his accented English.

"See you later, Chepe." He finished stowing his signs and drove off.

Chepe checked on his security detail, gave an all clear to Quint, and left. The team, minus Chucho, trudged up to the residence. Horacio said good night and trudged back down to the garage for his limo. Quint showed Leo to Mrs. P's room and said goodnight. Chucho was still in his office dealing with his equipment when Quint went to bed.

Chapter 22

Evidential Documentation

By noon, Chucho had put together a video of the activity in Nader's garage, rescuing Leo, and the actual sale of the weapons, properly time stamped and geo-located. Both SUV's license plates were recorded as well as a clear image of the grenade packing crate including the logo.

"Come see it," he said, serving himself a healthy portion of *huevos mexicanos* with *longanisa*, Quint's go-to meal.

Leo already sat at his place, looking a bit droopy, but in good spirits, if the speed of his shoveling in mouthfuls of spicy eggs was any indication. Quint, carried his fourth cup of coffee to the table and buttered another piece of toast. "Boys," he began, but was interrupted by Horacio's arrival, swinging his customary bag of *panes*.

"Good morning, *pues*—afternoon," he said in a cheerful voice.

"*Buenos tardes, Señor H,*" Leo replied.

Chucho turned from the stove smiling. "*Panes. Gracias.*"

Quint said, "Get yourself a plate, H." He noticed the man

looked positively refreshed, although he was probably the last to get to bed. "After breakfast, Chucho is taking us to the movies. He's got the video ready with, hopefully, enough evidence for Garza to call for an evidentiary hearing. Maybe have Nader detained. Once we determine what we've got, we'll go over there. I've called your brother. Sami can join us after four."

"Why do you want Sami?" Horacio asked.

"Illegal breaking and entering. Illegal surveillance."

"Why would the Americans care? Our crimes were perpetrated in Mexico."

"Hence we bring our attorney to keep the air clear."

"Would the U. S. have any jurisdiction over Nader?" Chucho asked.

"Good question, Chuch. I'm assuming if he's assigned to the embassy, he's under U.S. jurisdiction. That the man is selling arms to our enemies," Quint said, making air quotes, "should indict him. If so, we'll turn this over to Garza. Finally get back to our own operations."

"What *are* our operations, Mr. Quint?" Leo asked.

Quint snorted. "So you're on the team now, Leo? Another question for our attorney. What are the child labor laws here?"

"Easy, it's sixteen, but nobody pays attention to it."

"I'm a foreigner here, Leo. I have to obey the laws."

"Like you did last night?"

"So you wanted to be left trussed like a pig for slaughter—because that's what he would have done to you. I don't know what happened, but I know how Nader operates. You would have gone to the garage and been questioned. Every time he didn't believe you, he would pull out a fingernail or chop off a toe. He might have resorted to waterboarding. It was his favorite method back in Vietnam."

"Like surfing?" Leo's face clouded.

"Like drowning."

The boy blanched. He took his time ripping apart a *concha* to dunk in his chocolate.

"Leo, I would be happier if you went to school for a

149

profession. You're a smart kid. You could be whatever you want."

"But I need money, *señor*."

Quint pushed away from the table with his plate and cup and popped them into the dishwasher, "I want to talk to you about that. After we see the video, join me in my office and we'll figure out what to do with you. Everyone, clean up after yourselves. I'm going to make calls. I'll meet you in the IT office in fifteen minutes. We'll get this bastard."

A quarter hour later, the team convened around Chucho's computer. He pulled the video up on his second screen, a larger monitor than had come with the computer, rolled his chair to the side, and pushed play. They watched Quint pick the lock and enter the house, but Chucho had edited out the exploration beyond mounting the stairs. He had not included the conversation between Martinez and Quint until Martinez ran into the room and the camera picked up Leo on the floor bound and gagged. The video showed his rescue, then cut to Chepe's advance on the garage. There was no sound, but Chepe had gotten excellent shots of the markings on the crates, Nader bouncing a grenade, and his inspection of an assault rifle with the helper loading the crate behind him. The next segment detailed the sale in Ciudad Neza. Quint had made sure to get The Home Depot into a shot, establishing the location.

"Too bad we can't hear what they're saying at that exchange."

Quint stroked his chin, lost in thought. Eventually he said, "As far as I know, Nader doesn't speak Spanish so the buyer must speak English."

"Who do you suppose he is?" Horacio asked.

Chucho said, "I can tell you who the vehicle belongs to." He fished on his messy desktop, picked up a Post-it Note from a pile. "Somebody named Charro Navar Lovato. I found one woman with that name in Cuernavaca. So far, nothing else. Nader's SUV is rented by an import business with a U.S.

governmental agency IP address. Go figure."

"He's with the NSA. They have many bogus businesses."

"Bogus?" Leo asked.

"*La impostora,*" Chucho said.

"It's a front, Leo. The NSA often operates in secret. But let's get back to work here. Chucho, have you put this on a thumb-drive for me?"

"*Sí, jefe,* it's what we watched." He ejected the drive and handed it over to Quint.

"Thanks. Leo, let's have that chat. H, I'll be ready to go to the embassy in a half an hour. We'll probably have to wait to see Garza, but I'll call now."

Quint and Leo stepped into the office. Quint closed the door behind them, offered Leo a seat. The boy looked nervous. "Leo, there's no reason to be nervous. As long as you don't lie to me."

"*Sí,* Mr. Quint. What do you want to talk about?"

"About you. Who you are, where you come from. Why you aren't living at home or going to school. How you got caught up with Chuck Nader."

"That's easy. I picked his pocket. He caught me. He said he could use a boy for some work. But if I chose not to, he'd take me to the police."

"Yes, he's a *chantajista.* He blackmailed me when I was a soldier in Vietnam." Quint smiled at the boy. "But why were you trying to pickpocket him?"

"He had lots of money. I saw him talking to a man I know is *un rico* with the cartel, but because he spoke English, I figured he was a *tonto gabacho.*"

"Hmmm. You think all Americans are stupid?" Quint leveled his Quint squint on Leo.

The boy squirmed. Looking away, he stuttered, "N-no. Not *all* Americans."

"So the question is, why do you need to pickpocket? Why aren't you at home going to school?"

"My *padrasto*," he spat out the word, "kicked me out of the house. My father was killed. They found his body hanging from an overpass in Puebla with a couple of other guys. He'd been shot. *Mi mama* got involved with a real *estúpido*. Mean. I think he was with the group who killed my *papi*. I don't know. He kicked me out when I told *Mami* he was abusing my little sister. She's twelve. *Mami* sided with him." He stopped talking to gulp a couple deep breaths of air. "I couldn't protect her," he choked out, on the verge of tears.

"And here you are."

"Sí, aqui estoy."

"You say you're from Pueblo?"

"El estado. A little village. There was no work for me there. No one would take me in because they are afraid of the gangs."

"So you live in the *tianguis* in Tepito?"

"That's about it, Mr. Quint. When I make some money I rent a room to get a shower."

"Have you thought about your future? You don't plan on becoming a professional pickpocket do you?"

"There's only two options for me. *El carcel o el cartel*. *Pues,* the cartel means jail anyway. Or death. I'm not dumb. I wasn't a thief before I was forced."

"Have you talked to your mother or sister?"

"My sister. I call her whenever I can. He gets drunk. Hits Mami. He used to hit me. He turned Mami out. Veronica is left alone. He beats her and rapes her—says she needs to go with other men for money like her whore mother. He locks her in our house—doesn't let her go to school any more. I thought Nader would pay me. I could get an apartment and bring Roni there. I'd take care of her. Send her to school. She's really smart."

"Jeeze kid, this is a sad story. But it's not the story you told two nights ago. Shall we call Veronica?"

"Will you bring her here if I work for you?"

"That's jumping the gun, isn't it, Leo? But if I can confirm your story, Rosi will place her in a safe home. You met her.

That's what she does—rescues girls who are being abused. Shall we call her?" Quint picked up the receiver. "Number?"

Leo recited the number. A girl answered. He pushed the speaker button.

"*Roni, soy yo. Por favor, le habla al señor Quint. Dile la verdad. El nos ayudara.*"

"*Hola Veronica. Puedes confirmar quien es Leo?*"

She replied he was her brother. Was she in danger? Would she like Leo to come for her? She said yes in a quavering voice. Quint could hear her fear and her hopelessness as she described her ordeal.

"Don't be afraid. We'll get you to a safe home. I promise. My friend Rosi will call you soon to make arrangements.

"Will Leo come?"

"*Por supuesto, hermana. Hasta pronto. Chau.*"

Quint disconnected. "Okay, Leo, let's talk business. What can you do?"

Chapter 23

Garza Steps Up

Horacio knocked on the door. "Time to go, *jefe*."

"Leo, I've got to go now, but if you're serious about apprenticing with us, I'll give you a try. I'll pay you ten dollars a day and give you room and board. I expect you to go to school and maintain a B-average. If you steal, or I feel you are not honest, I'll throw you out, possibly right into jail. But I will do my best to help your sister. We'll get Rosi to talk to us tonight." He rolled away from his desk. "Can you make coffee? The security guards probably want some. Then go see what Chucho needs. He will be your supervisor."

"Okay, *jefe*." Leo trotted out of the office ahead of Quint. He heard him running up the stairs two at a time. The energy of youth, he thought.

"So you hired Leo?" Horacio asked as they got in the limo.

"Intern. I could give him Jade's room for now, feed him, try to teach him something. He can learn to cook when Mrs. P isn't here. If Chuch is agreeable, he can get some tutoring on the computer. He has to go to school and keep his grades up to a B-average or the deal is off. I'll give him a small salary. Maybe you can think of some things he could learn. If he's ever dishonest in anyway, he's out."

Quint gave Horacio the rundown on Veronica.

"You believe them?"

"I don't know, but Rosi will want to do an assessment. If it's true, she can rescue them both, Veronica and the mother. Her team can probably put the stepfather in jail. Leo says he's connected to a cartel. Thinks they killed his father."

Horacio considered Quint's report. "Unfortunately, this is becoming a common story. There are too few jobs. Fewer yet that pay enough to take care of a family. The gangs offer a decent living at the cost of the employee's humanity. But a lot of men take the jobs to save their loved ones. Kids with no options are seduced by the adventure and glamour of the *narco-corridos*. Big money in organized crime."

They lapsed into silence for a few blocks. Although a Saturday tangle in the Insurgentes roundabout and a jam at Reform left them stranded in a sea of vehicles for several minutes. Quint had finagled an appointment with the ambassador at four-forty. They had five minutes. Sami should already be there.

Horacio was a master at managing Mexico City traffic. They arrived at the guardhouse with a minute to spare and presented their identifications. Garza hadn't arrived. A young rosy-cheeked marine saluted Quint. A wave of sadness washed over him. Javie had been just like this kid. Full of life. The marine led him through the corridors to Garza's office. He felt old, jaded next to the boy. Mrs. Tomsky, in slacks under a sweater-set with her hair in a twist, showed him to the uncomfortable couch to wait. He should reach out to Javie's family with his condolences. The boy had everything to live for. Quint had allowed him to be murdered. He could have, no, should have put his foot down, refused to allow him to cross the border with Jade and Lily. He should have known the risks.

He did know, he thought, Because he knew exactly what risk Nader was. *Still is.* Isn't that why he was sitting here with a throwback to 1965 staring him down?

"I'm sorry, Mrs. Tomsky. Lost in thought. Is the big man ready to see me?" Quint asked, forcing a warm smile, which felt more like a rictus.

She smiled back. "Yes, Mr. Quint. Go in." She was probably pretty in 1965.

He lightly rapped on the door then walked in without waiting for Garza's invitation. "Mr. Ambassador, thank you for seeing me on such short notice. I'll try not to keep you too long. My attorney will join us in a few minutes, but I think we can start without him."

"I'm assuming you've invited Rafiq because you've acquired your information under unusual circumstances?" He cocked his head to the side and raised his eyebrows. "I'm guessing you may have pushed the boundaries of legality. But possibly not ours."

Quint tossed his head sideways and clicked his lips. "You got me, Garza. Here's our proof." He pulled the thumb-drive from his jacket pocket, handed it over.

"Take a chair. Tell me what we've got first. Can I pour you a drink? I have a feeling I'm going to need one before this interview is over." He chuckled and went to his credenza where today a polished silver tray held two cut-crystal decanters and several old fashioned glasses. "Bourbon or whisky?"

"Whisky, thanks."

Garza splashed about three fingers into each glass and handed one to Quint before sitting down. The curtains had been pulled across the window hiding the angel of independence.

"So what's our Nader doing?"

"Arms trading. Is the embassy missing any Chinese grenades or QBZ assault rifles?"

The ambassador's face turned pink then red as he cried out in shock. "What? You better have proof of this, Mr. Quint. This is a serious allegation."

"It's on the thumb-drive. I videoed the transaction,

although I don't know who the buyer is. We couldn't get close enough for sound. The buyer's license plate is registered to a Charro Navar Lovato in Cuernavaca. My partner, Rafiq's brother, says the name could be a man's or woman's."

The intercom buzzed. Mrs. Tomsky announced Sami. He stepped in, greeted Garza, who told him to sit. "Whisky?" Sami nodded.

"Sami, I was just telling the ambassador what I discussed with you earlier. We haven't watched the video. Ambassador, is there more I can tell you or would you like to watch then ask questions?"

"Let's watch." He plugged in the drive to a USB outlet, opened the file, then moved out of the way of the screen behind him so everyone could see. He hit play.

Quint watched Garza's reactions, not the video. Garza concentrated through to the end, then scrolled back to the beginning, watching, pausing to ask questions. "Where is this house? Is it Nader's?"

"Yes. Nader made another attack on my property, but when we showed up he ran, leaving behind a street kid he'd brought along. I suppose he planned on having the boy take the blame. I believe he was searching information on my operation. I don't really know.

"I made the kid a better offer. I sent him back to Nader as a CI. We got a call last night from Leo. I asked for the number, not knowing if Nader had placed listening devices. We called him back from another phone, which my IT guy got a trace on. I found the same phone number and an address in his pocket. Now you've seen what we found at the address."

He continued watching as we discovered Leo and untied him. "How did the boy manage to convey information?"

"Code. He called me *Papi*. I knew he was in trouble."

"Clever. I'm assuming you planted listening devices throughout the house after you broke in."

"It's one of my questions for Sami. I'm guessing the U.S. has no problem with me uncovering an enemy of the state, but Sami, is Mexico going to be upset I picked Nader's lock?"

Quint thought that for no other reason, including Sami in his business was downright uplifting. That laugh, his ogre laugh as Jade called it. He was laughing now. "I'm guessing this bad actor isn't going to call the cops to report his home was broken into, and a child he kidnapped was taken."

Garza grinned. "I suppose not." He continued watching until Nader inspected the assault rifle. "This is Chinese?"

"Probably not. Both Laos and Myanmar produce unauthorized knock-offs. Why?"

"I'm not sure what kinds of treaties we, or Mexico, have regarding arms, but I'm betting these weapons are illegal."

"I doubt a legitimate sale would take place in a dark parking lot in the middle of the night in Ciudad Neza," Sami said, laughing a fresh *haw haw haw*.

"Yes, that *was* a giveaway. Mr. Quint, do you think Nader has more?"

"Leo thinks so. We did not break into the locked room due to time constraints. I had to get the kid out. Nader suspected him."

Garza watched the sale twice more. "I wish we knew who the buyer is. He's probably a hired middleman, but by whom? Will you continue to look into this?"

"Are you asking my firm to look into this or are you asking for a favor, Ambassador?"

"I'll take this to the intelligence department, talk to them, find out what Nader is supposed to be doing. If their answer is what I think it's going to be, I'd like your outfit to work with ours, a joint task force. I won't tolerate traitors in our midst. You in?"

"Mr. Garza, I have a vested interest in putting this man behind bars. He's tried to kill me too many times."

Garza stood. "Then get your attorney to write up a contract." He pointed his chin at Sami. "Mr. Quint will be considered a consultant. You probably know how this works."

Sami reached out to shake Garza's hand, as did Quint. "Thank you, Ambassador. We'll get to the bottom of this. I'll be waiting for your people to contact me."

"Thank you. Good day to you. We'll be in touch," he said, showing them out of the office. Mrs. Tomsky was not at her desk.

Chapter 24

I'm too Old to Live Like This

"That's a positive turn of events. Maybe we'll pick up more contracts with the embassy," Horacio said as he steered the limo into the Insurgentes traffic.

"Takes a bit of financial worry off. Not that we wouldn't solve this one anyway."

"I hear you. What was Nader doing at the office the other night?"

"Ain't it obvious?" Quint grimaced into a snide chuckle. "He thinks I have something on him. He planted his listening devices. Spy vs. Spy. It would be funny if the game weren't deadly."

"Spy versus Spy?"

"Not a reader of *Mad Magazine*?"

Horacio's face blanked. He turned his concentration to the honking snarl in the roundabout. Quint wondered if they carried *Mad Magazine* at Sanborn's. He could use a good laugh right about now.

"When we get back, let's find out what Chucho has

recorded from our bugs. We should sweep the offices again, too."

They had turned into Roma. The Art Nouveau architecture crowding the treelined streets gave Quint a sense of calm and longevity, as if all were well with the world, and all would remain so. What a joke. Maybe he was in the wrong business. Maybe it was time to do something uplifting—work with children or grow carrots. Anything without death, destruction, hatred, greed. He'd begun his adult life fighting for idealism. He was going to keep the world free.

Freedom? Who was free? Not even the men like Nader, were truly free. His kind, like cockroaches, swarmed where they could thrive as they exploited a rotten situation, exploited the very concept of freedom. Nader had robbed Quint of freedom. He'd conned a kid with friendship, importance, heroin, then showed his true colors. Well, Leo wouldn't get drugs from Quint.

"Are you serious about Leo? Keeping him on?" Horacio asked, as he pulled into the alley.

"I don't know, H. I might be too old for a puppy." A wry grin spread across his face. "But I'll be damned if I'm going to do to Leo what Nader did to me. I'm not pretending to befriend him then dumping him on the police station's doorstep when I'm done with him."

H rolled to a stop by the service entrance door and turned to face his employer. "You aren't Nader, Quint."

"He was the one who turned me in, H. Charley Stone confirmed he didn't have anything to do with it."

"Let it go, *jefe*."

"But, H, don't you see? What's happening now has *everything* to do with it."

"Maybe, but better to stop the threat, move on, forget it. You'll never be free until you forgive that part of your life. Do it. Move on. You Protestants know about forgiveness. Come on, let's go up." He opened his door, stepped onto the cobbled drive, and saluted the security man who had appeared above the building's balustrade.

Quint lumbered out, looked up, raised his hand, quickly dropping it again. He felt old. Beaten down. Today, even with a contract coming in from the embassy, Quint had the blues.

He was just too old to live like this, he thought as he shuffled toward the back stairs. "I can't let it go until I know what Nader's beef with me is."

"*Jefe*, call Rosi. Go have that dinner with her."

"I'd probably fall asleep at the table."

"Better than cooking for the crew here."

"When does Mrs. P come back? Quint asked, as he huffed through the back door. *The altitude is getting to me.* "Grab a beer, H," he said, pulling a Superior out of the refrigerator as he passed. "Grab one for Chucho, too."

"And Leo?"

"Naw," he said, turning back to the open appliance, "I'll take him a Coke."

They took the drinks and a bag of spicy chips downstairs. The IT department door stood open. Leo popped out as soon as their shoes clomped onto the marble floor, headphones hanging around his neck.

"Hi, Quint! ¡*Hola Horacio! Qué onda?* Chu is teaching me how to run the software for the listening devices. Wait 'til you hear what we found out."

Chucho turned around in his chair. He pulled the headphones off his ears to hang around his neck like Leo. *That must be the thing.* "We've got some intel, Quint."

Quint dragged a folding chair over to the computer table and sat down. "Music to my ears. The bugs are working, I take it. H, grab a chair."

"Nader went ballistic when he found Leo gone this morning. We couldn't follow everything he said, but most were clearly *grocerias*. He put two and two together pretty quickly and started looking for the bugs. Why does he hate you so much? He said, 'Quint, you bastard, you're a dead man. I'll get you and that pretty girl of yours. She's going to hell to join her mother.' Then he stopped talking, *jefe*, but I could hear him moving around. He found the bugs where Leo was, and five of the bugs downstairs. When he pulled what he thought was the last he said—"

"Hold on Chuch, let's hear the tapes," Quint said.

"Right. Let me reset the file."

"Mr. Quint, Nader hates you. *Parece que lo superaste*—you bested him. *¿De verdad lo acusaste falsamente?*"

"Leo, I never accused him of anything, until now. Chucho, get that recording going."

"Here you go *jefe*," he said.

"...I've found the mics, Quint, this is the last one, but not the last you'll hear from me. I'm coming for you. You cost me, asshole. Now you're going to pay. It took me years to track you down after I got out of the pen, but all the time inside I planned how I would take you apart, carve you up. While I do it, I'm going to tell you all about your little gook girlfriend. What was her name? Tee? Twee? You better take a paternity test, bro'. But don't worry. I'll tell you all about it while you watch me kill JadeAnne like I killed her whore mother."

The recording played dead air. Quint rose half out of his chair, a murderous gleam in his eyes, as he turned toward the door. Horacio bounded up to grab Quint's shoulders. He settled him gently back onto the chair, saying, "It's what he wants. Calm down. Don't give him satisfaction. We'll get him, Quint."

Quint acquiesced, "You're right, H." His body slumped, rage coiling deep inside preparing to strike later. He sucked in a deep breath the way Jade taught him, letting the tension stream out with its release. "So what have you found out?"

Chucho cued up another file. "After he thought he'd gotten all the bugs, he called a guy. His supplier maybe." Chucho hit play. The sound of a phone line ringing then Nader's voice. "The exchange has been transacted. Meet me tomorrow night for your split... No, not here. The other place. Tell Mr. Chanthavong I can move as much as he can provide. There's a turf war brewing."

"So he found the bug in the phone. Too bad. We'd have both sides of the conversation. Did you get the number?"

Chucho grinned. "I did, *jefe*."

163

"Don't keep me in the dark, man, where did he call?"

"A number assigned to the U.S. embassy."

"Holy cow! It's a conspiracy. Give me that number." Quint held out his hand for the slip of paper Chucho offered. "I'll get this to Garza right now."

"There's more. He got a call a couple of hours later." Chucho played that clip.

"I'm glad you found the merchandise acceptable, sir. I appreciated the punctuality of your man, and the professionalism of our transaction." Several moments of static ensued before Nader came back on the line. "I'll let you know when the shipment arrives. I look forward to doing more business in the immediate future, *Señor El Muerte.*"

"*Jefe,* we got him."

"How so? Who is *El Muerte?*"

"*El diminutivo de Arturo Beltran,* how do you say it? The little name," Leo said.

"Nickname? For Arturo Beltrán?"

"They're stockpiling arms. I tell you, there's going to be a war," Chucho said. "I've hacked into some of their chatrooms. JadeAnne was right. Beltran Leyva and Los Zetas are getting friendly. You know—the enemy of my enemy is my friend? BLO and Sinaloa are going to war. Sinaloa and Los Zetas are already at war in the Gulf states."

Horacio's jaw dropped in alarm. "Can these organizations find out you've hacked them?"

"No, H. We're safe. I know what I'm doing."

"Do we have any more recordings?"

"You and Martinez put them in every room?"

"Yes."

"Then he's only just gotten up." Chucho tapped the keyboard. Another file played. Snoring.

Leo hooted. "Old guy needs his sleep."

"Careful dude, everyone needs sleep. Chucho did you catch any shut-eye?"

"No *jefe.* This was more important."

"You'll be no good to the team if you don't go home to

bed. I'm calling for food. Leo, you can go pick it up."

"Okay!"

"I better go with him to help carry everything. Where are we going?" Chucho asked.

"Quint searched his phone. "That *barbacoa* place. Gonzalitos. How many tacos each? Eight? With sides?"

"*Chido, jefe.* I want ten," Leo said.

"How about I buy two kilos of meat and a kilo of tortillas?"

"That works, *jefe*. With beans, rice, and a liter of salsa. Here, let me put in the order. " Horacio picked up the phone.

Leo and Chucho hauled several bags of food up the back stairs, calling to the security guards as they went up. It was nearly sunset. Chucho had kept watch on the short walk to Gonzalitos. No black SUVs with Nader's license plate, he reported privately to Quint.

While the boys picked up dinner, Quint called Garza on his private line with the new information. Garza hadn't wanted to believe his embassy could have gun runners. "Mr. Quint, this might have to do with the operation Mr. Nader is here to run."

"It might, Ambassador, but Nader's rant against me tells me something else is going on. Pull your Intelligence chief out. Have a chat. He'll know, and he'll have to tell you or be indicted too."

"You're not implying he's involved, are you?"

"I'm not implying anything until you've talked to him."

"I may not track him down before Monday."

"Call as soon as you have information. We already know Nader is setting up another sale to Arturo Beltrán."

Garza blew out his breath in a rush. "God help us. These cartel people are ruthless. We have to stop them."

"Frankly, Mr. Garza, it's what I was hired to do."

Chapter 25

Another B & E

Sunday, October 7, 2007

"*Soy yo*," Chucho announced when Quint answered his phone. "Nader just spoke to someone on the phone. They're meeting in an hour regarding a shipment."

"Where?"

"Airport."

"We're in the kitchen. Stay where you are, I'm coming down." He hung up. "Chepe, looks like we might be in for another adventure. You can give me the shift report on the way."

Chepe pulled out his phone. "Martinez? Call Ochoa. Get him over here. Paco and him can keep an eye on things. We've got a mission. Meet us in the *jefe's* office."

They clattered down to the office suite. Chucho was ready with his laptop queued to play the latest messages."

"Hey man, how'd you set this up? I thought you had to be close by to hear anything," Chepe said.

"I wired a recorder into a neighbor's electrical panel while you planted the bugs. I can access the recorder from here. No biggie."

"Mr. Quint, where'd you find this genius? I need a man like that."

"UNAM, Chepe. In the computer sciences department. Chuch is the wave of the future."

"I can introduce you to someone, Chepe."

"*¡Bien chido! compa*."

"Men, we're going back to Jardines de San Mateo to plant bugs in the garage. We are also going to open the locked room and photograph what we find. You driving tonight, Chepe?"

"Sure, bossman."

"Chuch, gather what you need, including a gun. Chepe, you need weapons?" He handed over the gun cabinet key. Chepe shook his head. "This isn't a stake-out, men, we'll have little time. You'll need to connect the new bugs to the box, or whatever it takes."

"That's what I'll do. But what about H and Leo?"

"Gone to Horacio's house for the night. H is going to take him to buy some clothes in the morning," Quint replied. "I'm running up for bottles of water. As soon as Martinez comes down, we're off."

They made it to Nader's in record time. It was the Sunday lull before the evening traffic picked up. Quint directed Chepe to pull over a couple blocks from the house. He sent Martinez to walk through the neighborhood to check everything out. Especially the house. They waited, two in Chepe's silver Volkswagen Jetta with one of Chepe's cousins leaning against it at the curb. Just a group of kids waiting for a friend. Quint's phone rang.

"Martinez, *dígame*."

"House and garage are dark; the car is gone. I'm in the *callejon*."

"We're on our way."

Chepe started the motor, Chepe's cousin jumped back in. They peeled out, making a U in the street. Chepe circled the block coming down the cross street to turn into the alley. Chucho sprang out with his tool pouch as the car stopped between a tall hedge and another garage several doors from Nader's. He found an electrical service panel and got to work. The others leaped the fence. Quint picked open the garden door to the garage. He let the others in then edged along the plantings to the back door and picked that lock, letting himself into the house. The locked room was just off the kitchen. He quickly picked it open. "Bingo," he said through the commlink. He got busy snapping photos. It took three minutes. He left the room untouched, the doors locked. Nader was into some deep shit. Quint had proof.

In the garage, Chepe and Martinez planted and tested the bugs. They photographed dozens of crates of ammo stacked up against the wall under the window. Quint opened a couple of the crates to shoot photos of the contents. More of the probably Chinese knockoffs.

The operation lasted ten minutes then they were back in the car on their way to Colonia Roma.

"Jefe, aren't we going to the airport to see who he's meeting?" Martinez asked.

"Naw, they'll be done. He'll either be at a bar picking up a hooker, or he'll be home soon."

"What about the office? He knows you took Leo."

"Yeah, what's your point? I say let 'em come. We'll all be there. Ready."

"He's got grenades."

"So do we." The Cheshire Cat grinned at his men.

Chapter 26

Success Breeds Success

Monday, October 8, 2007

In high spirits over a successful mission, Quint's team laughed at the ever more fantastical stories Chepe and Martinez told on the midnight ride back to Roma Norte.

"*Jefe*, next time, I want to go in too, okay?"

Quint glanced at Chucho, eyes gleaming in obvious admiration for the older men. Poor kid, he'd spent most of his life serving a master. *Well, it has paid off.* Chucho was proving to be an invaluable member of his organization. Quint just wished he could keep him safely in his computer den. He'd never forgive himself if harm came to the kid. But how could he stop him?

"Carrying a gun isn't excitement enough, Chuch?"

"*Pues*, not really. I'm stuck in the van. I want to have some stories to tell too."

"If Nader comes at us again, you'll have plenty to talk about," Quint replied as Martinez circled the neighborhood for the second time.

"Señor Quint, looks safe."

Quint nodded, tossing his key. "Chepe, unlock the door, but make it look like you're waiting for someone to answer. Chucho, be ready to run. Martinez, any activity across the street?"

Martinez texted the security team. From Quint's limited view from inside the truck, the block looked dark and quiet. Not many lights on in the apartment windows this late. Only his place was lit up like a marquee. But he couldn't see the building opposite.

Martinez's phone dinged. "No *jefe*. Get going, Chepe."

Chepe bounded out leaping to the door. He put on a show of knocking, turned around, dipped his head. Martinez laughed. "Chucho, *jefe*, your turn."

Once the alarm was reset, they relaxed upstairs, their beers and a line of grenades decorating the table. They complimented each other on a good surveillance job. Quint had not shared his findings with the team. Except for Horacio, he wouldn't reveal what he discovered until he sat with Garza and Sami. He looked at the clock. Too late to call H.

"Chepe, you're in charge. I doubt we'll see trouble tonight. I'm going to bed. Help yourselves if you get hungry. Chuch, you get your homework done?"

"*Sí, jefe*. I'm turning in, too. I want to research more about Nader before class."

"Good man. I'll make us all breakfast at seven. *Buenas noches*."

"*Buenas noches*," the men echoed. They went their separate ways, Chepe and Martinez bouncing grenades in their hands.

A dark cloud of loneliness engulfed Quint as soon as he shut his door. It wasn't too late to call Jade; maybe she'd be home and want to talk. He picked up the phone to tap the number, but it rang.

Quint's heart skipped a beat. "*Hola, Rosi.* I'm glad you've called."

"I was thinking about you, Jackman. It's not too late?"

"No, not at all. I was thinking about you, too," he replied, realizing he *had* been thinking of her.

"*Que bonito.* I was hoping you were free for dinner one night this week."

A sharp jolt of joy passed through him. He grinned. "I'd like that, Rosi. But I'm not sure if it's safe for you to come here yet."

"At my house," she said. An order, not a request. His grin broadened.

"When?"

"Tomorrow? Tuesday?"

"Tomorrow is a tentative yes, and I have something important to talk to you about anyway. You know Leo has a sister who is in trouble?"

"My brand of trouble. Yes, let's talk. How is Leo getting on?"

"At Horacio's right now. But he's worried about the girl. She needs extraction to a safe home."

"I've got meetings tomorrow until four or five. Can you brief me then?'

"Probably. I have to get in to see Garza. He'll dictate the time."

"As always. Okay, let me know as soon as you know. What did you find?"

"I'm keeping it under my hat until I see the ambassador. It's damning"

"Good for you, Quint. Let's try for dinner. It's late. I better let you get to sleep."

"Thanks for calling, Rosi. See you tomorrow."

The line went dead. Quint smiled into the shaft of moonlight angling between the curtains. Rosi had invited him to dinner. He kicked off his clothes and lay down. The memory of her kiss filled his dreams.

Chapter 27

Quint, Rafiq, & Stone—Solutions

Quint awoke feeling rested—no intrusions, attacks or emergencies. A good sign. He expected his day to go well. Garza would see him, Sami would be free to accompany him, and the slow process of stopping Nader would start. Everything would culminate in dinner with Rosi. Maybe Jade would call with the good news about her return.

His anxiety sloughed off down the shower drain. His reflection grinning back warmed him as he shaved. Yes. A good day. He'd make pancakes, eggs, and sausage for the crew. Or, if his luck held, he'd find Mrs. P already in the kitchen. It was just about seven. Quint gave himself an appraising look in the full-length mirror, approving of the peach-colored oxford cloth shirt. He almost looked professional.

Lady luck smiled. Mrs. P was stacking pancakes on a platter, the scrambled eggs with a mountain of bacon already on the table next to the salsa and a basket of tortillas.

Chepe sat at the table filling his plate. "Morning, bossman." He tipped his coffee cup in Quint's direction.

"Good morning, Chepe. Quiet night. Nothing to report?" He sat down. "Hello, Mrs. P. I'm glad to see you."

"Señor Quint, I am glad to be here. Chepe says things have quieted down."

"For the moment. Chepe's crew is standing guard. You know Chucho had an alarm system installed?" He regarded her quizzically. "How'd you get in?"

"Chucho showed me how to work the alarm. Wasn't he at work too early, Señor Quint?"

Chepe yawned. then said. "He was at work all night. That kid is determined to get everything on Nader."

"You're too hard on the boy, Señor Quint," Mrs. P said, her voice disapproving.

Quint threw up his hands. "Don't blame me, Señora! I told him to go to bed."

She harrumphed then poured more coffee into the men's cups. Yes, it was good to have her back.

The doorbell rang. Shortly, the clatter of shoes echoed up the stairs. Martinez ushered the day shift to the table and disappeared. The young men mumbled, "*Buenos,*" in unison. Like triplets, they slouched into the empty chairs.

"Doña, may I introduce my *primos* Flaco, Avandaro, and Alfonso. The day shift," Chepe said.

They mumbled again, something that to Quint, sounded vaguely like, "*Encantadadeconocerte,*" between shoveling bites of eggs into their mouths.

Chucho skidded into the room, twirled Mrs. P off her feet with a hug, and said, "It smells *muy rico* in here."

"You mean you've missed my food, Chucho?" she said, eyes twinkling.

"We've all missed your cooking, Mrs. P," Quint said. Turning to Chepe, he asked "Where's Martinez? We need to brief the new shift."

"I've sent him home. Nothing happened last night. There's nothing to report. I'll take my cousins down after we eat. Teach them the alarm. Whaddaya think? One patrolling the roof, one in the garden, the third resting inside in two hour shifts?"

"Sounds good, Chepe. Men, text if anything looks suspicious. I mean *anything*." Quint pushed back from the table. "I'm getting started. I've got a lot to do today. Chuch, drop by before you go to school. I want everything you've found out. Have you spoken with Qadir or Laith?"

"*Sí jefe*. Both."

"Okay. I'll see you later."

This was the part Quint hated. Administrative duty. Sitting at his desk doing busy work—reports, invoices, contracts, scheduling. Talking on the phone. It was still too early to call Mrs. Tomsky to get on Garza's calendar. He'd start with the contract. Get Garza's signature today. The sooner he took care of it, the sooner he'd get paid at the end of the job. Quint was familiar with the glacial speed of bureaucracy. He booted up.

Staring at the contract template, he realized he needed a new name. Although he drew funds from Senator Aguirre's trust, he couldn't use that name for this job. Quint needed an official Mexican corporation, an S.A de C.V. He doodled ideas on his notepad. He wondered if Jade would take Dylan's last name—Porras.

> *Jackman Quint Investigations, SA de CV
> *Jade & Jackman Services SA de CV
> *J. Quint and Daughter SA de CV
> *J. Quint and J. Stone Private Services SA de CV
> *Quint & Stone Investigations, Illegal Ops, Mayhem SA de CV
> *Quint and Porras—Services

What about Horacio? Chuch? Quint wondered what Chucho's last name was. He couldn't remember ever hearing it. But when this outfit got going, he'd be paying wages and taxes. Maybe Susana knew. Yet, what about her? He struck his pen through the list and picked up his phone.

"*Bueno*?" Susana Arias de Barrera's clear voice sounded

chipper.

"Hi! Quint here. How are You?"

"*Ay* Quint, this project is taking forever. *Lo siento, jefe.* I'll be at it for another month or six before I can come back to work full time. How are you doing with getting set up? Congratulations on getting that little girl back to her family." She inhaled a gulp of air.

Quint smiled. "Thanks, but that was all JadeAnne, Rosi, and Dafne Olabarrieta's doing. I was against it from the start. You know what happened?"

"Anibal Aguirre brought it on himself. Don't feel guilty—don't deny it. I know you, Mr. Quint."

"Me? I don't feel guilty—well, okay, for Jade being forced to pull the trigger."

"She's strong, like you. *Que pasa?*"

"I'm not trying to hurry you, Susana. Chuch said you're swamped. But I have a question. It's pretty dumb."

"I'm a depository of answers to dumb questions. Try me."

"What's Chucho's last name?"

"*Ay*, not so dumb. When he came to the senator, he was not exactly clear on his name. Apparently his mother changed last names along with her many boyfriends. We think his name was Jesús Arriaga, which comes from '*roto*' or broken, but he called himself Chucho—'mutt'." He was a darling boy, but he was a stray fifteen years ago."

"So if I hire him officially, he's Chucho or Jesús Arriaga?"

"No. The senator officially had his name changed to Aguirre—Chucho Aguirre Arriaga."

"He adopted the boy?"

"I don't think so. He was made his legal guardian. Ask Chucho. He might know. Why, are you adopting him?" Susana giggled.

"No, but if the kid continues to progress like he is now, I'll make him a partner. I think I'd better incorporate here in Mexico. You can help with that, can't you?"

"*Claro que si, jefe.* As soon as I come on board. Sami is taking care of your legal needs. Ask him to get the process started. It takes time."

"Good idea. I'm looking forward to you taking over the administration—our official business manager. Hurry back, Susana," Quint said, pausing. "One more thing, what should I call this organization?"

She laughed harder. "Quint's Folly?"

"Hey!" he yelped. "You think the senator's operation is a mistake?"

"No, no, *jefe, solo bromeaba*—just joking. You know you can win battles, but not this war, Quint."

"I know, but if we can get paid to put a dent in organized crime, we'll call it successful."

"Not to be discouraging, but it won't even be a dent."

"We cost the cartels money, that's a start."

"Yes, and I will be proud to run this noble operation. See you soon," she said, ending the call.

Quint contemplated the notepad. He jotted, 'Aguirre, Quint, Rafiq and Stone Services, SA de CV' then 'Aguirre, Arias-Barrera, Quint, Rafiq and Stone Solutions, SA de CV.'

"Solutions. That's it!" Quint and Rafiq Solutions SA de CV. Now all he had to do was figure out how to pay for it. The trust from Senator Aguirre would help, but not last forever. He expected the embassy contract to terminate when he unveiled the secret of the locked room—barely enough hours to cover the last few days' operating expenses.

He picked up the phone again. Jade would be up and caffeinated by now.

She answered on the second ring. "Hi, Dad. Good timing. We just finished breakfast. What's up?"

"Wondering how you're doing. Dylan still enjoying himself?"

"Ask him."

Quint heard the sounds of seagulls squabbling in the background then Dylan's voice.

"*Hola Quint,* I heard you all have had some excitement

176

lately. No one needs a doctor, I hope."

"Nope, we're all fine, but we could use some help getting this business off the ground. When you bringing our girl home?"

Dylan snorted. "You mean, when will that woman let me leave? I'm due back at work on the sixteenth. I'm hoping Jade is with me."

"So am I. Tell me what's going on."

"We're packing up the houseboat in between dinner parties and negotiations with her ex. He hasn't got enough money to buy her out. She'll probably lose most of her investment. The good news is, she has a couple who are willing to sign a three-year lease on the Sarasvati. After that they will have an option to buy, applying the lease payments to the purchase price. That is, *if* Jade decides to stay in Mexico. The wife runs a nursery specializing in orchids. It's how they met. Jade wasn't going to leave her plants to die."

"No, she loves the orchids like children."

"Just about—"

Quint heard Jade in the background. She grabbed the phone. "What! Dylan is telling lies again? I'm thrilled to have found Meadow. She and her husband live on a sailboat, but it's too small for their growing family. God, it's hard to leave Sausalito's waterfront community."

"And you're coming. Right!?"

"Yes Dad, but it may not be with Dyl on the fifteenth. Dex is being a jealous dick. Even though *he* dumped *me*."

"Dex doesn't want to buy you out. Work out a payment plan. But don't worry. I have a job for you. Susana says she has half a year before she'll be full-time. We have a lot to do. We'll need extra hands after she comes back.'

"I'm not anxious to be an office manager again, Dad."

"A temporary office manager. Then we'll see what we need. I'm going to ask H to be a partner. I'm incorporating. How does Quint and Rafiq Solutions SA de CV sound?"

"What about me? Quint, Rafiq and Stone Solutions"

"You want to be a partner? I'd be happy with that, but if

not managing operations, what?"

"Vice president."

Quint chuckled. "Chairman of the board?"

"Later," she quipped. "We've got to go soon, Dad. Another round of arguing with Dex."

"A couple minutes more, daughter." She sighed. "Your dad, your other dad," he corrected himself, "did not turn me in. It was Nader. Nader is running guns, selling to BLO. He knows I'm onto him. He's threatened us."

"Us? Us who?"

"You. Get on that plane with Dylan. Be very careful. Keep a look over your shoulder at all times. I'm meeting Garza today with proof of his actions. The threat should be eliminated soon, but your old boyfriend should assign a bodyguard to you. I'll pay from today through you getting on that plane."

"Oh, fuck, Dad. I don't have time for one of Dex's thugs to get in my way."

"You'll have more time if you stay alive, Jade. Do as I say. If Nader gets on a plane, I'll be right behind him."

"Sheesh! Okay."

"On another topic, what's the word on the hacking from Qadir?"

"Really, I have to go. I think he's talked to Chucho. I'll make sure he does this morning if they haven't yet. Bye, Dad. Love you."

The line went dead. "Love you too, JadeAnne."

He marked his calendar for the fifteenth. One week to solve the Nader problem, create an organizational chart, and get everyone to agree to their positions. Damn, he needed Susana.

Chapter 28

It's Up to Us

Horacio's booming laugh bounced down the hall. Quint stood up, stretched, popping several vertebrae. He stepped to the door, poking his head into the hall to catch his soon-to-be partner before he settled into the workroom. "Yo, H, join me. I've got a proposal for you."

"Coming *jefe*." He raised one finger. Quint recognized he was on the phone. He said goodbye as he trotted down the hall. "*Que pasó, jefe?* You look happy."

"I am. Jade says she's coming back. Dylan has to return to the hospital next Tuesday, so we should see them on Monday, latest." He added, "Hopefully."

"Did you tell her of the threat?"

"I did. I asked her to have her ex put a guard on her. She agreed against her wishes. But that's not what I want to talk to you about."

Horacio raised his eyebrows.

"First H, I need to incorporate this business, get everything legal. Pay wages. How would you like to come in as a partner?

You'll still get your salary, of course." Now Quint raised *his* eyebrows.

Horacio brought his hand to his chin. He gazed at the floor, brow furrowed. Quint's blood pressure ticked up a notch.

"I don't have a buy-in, Quint."

"Sure you do. You've got the ride."

Horacio's face broke into his wide ogre grin. "Then yes! I'm in." He reached across the desk and grasped Quint's outstretched hand. "What else did you have, *jefe*?"

Quint grinned back. "Sit down, *partner.* How does this sound? Quint, Rafiq and Stone—Solutions, SA de CV? In gold on the door?"

"¡*Guau!* I can see it now. What about Chuch?"

"After he finishes school. But Jade expressed interest. If she shows up next week, she can take over running this place until Susana is back. Leo can assist part-time. Mrs. P will do what she does. Everyone else we'll use on a contract basis. I thought I'd ask Sami to start drawing up the papers."

"What will Jade do after Susana takes over?"

"She wants to be Vice President. Whatever that means. She'll investigate, but I don't want her in the field. I'd make you Chief Operating Officer, but think about what you want and how you see the responsibilities for each person."

"A real corporation, eh, *jefe*?"

"Partner! If we want to work for the embassy, we have to be legit."

"Tru dat."

Quint checked his watch. It was nine. "Speaking of the embassy, we need to coordinate with Sami to meet with Garza today. Let me tell you what I discovered last night. Close the door."

"You found something. In the locked room?"

"Yep. Weapons U.S. Made. Military grade. Grenade launchers. M67 Fragmentation grenades. Stinger MANPADS. All kinds of rifles. The room was stacked with crates."

"¡*Hijole!* Did you bring home *unos recuerdos*? How do you say it?"

"Souvenirs? Scroll through the images." He tossed his cell.

Horacio scooped it out of the air in his giant paw and started to swipe. "Why's he selling Chinese guns if he's got these?"

"I'm guessing he's a Walmart of weapons."

Horacio roared with laughter.

Gotta love an ogre, Quint thought, grinning at his new partner.

"Have you called Garza yet?" H asked.

"No. Sami neither. I waited for you."

Horacio placed his hand over his heart. "I'm the first to know this?"

"And your brother will be second. Can you call him? I'll call Garza."

Horacio circled the immediate area looking for a parking space. Finally he found something by the restaurant, not far from the embassy's back gate. Quint and the Rafiq brothers clambered out of the limo deep in conversation. Sami had seen the photographs. He agreed the cache of arms was serious, but wasn't it a problem for the Mexican police?

Quint replied, "I don't know, Sami. If the man has this quantity of arms in Mexico, doesn't it mean he's got some pretty strong connections in both the U.S., probably military, and in immigration here? My country frowns on illegal weapons trading, especially when those weapons are going to criminals."

Horacio agreed, suggesting it was probably the Mexican police helping him move the goods. Sami agreed with a pithy, "Tru dat."

Quint saluted the marine on the gate. Another kid fresh out of training. Another Javie. He pulled out his passport. "I'm Jackman Quint, my partner Horacio Rafiq, and my attorney, Sami Rafiq to see the ambassador at four."

The guard checked his list against the men's documents then opened the gate as Mrs. Tomsky stepped from the building. "Good afternoon, Mr. Quint, Señores Rafiq. The ambassador is waiting. Please follow me."

Mrs. Tomsky knew the secret way to Garza's corner office, which included an elevator. She announced their arrival over the intercom then ushered them into the inner sanctum.

The ambassador stood, shaking hands with each. "Nice to see you today, Rafiq," he said to Horacio. "Congratulations on your partnership." Behind him the angel choked in the day's pollution.

"Sit. Sit. What shall I pour today?"

"I think it's a whisky day, Ambassador. Why don't I pour while you look at what our man Nader is keeping in his back bedroom."

Garza tipped his head, held out his hand for the phone. Quint stepped to the cocktail tray. Before he poured, he heard Garza's quiet gasp. A slight smile crossed his lips.

Quint handed out the tumblers of tawny liquid, a generous three fingers each. Taking his phone from the desk, he asked, "What do you think? These weapons aren't the usual U.S. made stock of the gun shops. No straw buyers picked these up in Arizona. These are military. Nader has some serious connections. I'm certain important men in our government will want to know about this." He took a gulp, savoring the fiery liquid as it warmed his throat then belly. "Proof enough to get an arrest warrant and ship him back to the states?"

"Mr. Quint, it's proof enough to get Robert Miller, our CIA bureau chief, in here." He punched the intercom. "Mrs. Tomsky, get Robert Miller up here right now."

"Ambassador, how do we know Miller isn't in on it, too?"

"We don't, Mr. Quint, but Miller heads the bureau. We have to start somewhere."

Ten minutes later, the bureau chief was ushered into the room. Garza pointed to the drinks tray and nodded toward the fourth chair. Miller poured himself a whisky before sitting down. Garza made introductions.

"Miller, you have a man on special assignment, Chuck Nader. We have evidence Mr. Nader is trafficking in arms.

What is his assignment here?"

Miller looked nonplussed. "Confidential."

"Not in this office." Garza's voice held a subtle threat.

Miller looked at Quint and the Rafiqs.

"They are authorized to hear what you have to say," Garza said.

"Operation Wide Receiver."

"What? What is that?" Quint asked.

"An ATF deal, started in 2006 under George W. Bush. They're tracking shipments of straw buys out of Arizona to find the end users."

Quint interjected. "Straw buys from gun dealers?" Miller nodded. Quint continued. "Ambassador, the weapons in those images did not come from gun stores."

"Mr. Miller, what can you tell us about Operation Wide Receiver? More importantly, how does an NSA operative fit in?"

"Tony, there's nothing more I can add. I've met Nader once or twice, but I assumed he was with ATF. You need to talk to Cesar Alejo. He's in charge at this end."

"What kind of man is he? Do you trust him?" Garza asked.

Miller took a sip of his whisky. After gently returning the tumbler to the edge of Garza's desk, he tipped his chin toward the window and cleared his throat. Quint leaned in, full attention on the bureau chief.

"Alejo is a methodical worker, but a bit of a zealot. He's smart, yet his drive to defend Mexico—the entire world—from the cartels clouds his judgement, in my opinion. He believes he's doing great good. While a stickler for the rules, he makes poor choices. From the little I know, this op is one of them."

Quint queued up the photos from the locked room and passed the phone to Miller. "Chief Miller, is it possible Alejo is involved with trafficking U.S. military armaments in Mexico?"

"What are you showing me, Mr. Quint?"

"Chuck Nader's stash of U. S. military arms at his home in the north of the city. In the garage, he has the Chinese-made guns and grenades. I saw QBZ-97s. On Friday night we surveilled Nader with an Hispanic man loading crates into a van. We tailed them to Ciudad Neza near the The Home Depot where he sold the shipment." Quint took the phone back to cue the video of the transaction. "Can you identify the helper or the buyers?"

Miller studied the video, rewinding it several times. "It's not Alejo. The helper looks familiar, but I can't place him. Sorry."

"Could the helper be an actor calling himself Señor El Muerte?"

"Not at all. That's the code name for the head of the Beltran Levya Organization. What's his involvement?"

Quint nodded. "Yes, that agrees with our phone tap. He wants more arms. A specific list. There's another recording. Maybe you can identify the voice? We planted bugs throughout his house. The next day we recorded this." He replayed the recording: S*ound of ringing. A male voice answers, "Bueno?"* Nader's voice, 'The exchange has been transacted. Meet me tomorrow night for your split... No, not here. The other place. Tell Mr. Chanthavong I can move as much as he can provide. There's a turf war brewing.'"

Everyone looked at Miller expectantly. "I don't know. It doesn't sound like Alejo."

Garza said, "Maybe not, but someone in the embassy is involved. Quint's IT man captured the number." He pushed a slip of paper across the desk. Miller picked it up. "It's assigned to your bureau. Alejo?"

Miller pulled his cell from his pocket and scrolled for a moment. "No, not Alejo. It's an unassigned number at the moment. Used to belong to Davidson, but he was reassigned to El Salvador. That desk has been empty for a couple of months."

"Find out who uses that desk," Garza demanded. "Keep it under your hat, Bob. I'd like you to investigate your bureau. Mr. Quint and Mr. Rafiq are investigating Nader for us. Please cooperate with each other." Garza tipped his glass toward the men. "By the way, I want to talk to Cesar Alejo. Bob, get him up here as soon as you can. Check my schedule with Mrs.

Tomsky."

"Sure, Tony. But may I ask why aren't we turning the arms sales over to the Mexicans? This isn't our jurisdiction. There's a question of the legality in obtaining the evidence. Where do we stand?"

Garza hooted. "That's rich, Bob, considering your agency's methods. But, you have a point. At the moment, this is undercover. We're exploring who and what. If we can legally obtain sufficient evidence of trafficking U. S. military weapons, we'll send this up the chain. Failing that, we'll turn our findings over to the Mexicans. That would be the Agencia Federales de Investigaciones, correct?"

"Isn't Nader's helper AFI?" Sami said, "He looks like an AFI agent I've run into."

Miller nodded, grimacing. "They're all on the take."

Garza frowned. "Then it's up to us, boys."

Chapter 29

Happy Hour

The meeting had lasted an hour. Quint tapped Rosi's number into his phone when they exited the embassy.

"Perfect timing, Jackman. I just finished up here. Are we getting together?"

"Absolutely. Shall I ask H to drop me off at your place?"

"I'm at the Maria Isabel on Reforma. I'll come for you."

"Don't bother. I'm outside the embassy. I'll be there in five minutes. Meet me at the bar."

"*Que amable*, Jackman. I'll order us drinks." She clicked off.

Horacio and Sami had continued walking toward the limo. Quint shouted, "I'm meeting Rosi over at the Maria Isobel. I'll see you tomorrow, H. Thanks Sami." He waved as he headed around the corner.

Although his walk was no more than two long, barely inclined blocks, the altitude combined with the heavy exhaust from traffic on eight-lane Reforma settling into the stratified yellow *contaminación*, had him gasping when he reached the

Maria Isabel. He bent over, put his hands on his knees, sucking in a few deep breaths before entering the elegant lobby. He hoped the air in the hotel was filtered. Maybe walking had been a shitty idea. How the hell did people live in this? But he'd been here long enough to know you just soldiered on. He considered wearing a mask like people in Beijing.

If the lobby was elegant, the bar was doubly so. Gleaming planked wooden floor in dark and light strips pulling his eyes in. Clusters of club chairs and low tables under bright but unobtrusive lighting. A curved bar glittering with crystal in front of floor-to-ceiling windows overlooking a lush green oasis in crowded Cuautémoc. Movement caught his eye. Rosi waving, her wide smile lighting up her face from a corner by the garden windows. Two drinks sat at the round table between the chairs. He waved back, a little flutter in his chest.

She stood to greet him with the typical Mexico City two cheek kisses. He pulled her into a hug then released her to give her the once-over. "Rosi, you look lovely as always. A sight for sore eyes."

"Thank you, Jackman, but it's because of the pollution— your sore eyes. You should carry eye drops. You're looking sharp yourself, by the way." She gestured to a chair conveniently positioned to take in the view of a cluster of country flags framed by the dark green of the trees with high-rises soaring above. Reseating herself, she picked up her glass. He did the same. Melodic jazz played in the background. "You'd never think twenty-one million people surround us, would you?" she mused. She wave her hand toward the tall glasses filled with something amber. "Spiced rum and ginger liqueur with honey, lime, a spritz of ginger ale garnished with mint."

"Does it have a name?"

She thought for a moment. "It's a spin-off of a spiced honey mojito. A *mojito en ti*." Her silver-bells laugh pealed.

Quint cocked his head, brow wrinkling, chuckling to cover his confusion.

"A play on words, Jackman. Taste it!" She held up her

187

glass to clink.

He tapped his to the rim. "*Buen provecho,*" he said, his smile sincere and warm. They sipped, keeping eye contact.

Rosi broke contact first. "How has your day gone? You saw Garza, obviously."

Quint set the spicy drink down. "It's been a wild day. I talked to Jade. She *is* coming back. Possibly by next week. Dylan has to be at work next Tuesday. I'm happy; I miss her. But that's not all, Rosi. I've decided to turn the operation into a business. There is so much opportunity here in Mexico. I already have a resident visa—why not? I asked Horacio to come in as my partner. Sami and I spent some time today going over potential structures for the organization. We have a contract with the embassy. After that the job I agreed to do for Aguirre. I'll hire Chucho and Susana. Take Leo on as a paid intern. What do you think?"

Rosi placed her hand on Quint's, resting on the chair arm. She looked him in the eye. "I think this is wonderful news. You'll be staying then." She squeezed his hand then relaxed back into her chair. "What happened with Tony today?"

"No, you first. How did your day go?"

"Typical Monday. We started with a meeting of the board, then lunch at a cute place in Condesa with a potential donor. He picked up the tab, but I'm not sure I sold him on our mission. His ideas seemed too conservative, more like a supporter of the system as it stands."

"You mean a horny patron of the sex trade."

"Exactly. If he ran his eyes up my leg or down my blouse one more time I was considering shooting him." She laughed irresistibly. Quint joined in. After another sip at the mojito, Rosi detailed the rest of the day.

Around them the bar filled. Waiters bustled about with drinks and scrumptious smelling *botanas*. Quint's stomach rumbled. He took a sip, concentrating on the flavors. The ginger added depth. He decided he liked it.

"Rosi, I wanted to talk to you about Leo's sister Veronica, or Roni, as he calls her. I think she's about twelve. As Leo's story goes, after the gang affiliated stepfather killed his father, he moved in and turned the mother out. He started preying on the girl, keeping her home. Raping her. Leo claims he beats the family. I spoke to Roni. She wants to get out, go back to school. I have no capacity to raise a little girl, but I thought you might be able to place her in a stable home. Leo is willing help pay for her keep with his wages. What do you think?"

"Since Roni lives at home with one living parent, the parent has to agree to putting her daughter in a foster home. That is, to do this legally. It would be different if she ran away. But Jackman if this is true, we've got to get the mother out too."

"I thought you'd say that. Aren't there shelters for people in situations like this?"

"*Claro que si*, Jackman. I place people regularly. I need to talk to the mother."

"I can't help you there. Leo was not forthcoming when I asked about her."

"Bring him over tomorrow—you'll see him, won't you?"

"Horacio is in charge."

"Then ask him bring Leo by after school. I planned on working in the office all day tomorrow." She sighed.

Quint took her hand. "What is it, Rosi?"

"Sometimes this work feels hopeless. These are just kids. The mother should have taken them and fled at the first sign the man was abusing them. People need education. The women to learn they don't need to depend on a man who wants to exploit them. There are programs—not just mine, which is primarily concerned with freeing and placing trafficking victims in rehabilitation centers, but shelters for abused families with programs to help mothers learn a trade. Some help them find housing or work to support their children. The men need to learn domestic violence of all kinds is not acceptable in modern society. The people who need the services the most are often the ones who don't know about them or won't go to them. Informing people of resources is the biggest part of my job. Jackman, I'm exhausted."

"I'm so sorry, Rosi. I know. It isn't enough to be good at the job. Odds are stacked against you every day. The evil rampant in our world is relentless." He lunged over to give her an awkward hug.

She rested her head on his shoulder for a beat. "*Ay*, I'm feeling sorry for myself. Your work is just as thankless. So what happened with Tony?" She gave him a little shove toward his chair.

Quint sat down. They clinked glasses again. He began his recap of the day.

"So the bureau chief doesn't think his agent, Alejo, is the type to be involved with Nader's gun running. He described him as 'methodical but a bit of a zealot'. I took that to mean a do-gooder. Alejo is running a secret U.S. mission to determine where U.S. weapons are going in Mexico. I can't tell you more, but Garza is looking into it." He swallowed the last of his *mojito en ti*. "Aren't you hungry? I'm starved. Where shall we go?"

"My house. I've slaved over a hot *horno*, oven, all day." She laughed then stood up, slipping her arm through Quint's.

They threaded their way through the throngs of young, well-dressed office workers and professionals congregating after work. Happy hour, he thought. He leaned into Rosi's ear. "Do they have happy hour here?"

She giggled. Quint could listen to the jingling of her laughter forever.

Chapter 30

Love Hurts

Rosi's two-story house squatted behind a high bougainvillea-covered wall between what looked like a McMansion and an apartment building on a quiet mixed residential street somewhere in San Angel. He wasn't sure. In fact, he was lost. But the din of the city had dropped to more of a gentle vibration. The air tasted a little cleaner. The electronic gate clanged behind them, Rosi pushed the garage door controller clipped to the visor. The door opened allowing them to drive inside before getting out of the car. A necessary safety feature with the increasing crime in the capitol. At the back door, Rosi entered another code to turn off the house alarm. He hadn't remembered the details from his last visit. Losing his grip or overwhelmed by his growing feelings for her?

"It feels so peaceful here, Rosi," he said, breaking the silence.

"It's the security, Jackman. I live in an upscale colonia on a quiet street, but we're still in Mexico City. We're still in Mexico. I live alone. Sometimes I shelter women running from the cartels." She flipped on a light.

"You do?"

She took his hand, leading him through a typical back hall into a large kitchen filled with colorful Talavera tilework and displayed dishware. She dropped her tote bag onto the long plank table, snagged a couple of beers out of the refrigerator, pointed one at him. "A beer while we wait for dinner?"

Quint took the mini Victorias from her and looked around for the opener.

"I'll get it," Rosi said, taking it from a drawer. She popped off the tops. He handed one to her. She touched the neck of his, said, "Cheers, Jackman," and swigged. "Now, about dinner..."

"I didn't know you cook. What are we having?"

"Cook? *Juevos* when I have to. No, I'm calling El Carmen Deli for delivery." Her gleeful laugh sent shivers up his spine. "Anything you don't eat?"

"Whatever you choose is great, Rosi. Surprise me."

"Good. Why don't you make yourself comfortable in the living room. Here's another beer," she said, handing him a fresh bottle. "I'll call in our order."

Quint wandered into a comfortable room with large windows overlooking a pretty garden strategically lit with flood lamps and pathway lights coming on as twilight deepened to night. He was settling into an easy chair when she joined him, carrying a plate of fresh cut vegetables and a bowl of some sort of dip on a tray. She deposited the snack on the coffee table, flipped on a few lamps, and the CD player. He didn't recognize the music.

"Dinner will arrive in a half hour. Help yourself to the *botana*. Now tell me everything."

"Nader is selling arms, as I said, but there's the complication I mentioned, Operation Wide Receiver. I'm worried Nader is involved in a possibly sanctioned arms sale. If he's actually doing something for the government, I can't put him behind bars—oh, did I tell you Jade's dad, Charley Stone, didn't turn me in?"

"He didn't? Who then?"

"Nader. He pretty much admitted it. He spewed his hate through the bugs we planted. He plans to kill me. Worse, he threatened Jade. I need to protect her, but I don't know how. Nader could go to California. I need to get proof he's double dealing or passing intel to the cartels. I can't bear thinking of him harming my girl." He stopped talking and lowered his head to his hands. When he spoke his voice broke. "Rosi, he said he killed Thuy. Why does this man hate me so much?"

She eased off the couch and went to Quint, rested her hand on his head for a moment then began a soft massage to his neck and shoulders. He first stiffened then slowly relaxed his tensed muscles.

The gate buzzer sounded.

"That must be the food, Jackman. I'll be right back." She hurried through the kitchen, stopping to say "*¿Dime?*" into the intercom before running out the back door.

Rosi was a courageous woman doing a righteous but dangerous job. She wasn't going to be impressed by a scared crybaby, Quint worried. She was tough. *God, I'm such fool. Why would she want me?* He should leave. Call for a taxi. Make up an excuse. Do what he always did when his feeling were showing—get out. His phone rang.

"Yeah."

"Don't come home. Your buddy has lookouts in the neighborhood. I've called Garza. He's sending a couple of men," H said.

"Has Nader been near the building?"

"No. No one has seen Nader, but Martinez recognized one of the men. We're on lockdown. Chepe's team is good."

"How many? Where? What are they doing?"

"Three cars staked out. Maybe five men. No one in the alley."

"You should get out. Take Chuch and Leo. Leave it to Chepe. Don't risk your lives to protect the building."

"Sorry, *socio.* This is a partnership. I'm not running away, it's my office now, too."

"Damn, H, I couldn't live with myself if any of you got

hurt because Nader has a bone to pick with me."

"We're gonna catch him, Quint. Stay put. I'll call later." He hung up.

Quint headed into the kitchen. The back door slammed. Rosi breezed in with two bags and dropped them onto the counter. "Come on, help me set the table."

"I, uh, there's an—"

"There's nothing you can do about it, whatever it is. You're enjoying dinner, then we'll figure it out, Jackman." She reminded him of his mother when he was a boy. No nonsense. Take charge.

She pushed him into the dining room, opened a cabinet. Plates, silverware, and two napkins appeared. She handed everything to him, pointing to the table. He set the places across from each other. Rosi added tall glasses and two candles before hurrying back to the kitchen. He heard her rustling through the bags. She reappeared shortly with three dishes trailing an enticing aroma of meat and cheese accented by smoky spices. She set the tray of steaming dishes onto the table. His stomach complained again. Not a growl, a roar.

She nodded at a chair. "Sit, Jackman. Please serve yourself." She took the opposite chair and spooned an herbed cheese onto slices of fresh baguette, topping it off with cherry tomatoes and black olives. Quint smelled the garlic. "*Queso Helénico*. My favorite take on *queso fundido*. That's a salad of beets with artichoke hearts. That," she pointed to what looked like *albóndigas*, "is *Albóndigas Zapotecas*, the best twist on meatballs made."

He dished up a plate of the meatballs and took a bite. An explosion of flavors burst across his tongue. "You're right. Don't tell Mrs. P I said this, but these *are* the best. What is the cheese?"

"Chihuahua cheese made by Mennonites. The meat is cooked in garlic and epazote then it's topped in a salsa made with four chiles."

"I can taste the *chipotle*. It's amazing Rosi, thank you." The food was making him feel better, stronger. "Rosi," he started, between bites, "H called. Nader's people are in my neighborhood. He called Garza who is sending a couple of guys, hopefully to catch Nader. But no one has seen him." He chewed another bite, thinking.

"What are you thinking?"

"I'm worried. He's a trickster. He could be distracting us so he can get on a plane to San Francisco."

"You love Jade. Of course you fear for her, but you aren't thinking clearly. You hired a bodyguard for her. Call. Ask her to go to her father's house for the night."

"Nader knows who Charley Stone is—"

"Or to a hotel. Jackman, call her now."

Quint picked up his phone, tapped in her number then punched on the speaker.

"Hi Dad, what's up?"

"I'm at Rosi's for dinner. We wanted to say hi."

That's wonderful. Hi, Rosi. Wha'd you make?"

"Delivery—his favorite."

"¡*Albóndigas*!" they chorused. Quint felt his ears heating up.

Rosie continued. "Jade, honey, your dad is worried about your safety. Nader has dropped off the radar. We think you, Pepper, and Dylan should go spend the night in a fancy San Francisco hotel."

"He told me Nader had made threats. Dad, Dex put Clarence on guard duty tonight. We'll be okay. You said yourself he's a lousy sniper."

"Jade, you should be afraid. He can't shoot for shit, but he can do other things. Put Clarence on. I'll tell him what he needs to do."

She said, "Are you crazy? Dex hired him. We've finally agreed on a payment schedule, by the way. You aren't butting in. Dex already doesn't like you."

"Did you get the price you wanted?" Rosi asked.

"Close. He's found a new partner to buy me out. I'll get half up front then two additional payments over the next six months. With the first, last, and security deposit, I'll have capital for our business. And the wedding."

"You'll save the rental money. Use it for your houseboat, Jade," Quint warned.

Rosi beamed. "Wedding! Quint you never said anything about a wedding. Congratulations. When?"

"Rosi, we've only known each other for a couple of months. We're waiting for at least a year, testing it out first. Dylan wants to open a private practice. I want to finish the job we started. Get that exposé written. Maybe a book. How are the dogs, by the way?"

"Living with H's family until things settle down," Quint replied. "And that reminds me, please warn Charley. Never mind. I'll call him. He may have some information for me."

"Where's Dylan?" Rosi asked.

"He went to Mollie Stones—the supermarket—for wine. We needed a rosé to go with our roasted veggies and wild rice. Speaking of dinner, aren't you two in the middle of yours? I'll let you get back to it. Bye, Rosi. Bye, Dad. Love you."

Rosi served herself the last of the salad. "Take the rest of the meatballs, Jackman, but save some room for house-baked *panes* and hot chocolate."

He put his fork down, pushed the plate aside. "I don't know that I could take another bite, Rosi."

"Help me put the food away then, and we'll take a stroll in the neighborhood. Always a good way to digest a meal."

"It's dangerous."

She laughed. "Jackman, he doesn't know where I live. Unless he followed me, how would he find out?"

"Property records."

"Not easily done in Mexico. They're not in my name. The house is in my daughter's name, which is different than mine. I use my mother's name and there are millions of Orozcos. Yesenia was a DelVacho growing up, but took her husband's name and dropped her father's. Two dynasties removed, you might say. One of them we wanted to disassociate from completely."

"Your ex?"

196

"*Sí.* A DelVacho. A corrupt, powerful family in the State of Mexico. We met at school. He was a sweet kid. But politics and the expectations of his family ruined him. We saw things differently. Our marriage only lasted six years. Yesenia was three. I had to fight to keep her. It was ugly, but I kept her with help from my parents. Yesenia and Bruce live in Toronto. He's an IT consultant. She teaches Spanish at a private high school."

"I had no idea. If the family is so powerful, how did she escape to Canada?"

"She's got her grandparents wrapped around her fingers. They will do anything for her. It doesn't hurt that Bruce has political aspirations. Let's take that walk."

Rosi took the dishtowel from Quint's hands and tossed it onto the counter. She led him into the back hall toward the door, but he circled her in an embrace. She smiled up at him. He bent to her full lips, kissing her lightly then deeply. His heart raced. He felt her heart racing, too, and closed his arms around her, worries quelled. The hallway disappeared. Nothing else existed. Only Rosi.

His phone rang. The moment dissipated like breath on glass. He fished the phone from his pocket. "I should take it, Rosi. It's Garza."

She hugged him and whispered, her voice husky, "Let it go to voice mail." She kissed him again but pulled away, and said, "Now for our walk. Come on, Jackman. The evening is lovely." Rosi slipped her hand into Quint's and drew him toward the street.

Walking arm-in-arm in silence, Quint admired the grand houses towering over their high walls shaded by the mature trees lining the neighborhood.

"That house," Rosi said, pointing to a Mediterranean style mansion, "is my favorite. it's as lovely inside as out. It's lucky I'm not attached to having a grand home. It's never going to happen for me."

"You could remarry someone rich."

"Generally the wealthy are the ones who don't want to change the societal status quo."

"You mean, it's the rich dudes who can afford to buy women."

"More or less. It's the men with the power who don't want to lose it." A gate opened ahead, spilling out a top-down sports car driven by a young man." He waved as he passed. "The neighbor's boy. He's a nice kid. Spoiled. The youngest of six. His oldest brother dated Yesenia for a while."

"You've live here for some time then?"

"Twenty years."

"You never wanted to remarry?"

"Are you asking?" she joked. "Let's go in an explore the idea."

Quint realized they'd circled back in front of Rosi's house. A shot of excitement zipped up his spine. His mouth watered. He swallowed. A night bird called in the distance.

"Take a test drive?" he quipped.

"Something like that."

Chapter 31

Finally—Evidence

Tuesday, October 9, 2007

Rosi dropped Quint at QRS Solutions at daybreak. Nothing stirred on the street; the apartments remained dark, the businesses closed, his digs included. Security invisible—no signs of invasion, battle, death.

"I texted; they're expecting me. I'll go upstairs, catch a couple hours more shut eye. Thanks for the evening, Rosi. Even if we didn't get much sleep." They giggled like naughty children. "Talk to you later?" he asked, then leaned over the gearbox to give her a kiss.

She turned to catch it full on. When they pulled away, she nodded. "Grrrreat!"

Quint winked at her. "Breakfast of Champions. Bye!"

He bolted the office door and was halfway up the interior stairs when the alarms wailed. *Damn!* He'd forgotten to turn off the system. So much for sneaking in. He tapped back down the stairs and ran for the panel. Martinez beat him.

"Ay *jefe,* it was a good night?" He winked as he punched in the code. The shrill electronic screams stopped. Chepe appeared.

"Morning Chepe, Martinez. So good, I forgot the alarm. Come into my office. Tell me what happened last night." He flipped on the lights. The men sprawled onto the couch. Quint swung his feet onto the desk. "We need some coffee," he mumbled, yawning. "So what happened?

"Nothing," Chepe reported. "Some guys hung around in cars. They left when the police drove by. I'm guessing you or Horacio called them?"

"Not me. H called me, said one of Nader's people was watching the office. You didn't recognize any of the others?"

"One of them. There were three cars: a late model white VW bug, license DF 287-TFC 09 Distrito Federal; a 2000 silver Nissan Tsuru, 509 LHY DF MEX; an older black Dodge Ram Charger, 729-ZUG DF MEX. Three kids in the VW, parked down the block, possibly letting off one after a night of it. I didn't see the car drive away. The Nissan parked across the street two doors down, the Ram across the boulevard kitty-corner to the building. I recognized Nader's helper from the other night. He's a cop. A dirty cop."

"How do you know, Chepe?"

"He's been around. I've been around. He was on the beat years ago in my neighborhood, shaking down the housewives for lunch money. Name's Nacho Trampoza."

Martinez added, "Now he's dealing arms with a *gabacho.* My guess? He's on the BLO payroll. Probably made the connection for Nader. What a loser."

Chepe growled, "A rich loser. Maybe Chuch can look into him.""Good idea." Quint pulled a lined pad from the desk, grabbed a pen, and handed them to Martinez. "Give me those plates again. Chuch can look them up. Speaking of Chucho, he went home with H and Leo?"

"No, bossman, he's upstairs sleeping. He's a hard worker, that kid," Chepe said.

"That he is. So Nader didn't come around?"

"No. But the bugs picked up something. Horacio called Garza with it. That's all I have, Mr. Quint."

"Anyone on duty now?"

"¿Como no? My sister's boy. He plans on going to the police academy. Likes the excitement of security work." Chepe made air quotes as he said "excitement".

The men snorted. Quint remembered how exciting even the dullest moments were when he first got to Saigon. He looked out the window. A faint line of grey lay over the apartment across the alley. "I doubt we'll be attacked now. It's getting light. Does your nephew have a car?" Chepe nodded. "Good. You guys can go home, get some sleep. The kid can finish the shift. Tell him to pass on their duties when the day shift comes on."

"Thanks, *jefe* . See you tonight," Martinez said. They got up. Chepe saluted as they stepped out the door.

Quint replayed his night with Rosi in the shower. She was a marvelous lover— enthusiastic, playful, no passive shrinking violet, she knew what she wanted and told him. Rosi delivered as good as she got. Their night had been no one-night-stand. She was clear on that. They'd talked all night, holding each other. Laughing, crying, loving. He'd never experienced anything like it. He'd loved Thuy. He had trusted her, and it had been beautiful, but that was puppy love compared to how he was feeling about Rosi Orozco. They meshed. Their bodies molded together perfectly. Two matching pieces of a puzzle. Their ideals, even their tastes in *albóndigas*. Quint lay in his bed for a little more sleep, his last thought of Rosi.

Insistent knocking pulled him from a dream. "Quint, *partner*, wake up."

"H? That you?" he croaked, eyes still closed.

"We've got a meeting with Garza and Alejo in ninety minutes. Chepe didn't tell you?"

"Christ! Thanks. I'm getting up. Any fresh coffee?"

"Mrs. P has it ready. Breakfast too. That good of a night,

eh?"

"Rosi is an amazing woman. Give me a few. I'll be right out. Chuch here?"

"Yes, but he's leaving for class soon. It's after nine."

Quint threw off the covers feeling the weight of his fifty-six years in every muscle, but he dragged himself into pressed clothes and shined shoes—*thank you, Mrs. P*—joining Horacio, Chucho and his housekeeper in the kitchen. As promised, a huge cup of steaming coffee sat at his place.

"What do you have for me, Chucho? Did you get the plates? What was the name of Nader's helper? Yeah, Nacho Trampoza."

"I did, boss. The VW is owned by a kid I go to school with. I called him. He said he was dropping off a friend who lives on the block—"

"Martinez was right then."

Chucho shrugged. "I don't know, but the Ram is registered to the wife of the man you are meeting this morning. Alejo, is it? The Nissan is registered to the embassy."

Quint frowned and banged his coffee cup on the table. "Great. Just fucking great. H, we have to play it like we are ignorant. Until we have some proof, anyway."

"I hear you, Quint. I'll watch Alejo. You ask questions. Do you want me to call Garza now to look into the Nissan? The embassy must assign cars to employees. There will be a record."

"No. We'll stay with him after Alejo is dismissed." He looked at the kitchen clock. "Mrs. P, that time correct?"

"Of course it is, Señor Quint. Why?"

"We better get a move-on then. Mrs. P, delicious as always. Thank you. See you for dinner?" He pushed his chair under the table.

"I will be here."

Mrs. P handed him a go-cup of freshly poured rocket fuel. The men headed down the back stairs to the limo.

Chapter 32

SAC Alejo

Chucho jumped out at the Insurgentes glorieta. Quint managed, "Thanks, Chuch. Have a good day at school," before horns honked and the door slammed. He turned to Horacio. "You think Alejo is involved? That's not how Miller described him. 'Bit of a zealot,' he said. A stickler for procedure, but makes poor choices. Going after me may be one of them."

"Hmmm. I don't know, Quint. Most superiors don't know their teams." He braked sharply, swerved, honking, around an idiot trying to turn left into the oncoming morning stampede down Reforma.

"Give me your thoughts. It's suspicious his wife's vehicle was parked across from our business. Do you think Nader has convinced the man we are helping the cartels?"

"It crossed my mind. If Nader is the manipulator you described, I'd believe anything of him." He slowed to make the left into the embassy's neighborhood and started trolling for parking, a nightmare at any time of day, but especially in the morning. This Tuesday was no exception. The curbs were jammed. The closer to the embassy, the worse it got. Cars blocked driveways, red zones, even stacked up double- and triple-parked.

"Christ, H. Why aren't these vehicles ticketed?" Quint asked, as they waited in line to get around two Mercedes and a Suburban triple parked blocking more than half the street.

"The police come, but the chauffeurs pull away to circle or pay *la mordita*. It's cheaper than paying valet parking."

They were moving again. "Is there valet parking?"

Horacio shrugged. He slid into a spot as another limo pulled out. "Parking juju. It's why Senator Aguirre hired me." He exploded into Shrek-like bellows of mirth. Jade was right about the Rafiq brothers resembling Shrek ogres. He was grinning as they hurried back to the entry gate.

A new fresh-faced marine greeted them, checked their IDs against the entry roster.

"Welcome to the United States, gentlemen. The ambassador is expecting you." He gestured toward the door. "Someone will escort you up."

Quint saluted, surprising the soldier, who quickly saluted in reply.

"Good morning, Mrs. Tomsky. What a lovely color sweater you're wearing today. Is he ready for us?"

The secretary smiled, obviously pleased by Quint's compliment. "Good morning, Mr. Quint, Señor Rafiq, please go right in." She pushed the intercom. "Your ten-thirty appointment is here."

"Gentlemen, pour yourselves some coffee. Alejo is on his way," Garza said.

"Thanks, Ambassador. Quickly, before he gets here, as you know, we were surveilled last night. Someone called the police. You?"

"No, I sent an embassy guard around. He reported nobody was watching your building, but it took almost an hour to get someone over there. Maybe one of the neighbors?"

"Must have been. But the good news, we identified the man we recorded helping Nader load up and sell in Neza. He's a cop, according to our team. A dirty cop. Nacho Trampoza. We also got the license plates." Quint paused to pour his cup. He seated himself in front of the desk. "The car is registered to the embassy. The Ram is registered to Alejo's wife." He passed a typewritten paper with the makes, models, and plate numbers to Garza.

The ambassador paled. "This is what I needed to start the day. So Alejo is dirty?"

"I don't know, Ambassador. We think we should keep this information under our hats for now. We'll assess his answers and investigate the information before we tip him off. The embassy has records of car usage?"

"Absolutely. The motor pool checks IDs. Employees check the vehicles out. It's probably on assignment to Alejo. If it's in the garage, we can send a tech down to take fingerprints."

"Let's hear what the man has to say first. I don't want to implicate him if this is one of Nader's shenanigans."

"Agreed, Mr. Quint, I've been mulling over the bugging tape your office sent me. What do you make of it?"

"Truthfully, Ambassador, I haven't heard it. I was out last night. I only heard about it this morning. Horacio hasn't heard it either. Can you fill us in?"

"It might be enough to call in the MPs. Unfortunately, I can't identify the voices. We aren't certain who is being threatened. Maybe you'll have better luck."

Garza swiveled his monitor and opened the file, clicking the *play* button. The sound quality was not great. Quint assumed the speaker was on a phone some distance from the bug. There was no telling what bug Nader hadn't found, but probably one placed high in a lamp or low under a piece of furniture. It didn't matter. He listened carefully.

"It sounds like Nader, but I wouldn't stake my claim on that. Horacio, could you get any of that?"

He shrugged. "Can you play it again, Mr. Ambassador?"

"Sure." Garza turned the volume up and tapped *play.*

First static then a bang, as though a door slammed. Garza stopped the replay. "Any possibility that was a gunshot?"

Quint shook his head. "Probably not, but we'll have it analyzed, Chucho can clean it up. Keep going."

Angry voices argued, but the words sounded indistinct at first. The voices got louder and the clarity improved.

"¡*Pendejo! Alg ... policía.*" the sound dropped out as though the speaker had turned away. Then Quint recognized a voice. Clear. Unmistakable, *Nader.* "Speak English," the recording garbled. "... not...police... Do what you were paid to do."

The other voice broke in, not garbled, but faint. Quint thought he must be standing in the hall or outside. "...your game. I kill the *gabacho,* you have me arrested?" the man shouted in accented English.

Nader's reply loud, threatening. He'd moved closer to the bug. "You destroy my deal with Beltrán, I won't need to have you arrested. The narcos will kill you."

"What if your (garbled) figures it out. Pendejo, using his ca..."

"We'll deal with him. Load the SUV." The sound warbled. Garza turned up his speakers again. Another bang. More unintelligible Spanish in the background interrupted by Nader. "The garage. Get to work." The rest faded to static, then silence.

Quint watched the men's reactions. Garza had shifted to stare out the window at the winged victory. It was what Quint hoped they'd have, but Horacio frowned, brow wrinkled, slight disgust playing across his face.

"You're thinking something, H."

Garza swiveled his chair to face the partners, interrupting. "He's implicated himself. You're convinced it's Nader?"

Horacio shifted in his chair, glancing at Quint. "Go on, H. Tell us."

"It's the Mexican cop, he's been hired to kill you. I think he was right—Nader called the cops. Too early. That noise in the background? Nader's new helpers."

Quint studied his coffee cup before looking up. The mid-morning sun cast a halo around Garza's head, silhouetting him.

It hurt Quint's sleep-deprived eyes. He shifted his glance to Horacio. "Something doesn't make sense. Why—"

A buzzer sounded followed by Mrs. Tomsky announcing Cesar Alejo. Garza stood to greet the CIA man as he entered the office. Quint craned around to take him in. Medium height and build, dark complexion, black, close-cropped hair. He wore a white dress shirt rolled over his elbows, collar opened with a red, white, and blue tie loosened, black polyester pants. His shoes gleamed. A career bureaucrat. He'd met plenty. The bureaucrats had a tendency to resemble each other. Not the kind of man who would naturally gravitate to a scum-bag like Nader, but possibly one who could be duped by him.

"Join us, Mr. Alejo. Please meet Mr. Quint and his partner, Mr. Rafiq. Grab a coffee."

"Good morning, Ambassador, gentlemen." He sat down. "I'm not sure why you've summoned me. How may I help?"

Garza sat up straight, fixing Alejo with a penetrating stare. Alejo squirmed slightly and looked away. Garza's voice commanded everyone's attention, "We are investigating irregularities, possibly malfeasance in conjunction with your Wide Receiver operation."

Quint studied the CIA man. Alejo's eyebrows shot up in surprise. "It's need-to-know from Washington." The set of his lips told Quint the man would not willingly divulge information.

Garza said, "You're in my house Alejo. I'm going to have to deal with the fallout if this goes sideways. If you are unwilling to start the conversation, allow me to share what I already know."

Alejo clamped his jaw. His nod was terse. Obviously Alejo did not want to co-operate.

"Mr. Alejo, you are the SAC—" he turned to Horacio to clarify. "Special agent in charge. It's an ATF op to track assault weapons sold in Mexico. The idea is to follow shipments to the end users, presumably the cartels, to eliminate them. Am I right so far?" He gave Alejo the proverbial bug-on-a-pin look. Quint was surprised the diplomat had it in him, but glad Garza wasn't grilling *him*.

Alejo remained silent.

"Mr. Alejo? You *are* in charge, are you not?"

"Yes, I head the op. Basically, Operation Wide Receiver *is* an attempt to staunch the flow of arms across the border into the hands of criminals. You may have heard of gunwalking?"

Quint nodded. Horacio and Garza shook their heads. "No, gunwalking?" Garza asked.

"It's a term for suspicious gun sales—walking—to Mexico. Wide Receiver initiated in Tucson a little over a year ago at a gun shop to monitor sales to straw buyers. You are familiar with this term?"

"Yes, third parties hired to purchase weapons for an unauthorized purchaser or in suspicious quantities," Garza explained. "Go on."

"The op was handled in a haphazard manner. ATF determined the most purchased weapons were the AR-15s, semi-automatic AK-pattern rifles and Colt 38s, but between ATF Tucson and MOC, Mexico City Operation, and Mexican Law enforcement, most of the weapons were lost. ATF planned interdiction or surveillance when the weapons reached the border, but it was a fiasco. The guns were supposed to have Raytheon tracking devices. No one followed up. The kingpin buyer was lost to another operation due to lack of inter-agency cooperation. Only sixty-four guns were recovered."

"So what are you doing here?" Quint asked.

Alejo swirled the dregs of his coffee. "I can't reveal that information, but my team, working with the Mexican Attorney General's office is looking into the issue of illegal arms trafficking. We are dedicated to stopping the rising criminal violence in Mexico."

Quint sneered, "Medina Mora? Isn't he our pal Garcia Luna's puppet?"

Garza frowned. "Mr. Quint, please. I want to hear the rest of the report. Mr. Alejo, I understand you have an operative on loan from NSA?"

"NSA? I don't think so, unless you mean Nader? I was

instructed he's a CIA advisor. An expert in weapons and arms trafficking."

"What exactly does he do for you?"

"Nader feels the way I do, Ambassador. These criminal organizations are destroying Mexico, which will have a huge impact on the United States and much of the rest of the world. Violence is rising. Thousands are being killed each year by our weapons. Our taskforce is committed to stopping the flow of arms into Mexico."

"Shouldn't you be at the border then?" Horacio asked, frowning.

"There are systems in place everywhere. We are training Mexican law enforcement in interdiction and surveillance. The Bush administration is investing millions. We shall succeed."

"What about the military grade weapons coming in? Who is stopping the thefts? Or the Chinese QBZ-97s and grenades coming in?"

Alejo's eyebrows knit, confusion played across his face. He wasn't faking it, the man didn't have the imagination, Quint thought. *Maybe he really doesn't know what Nader's up to.*

"Alejo, what kind of car do you drive?"

"What? I drive a Nissan assigned by motor pool. Why?"

"Do you have another vehicle?" Garza asked.

"Of course, I have two. My wife drives a VW. I've got a Ram I use for camping. What does this have to do with anything?'

"Where were you last night around nine?" Garza questioned.

"What? I was at home with my wife, reading a story to my five-year-old before bed." He stopped speaking, his jaw dropping. "Something happened with my Ram? Tell me what."

"Did you loan it to anyone, or was it stolen?"

"I loaned it to Agent Nader. His was in the shop."

Garza tipped his chin to Quint and Horacio. Quint grinned. *We're gonna get him now.*

"What about the Nissan. What's the license plate?" Alejo recited a number matching the plate on the surveillance car.

"Where was it last night? Did you loan that out, too?"

"Of course not. I parked in the driveway at home. Before you ask, no, the gates were locked. No one outside my family has the code."

Quint interrupted, "Alejo, you better change your gate code."

Chapter 33

Analysis and Intel

The partners agreed on one thing—Alejo came off as credulous. *With a stick up his butt.* An easy-mark for Nader. However, it might be an act; Garza ordered up an internal investigation into both. It hadn't been a wasted hour.

Horacio navigated the lunch-time commute by-passing the turn into Colonia Roma toward Navarte Poniente.

"Lunch with Sami?" Quint asked.

"*Sí.* The Lebanese place. He's got some papers for us to sign."

"The text you got."

"*Ay*, you heard that?"

"I'm not deaf yet."

"So is Alejo *estupido* or what? I didn't like him much," Horacio said.

Quint thought for a moment. It was unusual for Horacio to declare dislike. "Why? Too naive?"

"*No sé.* It's probably me. I met cops like him on the job. Think they'll make a difference—"

"Superior attitude. They'll do what no one else can."

"Exactly. Their way or no way."

"He a bureaucrat. Probably SAC because he sucks in the field." They got a laugh out of that.

Horacio wedged the limo into a space for a VW. Sami waited in front of the restaurant.

"Good timing. My neighbor just pulled out. I've got a table in the garden. Tea is ordered." He held the door for his brother and Quint. Inside he said, "Follow me." He raised his hand to a greying man in an apron and thrust his chin toward the window overlooking a patio with tables.

Their table was already laden with fresh pita bread, dips, salads, and a tray piled with wrap-style chicken sandwiches. Of course the tea and three small glasses painted in floral designs awaited them.

"Chicken shawarma," Horacio exclaimed. "And labneh. Good choices, brother."

Sami's eyes twinkled. "All your favorites, Horacio. Sit! Sit! Let's eat before it's dinnertime. Fill me in on the case."

The men ate, discussing Nader's agenda and possible illegal activities. Sami agreed to ask around about Operation Wide Receiver. He'd probably get more information than Quint would.

It was mid-afternoon before the meeting with Sami completed. They'd signed what Quint reckoned was a ream of legal mumbo jumbo allegedly making them a legal corporation. He closed his office door and settled in to contemplate the dust motes floating in the shafts of sun streaming onto his floor. Incorporating was the right thing to do, but right now a distraction from what was important—stopping Nader from killing him or anyone he loved. If only he knew why Nader was after him. Someone must know. He'd start with Laith, the most experienced of his hackers. If Laith couldn't find some dirt on Nader, he was probably SOL—shit out of luck. He dialed. A fat fly dive bombed his head. He waved it away.

"Computer office."

"Laith, please. Jackman Quint calling."

"Quint, old partner."

"Gonz? That you? What the hell're you doing answering your IT department phone?"

"You must have telepathy. The intern is scanning your invoice right now."

"The new SUV? What's the damage?

"Not bad, fifteen thousand. I found a three-year-old used Chevy Tahoe. Perfect condition, low mileage. Smoked windows. How are things down Mexico way?"

"Lucky I got a contract with the U.S. Embassy."

"Doing what?" Gonzo asked.

"Stopping Nader. It's why I called. Laith agreed to do some searches for me." He watched the fly circle in the light.

"You're not poaching my computer genius are you?"

"Nah, I've got my own and my girl has one, too. I put all three on the job. I still don't know why that rat bastard has a vendetta against me."

"Your crappy personality, bro'. Don't take it personally."

Quint frowned. "Seriously, he's threatened my daughter."

"Joking, dude. I'll pass you to Laith. Good luck, friend."

Quint listened to the buzzing fly. It was on the floor now in a pool of sunlight streaming through the glass door, flapping but no lift off. Walking in crazy circles, buzzing. Dying.

"Quint, man. Good timing."

"Yeah, Laith, I know about the invoice. What you got for me?"

"Invoice? Oh, Gonzo's SUV. No. I have something better. Hang on, let me get my notes."

Laith was back on the line in a beat. He launched into a biography of Nader. He'd researched everything from his first school to his prison term. Then it got a bit fuzzy.

"Laith, I'm impressed. Did you get into the employee records we spoke about?"

"I never give away my secrets, man. But I'll tell you, this guy has been into some serious shit. I'll send you everything I got from '68 through '75. You can decide what you need. That cat was real scum. Got paid for it, too. Finally, in '75 the agency decided he'd crossed the line when he was caught red-handed giving intel to the enemy. Only it was a plant, not an enemy agent. It took several months, but he went to prison for eighteen years. Mostly solitary."

"Not for trafficking? Did you find the agent's name?"

"No. A code-name only. Mr. Jack. Yeah drugs, too."

"Was he fired?"

"That's the odd thing, I couldn't find any termination records, but in 1994 there were records reinstating him to active duty. No duties specified, but he went to Bosnia. Looks like he made it back to Cambodia in '97. Records suggest he reconnected with some old opium contacts. He was pulled out then bounced around Africa until Afghanistan. He drops off the record in '06."

"No indication why?"

"Nothing, but what I did piece together from serval sources —every hot spot your boy went, weapons theft increased. Trafficking in military grade arms skyrocketed. I think he was sidelined, possibly given a deal—quit or go back to jail. There is proof he was organizing arms thefts, but it was sealed."

"How'd you get it?"

"Magic."

"Does your magic show who he's working for now?"

"I'll look. I've sent what I got, man. Hope it helps. I'll be in contact. Oh, hey, thanks for hooking me up with Qadir. He's top notch. A good resource. Your boy Chucho is one hella hacker too. Adios for now."

Quint glanced at the carpet by the door. The sun no longer beamed in. The fly lay lifeless in the shadow. Just like Nader when this was over.

He turned on his desk lamp. It seemed to be getting dark too early. He could barely see his notepad. He'd gone over and over the notes he'd made of Laith's intel. Everything about Nader was off. Not long after Quint, he went to prison for selling military secrets to an Asian, code-named Mr. Jack. Did

Nader think Quint was so stupid to use his first name as a code name? How could he ever be confused as Asian? No. Flimsy. Why hadn't he been fired? He'd been tried for seditious conspiracy. A clatter of shoes and voices in the hall broke his concentration. Chucho, Leo, and Horacio were joking about something in reception. He joined them.

"How were classes, boys?"

"Awesome," Leo said. "I like my school. Raafe is showing me around and introducing me. I already got an A on my maths homework." He beamed at Quint.

"That's great, Leo. After dinner, I want to talk to you. I have some news."

"About Roni?"

Quint nodded. "And Chuch, I need to see you now. How are things going with that assignment I gave you?"

"I have some information, *jefe*. I was on my way to tell you. Can you come to IT? See you later Leo, Horacio." He started down the hall.

"I'll talk to you later, H," Quint said. "Leo, I'm proud of you."

Chucho cleared the usual pile of computer books and magazines off the chair for Quint. When the desktop was visible he clicked on a file. A page of dates and notes popped open.

"What's all that?"

"I found a user name for Nader. His arms business is on Tor. This is the list of transactions I've found."

"Tor?"

"Yeah, the Torproject.org. Everyone says U.S. Intelligence developed it, but if you don't want anyone to know what you're doing, you use it. It's a browser like AOL has. "

"So there's no record of you being there?"

"Precisely. Tor makes sure there's no way for anyone to find out where I've gone. Don't worry, Nader won't ever know I've hacked his email."

"What's his email address?"

"It's a business name. Covert Tactical Sales. It's like the eBay of illegal arms. Here's one of Nader's emails." He wrote the address on an old envelope.

"You telling me I could just email him right now?"

"Sure, so long as you're using PGP for encryption. Or use his regular Gmail address." He added it to the envelope.

"I've hacked the server. Let me print these emails for you." Chucho clicked a few keys. The printer sprang to life, spitting out a couple of pages of dated conversations. He reached over to the shelf, grabbed the pages, handing them to Quint. "I could tell you more about what's here, but maybe you'd like to read them yourself. I'm pretty sure you're going to ask for transcripts of a couple other emails. Especially the one that might be arranging the theft of the rocket launchers we found."

"They were stolen then. Like we thought. Not part of the Wide Receiver Op?"

"No, *jefe*. You have proof in your hands."

Quint studied the printout. He felt almost giddy. Nader was organizing the theft of U.S. military weapons then selling them to Mexican cartels. He had copies of emails in his hands proving it. Garza kept intel on the op close to his chest. But now Quint had something to trade.

Chapter 34

A Set-Up for Blackmail?

Quint heard Mrs. P as she found the men in a huddle around Chucho's computer screens in the computer room. The room was silent beyond the thrum of electronics. Grainy black and white images playing across the three large monitors were hard to see, but one thing was certain, they were watching the commission of a murder. Mrs. P cleared her throat from the doorway. Four heads whipped around toward the noise. Chucho cut the feed.

"Mrs. P, Is it already dinnertime?"

"*Sí*, Señor Quint. *Chilis relleno* with tuna fish, your favorite jicama and orange salad, and *arroz mexicano*. Come. I have *quesadillas de hongos* to start. Coconut flan for dessert."

Leo's eyes widened; he licked his lips. "I'm starving!"

"Go help Mrs. P with the table, Leo. We'll be there in five minutes," Quint said. The housekeeper frowned. "We'll be up soon, Mrs. P. With big appetites."

"Señor Horacio, will you join us? *Hay mucha comida*."

He checked the clock. "*Gracias sí, Doña. Ya comieron en*

casa," he replied. His family had already eaten.

"You were expected, H? Better call your wife to apologize." Quint jerked his head toward the door.

Quint watched Horacio and Leo escort Mrs. P down the hall. Horacio stopped in his workroom to call home. Leo closed the stairs door behind them.

"Turn it back on, Chuch. Mrs. P is gone. I didn't want her to see that."

"Neither did I. I worked on the clarity while you talked. You'll be able to make out the man's face. Look."

After lightening the picture so the people were no longer in shadows, Chucho played the video again. More like ghosts, but now Quint could see the man aiming a handgun. He followed down the man's arm to his hand. The gun. A man running toward a gate. The arm flew up; the man crumpled, a dark stain blooming on his back. The shooter turned, holstering his gun. Nacho Trampoza. Behind him, stepping from the shadows, a profile. Quint gaped. It looked like him. He shuddered, jiggling his fingers nervously against his thigh. Nader wasn't above blackmail.

"*Jefe*, that's the guy from Nader's garage. Who did he kill?"

"I don't know who the victim is, but this was an execution. The shooter is Trampoza, a dirty cop. He's on BLO's payroll. What about the profile coming out of the shadows? Someone else was there. Can you do your magic? Make him visible?"

"I can try. He looks kinda like you, boss. Shape of his head. His nose. Is it Nader?"

"Whoa, Chuch! You think Nader and I look alike? I don't have a pot belly or steel gray hair."

Chuch tapped at his keyboard, making the image larger but not much clearer. "No, Mr. Quint, not in person, but you've both got angular faces and light hair in black and white. Your noses are similar, too. And short hair with a wave in front. See, like this guy in the shadows. You can see the wave."

"Yeah," Quint said, running his hand through the wave over his forehead. I think we are supposed to think this is me.

Can you tell when the video was made?"

"No, *jefe*. But I could see if I can get help at school. I don't think it's old—just amateur."

"I don't want this to go to school. Could that man be Nader?" Quint paced as he studied the computer screen.

"I guess so. I can't see him well enough. Why?"

He stopped pacing directly in front of the screen and leaned in, shifting his weight foot to foot. "The jacket. See? I don't own a jacket like that. I think whatever is going on here, Nader means to implicate me. But Chuch, he'll try blackmail first. It's his MO. Send the video to Laith and Qadir. Maybe one of them has more sophisticated equipment to clean it up. If that's Nader, it's all the proof we need to get a warrant."

"On it, *jefe*. Can we go eat? I'm starved."

"Send the file first. I'll let Chepe in. He can see the file after dinner."

Chucho's stomach grumbled. "Already done."

Chapter 35

History repeats

Thursday, October 11, 2007

Quint didn't feel any closer to shutting down Nader's arms trafficking, and he still puzzled over the man's vendetta against him. He spent the week intelligence-gathering, which was interesting enough, but the administrative work? Treading water. That's all. Nader must have found the last bugs, because there were no more threats or admissions of law breaking. No more videos or surveillance of what Quint was becoming accustomed to think of as the QRS Solutions office. He occasionally caught himself drumming his fingers, impatient for one of the IT departments to identify who the profile in the video belonged to. He absently stirred another spoon of sugar into his coffee. To top things off, Garza hadn't yet turned up anything through his internal investigation. The operation stalled. Not even Rosi had been available for more than a couple of phone calls. Hell, all he'd really done was send a wire transfer to Gonzo for the SUV. A big hit to the bank balance.

The inactivity was killing him. Quint was a man of action, not an administrative grunt. He checked the calendar again. Three more days until Jade came home. He looked forward to handing off some of the paperwork. He itched to get back into the field—wrap it up. When he put Nader away, it wouldn't matter much what the man's beef was with him. He could get back to work, make some cash instead of spending it. Chepe's crew didn't come cheap. He looked at the clock. The day shift would be here any minute. He should get busy on breakfast.

Quint put a steaming basket of tortillas on the table next to a bowl of scrambled eggs, and a hill of bacon strips on a platter. Mrs. P's *salsa mexicana* filled a painted clay bowl. The coffee was fresh. He was setting out the plates when the doorbell buzzed. Chepe's nephew would get it; what was his name? Quint was still trying to remember as the sound of cattle hooves clattered up the stairs, bursting into the residence. Chucho was with the security men. Good.

"¡*Buenos días, jefe*!" the men shouted in unison, a little too chipper for Quint's state of mind.

"Morning to you, too, although, I'm not so sure how good it is. Serve yourselves. Your nephew standing guard?" Chepe nodded.

Five chairs scraped as the security team and Chucho settled into eat. Quint contemplated his coffee while the men passed the trays and poured their mugs of coffee.

"What's the matter, *jefe*?" Chucho asked. "You look worried."

Chepe straightened up, a tortilla full of salsa dripping egg hallway to his mouth. "Anything we need to know, Quint?"

"Men, I have a hunch something is coming down. Chuch, share what you found online."

"The video?" Chuch asked and Quint nodded. "Yeah, well, I stumbled on a video of that cop shooting an unidentified victim. A man in profile watching the assassination looked a lot like Mr. Quint, but I sent it off to a couple of IT guys I know. I didn't tell you yet, *jefe*, because I just got confirmation this morning. It's a fake. There's no man in the shadows. It's a cut-out, like made from paper."

"What do you mean? They put an advertising poster in the picture?"

"Something like that. You said it wasn't your jacket. Laith has better software. He said there's no body, only a picture. I don't know how else they could have done it. He also said this isn't CCTV. He thinks it's a set-up, just like you said last night."

"Bossman, I'm not following." Chepe said. "Someone made a video of Trampoza shooting a man and put a carboard dummy in it that looks like you?"

Chucho thumbs upped. "Digitally, but that's what the other IT department said. The shooting is fake, too. It's all fake."

"Hey Chepe, we need to get a camera and do this. I can think of a bunch of uses for fake videos," Martinez said, through a mouthful of breakfast.

"Like blackmail," Quint sneered. "I don't have proof, but I think that's Nader's intention. Possibly to eliminate Trampoza as well. The cop has done what Nader needed—given him access to BLO. Knowing how he operates, he won't want to be sharing the profits. I saw it before—" Quint stopped speaking. His lips squeezed into tight disgust. "It's exactly what he did to me."

All eyes turned to Quint. He'd never shared his complicity in the opium business. He'd originally been forced to participate, but he'd profited. No, he hadn't been an innocent in the business. When the payoffs started coming in, he was willing to break the law. He'd been Nader's Trampoza. Greedy and willing. His stomach soured. Nader had busted him but he'd paid his debt, hadn't he? Society may have forgiven him, but Nader wasn't going to. Nader didn't turn him in to serve time—he was supposed to die. How many times during his arrest and incarceration did guys come at him? But Quint didn't have time to think about past history, he needed to make sure history didn't repeat itself.

"I wish we knew who the other man is. But men, this is

what's bothering me. We need to be particularly vigilant. Nader is coming. I feel it. Chucho, monitor everything. That video is a preview of what I'm to expect."

"You want me to add security?" Chepe asked.

"I'm not sure he'll try attacking us here again, Chepe, but I want one of you to come with me when I go out. You're armed?"

"*Por supuesto.*"

"Good. So Chep, after we finish, bring the team down—and take this plate to your nephew, he's probably hungry. We'll look at the video. I'm going to get started."

Quint shoved from the table, catching himself on the edge of the counter, his muscles rigid and his head light. This wasn't combat—Nader was toying with him. Quint didn't have any more time to muck around. He needed to stop the maniac before Jade came home.

Chapter 36

A Morning of Communications

Quint heard the stairs door slam. Rubber soles whapped into the workroom. He punched the intercom.

H? That you?

Sí, soy yo. Morning.

Got a minute?

On my way.

"New developments on the video." Quint shifted a shoulder toward the couch. Horacio sat down, setting his coffee onto the end table.

"I got the lowdown upstairs. Nader recorded a fake video with Trampoza, a digitized figure? A fake shooting? Why?'

"I'm no psychologist, but frankly?" Quint cast a penetrating look on his partner. "Nader is mentally deranged."

"It's taken you this long to figure that out?" Horacio guffawed. "The whole crew thinks he's crazy."

"Crazy like a rattlesnake. He's determined to sink his fangs into me."

"Tru dat. So?"

"I thought it was blackmail, but it's a message. This, or a close version of it, will arrive in my inbox before Monday."

"Why Monday?"

"Jade comes home Monday."

That's right. I'd forgotten the date. But how do you associate the video with JadeAnne? Did she get it? Have you talked to her?"

"No. I'll call her today. Listen. Laith did some work on it. Says it's a fake killing. The shadow figure is a digital image. I'm guessing he plans on using this in several ways: one, to have us get Trampoza arrested—or kill him. Nader probably has someone who will shove a shiv into his neck before he can get to trial. It's what he planned on doing to me. I knew too much. But I didn't die." He craned his neck around and pulled on his shirt collar. A wormy-looking scar ran from his ear to his shoulder. "The attacker probably reported I was dead. Then here I am in Mexico City thirty-three years later."

"We figured he pegged you for his arrest and stint in penitentiary."

Quint grimaced. "Bingo."

"*Pues,* beyond accusing Trampoza, what—"

"We know blackmail. Back off or he'll have me arrested for murdering Trampoza?"

Horacio thought a moment. "Flimsy. Garza won't go for that. When was the video made?"

"I don't know, but Chuch and Laith think it's a prototype or rehearsal."

"The other option?" Horacio said.

"The victim is Jade, and I'm made to watch like Nader threatened."

The clock's second hand continued its clicks, a steady heartbeat inexorably counting down the silence.

H shifted on the settee. "We should turn this over to Garza. Do we have any intel on where he is?"

Quint tapped his phone, put it to his ear. He looked at Horacio. "Chuch, do we know where Nader is? I'm here with

H. You're on speaker."

"*Buenos días. Sí.* He's at home making calls."

Horacio said, "How do you know?"

"Martinez tapped his phone."

"When did he do that? Quint, did you know?"

"Wednesday morning early before I went to class. I helped him trick the truck out with TelMex logos. It was okay, wasn't it, *jefe*? We thought it would help."

"What has Martinez heard?"

"I don't know. When he identified Nader's line at the junction box, he attached a mini recorder on it. He has to go back up the pole to get the tape. He placed a bug so we know the recorder clicks on. One of Chepe's uncles is watching the house, too."

"What the hell, Chuch? Chepe and Martinez are running their own investigation?"

"*Jefe*, you asked for three men during the day, but you and H have been here. He left two men and sent the third to be an advanced warning system. He watches the house and follows Nader when he goes out. He'll call if Nader is coming our way."

"What about at night?"

"Chepe has family up there. The young cousins are keeping an eye on the two exits from the neighborhood. Street basketball at one corner. Teens hanging out at the seedy end of *la vecindad*."

Quint laughed. "Chepe and Martinez have a regular spy ring. When did they plan on telling me?"

"As soon as they have something, *jefe*. All Nader has done since Tuesday is buy food."

"And Trampoza?"

"*No sé.*"

"Thanks, Chucho." He disconnected.

"I'm surprised. I'm not sure what to think, H. I wonder if Chepe's going to bill me for the extra manpower. Speaking of money, I didn't tell you. Gonzo's SUV cost me $15,000. I wired it the other day."

"We going to have enough to make it until we bill the embassy?"

"I'll worry about that when Nader is behind bars. I've got to read this transcript of emails. What are you working on?"

"I asked Sami to nose around for dirt on Trampoza this morning. I've been connecting with some old friends from the force. I'll have lunch with a couple of guys I know who worked with Trampoza. After, I'll read the records of disciplinary actions and complaints against him. Gomez and I always got along. He's in charge of records."

"Sounds good. Chucho is off school today. He and I are going to do a little hacking—after I call Jade." He checked his watch. "Which I'll do now, before she goes out."

Horacio collected his mug and rose to go. "More coffee, Quint?"

"Please. Save some time to meet with me this afternoon before quitting."

"Will do."

He knew it was going to be another long day of administrative thumb-twiddling. He better make a list. If Susana were here, he'd have her type an agenda, dial the calls, manage the employees, leaving him with the interesting bits. Quint wondered if he was cut out to be the COO of a company. Maybe Horacio was better suited for that role. But that would leave him the odious task of finding clients—the front man. Quint sighed then fished a ruled pad from under the pile of accumulated notes, mail, messages, and receipts. He started a list.

>*Call Jade
>*Return Charley Stone's call
>*Call Garza for an appointment
>*Finish reading the emails and meet with Chuch
>*Get a briefing on Qadir's investigation into

Nader
*Call Chepe
*Arrange with Mrs. P to clean and shop
*Figure out what a CEO does
*Dinner with Rosi?

Looking at the list, it didn't feel so oppressive. He tapped the number for Jade's landline. It rang twice.

"Dylan speaking."

"It's Quint. How are things going? Where's our girl?"

"Hey, man, good to hear your voice. Is everything okay?"

"Things have been quiet for the past couple of days. Is the bodyguard on duty?"

"Jade hates having him follow her around. Especially because he's buddies with Dex. She says he's spying on us."

"Where is she?

"Driving him crazy chasing her around the track while she runs."

"My daughter reminds me of me. How's Pepper?"

"Upset by all the packing. Twice he's gotten out and gone to the office. He curls up under Jade's old desk. Dex said he's going to keep him, upsetting her. She's questioning the move. But it's too late to back out now. All the contracts are signed; she's received the first payment. Half her stuff is packed and stored. We agreed we'd come back for what we need when we find a place to live. She'll sell the rest. She's renting the place partially furnished."

"That's smart. By the way, has Jade received any videos by email?"

"Not that I know of. Why?"

"One of Nader's tricks. It's a fake. She's not to worry. I think it's some sort of warning to me. I wouldn't mind talking to Qadir, though. Maybe she could tell him to call."

"You can call him."

"Don't want to upset Dex. You two are still coming on Monday?"

"That's the plan. Mexicana out of San Francisco, Flight

1526 arriving at 4:42. You picking us up, or shall I ask someone else? We'll have a lot of luggage."

"I plan on being there. I'll ask H for the limo, but if something happens, he'll come or I'll call Seeger and Dafne. Don't worry, someone will meet you."

"Thanks, Quint. Jade will kill me if I don't ask how your date with Rosi went."

"Tell her it went well. We have a dinner date tonight."

"Twice in a week? It went better than well. Good for you. She's lovely."

"She is. Please give Jade a hug. Pat the dog. I'll see you soon. Monday at 4:42."

The thought of Jade's homecoming lifted Quint's spirits. The day didn't feel so claustrophobic. He turned to the next task with a modicum of optimism. Charley Stone had some news for him.

Again he got a message machine. Maybe he should call the office, but Charley may not be as forthcoming from his 30th floor San Francisco corner office with magnificent bay views. He left a message asking Charley to email him with the highlights of his report when he had time—he'd be out until late tonight. He crossed his first two tasks off the list. Next was an appointment with Garza. In light of the new information about Martinez wiretapping the phone and Chepe arranging neighborhood surveillance, he'd be better off seeing Garza tomorrow. He texted: *H, you free to see Garza tomorrow if I can get an appointment? Anytime. Let me know.*

Horacio replied: *Will do.*

He called Mrs. Tomsky. The ambassador would see them at two. He ticked it off his list then stood up to stretch and refresh his coffee. Maybe Mrs. P had arrived. He'd brew a new pot of coffee while they planned Jade's homecoming. He trudged up the stairs.

The housekeeper hadn't shown up. One of the security men sat at the table with fresh coffee, talking on his phone. He hung up when Quint came in.

"Sorry *jefe*, I'm on my break and we needed some coffee. It's alright I made it?"

"Sure, man, you saved me having to do it," Quint said while filling his cup. "Anything going on?"

"Nothing. Normal neighborhood activity."

Quint thanked him then trudged back down the steep stairs to his desk. He couldn't put it off any longer. The list of Nader's emails awaited him. Why he dreaded reading it, he didn't understand. Maybe he feared the truth, but now was the time. No one was going to interrupt him. If the emails revealed anything illegal on Nader's part, he'd have Garza's proof.

Chapter 37

Email Evidence

from: <ctsnader@gmail.com>
to: <lonewolff@gmail.com>
date: October 3, 2007 4:27 PM
subject: Project Update
mailed-by: gmail.com
signed-by: gmail.com
security: Standard encryption (TLS)

Received shipment. Part missing.
Full payment when received.
Same shipping arrangements.
~Chuck

from: <lonewolff@gmail.com>
to: <ctsnader@gmail.com>
date: October 3, 2007 6:28 PM
subject: Re: Project Update
mailed-by: gmail.com
signed-by: gmail.com
security: Standard encryption (TLS)

Don't fuck with me, Nader. Wire the payment. You'll get the grenades when I get the money.

from: <ctsnader@gmail.com>
to: <lonewolff@gmail.com>
date: October 4, 2007 2:12 AM
subject: Re: Project Update
mailed-by: gmail.com
signed-by: gmail.com
security: Standard encryption (TLS)

That wasn't our arrangement. We'll follow our agreement or I'll find a new supplier.

from: <lonewolff@gmail.com>
to: <ctsnader@gmail.com>
date: October 3, 2007 7:47 AM
subject: Re: Project Update
mailed-by: gmail.com
signed-by: gmail.com
security: Standard encryption (TLS)

Are you threatening me?

from: <ctsnader@gmail.com>
to: <Trampoza@gmail.mx>
date: October 5, 2007 11: 00 AM
subject: Require your help
mailed-by: gmail.com
signed-by: gmail.com
security: Standard encryption (TLS)

Deal set. Come to warehouse Friday at 9

from: <Trampoza@gmail.mx>
to: <ctsnader@gmail.com>
date: October 5, 2007 12:17 PM
subject: Re: Require your help
mailed-by: gmail.com
signed-by: gmail.com
security: Standard encryption (TLS)

Need another man?

from: <ctsnader@gmail.com>
to: <Trampoza@gmail.mx>
date: October 5, 2007 12: 51 AM
subject: Require your help
mailed-by: gmail.com
signed-by: gmail.com
security: Standard encryption (TLS)

No. Bring your equipment.

Quint read through the thirty or thirty-five emails. Nader engaged in thinly veiled conversations with Trampoza about the arms deals and some of the attacks on Quint. Nader described the video in an email to Trampoza dated the 7th as "a good rehearsal." If nothing else, he could cause Nader some grief for harassment. Chuch was right. Quint had a list of emails for him to look into. Top name—lonewolff. Whoever lonewolff was, he supplied the grenade launchers, Quint was sure of it. Chucho needed to find out who that joker was. Quint could shut him down with a couple of calls if he was military.

It frustrated him he couldn't see the correspondence on that Tor thing. Why didn't Nader use it for all his email if it was untraceable? Trampoza probably wasn't too computer savvy, but lonewolff? The arms brokers, Mr. Chanthavong and someone called Mr. Chin? Well, he would get to the bottom of it with Chucho's help.

He stood up to stretch and search out a fresh cup of coffee. He gazed through the window at his private patio, realizing the patch of visible sky was actually blue. He stepped outside. A warm, clear day greeted him. How did office workers stand being inside under electric lights all day? He'd go up. Speak to Mrs. P about getting ready for Jade's arrival and see if Chucho wanted to go grab some lunch. He had a hankering to sit in a sunny restaurant patio with a torta or some enchiladas.

Upstairs, Mrs. P hummed along with an old standard on the radio as she patted out tortillas from a bowl of masa.

"Good morning Mrs. P," he said as he entered the kitchen.

She jumped, exhaling sharply. "*Ay*, Señor Quint, you startled me."

"*Lo siento,* I didn't mean to scare you. You're just who I wanted to see. What are you making?"

"Masa for *panuchos yucatecos* for dinner. You will want to eat when Mr. Chepe and Mr. Martinez arrive, *¿sí*?"

"Mrs. P, you're a mind reader. I thought I'd invite Chucho out for lunch. Horacio has a lunch meeting. It's a fine day. We've been inside too much. Would it be an imposition to ask you to make tortas for the security men?"

"*Ya listo. Tortas de atun y ensalada de jicama y naranjo.*"

"What would I do without you, Mrs. P? By the way, did I tell you JadeAnne comes home on Monday? We're picking her up at the airport around five o'clock. You'll be here when we arrive?"

"The señorita is coming home! Of course I'll be here. I'll prepare her favorite supper with *crepas de cajeta* for dessert."

"What did a man like me ever do to deserve you, Mrs. P?"

"I was going to have the weekend off, Mr. Quint, but if it's all right, I'll take the afternoon until dinner and plan on working Sunday to grocery shop and clean the residence for the señorita."

"Thank you for reminding me; I forgot about the cleaning. I'd really appreciate anything you can do to make her homecoming happy. Have you considered moving back in when Jade comes—once we've dealt with our current problems, I mean."

"I plan on it. How is your investigation going? Chucho says he found some critical information on that internet."

"It's true. Chucho is a magician. I may have enough to take to the ambassador."

"*Pues, buenos suerte*, señor." Mrs. P tested another ball of masa. She deemed it the correct consistency then scooped the dough from the bowl, wrapped it in a double layer of plastic, and put it into the refrigerator. "So it doesn't dry out." She pulled her sweater and handbag from behind the door and wished Quint a pleasant afternoon.

He grinned. His housekeeper was a marvel. At least now that she'd fully embraced him. No more spying or lies, Mrs. P was an ally Quint couldn't imagine doing without. He hurried downstairs to get Chucho and find a sunny patio. They had some interesting emails to discuss and some planning to do.

Chapter 38

Chucho Makes a Date

Chucho knew a charming café within close walking distance. The patio was surrounded by tall shrubs and wooden fencing. Metal tables filled the open space, some with colorful umbrellas, others in the dappled shade of a row of jacarandas at the back. They claimed one of those tables. Quint positioned himself to face the entrance. Nader could be coming for him at any moment. He wasn't letting his guard slip.

A cute waitress flirted with Chucho as she took their orders. She looked to be about his age. After she went inside to put in the orders, Chuch admitted she was in one of his classes. She'd mentioned the café.

"She an attractive young woman," Quint said.

"Yeah, I kind of want to ask her out."

"Why don't you? She's in your class? Is she a computer whiz, too?"

"Better than I am. But I think she has a boyfriend."

"So what? Ask her to coffee. Find out if she has someone. Take her in your new Beemer when we get it."

"You found one!"

"Not yet, but H is looking. Go for a coffee date on campus first. It's safe and sufficiently impersonal enough she'll probably say yes. It's what I'd do. If it turns out she's single, ask her for dinner and a film. Girls like that."

The waitress returned with their drinks. "Magalí, this is my *jefe, Señor Quint.*"

Quint stood. They shook hands. "Nice to meet you, Magalí. I'm impressed with your course at UNAM. Chuch is invaluable to my organization. How much longer do you have to graduate?"

She smiled. "Two more years, señor. Chucho is top of the class. I better get your lunches. Nice to meet you." She sashayed off.

"See that walk, Chucho? She wants you to ask her out." They laughed. "Call her after work. You'll see. Speaking of work, I read the emails. You know what I'm going to ask—"

"Will I hack Trampoza and that lonewolff address? Who else? The Chinese guy?"

"Don't bother with him. It's clear what's going on. He sold Nader the Chinese grenades. Probably the rifles, too."

"I already hacked into Trampoza's server. He never deletes anything— made it easy. I found the emails introducing Nader and his weapons. There's been talk about the coming war with Sinaloa. What they need to stockpile. Trampoza knows about the weapons in Nader's locked room. He told the Beltráns they're stolen. He gave whoever he's talking to an inventory. Hinted he might be able to secure the weapons without paying."

Quint was sipping his *horchata* when Chucho revealed this last. He nearly choked, spraying *horchata* all over the table. He swallowed. "You mean, Trampoza is suggesting stealing the stockpile, or killing Nader for it?"

"His contact said something like, 'it has to look like an accident'. Trampoza said that was easy. The contact asked if Nader could get more, or if he, Trampoza, had a connection with the seller. To this the cop said no. I don't think Trampoza is handy with the computer."

"I don't either. This is good stuff, Chuch. It confirms what we thought—stolen arms for a coming cartel war. What about the seller? lonewolff@gmail.com."

"His name is Specialist Wolfgang Becker-Hurtaldo. He's a Specialist in the U. S. Army stationed at Yuma Proving Ground Army Base in Arizona. That's where the weapons are tested. It has a depot of every kind of weapon. He works there."

"Find out his superior officer, Chuch. I think I'll give him a call. I'll need all the emails like you gave me for Nader."

"I've already printed lonewolff and Trampoza separately."

"Good man. How's your lunch?"

"*Muy rico*. Yours?"

"Same. Thanks for bringing me here." The waitress finished serving a nearby table, and Quint signaled for the check. Magalí nodded, headed inside, returning shortly with her card reader.

"Lunch was delicious, thank you," Quint said as he scrawled a few loops on the machine. "We'll definitely come often." He handed it back and rose to leave.

Magalí turned to Chucho, giving him a flirtatious smile. "I'm so glad you brought your boss by. See you in class?"

"See you at class. Um, would you like to have a coffee with me after school in the student cafeteria one day?"

Her smile lit up her face. With eyes twinkling, she said, "Sure. Monday after Carrera's class?"

"See you then." Chucho waved and hurried after Quint.

Chapter 39

Someone to Do the Job

"I don't like it. Nader's been too quiet," Horacio said. "There hasn't been an email since the seventh. Our bugs haven't picked up anything—"

Quint shrugged. "H, he had the place swept. We knew he'd find them."

The team congregated in Quint's office. The day waned, electric lights casting a warm glow, but tension filled the room.

Chepe paused mid-stride in his pacing. "But my *halcones* haven't seen his SUV, and our stakeout hasn't reported any movement. It's like he doesn't exist. Or he disappears like Harry Potter."

"I agree, he's like a ghost. Maybe Specialist Wolfgang Becker-Hurtaldo got him. He threatened Nader."

Martinez popped the top off another Corona. "The phone tap proves he's home. He's ordered food and talked to someone he calls Butchie or Butcher. I'm guessing he's an NSA buddy or his cellmate. You heard the tape. They shoot the shit. I'm guessing he's using burner phones for business. He must be working in *la madrugada* when our watchers are sleeping, but the security guys already take two ten-hour shifts: five a.m. to three p.m. and three to one a.m. If we want 24-hour surveillance, we add a man or use cameras."

"Play it again, Martinez?"

Martinez rewound then punched play on the mini-recorder. For ancient equipment, the sound was clear:

Nader: Yeah.

Butchie: Hey Chuck, what's going on?

Nader: Not much. How about you, Butchie? Any news?

Butchie: Work is slow. Our friend got transferred. I'm hanging loose.

Nader: Takin a break, that's good news.

Butchie: I thought I'd visit California. They say October is the best weather on the San Francisco bay. Maybe learn to scuba dive.

Nader: Lot's to do in the Bay Area, but the water up there is too cold. Anyway, I owe you one. Fly down here on your way home. We'll go over to Cancun and dive together.

Butchie: Sounds good, bro. I'll come collect on that offer. Anything I can bring you?

Nader: Maybe some of that San Francisco sourdough bread. And plenty of photos.

Butchie: You got it man. I'll send my itinerary.

Nader: Thanks Butcher. See you soon.

The line went dead. The men looked at each other. Horacio shook his head. Chepe shrugged. Martinez' face was blank. His English was too limited to understand much. Only Chucho lit up, grinning.

"Chuch, what's with the face?"

"*Jefe*, think about it. The guy's name is B-U-T-C-H-E-R. Doesn't that mean *carnicero*? And he's going to California? Then Nader says he owes him something—to bring photos? I think Butcher is an assassin."

Quint shivered as chills raced through him. Nader didn't need to go anywhere. He had someone to do the job for him.

"Chucho, can you search right now for news of Becker-Hurtaldo—the friend that got transferred? Maybe it was to the morgue. If that's correct, I'm flying to San Francisco tonight."

"On it, *jefe,*" he said, as he trotted out of Quint's office.

"I don't understand, bossman, why would you go there?"

Horacio interjected. "Quint's daughter is there. Nader threatened to kill her." He leaned forward and scrutinized his partner. "Quint, you checked your email for the video recently?"

Quint shouted after his IT specialist. "Check my email, too!"

The tension thickened like a custard cooking. The team held its collective breath until Chucho called over the intercom. "*Jefe,* no video, but I sent you a newspaper article from the Yuma Daily News dated today."

Quint clicked open his email to retrieve Chucho's message. The front page headline read, "U.S. Army Yuma Proving Ground weapons Specialist Found Dead." Quint skimmed the short paragraph then read it aloud. "Army Specialist Wolfgang 'Wolf' Becker, 34, was found dead in an arroyo near the weapons testing ground with a knife wound to his throat early Thursday morning after being reported missing on October fifth. The knife was found near the body, but the killer has not been identified. Becker's wallet, watch, and iPhone were intact. Sources suggest Becker may have been involved with recent thefts of weapons, including several Stinger MANPADS, cases of grenade launchers and M16 assault rifles. Base police are looking into the thefts."

"Good call, Chuch. *Carnicero*-the Butcher. But there's a lot of maybes. Maybe the California bit was to get you out of town. Maybe it's a set-up to cause confusion so he can attack here. We have enough now to go to Garza," Horacio counseled.

"Appointment at four tomorrow." Quint's voice sounded flat.

Horacio shot his partner a worried look. "Then let's get the evidence prepared for the meeting. Martinez, when did that call come through?"

"Not sure. I'm guessing sometime this afternoon."

"But he's been dead for a week?" Horacio said.

"'Transferred' is code for discovered? I don't know, but the article and the call are no coincidence," Chepe said.

"No. Probably not," Horacio agreed.

Quint slumped in front of his monitor, scrolling. He suddenly straightened up. "Men, I think I know what Nader's motivation is." He paused, reread something, then said, "H, I got a message from Jade's father today. He got hold of transcripts from Nader's trial and some documents submitted as exhibits from an expert witness for the defense. A psychiatrist. He testified Nader is bipolar, paranoid, and delusional. In evaluation, Charley Stone said he ranted about me stealing his woman. He accused me of trying to take down his organization. The transcripts document Nader accusing me of turning him in, which I'd already guessed, for crimes I committed. Of course, I was in the pen at the time he claimed this went on. There's more. Allegedly I stole his woman and kidnapped his child before they got him on meds to put him on trial." He shook his head in disbelief.

"I guess he's off his meds again," Chepe said, obviously attempting to add levity to the moment. No one laughed.

"I feel him coming. Men, I can feel it. We need to be ready." The doorbell rang. Quint checked the time—Rosi. He'd forgotten their date. "It's Rosi. I'll invite her to dinner. You men, go up. Mrs. P has it ready. We'll organize a defense while we eat. Let's go."

Chapter 40

I Can Feel It Coming

By the end of dinner, something resembling a plan was in place. Chepe called some cousins to patrol the neighborhood. Martinez supplied everyone with burner phones and weapons from the stash in his utility truck. The day shift was sent to Jardines de San Mateo in Rosi's car to monitor Nader's movements, relieving Chepe's people already staked out. Horacio was tasked to collect Chepe's uncle, a cop, to protect them, then drive Mrs. P and Rosi to San Angel. H agreed the limo was too identifiable. He'd garage it and taxi back. Martinez changed the signage on his truck to a commercial laundry service then parked it around the corner by the park. Chepe moved his car into a neighbor's driveway behind the gate. Finally, Quint issued weapons and instructions to his team.

Dinner's Yucatecan chicken stuffed cornmeal dumplings lumped in his stomach, making him feel heavy and nauseous. They probably had been delicious, but tension killed his taste buds. The men seemed to enjoy them. Mrs. P left happy, if not a little afraid. Rosi said she'd take good care of the housekeeper. She winked and gave Quint a kiss he ought to remember. All he could think of was Jade. He escaped to his office, pulled his curtains closed, and called Dex Trouette, Jade's former business partner.

"Trouette."

"Dex, this is Jackman Quint."

"Quint. Thanks for the payment. What can I do you for?"

"Get Jade, Dylan, and the dog to somewhere safe. I'm emailing you some documents now that explain. They'll back up the bizarre tale I'm going to tell you."

"She's not going to do anything I say, man."

"Bodily carry her away if you have to. Go to the police. Place the three of them into protective custody. An assassin who goes by Butcher or Butchie has been hired by a man named Chuck Nader to kill her. Charley Stone can verify information on Nader. Are you looking at the documents?"

"This is crazy. I doubt the police will listen to me, but I'll go for Jade now."

"I'll call Charley and ask him to meet you at the dock."

"Why not send them to him?"

"Nader knows him. We all served in Vietnam together."

"This is some beef from the '60s?"

"Seventies, but yes. Thanks for caring for my girl, Dex." Quint ended the call.

Charley agreed to meet Dex. He promised to text when Jade was safe.

Quint slumped into his chair, exhausted. Garza wasn't answering. It was down to waiting. The silence was uncanny. Quint could always hear the noises: sirens, backfires or doors slamming, laughter, arguments, TVs, music. The city was holding its breath waiting for the attack. Tonight? Nothing. He hauled himself up, turned off the lights, crept past reception, nodding to the shadow of H's retired cop friend working sentry duty at the door, and dragged up to the residence. He really wanted a shot of whisky. No, if he were he honest, he really wanted to be free. Free of Chuck Nader. Free to live without violence or fear.

His post was the living room, watching the connecting roofs to the south, along the alley and garden to the garage. He positioned himself at the window behind Jade's potted palm with a pair of binoculars and his infrared goggles. It was like the jungle all over again. Fighting for freedom. Again and again and again. His life had been a continuous struggle for freedom from something.

He scoffed softly. Freedom? Who was free? Not even men like Nader were truly free. His kind, like cockroaches, swarmed where they could thrive as they exploited a rotten situation, exploited the very concept of freedom. Nader had robbed Quint of his. He'd conned a kid with friendship, importance, and heroin then showed his true colors when Quint was addicted to drugs. Just like his country. A lot of promises. A lot of rhetoric. He saw what happened when the NVA launched their final campaign to claim South Vietnam. America pulled out, leaving the people they'd come to save to bear the brunt. Thuy. She hadn't needed to die. Quint could have gotten them to America. But Nader lied, cheated, betrayed. Did he really rape her? Father Jade? Kill her? Quint didn't believe much of what Nader claimed. He was a sociopath who loved mayhem. But Quint was tired of mayhem.

Nader had suffered, too. Mental illness. Surely that robbed him of his freedom. And Quint knew what prison did. His phone dinged. Texts.

Team #1 *Nader's on the move*

Team #2 *We're behind him*

He texted his men on site: *It's started—thirty minutes.*

He texted Garza. *Send the police to my office.*

No, Nader wasn't getting a pass, He'd fucked up Quint's life. Now he'd pay. Maybe Quint would never be free, but he'd make sure he and his were free of Chuck Nader.

A surge of energy bolted through him. After the agonizing days of office administration, he finally felt alive. Purposeful.

Quint straightened up, put on the goggles. His domain turned to a Martian landscape, green, a bit fuzzy, weird shaped formations poking up where pipes and chimneys stood during the day. Nothing moved. A few lights from the apartment across the way shown like brilliant suns, but mostly greenish shadows pressed into the roofs then sank into the alley. The kitchen clock thundered the seconds through the silent house. Twenty minutes.

Another text arrived.

Dex: *It was a hassle, but Stone got them to a hotel. All are safe for now.*

Quint texted back: *Thanks. Shit is about to hit the fan.*

Dex: *Good luck man.*

Ten minutes. Quint clicked his commlink twice: Ready? The men, in pre-arranged order, replied: one click. Yes.

He prayed Nader didn't try out one of his stolen Stingers. Chepe and Martinez were on the ground with grenades. Chucho and Horacio carried them, too. H's cop buddies carried their service revolvers along with an assortment of semi-automatic rifles. He'd finally relented; Chucho carried the Uzi.

God, let them keep the battle on the street.

Suddenly, the silence rent with screeching tires, car doors slamming.

H texted: *Trampoza and three guys entering the callejon*

Quint bolted for the back door. He wasn't going to kill the dirty cop, he was going to have him arrested. No one would do anything until Nader arrived. Unless they had to.

Trampoza's team crept around the garage toward the walled garden. Quint watched as Trampoza hand-signaled the men to their stations. The first, carrying a coiled length of rope, to the corner of the wall behind the tree; the man wearing a hoodie crept up the back stairs; the last to the gate. They all carried semi-automatic weapons slung over their shoulders. None of Trampoza's men looked familiar under the infrared glasses, but Quint recognized their movements. Police or military? Trampoza pulled a balaclava from his jacket pocket, yanking it over his head. The third man donned his own. The attackers headed to their assigned stations. Did Trampoza think they would breach the wall? They were in for a surprise. They might get over the jagged glass, but the razor wire hidden in the foliage would be a problem, and so would the barbed wire extending up from the top. Electrified, as was the gate. He'd already flipped the switch.

Trampoza watched from the alley as his men took their positions then slinked back behind the garage toward the street. What was he up to? Quint hadn't noticed him communicate with anyone, but it might have been a click or buzz from a device in a pocket. Maybe Nader had arrived. He texted the roof team. Two clicks—no. He called Chepe. "Nader?"

"No, bossman. Not yet. Anything on your side?"

"Trampoza. Three men. Armed. Two to come over the wall. The third on the stairs. It looks like they're waiting for something. Nader, probably, just like us."

"Trampoza?" Chepe inquired.

"Scuttled out of sight after his men were in position. *Cucaracha.*"

"No, Chucho's text says he's gotten back into his vehicle."

"Wearing the balaclava? Now that's not going to attract attention on the street."

They snickered. "*Nacos,*" Chepe said. "What's taking Nader so long? He's six minutes behind."

"Lemme check with the roof team." Quint tapped the communication device. "Any sign of Nader from up there?"

Two clicks.

"Chepe, they can't see his SUV. Is there any possibility he could be in the park with a Stinger?"

"Anything is possible, but he'd have to be a magician to hit us. He'd take out the apartment building first, or most of our block."

"That's what worries me. You have anyone on the park?"

"Two men. Texting now."

Quint listened to dead air for a minute until Chepe returned. "Bossman, the SUV is in the park. Nader has two guys with him. My cousin pulled past on his motorcycle. Said they're unloading something from a crate."

"Did he see any marking on the crate?"

"He couldn't make out what it said. Too dark, but their jacket pockets bulge."

"Grenades." Quint texted the entire team.

"Martinez says they're on the move. Two headed his way. One up the street in front."

"With pockets full of grenades?" They snickered again.

"Keep me posted," Quint said.

Quint alerted his team to be on the lookout for Nader. It surprised him Nader would wander from his SUV. That wasn't his usual practice. He always stayed close to his quick exit. Maybe he planned to escape in Trampoza's vehicle, he considered while he stationed himself in the corner bedroom with the view of the roof and street. He had a middling view of the block through the trees, but the night goggles helped. He held his gaze on a spot about three quarters down the block. Movement on the sidewalk caught his eye. He couldn't make out a face, but the familiar gait identified Nader. A telescope over his shoulder. Just back from a jaunty stroll through the park to look at the stars before bed. All he needed was a little dog on a leash, the bulges in his pockets tennis balls for a game of catch.

Nader closed in on the office building. Quint saw him clearly now, speaking to someone on the phone as he walked. It wasn't a telescope. He texted Chucho and asked if Trampoza was on the phone. One click. Quint sucked in a breath. Only moments to go. Nader crossed the street, disappearing from sight. Thirty more seconds and H's cop friends would converge on the car. He sent out a text: *everyone ready?* Clicks poured in.

Sirens wailed in the distance, coming in their direction. The backdoor window shattered. The door banged opened before a thud on the landing shook the house. Horacio thundered after the hoodie wearing interloper, shouting. Quint watched the alley from his perch behind the palm. The man at the gate grabbed the top. He jumped marionette-like before dropping to the ground. He couldn't see the man with the rope, but Quint's lookout on the roof of the apartment building reared up shouting a warning. Too late, the garden lights flickered. The attacker grabbed the electrified wire. Quint bolted for the kitchen. The ruckus was getting louder, coming closer. No thug was going to disturb the peace and organization of his housekeeper's kitchen.

He met the fight at the pantry door. Trampoza's man had one hand grasping at Horacio's throat with a large can of tomato juice in the other. Quint batted away his hand quashing the thugs' attempt to bean Horacio with the can. Quint grinned as Horacio balled his fist, sending an uppercut into the man's chin. The thug flew backwards into his arms. He had the man down, arms locked behind his back before the man knew what hit him. H pulled a couple of long tie wraps from somewhere to bind his wrists and ankles.

"Mrs. P isn't going to like what this clown did to her pantry, *jefe*," Horacio said, over the whoops and wailing of the sirens.

Quint let out a hoot. "Tru dat." He dragged the man into the pantry rubble then backed out, locking the door. "Get going. Your guys are grabbing Nader."

They clattered down the wooden steps, running around the garage to the street. Blue lights flashed from the roofs of five patrol cars, cutting-off the block, Trampoza's vehicle caught in the middle of the fray. A Silver Nissan Tsuru. Trampoza was on his belly in the street. A young cop kneeled on his back, holding him down as he roared obscenities between identifying himself as police. Quint couldn't see any other detainees.

"Where's Nader?" he shouted over the mayhem.

Dumfounded, Horacio gaped. "Not here." He pulled out his phone and thumbed a message. The phone dinged. "Chucho said Nader never appeared. His men didn't come either."

Quint clenched his fists and howled at the night sky. "You mean two men with hand grenades and one with a grenade launcher are loose in the neighborhood? H, notify whoever is in charge here." He pulled the commlink from his pocket, yelled into it. "Everyone—into the street. Now! Get away from the building. Get away from the building!" He ran toward the alley.

His phone buzzed. "Yeah," he gasped.

"Bossman, Nader ran. He must have contacted his men. Martinez saw them turn around and run back toward the park. Confirmed the SUV peeled outta there like it was on fire. My cousin followed them. We'll know more when he reports in."

"The man on the motorcycle, Chepe? I hope he's careful." Quint disconnected and ran into the alley.

It was already filled with police. He needed to catch Nader, not spend the evening giving statements. Yet, he needed the information Trampoza's men were providing. It could be essential. Luckily neither had been electrocuted to death, although the man who grabbed the gate sported severe burns across his palms. The other man looked dazed but unharmed. Must have hit his head on the pavement when he fell. Horacio was already interrogating the pair with one of his old friends from the force when Quint interrupted.

"Who are they? What were they supposed to do?"

The officer jerked his thumb toward Quint. "Who the hell is this?"

"My business partner, Jackman Quint, Raf. Quint, Rafael Mendoza, my partner from the precinct."

The men shook. Quint asked, "So who are these jokers?"

Raf said, "Two-bit players. Hired muscle. Hired guns. We've met before, haven't we, boys?"

The men snarled unintelligibly. Quint picked up "*chigate pendejo*" and a couple other ripe epithets.

"What was the job?"

"They clammed up when I asked. With the weapons they're carrying, I think assassination. Too much hardware for a typical B & E." Raf kicked the closest man. "Hey asswipe, what was the plan tonight?"

The man responded with, "Ask Trampoza."

"Oh, we will. Don't worry about that."

The other man piped up, "Where's Beni?"

Horacio said, "Beni, the guy broke in? He's safe." He turned to Raf, cocked his chin toward the back door. "Locked in our pantry."

Raf sent two officers to retrieve Beni. While he gave orders, Quint motioned H aside. "Trampoza is driving Alejo's car again. Something fishy going on."

The officers half dragged the trussed Beni down the stairs. He swore, shouting, calling down the wrath of the heavens on the police, and especially Trampoza. He was the one to interrogate.

The officers added Beni to the huddle. Raf started the questioning, letting up when Horacio asked to intervene. Beni took one look at H and tried to crabwalk away. H grabbed the neck of his tee-shirt and twisted. "What were you supposed to do here tonight?"

"Ask that fuck Trampoza. He got us into this. Said an easy job. B & E grab the cash in the safe. Get out."

"A lot of weapons for robbery. Were you going to shoot the safe open? Why were you going upstairs? Trampoza cased the place—he knows where the safe is."

"Ask him. He gave us the guns and told us what to do. That's it." He shut up.

Quint studied the men while Raf and H interrogated. He recognized gang tattoos, probably received in prison. One had BELTRAN tattooed up his arm. He pushed into the conversation. In halting Spanish he asked, "Does your boss Hector Beltrán know you're breaking into gringo's houses? Gringos he's dined with? I bet he wouldn't like that. Shall I call him?" He pulled out the phone. "Tell him what you've been up to?"

251

The detainees had the decency to look scared. Good. It meant this was all Nader. But he'd crawled back under his rock.

Chapter 41

New Complications

Friday, October 12, 2007

Under cover of the mayhem around them, the partners slipped into the street to meet Chepe and Martinez. The danger at home was over for tonight, Quint thought. They piled into Martinez' truck. After he and Horacio paid a visit to the cockroach, he might drive Rosi's car back to her. He smiled at the memory of her arms, her kisses. Her body on his.

"Quint are you listening to me?" H shouted over the noisy truck.

"Sorry, H. Thinking about that video. Can you find out if the police have it yet? I think this was the set up to take Trampoza out. If they have the video, it proves my theory. Anyone in the precinct dirty you know of? Maybe the dirty cop with a knife, or the interrogator who beats him to death with his stick." He grabbed the edge of a supply cabinet as the truck made a sharp right turn.

"Nader is planning to take him out, you think?"

"Makes sense. It might have been Trampoza killed the supplier."

"I don't see Trampoza using a knife," H said, shaking his head.

"And the conversation wouldn't make sense if it was him. You're right. But he set me up to land in prison. Thinking back, I had several close brushes with death after I was arrested. The cop has fulfilled his usefulness. Trampoza knows way too much about Nader's business."

"I agree with you there."

Again they were jostled by sudden braking and a chorus of horns. Quint leaned toward the cab and shouted, "Take it easy, Martinez. Or put in seat belts." He turned back to Horacio. "Text Raf. Ask about the video. I'm worried. A video with Trampoza allegedly killing a man with something that looks like me observing can't be good. Also bad, Trampoza driving Alejo's car."

"Not the first time."

"You really think Alejo is going to loan out his car after he's been called out for it? Not unless he's stupid or has a wish to go to prison."

"But you're thinking—" Again Martinez jammed on the brakes and the horn. H slid into Quint. "Sorry, man." He pushed himself back to his spot on the bench. "You don't think Alejo is involved in the arms trafficking, do you?"

Quint shook his head. "Not at all. He's been duped, manipulated. Now he's implicated in whatever is going on. Or he's dead. Killed by Trampoza. That has a nice synchronicity to it."

"You didn't kill someone for him." Horacio looked dubious.

"No, but I've thought about killing Nader."

"Why didn't you?"

The truck surged forward, accelerating. The ride smoothed out. Chepe pushed back the curtain separating cab and cargo. "Bossman, are you sure this is a good idea? We could turn around."

"I agree, Quint. A fool's journey. I don't see what we might gain."

"I want to know why he has it in for me before I kill him."

"You ain't goin to kill the bastard, bossman. You're going to get him arrested. Put him back where he belongs."

"Boys, I have suspicions but no proof of anything except he's selling arms. For all I know, his business is legit."

"Then let the legal system sort it out," Martinez said.

"H, did he really say that?" Quint shouted. "No good. Nader will buy his way out."

"I meant the U.S. legal system."

Horacio made a disparaging sound. "It's why I left the force. But that crew out there today was the exception. Raf is a stand-up guy."

"What are you saying, H?"

"Try the ambassador again."

The utility truck exited, jogging along the surface streets into Nader's neighborhood. "You won't change your mind, Mr. Quint?"

It was late. The residential district had gone to bed. Few lights showed at gates. The streets lined with parked cars. Martinez circled, passing Chepe's cousin on the stakeout. He flashed his brights once and turned the corner, parking beyond a street light. In a moment a thin shadow rapped on the passenger window. Chepe grinned. He rolled it down and greeted the man with a high five. "How's it going, Gordo? I'll let you in." He hustled to the back to unlock the door, following Gordo inside. Martinez pushed through from the front and secured the curtain.

Gordo gave Chepe a bear hug. "*Primo!* So good to see you. I worried when that bastard loaded a grenade launcher into the SUV. I left you a message. What the hell happened? I followed him over to Roma. He had two guys. Lots of guns, but I couldn't get close enough to listen. Nader took off into the neighborhood with the launcher. The other two went the other

way. I trailed them until I saw all the cops. Came back here."
He shrugged. "Didn't know what else to do."

As Gordo talked he gesticulated and paced. The truck
rocked. The guy was like a speed freak, Quint thought.

"Sit down, man," Martinez said, pointing to a crate. Gordo
sat, but fidgeted continuously. "What are you on, *cuñado*?
Meth?"

Gordo laughed and shook his head. "Black coffee."

Chepe interrupted. "Gordo, can you tell us what you've
seen in the last few days?"

"Hold on, before he reports, let me change out the truck.
Gordo, help me." Martinez got up, pulled some magnetic signs
from the cabinet. He thrust half into Gordo's arms. They
crawled out. Inside the men remained silent listening to the odd
rip and slap of changing signs. In moments they were back.

Chepe asked, "What are we?"

"Painting company. Local address. Phone. Now tell us
what our pal Nader has been up to, Gordo."

Nader hadn't been out for a couple of days, but several
people visited him. Quint doubted they were old friends. He
hadn't caught Gordo's business, but the man's surveillance
skills were good. He handed Quint a list of visiting vehicles:
make, model and license plates with a description of the
drivers. Trampoza roared up on Thursday in a Mastretta-MXT-
lg. "It's still inside the gate. He left in the Nissan." He
described Alejo and his Nissan Tsuru. "It was dark. Too dark to
be sure, but it looked like the Mastretta driver helped Nader
haul a bag out of the house. They dumped it in the trunk of the
Nissan and the sports car guy drove it off. I saw his face as he
drove by."

"This guy?" Quint grilled. He held out his phone with
Trampoza's image glowing in the semi-dark.

"That's him. The other guy hadn't come out by the time I
left at daybreak."

Quint shuffled out of the truck, patting his concealed

holster. "I'm checking on the garage."

Horacio followed. "I've got your six, partner. And a few transmitters from Chucho." He hefted an M-16 over his shoulder.

Quint snickered as they slipped into the dark alley.

At the garage, Quint climbed on the garbage bin to peer through the window. The SUV was there, nothing much else. He shined the phone's flashlight, but it wasn't strong enough to see. Where were the crates of grenades and guns? All sold?

"Got a flashlight, H?" he whispered.

Horacio passed him a mini Maglite. Quint shined it down. The garage wasn't empty of crates, but the supply had diminished considerably. How had Nader gone out without any of Chepe's gang seeing him? He shined the light around. Something moved. He passed the light over the corner by the door again. Not a crate. Something bound in plastic with cord. It moved. Rats?

"H. Something is moving in there. We've got to go in."

"You thinking Alejo?"

"Not much chance of that, but we can hope." He jumped off the bin. They sidled around to the garden gate. Horacio picked the lock. They let themselves in. Quint checked for alarms. None. He signaled OK. Horacio picked the door lock then posted himself outside in a shadow. Quint pulled his gun, slowly entering the garage through a small opening. Something was blocking the door. He could hear the muffled sounds of someone moaning. The Maglite revealed a body tied into a large heavy-duty plastic bag. He opened his pocket knife to slit the bag.

A bloodied face stared back at him, eyes wide in pain or terror. He was gagged. Quint slit the bag all the way down. He sliced through the cords tying the man in, leaving the gag in place. It was not Alejo, but he didn't recognize him. He patted him down, no weapons. He removed the gag.

"Think you can walk?"

The man whispered, *sí*. Quint helped him up. He groaned. The man was a bloody mess. He wasn't going to walk anywhere. Blood soaked his jeans and seeped from his side.

"My brother," he croaked

"There's someone else?" The man nodded. Pointed a shaking finger to the SUV.

Gently, Quint leaned the man against a short stack of crates and, gun ready, moved around the SUV. The other body was on the floor. He slit open the bag. Dead. His head a bloody pulp. The wounded man would ID him.

He returned to the injured man, weaving his arm around the man's back and armpit. "I'm sorry, *amigo*. Let's go."

They half carried him to Martinez' truck and laid him on the plastic bag on the floor. He'd fainted.

"Martinez, this man needs a hospital—now. His brother is still back there dead. I'm betting these are the guys Nader hired to attack us tonight. H. Call Raf. I'll phone the ambassador again. Gordo, you need to watch the garage. Chepe, can you get Gordo some help? Call Chepe if Nader appears. Don't get caught. We'll have the police here as soon as we can get them. Let's get going."

Martinez turned over the engine and rolled away from the curb. Horacio was already talking on the burner. Quint tapped speed dial. Rosi would get the ambassador's attention if he couldn't.

Chapter 42

Alejo Holds His Head

Horacio flashed his old badge at the attendant in the local emergency room, barking orders. The doctor snapped his fingers and the bloody man was whisked away on a gurney, disappearing behind dark curtains.

The doctor rounded on Quint, shoving a clipboard into his hands. "Patient's name? Your contact information?"

Nonplussed, Horacio handed it back. "Ask him. Undercover operation—found him tied in the bag bleeding to death. He's yours now." He stalked off with Chepe at his heels.

They jumped into the truck and Martinez patched out, roaring toward the *Periférico*.

"What's happened?" H shouted over the engine.

"Garza called. He contacted Alejo. Wife claims he left several hours ago in the Tsuru with the cop. He hasn't come home. Garza is on his way to the precinct. Raf has Trampoza in protective custody—not letting anyone near him before Garza arrives. We're going there now."

"Where's the car?" Chepe asked.

"Probably still on the street outside the office." Quint scratched his chin. "You don't suppose he's rigged a bomb?"

"Wrong side of the street. But I'll bet you a hundred pesos Alejo is in the trunk," Horacio said.

"Risky bet. Let's go see. Hey, Martinez, make a detour back to the office. We want to check on the Nissan."

"You got it, Mr. Quint," came from the front seat.

Traffic was light this late at night and Martinez knew the quickest routes. They hit only one slowdown, skirting past Zona Rosa. The clubs would be active, it was Friday night, after all. Well, Saturday morning. Quint felt the truck pitch into the glorieta then surge into Roma. They'd be home in moments. "Pull up behind the Nissan. Chepe, Martinez have a tire iron back here?"

"Sure thing, bossman." He lurched into the back to a tool carrier, pulled out the tire iron and a heavy wrench. "Just in case we need to bash a window at the same time." He was enjoying this.

Martinez slowed to a stop. Quint bounced up. The Nissan still parked at the curb. In the States, it would have been removed as evidence by now. In Mexico City it might be missing its tires by morning.

"Lemme out, Chepe," he said.

Quint held up his hand to stop Chepe from popping the trunk with the tire iron. "Don't touch the vehicle, men." He pulled on a pair of plastic gloves. He proceeded to photograph the vehicle from various vantage points, then inspected the interior through the windows. Nothing inside, but he tried the doors. Locked.

"Okay, Chepe, let's do it." He grinned. "We got probable cause; this car has been used in the commission of a crime."

Chepe wielded the tire iron, popping the trunk open as though he was knocking the top off a cold Corona."

The laughing stopped. Quint edged to the gaping maw. He prodded the plastic bag with his index finger, felt a head. He whipped out his knife, stabbed at the bag, slicing it open, folding it back. Alejo looked up from his chest, mouth a rictus grinning from the protection of his arms. Quint gasped.

Martinez mumbled something.

"Wha'd you say, man? Speak up."

Martinez stepped back, face pallid an odd color of grey-green. "Gang killing. Or supposed to look like it. Up there? Zetas." He put his hand to his mouth, turned away from the grizzly torso clutching it's head.

"We know who did it," Quint said, already dialing Garza.

Chepe dialed Raf.

Garza took no time calling out the dogs. In fifteen minutes, a contingent of U.S. Marine Security Guards arrived in an SUV, followed by a black car carrying several suits. "DS," Quint muttered.

"What?" H asked.

"Bureau of Diplomatic Security." He strolled to the official in charge.

"Jackman Quint," he said, holding out his hand.

The man looked through him. He shooed the marines out of the way to gaze at the body then turned around, barking orders at the assembled men. Next he huddled with his clones for what was probably a pep talk. It was going to be a long night.

Another car arrived. Quint and Horacio stepped forward to greet Ambassador Garza as he got out of the shiny Buick. The passenger door slammed. Quint turned. It was Robert Miller. Thank God. Alejo's boss would be able to handle this. Miller nodded to Quint before joining the huddle.

Garza's skin sagged; the bags under his eyes wore black backpacks. Quint noticed his attempts to avoid looking at Alejo. Miller yelled, "Somebody lower that trunk lid." Garza brightened slightly.

"Ambassador, you should go home. Try to sleep," Quint

said, laying his hand on Garza's shoulder. "You've had a long day."

"And it's getting longer, Quint. What happened here?"

"Why don't you join us in the residence—" he pointed across the street— "for a nightcap. We'll give you the rundown. We're pretty sure we know who killed Alejo."

"A drink would be nice, thanks. Is there any question about the perpetrator—Trampoza."

They started across the street. "Chepe, Martinez, come with us," Horacio called to the men.

Miller looked around. He beckoned to Quint. "What happened here?"

"We're taking the ambassador to the residence for a whisky and debriefing. Why don't you come?" Quint shrugged, tipping his head toward his property.

"Thanks, Mr. Quint. I better stay here—supervise this clown act." He rolled his eyes toward the suits. "Administrative. Didn't have field officers handy when the call came. Murder isn't the usual type of crime we see at the U.S. Embassy. Thanks though. You go on. Tony looks done in. Please tape your statements."

"Of course. Thanks for handling this. It's been a shitshow all night."

I'll need you to make official statements tomorrow. We'll probably have to bring in the local constabulary."

"My partner brought in a good team earlier. We think Trampoza did the dirty work at Nader's behest. They're holding Trampoza under guard to keep him safe until he's interrogated. Miller, we want Nader. The Mexicans can deal with their bad seed."

"I hear you. Go tell Garza what went on. Do you have any proof Nader committed a crime?"

"Fresh dead body in his garage packed in the same plastic bag. My man called the cops already. I don't know the status. We took the other man to a hospital."

"Christ almighty. Go on, get Garza a drink." He turned back to the DS men, "It was not Los Zetas."

Chapter 43

Garza Finally Believes

Saturday, October 13, 2007

The ambassador sank into an easy chair with a quiet groan after the climb up the steep stairs from the office. "You should install an elevator, Quint. That's a hike."

Quint chuckled. "That's what our housekeeper says, too." He poured Garza a triple whisky. "This will make you feel better. You know, the rest of us hope the exercise will keep us young and fit. The young ones take the steps at a bound." He clinked glasses with Garza.

Horacio tipped his bottle of Corona from across the room. "I'm with you, Ambassador. We need an elevator. I'll put it on the supply list for when the embassy check comes in." They got a laugh out of that.

"Seriously, men. What happened here? Alejo isn't just dead; he's mutilated. Who does something like that? His poor family."

Quint's lips turned down as his face grew serious. "Nader.

He sees a situation, figures out how to profit from it."

"You think Nader killed Alejo? But why so brutally?"

"No. I think Nader told Trampoza to kill him. Make it appear to be a cartel killing. Alejo's job was to go after the gangs."

"Alejo. Alejo," Garza said, his voice pensive. "You know Alejo means 'man's defender' combined from Spanish and Greek origins. How did he not defend himself?"

"You passed us the info he left with Trampoza. Did Señora Alejo say what time?"

Garza pondered his glass for a moment. "Around seven. She was irritated Trampoza took him from his dinner table. Oh, dear." He stiffened with a stricken face. "What will I tell his wife?"

"Let the embassy pay for the funeral."

"Yes, that would help. Did she hear anything Trampoza said about why Alejo was needed?"

"I asked her that. She said 'the cop' was an errand boy, said Nader needed her husband regarding some new information—a break in the investigation. As they left she heard Trampoza say, 'follow me, we're going north'."

"*Pues*, Alejo drove himself to Jardines de San Mateo," H mused out loud.

"Why wouldn't he? His consultant had something important. Alejo probably had no idea where Nader had holed up," Quint said. "Ambassador, had anyone discussed our suspicions about Nader with him?"

"I doubt it. Miller said he'd look into Nader, but I don't know that the two met. I'll text him." The reply came almost instantly. "He says no."

"We can assume, then, Alejo believed Nader was working with, and I emphasize with, him. I'd wager he didn't believe Nader was making illegal arms sales," Quint said. "But I'd bet all or nothing Nader terminated Alejo to protect his operation."

"Slow down, Mr. Quint. Let's not jump to conclusions too quickly."

"Educated guess. Let me take you on a little trip back to

Vietnam. You were there. You know the kinds of things that went on. Nader 'borrowed' me from the Rangers... " Quint gave Garza the quick and dirty version of his association with Nader. "I was a naive kid when Nader got hold of me. But I was smart. Capable. Nader took me under his wing. Pretty soon, I'd become complicit. I knew all about his illegal opium dealing. I guessed he was passing sensitive information to the North Vietnamese. I wanted out. In short, I became a liability. The only other person who knew what I was doing is my daughter's adoptive father. I accused him of having me arrested. It wasn't Charley Stone."

Garza studied Quint. "It was Nader."

"And three attempts were made on my life before the trial was over. Until now, I didn't associate it with Nader, but now I see that's what he does. The police have Trampoza. He knows everything. Again, I'll place my money on his short life expectancy. Don't be surprised if he's dead in the morning."

"Raf won't let that happen, Quint. I briefed him. Trampoza will have round-the-clock protection until he's convicted."

"Ambassador, it's likely he killed Alejo. Can we get hold of him, have him tried stateside?"

"I was thinking the same thing. It's not usual."

"Is there any sort of state's evidence loophole here? H?"

"Homicide is a state level crime. Each state has its own code. He may not even see a judge. One problem, Trampoza was taken into custody purely on suspicion. He'll probably be released, show up to defend himself at a later date."

"Mr. Rafiq is correct. The system is based on Napoleonic Law. It doesn't work like ours. Calderon is making major amendments to the judicial system, but we won't see any changes before next year. Let's hope Trampoza is smart enough to bargain Nader's involvement for his own. Whether he'll receive leniency or not I can't say, but I worry we won't get the truth without some compromises."

Quint slumped in his chair, hand rubbing his forehead. The situation looked bleak. H retrieved the bottle and offered the men another tot. Garza threw his back. He held up the glass for more. Quint shook his head, levered himself from the low chair with his arms, disappearing into the kitchen, returning with a beer. "Mr. Garza, there's quite a bit more. It's been a long, eventful day."

He proceeded to detail the attempted attack on the property; the trip to Nader's; the dead man wrapped similarly to Alejo; the wounded man taken to the hospital. "The dead man was impossible to recognize, except by the say so of the injured victim in the garage. But my man, Martinez, recognized him as one of the men with Nader and the grenades. I believe he took photographs. It may be the only break we get."

Horacio said, "If he isn't dead. He lost a lot of blood."

"Mr. Quint," Garza said, "my life has gone haywire since you people arrived on my doorstep. Rosi insists you're an avenger of justice, but why did you have to come here?"

Quint shrugged. "Someone has to do it."

The ambassador rose. "Well, if I must have trouble, I'm glad you've got my back. Am I up to speed? I want to go to bed."

Quint chuckled. "Me too, Ambassador. H, take him to his car. Go home. There's nothing more we can do tonight." He nodded at the bottom of the stairs toward the offices. "H, pull Chucho away from his computer. He needs to go home, get some sleep." Horacio nodded.

"Your son?" Garza asked Horacio.

"Our IT department," Quint said.

"I'll be one moment, Mr. Ambassador," Horacio said, hurrying toward the computer room.

Quint walked Garza to the corner. A marine greeted them at the door. Quint could see another on guard at the entry to the alley. The Nissan was gone, impounded by the embassy. The rest of the circus had packed up, moved on.

Horacio and Chucho joined them at the ambassador's car.

"Good night then, Mr. Quint."

"To you too, sir."

Chapter 44

The Pieces Are Coming Together

Quint dreamed of explosions, guts splattering, blood. An immense sasquatch with gnashing fangs pursued him. He wanted to hide, but he had to find somebody. He had to protect somebody, but he didn't have a weapon. He ran and ran; the path narrowed. Suddenly he was trapped in a cave with barred windows. The inmates were coming for him. The mob ran by. Not him. They were on the edge of a marsh. He ran with them through the sea grass—a Stinger—get them out. Get them out! He raised the alarm...

Quint batted at the shrill noise. The alarm ceased. Seven a.m. had arrived too soon. The nightshift would be leaving, the dayshift coming on. He was supposed to make breakfast. Rolling into a sitting position, his head felt like it exploded. His stomach churned, making him queasy. He determined he'd need aspirin or a shot of hair of the dog to get going. Sleep would be good, but the dread Quint felt would prevent that. God, his head pounded.

A handful of Advil he found in the bathroom and a cold

shower, got him moving. When he arrived in the kitchen, Martinez was serving flapjacks to a tableful of strangers. No, there was Chepe, chipper as always. Gordo, dark circles under his eyes.

"Morning, Bossman," Chepe said.

"Morning, *jefe*. How many do you want?"

Quint grunted, "Mornin' men. No thanks, Martinez. I'll grab coffee. Fresh?"

"*Por supuesto.*"

Quint sat down with his mug. The faces started to clear. He nodded to Gordo. "How did the rest of the night go?"

Chepe tapped his fork on his plate, everyone turned to him. The chatter stopped. "*Compas*, get whatever you need. Let's start the meeting."

Martinez set a mounded platter of scrambled eggs on the table next to the tower of pancakes, two bottles of syrup, and a chunk of butter in a bowl. "*Jefe, hay salsa?*" he asked.

"Covered containers in the fridge," Quint mumbled.

The men served themselves while Martinez plunked down the salsa, coffee, and orange juice.

For several moments the only noise was the clatter of cutlery and smack of eating. Chepe broke the feeding fest with another tap on his plate. "Everybody, listen up. This is our *jefe*, Quint. Quint—you know Martinez and Gordo. The good looking one is Chulo." He pointed to a decidedly homely youth. "That's Lolo. The old coot is Tío."

Quint dipped his head, acknowledging the crew. He really wanted a beer. The coffee wasn't cutting it. "Thanks for your help, men. I appreciate it. Chepe, you have reports?"

Chepe and Martinez summarized the activity from the night before. Quint didn't note anything new in their report. Gordo maintained the man taken to the hospital was the man unpacking the launcher from Nader's vehicle.

Gordo reiterated what he'd said before about Alejo arriving and a large bag being carried out to the trunk of his car. He added the part where Trampoza stopped at a house in Naucalpan and picked up Nader's accomplices. He slid over a paper with the addresses of two locations. "The other one is a warehouse off the *Periférico* in Tacuba. Where he got the arms."

Quint straightened up. "Why didn't he bring guns from Nader's place?"

"They've been moving them to this warehouse all week. We think it's been the visitors taking the loads. The garage is almost empty. The guns and Stingers are gone from the house. Lolo, Chulo and I followed them on Thursday. We broke in. To the house, too." He fiddled with his phone. "Give me your number; I'll send you the photos I took."

"Yeah, but you can't see what's going on in the garage. Have you done this kind of work before, Gordo?"

"Military intelligence. Tío is a retired cop."

"Good team you've put together, Chepe. And these two?" Quint looked at Chulo and Lolo.

"Our cousins. Tío's kids. Different moms. Lolo is at the police academy. Chulo is about to graduate in criminal justice from UNAM. I've got a law degree, but this is more fun." Gordo's grin lopsided, lifting Quint's spirits.

Chepe interjected with, "Let's get to business, people. Some of us need to sleep before our shift tonight. Lolo and Chulo will be on duty here today. I've got a team on Nader's house and a man on the warehouse. As of arriving, we do not know where Nader is. The house is empty."

"He wasn't arrested last night for murdering the man in the garage?"

"No police showed up. The dead guy is still on the garage floor. I personally went through the house before dawn. No one is there."

"So he drove back with the launcher and the two men. Killed one, left one to bleed out in a plastic bag, then, without his vehicle, left."

"Mr. Quint. You're forgetting the cop's sports car. It's gone."

"Well, that car should be easy to find."

"Not in a garage, bossman. But don't worry, the team will

find him. Come on, men, finish up your breakfast. Chulo, you're on the first lunch break.11:30-12:15. Tío is in charge. Martinez, Gordo? Ready to head home?"

"See you tonight. I'm at the end of my phone if you need me." Quint poured the last of the coffee into his mug. The living room looked more inviting with sun angling across from the southeastern most window. He pulled up a chair to the window and tapped in Garza's number.

"Good morning, Mr. Quint. Please don't give me bad news."

"I may not deliver on that. Nader's whereabouts are unknown. We know he went back to Jardines de San Mateo last night, the SUV is there with the body. But Gordo went through the house before dawn. He's gone. Took Trampoza's sportscar. Probably before Gordo got back from Roma. A vision of running through marsh grass fleeted through his memory. I'm worried he's on his way to California. After Jade. Can you do anything? Flag his passport?"

"Miller took care of that last night. It's unlikely he'll be flagged on this side of the border, but he won't make it through immigration. Of course, if he jumps the border, we have no way to know."

"I'm thinking of going to protect her."

"How would you do that? Risk getting both of you killed, or being arrested? Better to contact the authorities from here."

"I've done that. She and her boyfriend have been moved to a safe place with security."

"Then you've done what you can. I should get going. Don't want to be late."

"One more thing. Gordo said the military weapons are no longer in the house. I saw the garage was almost empty. He says Nader has a warehouse where the weapons have been moved. My guess is, Nader won't be back to his house. The police did not investigate the anonymous tip. Maybe DS can stop by. Let them find the body. You can get a warrant."

A knife blade of sunshine cut across the room. Above the roofs stretched empty light-blue sky to his horizon. Not very far, but enough that he felt small. Inconsequential. Did his work really make a difference?

"...Mr. Quint? You still with me?"

He snapped back to the conversation. "Yes, Ambassador. I'm sorry, you were saying?"

"I'll talk to the powers that be. It would be far better if we took care of Nader rather than Mexico."

"I'm texting you two addresses and the vehicle's plate number now. Tacuba is the warehouse. The other is where Trampoza picked up the men who were taken into custody in my alley. My people are tracking Nader's movements. I'll follow up on the hospitalized man."

"Thanks Quint."

Quint disconnected the call. The spear of sun had broadened into a warm shaft illuminating his chair. He closed his eyes against the bright light, sinking into oblivion.

Chapter 45

Rat Trap

Quint bubbled up to consciousness from another disturbing dream. Disoriented, he swatted at the thing grabbing at him. Chucho shook his shoulder harder. "*Jefe*, Mr. Quint! Wake up. Wake up!"

His eyes slowly registered the young man's serious countenance. "Chuch?" he sputtered then cleared his throat. "What time is it?"

The day's sun had overheated the room to a stuffy oven. He tossed his arm over his eyes. Mrs. P would have pulled the shears and opened a window earlier.

"Four, *jefe*. There've been developments. Horacio says you need to come."

Quint muttered, "What happened?" He dropped his arm. The headache was only a soft tapping now, but his stomach grumbled. His mouth tasted like a desert. "Bad news? Tell me while I eat something."

Chucho handed over a steaming cup of coffee. "I poured a bowl of cereal for you. We have only a few minutes. There are *panes.* Hurry."

"For what?" He groaned as he lumbered out of the chair. Everything hurt; had he been runover by a truck?

"The ambassador needs us."

Chucho's years as Senator Aguirre's houseman showed. A place at the table was set with everything Quint needed, including a sliced banana for his Wheaties and a tall glass of fresh orange juice. A bottle of rum sat next to it. He snorted.

"To chase away last night, *jefe.*"

"Garza can drink me under the table. It didn't help my stomach was empty."

"Or it was four a.m. Horacio told me."

Quint dumped the bananas onto his cereal, doused the bowl in milk, and slurped bites while Chucho summarized the news. Chepe's team reported a small moving van pulling into Nader's yard. Two movers in white overalls disappeared into the house with folded boxes. About thirty minutes later, they began to ferry filled boxes to the vehicle. They noticed a third man, not in coveralls, carrying two suitcases. They could not identify the man as Nader.

"So Nader is moving out. On the run, I guess. What happened?"

"Chepe's guy with the motorcycle—"

"You mean Gordo?"

Chucho shrugged. Quint dumped a dollop of rum into the OJ and swigged at the glass. "This is what I know. The van went to Tacuba to a warehouse. H says you know about the warehouse." Quint nodded. He swallowed the remainder of his now-soggy cereal.

"They unloaded. The movers left. Chepe's man saw the sportscar when they opened the doors to back the moving van in."

"Chuch, cut to the chase. Where is Nader?"

"That's just it, *jefe,* we don't know."

"What time was this?"

"Around *medio día.*"

Quint roared, "And you all waited four hours to tell me?"

The backdoor banged, followed by clopping steps in the hall. Horacio appeared in the doorway. "Calm down, partner. We got the report about ninety minutes ago and called Garza. The warrant for the house came through. He sent a couple of marines to investigate the warehouse. Let's go. We're meeting them in Tacuba. The gear is in the limo. Get your gun."

Quint pushed away from the table and bolted for his room. Horacio called after him, "Meet us in the garage."

He strapped on his holster, checked the magazine, flipped on the safety. He filled the pockets of a dark jacket with ammo, tied on his combat shoes, then rattled down the back stairs to the waiting car.

Horacio patrolled the Tacuba neighborhood for potential *halcones*. If Nader had scouts watching the street, they'd be walking into a trap. H dragged his chauffer's cap low on his face. The cap, over his reflecting aviator glasses, obscured his face, and the dark, smoked-glass windows meant no one could see Quint decked out in bulletproof vests. Horacio had slapped false magnetic plates over the limo's real ones. Good thinking, Quint thought. Martinez was a good influence on his team.

He felt the electric excitement of battle zinging through his nervous system. They waited at the mouth of a driveway running along a seedy night club within binocular view of the only vehicle egress from the property, for the embassy team to arrive. They saw no suspicious loiterers. Quint was ready—all except for Leo, who did not have a vest or gun. Leo should have stayed at the office, manned the phones.

"H, I'm worried about Leo. We should have left him. He's not ready."

"No, Mr. Quint! I'm ready. I can shoot." The boy bounced forward on his seat.

"Leo, we don't want any shooting. We don't know what we're going to find, anyway Nader will recognize you. I need you here on lookout. You can help Chucho. You may not leave this car."

"B-b-but, I'm the *comadreja*, the weasel. I can get in through that window in back and let you know what's happening."

"That's what the trained marines are for. You're going to work the comms." Quint fished around in a duffle. He grabbed several communications devices, tossing one to each. "Chucho will work his magic on the computer. You'll keep us informed of enemy movements. I promise I'll get you weapons training, but until you're eighteen, you aren't going to battle."

"Mr. Quint," the boy whined.

"This is boot camp, Leo. Accept your assignment with, 'Yes, sir', or go to the stockade. Your choice."

Leo sat back, sulking. Quint tried to remember what it was like to be fourteen, barely out of puberty. Getting away from his father and brothers, came to mind. He spent most of his free time in the library.

A squawk came from Quint's helmet. He put it on, adjusted his mic. "See something, H?"

Horacio detailed the SUV that just passed. Six men inside. US diplomat plates. "Must be our guys. It's passed the warehouse. Turning at the corner toward the back."

Chucho madly typed, pulling up CCTV footage of the neighborhood on his laptop screen. He followed the vehicle as it appeared and disappeared camera to camera.

Leo narrated, "Behind the warehouse now. Passing. Hold on, now it's turning into a gate a couple of buildings away. I can't see it anymore."

Quint's phone rang. He checked the screen, Garza. "Quint."

"I'm behind the warehouse with Miller and five men. Saw you in front."

"Is Nader inside?"

"I hoped you'd know."

Quint held the phone away. "H, any further intel on Nader?"

"Chepe texted. Their guy sent this. Check your text."

Quint swiped open the app. An image waited. He clicked

275

on it. "Garza, I'm looking at an image shot in the last hour. Nader, entering the warehouse. I just forwarded it to you."

"This should be easy then. Miller will stay here. Two of my guys are moving around to the back, another two to the side. I'll come around with the rest. One can go in with you, and the others can take the delivery door."

"Who got the warrant?"

"Miller. Nader was working for his bureau. He's running the op."

"Don't let your people kill him. Death is too good for the *pendejo*."

"I hear you, Quint. Orders to wound, not kill. I'm coming around now." He hung up.

Chapter 46

Boobytrapped

Garza's marine hefted a ram at the locked entry. Garza nodded as Quint and Horacio moved into position behind the marine at the door. The marine was clad in a full protective gear. Quint hoped it wouldn't be needed. Garza held up a finger. "On three," he whispered. A second finger came up. He cocked his head, listening to the communication link. Quint held his breath, his heart hammering.

"Three!"

A deafening noise rose as three battering rams shattered open the doors around the building. The marines thundered down a short hallway, Quint and Horacio behind him, to a reception room with several offices off it. They each kicked in a door, weapons ready.

"¡*Vacio!*"

"Clear!"

"¡*Vacio!*"

Quint could hear the other teams now, as they cleared the mostly empty warehouse space. Two marines cautiously moved down an aisle along the back wall between stacks of crates. The weapons. Many, many more than Quint had seen at Nader's house.

Quint assessed the layout: north end two forklifts parked nose to nose, to the east, several chains with hooks hung from the two-story ceiling just inside the rollup door over Trampoza's sportscar. A set of stairs ran up to a second floor, which covered about a quarter of the main floor. The back entrance came in through a narrow hall next to the stairs. Interior windows overlooked the warehouse floor. It must have been the executive office, now dark. If he'd been in Nader's shoes, he'd be shooting from those windows.

Quint and the marine cleared the storage closets and the equipment rooms built-in under the second floor, working toward the stairs. Horacio and a team crept up the carpeted stairs. The atmosphere in the warehouse reeked of fear. The building was too still, too quiet. No one could have slept through the noise of the battering rams. Maybe Nader wasn't here, after all. He stepped back onto the warehouse floor to inspect the boxes clustered near the rollup door.

Clothing, some files, a few books. Grenades. He straightened up, tapping his commlink. Movement caught his peripheral vision. He dove behind the sportscar, M16 swinging up to the interior window as the glass shattered. A spray of bullets strafed the car and metal rollup door.

The sounds of shouting and boots on wooden flooring echoed down the stairwell. Shots fired. Quint expected Nader to be dead or dying in a pool of his own foul blood. He held his aim ready, watching the windows.

Suddenly a brilliant flash then the deafening bang. The southern two windows exploded out, glass tinkling onto the warehouse floor, smoke billowing from the broken windows. Fire raced up the dry wood walls.

Quint was running for the stairs before he knew what he was doing, shouting, "Horacio! H! H!" Thundering into the stairwell two marines on his heels. A body lay head down across the top most steps. Flames roared from what had been the doorway into the windowed office. Quint pounded to the landing yelling into the commlink. "Ambulance! Get an ambulance!"

It was Horacio. Quint leaped two stairs at a time to his partner. Horacio groaned. Quint yelled, "He's alive! Hurry, Chucho. Get the *bomberos*, too."

The marines pulled their jackets over their faces as they raced through the burning doorway, weapons ready to fire. The roaring of the spreading fire drowned out any sounds, but in moments, one of the men dragged a comrade through the flames. Then the second marine appeared with another over his shoulder. Dead. He shouted, "Target has escaped. The room is empty. The door was rigged."

Nader escaped? How? Horacio was sitting up, now. The flames approached the stairs. They had to get out of the warehouse as far away as possible before the entire place went up. The ammo and grenades were going to take out the entire *colonia*. "Can you walk, H?" He grabbed his partner, pulled him to his feet. Horacio shook and stumbled, but Quint managed to get him down the stairs.

Miller and Garza met them in the street. Two marines carried the dead, while the remaining man had the good sense to haul out as many boxes of grenades as he could. H safely outside, he ran back to help.

Inside, the fire raged, fueled by the broken windows and open delivery door. How did Nader get out? Quint bent to heft a box of ammo. He heard three pops. Not enough for ammo to have caught fire. Then a bang from the back. He shoved the box outside, dropping it as he raced to the corner. Nothing. Blank wall. The sound had come from the other side. He skirted the back edging around the north corner. A small gated enclosure with a garbage dumpster inside gaped open. Eight feet above, a narrow window overlooked the garbage area, its shattered glass sparkling around the body draped over the dumpster, bleeding out.

"Leo, no!" Quint gasped. "I got you kid. I got you, hang on." He scooped the boy off the skip and cradled him against his chest. Leo's breath labored, his heartbeat weak. Quint whispered, "What were you doing here, Leo?"

Leo, his voice barely audible, replied, "I knew he'd come out the window. I shot him, *jefe*. I did my part for the team." His eyes closed. Quint felt the boy's life draining from his young body.

He rounded the building carrying Leo. An ambulance screamed up. "Hold on, Leo. Here's the ambulance. You'll make it. Just hold on kid... " He felt the body relax.

Leo was gone.

Chapter 47

Gossip Travels Fast

Mayhem reigned in the local emergency room. Horacio was thankfully not bleeding or otherwise showing signs of dying anytime soon. He and Quint waited in an alcove, Quint pacing, H on a gurney. Gunshot wounds, knifings, beatings, a victim of a car accident, another doused with acid—a typical Saturday night in Tacuba, a nurse said.

Horacio wasn't doing well. He had spots of second degree burns on his chin, cheeks and hands where he had held them up when the blast threw him backwards. The tactical gear and helmet had saved his life, but it was a miracle he hadn't broken his neck or back when he landed. "I've had worse Quint. It only hurts when I laugh."

Quint knew he was lying. A wave of guilt washed over him. If it weren't for him—*and fucking Vietnam*—his partner would be at home with his family right now. Young Leo would be alive. What was he going to say to the Rafiqs? Only a couple of weeks, but Leo had become part of the family. He owed the boy. The kid was trying to prove himself to them. H would recover, although he might have a few new scars.

"H, how you doing?"

"My ears are ringing. My head is pounding. I can't sit up, I start spinning."

"I'll go see what's keeping the doctor."

"This must be what Dylan's shift is like over in Iztapalapa."

Someone let out a yowl that sounded like a cat being run over. A scuffle started in the hall outside the alcove between two boys in drooping pants with different colored bandanas like tails flapping from back pockets. Quint stepped between them, pushing them apart. "Cut it out, boys. A man's dying here. Have some respect."

The boys gawked at Horacio. One mumbled, "Sorry, man." The other backed away and joined a pod of identical wannabes.

"What happened to him?"

"Bomb blast."

"Is he going to die?"

"He might already be dead, the doctor is taking so long."

Horacio let out a loud, shuddering sigh and fell still. The boy stared, horrified. It was all Quint could do to keep a serious face.

The doctor scurried in his direction. He stepped into the man's trajectory, stopping him. The boy shrank back, slinking past the red bandanas to his side of the waiting room.

"Doctor, it's been two hours. My partner has survived a bomb blast, are you going to let him die here in the hospital?" Quint said, leading the doctor into the alcove.

"A bomb blast? That fire over in the warehouse?"

"That's the one. News travels fast."

"Had another man in with minor burns and a concussion. Disappeared before I could get him into a bed."

"Well, this is Horacio Rafiq, and he isn't going anywhere until you've seen him."

The doctor check H's burns. Two looked serious, he said. A *centavo* sized spot on his left cheek and a sear across the inside of his right wrist, which was beginning to blister. He called for

282

a nurse with tray of ointment and burn bandages. He gently cleaned the burns before bandaging them, then gave Quint instructions for two bandage changes and cleanings daily, removing as much burned skin as possible.

"Doctor, he was thrown six feet backwards onto the stairs. Hit his head."

"Mr. Rafiq, what were you doing before you hit your head?"

"Chasing a criminal to arrest him."

"Do you remember what happened?"

"I approached the door. Woke up on the stairs, burned."

"Do you know how you got here?"

"In the ambulance with my partner."

"Okay, you might have a concussion, but you aren't disoriented." He looked at Horacio's tactical gear, and asked, "Were you wearing a helmet?"

"Yes."

"I don't think you need a CT scan, but if by tomorrow morning you have any of these symptoms, see your doctor." He rattled off a list.

"My head is pounding."

"I'm sure it is. Do you feel weak or dizzy when you sit up? Your ears are ringing as well."

"How did you know?"

"The noise of an explosion can trigger tinnitus. It will go away. You need rest, no stress, no alcohol. Don't drive a vehicle until your symptoms have gone away. I recommend you go to your own doctor in the morning." He turned to leave.

"So he's not being admitted?" Quint asked.

"No. Take your partner home."

Quint smiled. "Yes, Doctor. We're on our way." He grabbed a wheelchair tucked into a corner of the room, helped Horacio into it, and wheeled him out of the hospital. He'd arranged the bill to be sent to the office.

"Chucho, can you come get us? Where are you?"

"I'm parked a few blocks away. I'll be right there. H is okay?"

"He'll live. But he won't be driving for a while so I'll have to rely on you. Do you have a driving license yet?"

"Yes. Got it two weeks ago."

"Then hurry up. This hospital is a nightmare."

In moments the limo pulled up to the curb. Chucho jumped out to help Horacio while Quint pushed the chair back inside. He saw the doctor again and hurried over to him. "Doctor, you treated another man came from the same explosion?"

"Yes, but why do you want to know?"

"Did he give you a name or address?"

"I can't tell you about another patient."

"I think it's the man who planted the bomb. The one we are after." He fished a badge from his pocket and flashed it at the doctor with a photo ID classifying him as a U.S. Embassy DS officer. He kept his thumb over the face. The ID belonged to one of the suits who'd shown up to inspect Alejo's car.

The doctor led him to reception. He ordered the nurse on duty to find the name and address. It wasn't Nader. He called himself Bill Smith. The woman said the man paid cash. Quint showed an image of Nader to the intake nurse. She nodded and pushed a copy of the intake forms toward him. He jotted down the listed address and slipped in in his pocket.

Chapter 48

He's in the Wind

Sunday, October 14, 2007

It was after midnight when Quint trudged up the back stairs. Chucho had tucked the limo into the garage. He was alarming it while Quint unlocked the back door and checked the residence's alarm panel. Green light. The system was off. His phone buzzed in his pocket. A text from Chepe. He sent a thumbs-up. Pouring a stiff drink was first priority. He grabbed a bottle from the pantry on his way into the kitchen.

"Chuch, you want a drink?" he called out when the door slammed.

"You know it, *jefe*," the young man said, throwing himself into a chair.

Quint set a bottle of Rancho Victoria Premio onto the table and rummaged in a cabinet for two tequila shot glasses, which he plunked down at their places with a lime, knife, and round wooden cutting board. "You pour. I'll cut the lime."

"To Horacio's health," Chucho said. He shot back the

amber liquid.

"To H's health," Quint echoed, drinking his. He poured a second round and lifted his glass. "To catching that bastard Nader. I want him in a six by nine solitary cell with no possibility of parole."

"I'll drink to that," Chepe said as he trotted into the room.

"Get a glass, Chepe." Quint pointed to the cupboard. "Call Martinez. Nader isn't going to bother us tonight."

Chepe sent a text. In moments Martinez burst through the back door to join them in the kitchen. Chepe filled their glasses then held his aloft. "To stomping on that cockroach!"

"And to Leo. I couldn't keep him in the limo, *jefe*. I'm so sorry," Chuch said, face stricken. He poured another round then held up his glass. "To the bravest kid on the team."

"To Leo," the men echoed.

They drank then clunked down the empty shot glasses, a wave of emotion rolling through the group as the men sat in silence. Chucho swiped across his eyes.

Chepe broke the oppressive sadness. "Tell us what happened today, bossman."

Quint poured another round before launching into the story.

"*Jefe*, let me see that paper," Chucho asked.

Quint pulled it from his jacket, sliding it across the table. Chucho booted up the ever-present laptop. He copied the address into a browser and a map popped onto the screen. The address turned out to be a wholesale clothing market on Calle de la Roldán near the Merced Market. He read out the address, turning the screen so the others could see the map.

"You think it's legit?" Martinez asked.

"Probably not. You know he's just moved over to his warehouse. When would he have time to rent a place downtown?"

"That's the thing, bossman, he was down there the other day. Gordo tailed him Thursday. He couldn't see the specific destination, but Nader went inside that clothing wholesaler. Maybe there's an apartment upstairs."

Chucho looked at the area map again. "It's an office. It's

where he transacts his business."

"Holy shit! Chuch, I think you've got something." Quint grinned. "He wouldn't bring his kind of client to his home if he had any sense."

Martinez frowned. "Then why did he go to the warehouse?"

"Martinez, if the bossman doesn't need us, let's go find out what's down there. Lolo's still on duty. You got that ragpicker sign in the truck?"

"Sure, got 'em all. Mr. Quint?"

"Gentlemen, go on down. Observe the neighborhood, but under no circumstances enter the address. We've had enough hospitals for today. The man is an ace with booby traps and a paranoid son of a bitch. If he's in there, he's got protections in place."

"Okay, Bossman. We'll get you some photos. Report back at eight for breakfast. Come on, Martinez. Let's change the signs. We'll find out what's going on down at the markets."

"Chuch, I'm bushed. I've got to hit the hay. You should too. Sleep in. You've earned it." He offered his computer specialist a wan smile.

"Thanks, Mr. Quint. It wasn't your fault about Leo—or Horacio. H's going to be fine."

"It wasn't your fault either. Leo was determined to prove he was one of us, but Horacio'd be better if I hadn't dragged him, or any of you, into this. Leo would still alive. But you're right. Sleep is what I need. I've been up too long." He staggered to his feet. "Good night, Chucho."

"You too, *jefe*. I'll make sure Lolo has what he needs. I'll set the alarm. We came willingly, Mr. Quint."

The bedroom was stuffy from the day's sun; he'd forgotten to close the blinds. Quint cranked open the window. He stood in the rush of cool night air, wishing he was sitting in Rosi's flower-scented garden under the stars with her. He stood her up for dinner Friday. Now it was Sunday. He hadn't even called her, he thought as he thumbed through the messages in voicemail. All two of them. Both from Rosi. He listened. "Call when you get in. No matter how late." *Well, she asked for it.* He dialed.

"Jackman, thank God," Rosi said, picking up on the first ring. "What happened? Can you talk?"

"I'm exhausted. Long day, but I wanted to hear your voice before I fall over. What are you doing up so late anyway?"

"Wringing my hands, watching the telephone. Is it over?"

"No. He's in the wind. He got away. Leo is dead, Horacio has a concussion and some pretty bad burns from one of Nader's little boobytraps."

"Oh, Jackman, I'm so sorry. I wish I were there with you."

"Me too, Rosi, but I'll carry this pain for a long time. Maybe tomorrow we can finally have dinner?"

"Yes. Let's go somewhere beautiful and quiet. You can tell me about what happened then. Go to sleep, *amor.* Things will look brighter in the daylight."

"Rosi Orozco, you are the tonic I needed. Thank you. Sweet dreams until tomorrow." He hung up, shook his clothes off, and crawled between the sheets.

The whine of the vacuum cleaner woke Quint. Who would be—*Mrs. P.* That's right, the housekeeper arranged to get the house ready for Jade. But seven a.m.? He rolled onto his stomach, dragged his pillow onto his head, and drifted off again. The next thing he knew, someone was knocking at this door, inviting him to breakfast. "Yeah, okay, gimme a minute," he growled.

"Good morning, Señor Quint. Mr. Chepe and Mr. Martinez are already here."

"Mrs. P, thank you. I'll be right there."

"Bossman. *Buenos días.* Look at this breakfast!" Chepe said, as Quint stepped through the kitchen door. "I want to steal Mrs. Pérez. Take her home with me."

Martinez laughed, making some noises around his mouthful that may have been agreement. Mrs. P blushed.

"Not on a bet, Chepe. Mrs. P is my household fairy. She

does more than feed us, she waves her wand and turns this place into a home. I'd never give her up." Quint winked at Mrs. P. She handed him a plate of her special *huevos rancheros* over *hoja santa,* a slightly peppery mint flavored leaf tinged with licorice that turned her egg dish into something out of this world. He sat down and dug in. She poured him a large mug of coffee. After a couple of bites, he asked "How did it go, men?"

Martinez grinned. "The panels worked perfect. The street is a garment area—discount, second hand, wholesale."

"*Pendejo,* he means how did the operation go?" Chepe said. "Great, Bossman. It went great. We parked around the corner; strolled the street. Lots of activity all night because some of the places have market stalls. Sunday is a big day. We talked to a few people about the market and the street. Found out most of the places above the street level stores are either offices for the stores or private offices for mostly market related firms. People agreed that only a few places are apartments. Mostly those have the owner's family living in them. A neighbor said above the clothes place there's an importer of something he wasn't sure. Chinese stuff." He winked.

"We brought the truck across the street and watched." Martinez added, a smug look on his face. Chepe had the same.

"And?"

"It's Nader. We saw him when he opened the curtains. Got a shot." He cued up the photos then handed his phone to Quint. "Swipe left."

Quint scrolled through a half dozen photos of Nader. He appeared to be ill, pale, and a bit disoriented. Several images depicted him stumbling, his expression vacant like he didn't know what he was doing. "Where'd he go?"

"Coffee. He's got a head injury. Scroll fast. You'll see how he staggers. He looks lost."

"I was thinking the same thing, Chepe. He should have stayed in the hospital. This it?"

"No. He had an altercation with a guy because the man tried to help him. I couldn't shoot, but I heard it. Nader is paranoid. Thought the man was going to attack him or do some sort of harm."

"That'd be the Nader I know."

"Bossman, he accused the man of being your agent."

"That's not good. Then what?"

"He ranted about 'his girl'. He'd teach 'that traitor, Quint what it felt like'. What's he talking about?"

An ominous storm cloud settled over Quint. He sent a quick text to Garza.

The story was far from over.

Chapter 49

You Took My Life Away

The office felt dreary, dark and empty. Quint flipped on lights as he proceeded down the hall. Chucho would wake up soon, but Quint had nothing for him to do. Maybe he should give the kid a day off. He poked his head into the computer room listening to the faint hum of the various machines. He was avoiding the inevitable. His desk awaited him with the lengthening list of calls to make. First to Horacio.

"*Bueno*," Amina Rafiq answered.

"*Buenos días, Amina. ¿Como es Horacio?*" Quint said. He had rarely spoken to Horacio's wife and was at a loss for words. His telephone Spanish was weak.

"*Señor, mi marido duerma. Vamos al doctor mas tarde.*" Her tone shouted displeasure. Another vote on Quint's culpability.

"Please don't wake him then. Will you have him call me after the visit?"

"Of course, Mr. Quint. *Adios.*" She hung up.

Quint slumped into his executive chair. Mrs. Rafiq told him

off as eloquently as if she'd given a speech. He wanted to placate her, explain, make her understand. He hadn't invited H to be his partner for his driving skills. This was why Amina Rafiq was kept away from her husband's work.

He hoped his next call would be more productive. He picked up the receiver and dialed. "Ambassador, it's Quint."

"Good morning. I thought you might call. How is Mr. Rafiq? Any more news on Nader?"

A bird trilled in the bougainvillea outside. The day was pleasant and Sunday clear. A day to visit a park. Feed swans, not chase down killers or worry about his team. "Ambassador, we got him home last night with mostly minor burns and the possibility of a concussion. He wasn't feeling too great, but Nader is feeling worse."

"What do you mean? What's the intelligence on him?"

"The doctor who treated Horacio yesterday mentioned he'd treated another victim of the blast. Described Nader. I got an address. You saw my text?"

"I did. Garment district. Paranoid."

"Yes. My security team ran surveillance overnight. They ID'd him in the morning."

"What did your men say?"

"He's sick. Pale. stumbling and shouting paranoid nonsense at anyone trying to help him. They shot photos. Check your email. I'm sending them now. Nader is concussed by his own trap. We haven't taken further steps. I thought I'd better check in with you first."

"Thank you. Let me get that address again."

Quint rattled it off. "Did DS go to the house?"

"Yes. We found the dead man. The accomplice had checked himself out of the clinic."

"Any weapons?"

"Some assault rifles and grenades. Chinese, as you reported. The house was empty of the stolen weapons. Our investigators spoke with representatives at the Yuma Proving Grounds. They're working on an inventory, but we won't have anything definitive for a week. That said, they've identified the body of Specialist Becker. It doesn't prove anything, Quint. Perhaps forensics will point back to Nader, but it's unlikely Nader actually killed him."

"True. But we both know he was behind it."

"I need something admissible in court," Garza said.

"Maybe the Butcher guy will turn state's evidence. Although we have no intel on him. What about the body in his garage? Isn't that enough?"

"That's Mexico's problem not ours. I contacted Miller. He's going after a warrant for the address."

"Do you authorize my team to watch him?"

"Absolutely. Tail his every movement."

"Okay, consider it done—" Quint's cell phone rang. "Hang on, Ambassador. It's my man in the field on the other line."

"Speak to me, Gordo." The connection sounded bad. Like being in a wind tunnel.

"It's Tío, but I'm with Gordo. Chepe assigned us to your man. He's on the move."

"What? I can't hear you." The wind died down. "Now I can hear. Where are you?"

"On the back of Gordo's motorcycle waiting at a stoplight five cars behind the subject."

"Going where?"

"Headed toward Circuito." Quint heard the rev of the engine. The rushing wind started up again. "Keep me posted," he shouted then disconnected.

"Ambassador, still with me?"

"Yes. Nader's on the move?"

"Sounds like it. Stay by your phone. I'll call as soon as I get an address." He hung up.

There was nothing to do but wait.

The stairs door slammed. Chucho. He listened to the plop of rubber soles on marble and yelled, "Good morning. Come in," when the footsteps reached his door.

"Morning *jefe*. Whasup?" He grinned, pleased with his American slang.

"Nader is on the move."

"¡*Guau!* What did I miss?"

"Sit down. I'll tell you." Chucho thumped onto the settee with his mug. "That coffee?"

"*Sí.* Fresh too. You want I get you some?"

"Please." Chucho sprinted back to the stairs, returning in two minutes with a thermos and mug.

"Good thinking, Chuch. It's like this..." He narrated the events from the time Chuch went to bed. "Gordo and Tío are following him on the motorcycle. We're waiting for a callback."

"If Nader has a head injury, he shouldn't be driving. What's the story about his girl? Nader has children?"

"Ravings of a madman. He told me over one of your bugs, he had dated JadeAnne's mother before me and accused me of stealing her away from me. If it's true, she never said anything to me."

"It couldn't be true. What would a woman see in him?" Chucho laughed. Quint joined him.

He was right, what would a nice girl see in someone like Nader? Money? Surely not his looks unless she was inordinately fond of waves of hair over a man's forehead. Quint blew across the steaming mug. Smelling the coffee gave him a jolt. He sipped gingerly. Chucho fooled around on his cell phone. The little bird sang it's heart out in the vine.

Quint caught himself watching the minute hand tick around the face of his wall clock. He looked into the patio. The damaged plants and broken pot from the altercation the week before remained. "Hey Chuch, isn't that gardener, Tonalli, supposed to come every week?" He looked into the patio. Chucho's gaze followed.

"You've forgotten. He's out at the senator's farm helping with the transition."

"That's right. I can't keep track of all the senator's people and I had little contact with the gardener. We need our office manager. Jade might do it, when she gets here tomorrow, but

Susana is the best."

"Tomorrow? Not the best time to come."

"No. Not the best time." Quint stopped talking.

Eventually he told Chucho to bring the limo around. The clock was the only sound in the room. Quint drummed his fingers on the desktop filling the dead space with jerky syncopation. The urge came over him to smoke a cigarette. God! He hadn't smoked in over thirty years. What was up with that? Where was Nader leading his men?

The cell finally rang.

"Quint. He's gone to a house in San Angel."

That dark premonition from breakfast smothered down on him. He howled. "Rosi!" The bird flew off.

"A woman came to the door. He bullied his way in shouting crazy things. Who is she?"

"*Tío*, stay on him. I'm on my way." He sprang out of his chair. What was Nader doing? What should he do? The bottom was falling out of his world.

"*Jefe*, you look sick. Do you need something? What about Rosi?"

Quint bellowed, "He's got Rosi, Chucho. How? How did he know about Rosi?" He kicked the waste bin, sending it flying. Chucho righted it. "He'll call to gloat. He's going to kill her. I know it. That's what he wants—to make me suffer. He couldn't get Jade, but how did he know about Rosi?" His fist rose and pounded the door.

"Give me the key, I'll get some guns. We have to go rescue her," Chucho said, springing off the settee. He held out a hand.

Quint's finger came up. First he had to call Garza. He fished in the desk, tossed the keys to Chucho with one hand and pressed the ambassador's number with the other.

"*Buen—*"

"Garza, he's at Rosi's. They followed him to San Angel. We've got to stop him."

"Slow down, Quint. What's happened?"

"Nader has gone after Rosi," he shouted. "To get to me. I've got to go. I've got to save her."

"We've got the warrant. I'm organizing a detail as we speak. Meet me behind the house. There's a *callejon* running along the *Periféico* wall. It intersects with a track running over the hill into Rosi's property. We'll stage from there. I'm ten minutes behind you. Get going."

"You're coming?"

"We're talking Rosi Orozco here. Get going."

"Ten-four. Out." He put down the phone then made a mental list of what they needed. The tactical gear. Guns. Luck and Speed.

He tapped Chepe in the phone list.

"Yo, Bossman."

"Nader has Rosi. I'll bring weapons and gear." Quint rattled off the address. "I'll text with directions to the staging area."

"We're on our way."

His phone buzzed. A text. He swiped it open to see a photo of Rosi tied to a chair, gagged. His heart raced. He felt sick. They had to get going!

The front door slammed. Quint heard Chucho running toward him. He yelled, "Chucho, I've contacted Chepe and Garza. Find the access road along the *Periférico*. How do we get onto it?" He gave Chucho the address and sprinted to the storage room for the gear. "You load the weapons?"

"By the door, *jefe*," he yelled back.

Quint grabbed the bags and hauled them to the door. Out of habit, he cautiously opened it, checking up and down the block. The limo parked in front, trunk popped. He hauled the gear, tossed it in, then ran back for the arsenal. Chucho had chosen well. He picked up the cases as Chucho ran up, grabbed the rest. They hustled the weapons into the car.

Quint drove fast, weaving through the moderate Sunday mid-day traffic, running the occasional red light. Horns honked, brakes squealed, tires skidded, but seventeen interminable minutes later they'd turned onto the narrow access road and joined the embassy team. Two marines had gone ahead to scout. Garza flapped about, wringing his hands. He was useless, Quint decided. But he loved the woman, too. Had for a long time. Rosi is probably why Garza remained at his post in Mexico City, he thought.

Miller tapped his shoulder. "Quint, this is what we're doing." He detailed the operation. "We don't know for sure he's there, but Señora Orozco isn't picking up."

Quint held up the photo Nader had texted. "Proof."

"Any demands?" Quint shook his head. Miller nodded, pursing his lips. He continued. "Do you know where they are in the house?"

"Living room. Lots of windows." The hum and rush of air from the *Periférico* played an ominous soundtrack. Quint felt stiff, off-kilter. "We go in the back off one the bedrooms and through the garage side door. There's a door into the back hallway. Have ladders? She's got a high wall surrounding her place."

Martinez's truck rumbled up, sporting highway maintenance signs. Four men jumped wearing the reflective overalls, boots, and orange helmets of a crew. Quint waved them over.

"Where do you want Chepe and Martinez's people?"

"Got cones, Martinez?" Miller asked, looking the team over. They'd pass as a road crew.

"*Por supuesto, jefe.*"

"Then go set up blocks on either side of the house, out of sight, he's got her in the living room. Don't let anyone through."

"Miller, I want my men in vests. Nader is dangerous, armed, vicious, and sick."

"Agreed. You have them?"

"Men, in the limo, vests, assault rifles. Ammo. You got tools, Martinez?"

The man nodded, grinning. "We'll set up to clear a sewer drain."

Chepe laughed and Quint cracked a smile. "Miller,

anything else?"

"Yeah, you men know how to use these things?" he asked as Gordo carried four M-16s to the others.

Chepe hooted, calling out his military ID and unit. Miller held up his thumb p before huddling with the two scouts.

Quint put on his vest and helmet, checked his weapon, and tested the commlink. "Chucho, put on a vest. You run the comms. I don't want you anywhere near this op. I'm not losing another man," he said, listening. Static. "Chucho, do you hear me?"

Chucho poked his head out of the embassy's van. "*Sí, jefe.*"

"What are you doing in there?"

"Helping run the communications. You should see the set up they have."

"Get your vest on and don't leave this site," Quint ordered. "No matter what."

Chucho trotted through the dead weeds to the limo for the vest.

Quint's phone buzzed again.

Nader: *It's the day of reckoning, soldier. We're gonna settle this mano a mano. You have thirty minutes to walk through the front door. Alone. Unarmed.*

Quint: *I'm on my way, but Chuck, why do you hate me so much?*

Nader: *We'll talk about it before I kill you.*

Quint: *You'll release Rosi first.*

Nader: *If you mean she dies first while you watch, yeah.*

Quint flagged Miller, who hurried away from his huddle with Garza. He showed the CIA man the texts.

"This changes our tactics. I need you to go in. You'll be armed. My men will be inside covering you. This is what you're going to do: get in that limo. Drive around to the front where he can see you. Walk up through the front door. Men outside will cover you. The men inside will handle it when you get in. Try to get him talking facing away from the back. You know the layout. Give the men a chance to get in and grab him."

"I don't want him killed, Miller."

"I don't get it. The man hates you and plans to kill you. Here's your chance to get rid of him."

Quint sneered, his face turning ugly. "Not my way, man. I want Nader punished in prison hell. For life."

"This I understand. Okay hang loose for fifteen minutes while we get into position. Then head in."

"Yes, sir," Quint said.

Ten minutes later another text came in.

Nader: *What's taking so long? Maybe I'll take a bite of your peach while you make me wait. Is the bitch as tasty as she looks?*

Quint let it go. He inhaled a deep breath and held it like Jade taught him. 6...7...8...then let it out slowly to another eight heartbeats. Immediately his blood pressure dropped. He slid behind the wheel. Another text. He ignored it. He circled around, backtracking to the city street, turned right, drove to the next corner, and made another right. Chepe moved the cones. He was through.

The limo purred to the corner. It really was a lovely vehicle to drive. He stopped, turned the key, let the door bang behind him. His phone rang.

"I'm here, Nader. I want to speak to Rosi."

"You're in no position to ask for favors, asshole. You should have thought about that back in '75."

"Chuck, I don't know what you think I did, except pack body bags with your heroin. I was already doing time in '75. But you know that, don't you? Let me speak to Rosi. I'm not coming in until I know she's okay." Quint heard Nader's ragged breath. He pictured the sounds as gnashing teeth.

"Liar! You know what you did." Nader was yelling now. Quint could hear him in the street. "You stole my woman and sent me to prison." His shouting was morphing from anger to hysteria. The man was a lunatic. "YOU TOOK MY LIFE AWAY!"

Quint hung up. He pushed through the gate and approached the front door. The phone rang. He didn't answer. He kept his gait even, measured, his head lifted, but his eyes flitted across the yard. One man in the bushes, another at the corner of the house, a third had made it to the entry. He nodded as Quint passed. This was it. A mentally unstable criminal was going to blast him. *God, let the vest work!*

"Welcome, Quint. Come in," Nader sneered, waving him toward a chair placed across from a terrified Rosi. He stepped forward, gun trained on Quint. "Arms up. I don't trust you. A sneaky kid. Going behind my back. You turned me in." Nader patted him down while he talked, his back to the kitchen. Quint watched a marine slip into position.

"Chuck. I confirmed it. You sold opium to an undercover agent. It's in your court records. We can call, have the transcripts faxed over, if it will help."

Nader shoved Quint into the chair, roaring "You were in that hospital stealing my woman from me. I visited you, I saw it. You got out. The army put you on death duty. I watched you take my girl away—"

"Thuy? Are you saying I took Thuy from you? You're paranoia has turned delusional. I was in the hospital a year before death duty."

"You ruined my life! She was supposed to be with me." He lunged, gun aimed, but Quint jumped out of the chair. Nader stumbled on the edge of the rug. His shot went wild.

Quint ducked and pulled a gun from his boot, one eye on Nader, the other on Rosi. She struggled against the tie wraps holding her to the chair, her face bone-white, eyes wide with fear.

Nader caught himself, swung the gun back but stopped, a chilling sound bubbling out of his throat. Laughter? He aimed at Rosi. An oily smirk spreading across his face. "Now *you'll* know how it feels, Jackman Quint."

A piercing howl came from the hallway, "Nooooooooooo!" Garza leapt into the room with a gun aimed at Nader. Squeezed the trigger. The shot went wild. Nader's gun was up, aimed. The old Colt blasted once, twice—Garza was down. The muzzle swung back toward Rosi. Quint spun, shot. Nader dropped like the sack of garbage he was, but Quint didn't have time to mourn his old CO. He ran to Rosi, pulled away the gag, then slit the ties binding her to the chair.

She screamed, "Tony, Tony!" as she crawled to him and gathered the ambassador into her arms rocking him, whispering, almost crooning to her old friend.

He smiled up at her, his face drained of blood. "I've regretted everything, Rosi. What I did…"

She put her fingers to his lips. "Shhh. Save your strength, my dear friend."

"I have to. I have to tell you."

"I know, Tony." She bent and kissed him.

He spoke again, barely audible, "I love you, Rosi. I've always loved you."

Quint watched as the blood pumping out of his chest dwindled to a trickle. *Why hadn't he put on a vest?* He reached for Rosi, lifted her from the floor. He held her as they wept. Around them swirled the confusion of aftermath. The mop-up had begun.

Chapter 50

Homecoming

Monday, October 15, 2007

Rosi rolled over, snuggled closer to Quint. He snaked his arm around her warm torso and pulled her in. She sighed, relaxing into his chest. Quint smelled roses. A ray of bright sun slit the curtain, casting a halo around their heads. He closed his eyes and sank back into his dreams.

Something joggled Quint. Someone wanted him, but he was so comfortable curled in his patch of sun. He shifted away from the prodding, the voice insistent, "Jackman. Jackman! You're snoring. Wake up."

"Huh? Wha—" Quint opened his eyes.

Rosi's lopsided grin filled his vision. "*Estabas roncando.*"

"Good morning," he murmured. "What was I doing?"

"It's afternoon. You were snoring loud enough to wake the neighborhood."

He chuckled. "So you know my bad quality now."

She rolled out of bed, padded to the window, swept the

curtain aside to flood the room with light. "It's past one. We're due at the airport at four-something. I still have to go back to my house." Her voice dropped, caught in her throat. A small sob escaped. "*Ay*, Jackman, he's gone. Tony has been a good friend to me for so long. What will I do without him?"

Quint watched a tear trace the contour of her lovely cheek. He felt the warm prickling in his own eyes. Tony Garza was becoming a friend to him too. Now he'd lost two—the ambassador. Young Leo. He shoved off the covers, rolled his feet to the floor to join Rosi at the window where she contemplated the little garden below. He encircled her in his arms and kissed her neck. "I'm so sorry. I-I don't know what to say. I've caused so much pain to so many—"

Rosi pulled away, spun to face him. "No, Quint. Chuck Nader caused this, spreading his greed across the planet. You have not caused the pain."

He hung his head. "But if it weren't for me, Leo would grow up, have a life. Horacio wouldn't be suffering. Tony would—"

She grabbed his shoulders, her eyes boring into his. "You don't hear me, Jackman," she said, softly. "Each player in this tragedy has chosen his own path. Nader was a greedy sociopath. You didn't bring him to Mexico. You didn't send him to prison. He ranted all about the terrible things you'd done. Paranoid, delusional ranting. Put this on Nader if you want to assign blame. He spent thirty-three years with festering hatred toward you. Because you had a future."

A breeze blew the sheers around them. Quint looked down at this beautiful wise woman. He wanted to believe her. "He talked to you?"

"In English. Shouting. Raving. You had everything—youth, intelligence, a beautiful woman, and the Army to protect you. His operation was crumbling. The NVA had used him. They didn't need him anymore. Nader had spies everywhere. But you knew the most about his operations. He hated you for it. If you turned on him, he would probably be executed. A traitor to his country."

"He had me arrested—"

"But you weren't killed. You were right, he said he took out a contract on you."

"And Thuy? What about her? He said—" Quint gulped, stifling the sob that threatened to erupt.

"She rejected him. She loved you. When you disappeared, he pestered her. She made her way back to her village to have the baby. Nader couldn't find her. Her death isn't on you, Jackman."

"And you, Rosi. How—"

"*Ay*, he gloated. It was impractical to go to California. He wanted you to watch him kill Jade, but he had business here. Anyway, how was he going to get you there? Obviously he didn't know you, Quint. But what would a man like that know about love and loyalty? There's a bug in the bedroom. He heard us on the phone. He laughed at how easy it was to follow me from my office."

"But I had the residence swept..." He slumped against the bed, his eyes glazing. The long moment of silence was broken by the ubiquitous call of the water vendor announcing his wares.

"I could use some coffee," he said.

Mrs. P whirled around the kitchen, a dervish of culinary activity. Quint licked his lips. "What is that smell, Mrs. P? *¡Muy rico!*"

"Good afternoon, Señora Pérez. Is this the welcome home dinner, you're making?"

"*Buenas tardes*, Señorita Rosita. Will you be joining us tonight? I'm preparing Señorita Jade's favorite, chicken breasts stuffed with fresh goat cheese in red mole with broad beans and chayote." She turned back to the stove, shook the cast iron skillet slowly toasting peppercorns, cinnamon sticks, cloves, and some sort of round seed or berry Quint didn't recognize, as the kitchen perfumed with sweet spicy steam. He recognized the tomatoes and onions cooking in the other pan. His stomach growled.

"Will we be in your way, Mrs. P? I'm starving. You, Rosi?"

"Shriveling into a sack of bones. But let's go out. Stop bothering the señora."

"No, *quedanse ustedes,* I've got a plate of *chilis rellenos con atun y una ensalada* for you. Help yourselves to coffee. I'll get the *asada* done and serve you. Sit!"

Quint held up the carafe and a mug. "Coffee?"

"Black, please, two sugars—I need a little jolt of energy today." She sat down rubbing at the still-red marks on her wrists from the plastic ties.

Quint placed her coffee in front of her, giving it a last clacking stir. "Still hurt?"

"I'll grab some bracelets when we go. No one will be the wiser."

"Then you've agreed to stay here until your carpet is cleaned?"

"Yes. I dread going back. My home was violated. Tony—" She swallowed her emotion but radiated deep sadness. Mrs. P delivered the chili rellenos and leaned down to give Rosi a gentle hug.

Quint served them portions of the tuna-stuffed poblanos. "I understand, Rosi, but the embassy's investigation will have finished. There's not much evidence to process; the house will be put back to rights in no time."

"It will never be the same, Quint. I will never be able to erase the sight of that madman killing my dear friend. Of Tony bleeding to death in my arms."

Mrs. P's chin dropped. Her lips formed a surprised O. She squeezed Rosi's hand and set the salad onto the table.

"No, it won't ever be the same," he agreed, his face stinging with embarrassment.

Rosi placed her hand on his arm. "It's not your fault, Jackman." She cut into her poblano, tasting the creamy tuna filling. "Delicious, Mrs. P."

Quint composed himself. "We'll need to give statements at some point." No one answered.

They chewed in silence while Mrs. P jabbered on about dinner, the cake, fancy cocktails and who should be invited. Apparently she bought colorful *papel picado* to decorate the dining room, and Chucho agreed to help set it all up.

"Did I hear my name? Hi Mrs. P, the ambrosial scents of your cooking woke me up. What are we having?"

"Coffee with tuna chilies. The good stuff is for the welcome home party. Sleep well?"

"Best in weeks, *jefe. Hola, Rosi.* I'm really sorry for your loss. Ambassador Garza always treated me, the senator's houseboy, like I was somebody." Chucho's face scrunched up. He and Rosi sniffed in unison.

She took his hand. "You *are* somebody, Chucho. Come, seat your important self here with us. Mrs. P, pass Chuch a plate?"

Rosi's weepy eyes flooded at the sight of Tony Garza's blood staining her carpet. Quint knew he should have gotten her list and come alone, but she insisted.

"Don't look, *cariña,* just come with me. We'll get your clothes and necessities. Close your eyes. Let me lead you."

The house was a mini-disaster. Blood, finger print powder, as if they didn't know who was involved, upturned furniture, one of the living room drapes pulled off its track, the dining room window peppered with bullet holes and spiderwebbed with cracks. When did that happen? Quint wondered. Rosi would have insurance. Quint would post a security man until the house was repaired. Tío, maybe. They reached her room. At least that remined untouched.

Rosi pulled a couple of suitcases from a closet and dumped the contents of her dresser into the large one. She did not speak. Quint could feel her pain, confusion and trepidation. They weren't ready for moving in together. Were they? But he was at fault. He had to offer her a safe home until hers was habitable again.

She moved to her bathroom to collect her toiletries,

makeup, and hair products. These filled the smaller case. She shoved the case into Quint's hands then shuffled to the walk-in closet and began sifting through her hanging clothes, pulling several dresses, a suit, a stack of pants, blouses and some sweaters off hangers and piling them into Quint's arms.

"You better bring the hangers, too," he said.

"Get me another bag for my shoes."

Obedient, Quint dumped the clothing on the bed, searched out a large flowered tote from the storage closet. Rosi took it from him and filled it with shoes. Quint started packing her hanging clothes in garment bags while Rosi collected her jewelry. He wondered where everything was going to fit.

He turned his Quint grin on her. "Rosi, it's damned lucky I don't have more than two pairs of pants."

She smiled, finally. "That's it. Oh, except for the files. I can use your empty office, can't I?"

"Of course."

"Then, haul my clothes into the car. I'll meet you back in Roma."

"Yes, Ma'am," he replied.

Quint drove the limo into the garage. Rosi pulled into the delivery area. *I should put an electric gate across the mouth of the alley.* He texted Chucho to help move Rosi's things into his room. They had to hurry, Jade was landing in two hours.

Mrs. P had put up the decorations. The cake was frosted. Horacio sat at the table with a tamarind soda and took notes on the party plan the housekeeper patiently explained.

"H! What are you doing out of bed?"

"Clean bill of health from the doctor yesterday. I called. Didn't you see my message?"

"We were busy with some other things, Horacio," Rosi said, glancing at the pile of clothes she carried. "I'm so glad you're okay. Forgive us?"

"Chucho filled me in. You should have called me, Quint." He frowned then grinned. "It's over. Jade is coming home today. Let's celebrate."

Quint grinned, too. "Let's celebrate! H, you driving us to the airport?"

"You bet partner."

Per Mrs. P's instructions, the crowd piled out at the front door. Pepper barked with joy as the door swung open and Mrs. P welcomed them in. The men hauled Jade's many suitcases into reception leaving them for later at Mrs. P's behest. She ushered everyone upstairs for "a little refreshment", linking arms with JadeAnne and Dylan. They led the crowd.

The landing door swung open. A cheer rose. "¡*Bienvenidos*!"

Everyone was there. Mrs. P had invited Dylan's brother and fiancée, Seeger and Dafne, his parents, Dafne's mother Dorotea, and Susana. Even the dogs. Maya's now quite large pups, danced around Pepper as he crooned his joy. Quint's heart swelled at the outpouring of love for his daughter and Dylan.

Quint pulled Rosi close, and grabbed JadeAnne, hugging them both.

"Welcome home!"

Mrs. P ushered everyone in to the bar Chucho had set up in the corner of the living room. Cumbia's played through speakers powered by Chucho's phone. While Chucho poured the drinks, Mrs. P set out a feast of *botanas* and the excitement of the homecoming took over. Quint sat next to Jade's potted palm and smiled as he watched his daughter circulate, laughing, confident. She'd changed somehow. Dylan, too. They were at ease, happy. They'd crossed some sort of line—settled into one another. The love passing between them had grown, matured, deepened. They'd become true companions.

In a few minutes, everyone had a drink and the greetings ended. People were settling in to visit and nosh before dinner. Even Mrs. P had made herself comfortable on the couch between Dylan's dad, Eladio, and Dafne. Quint hefted himself from his chair and held up his tequila, loudly clearing his throat. Slowly the room quieted and all eyes turned to him.

"Here's to JadeAnne and Dylan. It wasn't a home here without you. We've all missed you," he said.

Everyone cheered.

Jade jumped up from her ottoman, yanking Dylan behind her. She tapped her fork against her wine glass. "Everybody! Family! Dylan and I have an announcement." She took his hand and leaned into him as the room expectantly held its breath. Jade smiled up at her boyfriend.

Quint's heart swelled. He knew what was coming.

Dylan pulled Jade close. "I've asked Jade to marry me. She said yes!"

The group exploded into a joyous uproar. Hugs, kisses, congratulations abounded. And the party kicked into gear.

Finally. The residence was a home.

Coming in 2024

Kickback

A Dafne Olabarrieta Mexico Mystery

Book 1

Dafne has taken over the daily operations of the Olabarietta real estate empire with a substantial increase in compensation to go with her new status. Her husband Seeger Porras has shot up the corporate ladder, and life is coming up dahlias in Mexico City. But when Dafne gets a cryptic text from Alba, her best Uni mate, then finds her dead, she is compelled to follow the story Alba was investigating to uncover her killer. Determined to find justice for Alba's daughter, Dafne lands in a nightmare of governmental fraud. With millions in phony contracts and kickbacks to protect, what will justice cost? The conspirators have built a lucrative financial pipeline—right into the Governor's office and will go to extremes to keep it flowing. Alba got in their way. Will Dafne?

About Ana Manwaring

Ana Manwaring is the award winning author of the JadeAnne Stone Mexico Adventures, a memoir of living in Mexico, Gold Book Award Saints and Skeletons, three volumes of poetry as well as many essays, short stories and flash memoirs.

Ana teaches creative writing and autobiographical writing in California's wine country. She is the founder of JAM Manuscript Consulting where she coaches writers, assists in developing projects and copyedits. When Ana isn't helping other writers, she posts book reviews and tips on writing craft and the business of writing at www.anamanwariing.com/blogs/Building a Better Story, and produces the North Bay Poetics, a monthly poetry event.

She's branded cattle in Hollister, lived on houseboats, consulted brujos, visited every California mission, worked for a PI, swum with dolphins, and out-run gun totin' maniacs on lonely Mexican highways —the inspiration for The JadeAnne Stone Mexico Adventures. Read about her transformative experiences living in Mexico at www.saintsandskeletons.com.

With a B.A. in English and Education and an M.A. in Linguistics, Ana is finally able to answer her mother's question, "What are you planning to do with that expensive education?" Be a paperback writer.

If you had as much fun reading Backlash as I did writing it, please consider going to your favorite online bookseller and leaving a review. Reviews help authors continue to write their books for your enjoyment. And I'd really appreciate it!

To find out about new books and upcoming events, please take a moment to sign up on my mailing list at www.anamanwaring.com. To connect with me, find all my information at
www.linktr.ee/anamanwaring

Printed in the USA
CPSIA information can be obtained
at www.ICGtesting.com
JSHW020743221023
50375JS00001B/29